OUT OF CRISIS

OUT OF CRISIS

RICHARD CALDWELL

Indigo River Publishing

Indigo River Publishing
3 West Garden Street, Ste. 718
Pensacola, FL 32502
www.indigoriverpublishing.com

Out of Crisis | Richard Caldwell, author
ISBN ISBN: 978-1-950906-76-5 | LCCN: 2020944610
Edited by Deborah Froese and Regina Cornell
Cover and interior design by Robin Vuchnich

Special discounts are available on quantity purchases by corporations, associations, and others. For details, contact the publisher at the address above.

Orders by US trade bookstores and wholesalers: Please contact the publisher at the address above.

With Indigo River Publishing, you can always expect great books, strong voices, and meaningful messages. Most importantly, you'll always find . . . words worth reading.

For Trisha

It felt like God was making a martini. The first tremor savagely shook the ground, and everything standing on it, for three seconds.

Prologue

Washington, DC
Shortly after the United States obliterated the capital of North Korea and its brutish dictator

WITHIN THE BOWELS of the United States Department of State, a brilliant young analyst rocketed out of the political and administrative morass of the civil service system and into a position of authority and impact.

Near the end of the first quarter of the twenty-first century, the United States was the target of a series of horrific terrorist attacks. These incidents were orchestrated by a fanatical group of Middle Eastern religious extremists who used technical ruses to attribute them to the Democratic People's Republic of Korea—the DPRK—more commonly known as North Korea. Their objective was to instigate a war between the United States and Pyongyang forces. The plan assumed that such a conflict would expand to include Russia and China, resulting in an all-out nuclear slugfest. Out of the ashes of humanity's remains would rise a new, global Islamic caliphate and a caliph who would take his place as the rightful ruler of the entire world.

Following the second terrorist attack, the POTUS directed then–Secretary of State Robert "Bulldog" Pitts to develop a plan that would allow the US to engage and destroy the DPRK military infrastructure while minimizing collateral damage and civilian casualties. The action would have to be executed without instigating retaliation from other world powers, a near-impossible feat. The task was punted to David Stakley, a team leader in the Intelligence and Research Division of the State Department.

Leveraging a serendipitous flash of pure genius, David and his team conceived a strategy that brought the rabid dictatorship to its knees. And through the development of the Asian Independent Free Trade Union, AIFTU, it actually bonded the United States, Russia, and China into a partnership the likes of which had never been seen before.

It also endeared him to President Matthew Sheppard. Upon the Bulldog's resignation due to a massive but nonfatal heart attack, David was nominated and subsequently confirmed as the new secretary of state. At thirty-nine, he was the youngest SecState since the creation of the office in 1789.

David was elated and beamed with justifiable pride throughout the confirmation ceremony. But during the obligatory round of congratulatory handshakes, he couldn't help noticing the aloof demeanor and cold, almost distasteful expression emanating from the vice president.

Something just wasn't right.

1

Grand Teton National Park
The day before the day of

JEREMY RICHARDS BACKED HIS 1997 Airstream Excella into site 72 at the Colter Bay Village Campground around 4:00 p.m. on June 20.

He turned to his wife. "Judy, hop out and guide me back. I can't see the electrical hookups in the mirror. I don't want to start our vacation by explaining to some ranger how I managed to short out the entire park." He thumbed his twins in the back seat of the extended cab and grinned. "Take those two chimps with you. I'm starting to think that a felony charge wouldn't be all that bad."

Judy laughed and jumped out of the cab.

Jeremy, his wife Judy, and their twelve-year-old twin daughters, Ellis and Fiona, had driven eight hours a day for three days to get to the Grand Tetons from their home in Nashville, Tennessee. Jeremy and Judy had more or less shared the driving, while the twins did what twelve-year-old girls do. That mainly consisted of singing along to whatever teen boy band played inside their earbuds. And bitching. They had managed to make whining a team sport. Judy compared traveling with the twins to transporting serial killers from one prison to another.

Jeremy had to admit: without a heavy dose of Dramamine, eight hours was a long time for a kid to sit still. Not that he would ever consider medicating the girls. Himself, maybe. Pop a couple of Xanax or knock back a double Scotch, toss Judy the keys, and wake up somewhere in Wyoming.

Yeah, that would go over like a pork chop on Ramadan.

Colter Bay was part of Jackson Lake, which sat in the middle of Grand Teton National Park in Northwest Wyoming. The park and neighboring Yellowstone contained ostensibly the most beautiful scenery in the United States. The campground was situated almost seven thousand feet above sea level, surrounded by the snowcapped Teton mountains, towering fir trees, and crystal-clear streams feeding an equally pristine lake.

Jeremy was a thirty-eight-year-old professional baseball player trapped inside the body of a Morgan Stanley financial advisor. But that's the way life went for most folks. He and Judy were born and raised near Murfreesboro, about thirty miles southeast of Nashville. They had grown up together, lived on the same potholed country road, and attended the same grammar and high schools. In fact, Jeremy could not remember a time when Judy wasn't around.

The year the twins turned ten, Judy bought Jeremy a new, fire-engine-red Ford F-250 and the Airstream camping trailer as an early birthday present. She had been stashing money away each payday ever since she started working full time.

Jeremy was beyond appreciative. In addition to being the most lavish gifts he had ever received, he was in awe of Judy's quiet determination to purchase them.

From that point forward, he, Judy, and the twins would hitch up the Airstream almost once a month and go camping at one of the state or national parks in Alabama, Georgia, or Tennessee. Anything within a four-hour drive became a weekend getaway. They had also started planning a cross-country road trip and an extended excursion somewhere in the Northwest. They'd decided that Grand Teton National Park in Wyoming would be the perfect destination.

Their timing could not have been worse.

2

Washington, DC; the Foggy Bottom District
Two years before the day of

DAVID STAKLEY AND MARK LITTLETON, the US ambassador to Mexico, sat across from one another at a small, round conference table in David's office. David preferred a more informal setting over the traditional "have a seat in the chair across from my desk" approach practiced by many of his counterparts.

David leaned forward. "Mark, you're aware of the situation in the Yucatán Peninsula. The boss is getting a lot of flack about the increasing violence down there. It used to be a place where twentysomethings could go, smoke a little weed, show a little skin, and raise hell for a week. But in the last six months, there have been four brutal—and I mean brutal—kidnappings. Those are just the ones we know of."

"Yeah, it's bad and getting worse," Mark replied. "We've been talking to the *federales* about the latest incident. There are whispers on the street about an especially brutal beast they're calling El Choppo. He earned this moniker from the calling card he always sends to his marks: a body part. They haven't been able to finger the culprits. According to my contact, they suspect some kind of link to an organized crime family on the east coast and, get this, possibly even to the CIA. I was hoping to get additional details before our meeting, but—"

David's desk phone buzzed. He straightened. That rarely happened. Not while he was in a meeting. His administrative assistant, Trish, was rabidly protective of his time. She would never allow him to be interrupted unless she deemed a call *über*important or from one of the handfuls of top government officials he had on his "straight through" list.

The phone buzzed again. "Excuse me, Mark." David strode to his desk and reached for the receiver.

"Sir, you have a call on line six." A hint of urgency colored Trish's voice. "Line six" was David and Trish's code for an encrypted circuit with a confidential number. Only the directors of the CIA, FBI, and NSA; President Matt Sheppard, a close personal friend; and a scant few others knew what it was.

"He identified himself as Judson Ballard, and he dialed direct," Trish added.

David had not given his number to Judson Ballard. He had never even met the man.

He held the receiver to his chest and turned his attention back to his visitor. "Mark, I don't normally do this, but I have to take this call. If you don't mind, press the pause button on our discussion, and Trish will rustle up some coffee. But don't leave. I'll be with you as soon as I can get off the hot seat."

Mark stood. "No problem at all, Mr. Secretary. I'm here to serve. Besides, that will give me a little time to compose my response to the kidnappings." With that, he headed for the reception area.

As Mark closed the office door, David pressed the key for line six. "Good morning, this is David Stakley."

"Mr. Secretary, I know you are incredibly busy, and I humbly apologize for barging in on you telephonically." The voice carried a distinctive central Texas twang David recognized from hearing Judson expound his political and social perspectives on television talk shows.

"No problem. What can I do for you?"

"I have to discuss a matter of national importance with you. It will undoubtedly be the most pivotal discussion you have ever had."

Pivotal? David slid into his chair and leaned forward, focusing on his desktop speakerphone.

"By the way," Judson continued, "may I call you David? I zealously adhere to etiquette and protocol in any public setting, but sometimes, for the sake of conversational expediency, it makes more sense to skirt formalities."

"By all means, sir. David is just fine."

"In that case, why don't you drop the 'sir' and just call me Judson."

"All right then, Judson. To what do I owe the honor?"

"David, I know you have to be in a semi-important meeting in little more than an hour, and I just interrupted one . . ."

How the hell does he know that?

". . . so I'll cut to the chase," Judson said. "Since you're familiar with my reputation, I'll walk a little farther out on the limb and assume that you're also familiar with an organization I started a few years ago. Envision-2100. I'm currently serving as the president of its board of directors. Does that name ring a bell as well?"

David leaned back in the goatskin chair he had inherited from his predecessor, Bulldog Pitts, and considered his caller. Judson was one of the wealthiest and most politically powerful men in the United States. With a net worth bumping $90 billion, he was reputedly the fifth-wealthiest person on the planet.

"Of course the name rings a bell," David replied. "I would be a piss-poor excuse for a SecState if I hadn't at least heard of Envision-2100. I will admit, I only know what I see on the news and on social media. I don't have any firsthand knowledge. As an organization, Envision-2100 hasn't bubbled up on any intelligence briefings, but I'm told that it's teeming with financial heavy hitters. Word around the campfire is that Envision-2100, at least in the past, has intentionally kept a low profile, but that it's positioning itself to start swinging the bat politically."

"Well, at least we have some name recognition, and that's a pretty fair assessment of where the organization stands right now," Judson said. "As I mentioned, I currently serve as president of the Envision-2100 board. There are four other board members, and we rotate the position of president every twelve months. Envision-2100 is still in its infancy compared to similar organizations, although, in the strictest sense, there aren't any genuinely similar organizations.

"We officially formed our charter five years ago. Since then, we have grown to several thousand dues-paying members. And, David, the dues are staggering. But as you'll see, or at least as I hope you'll see, they are for a cause noble beyond that of any other organization's in the history of this country. That is not empty rhetoric.

"Enough of the buildup already. I said I would cut to the chase, and here I go, off on a tangent. David, my board wants to make you an offer. Perhaps enlist you in our cause is a better way to phrase it, and even that falls short of what I'm trying to say. But I can't go any deeper into the weeds at this point. We want to do so over an extended lunch, and time is of the essence. You don't have anything on your schedule of real importance after eleven next Tuesday. How about I have our copter pick you up at eleven thirty, sharp, at your heliport?"

David's brow scrunched into a mask of apprehension. Not at what Ballard had told him about Envision-2100—most of that was public knowledge—but at the fact that Ballard had been able to slip by the standard screening process. God only knew what else Ballard had access to. He and Trish needed to talk.

"Judson, I'm flattered that you've taken the time to reach out to me personally. But I have to admit, I'm concerned. How in the hell did you get my private number? Only a dozen people in DC—in the country, for that matter—have it. Even more puzzling, and quite frankly alarming, is what you know about my schedule. It appears there is a leak in my front office.

"As for the helicopter, you do realize that Foggy Bottom, and all of DC, is in restricted airspace. And finally, why me? Why are you approaching me with whatever it is you have in mind?"

David swiveled in his chair and gazed out the window. From his fourth-story office in the Harry S. Truman Federal Building, he could see the Theodore Roosevelt Bridge, where I-66 crossed the Potomac River. As usual, the traffic heading into DC this time of day was dismal. Outbound traffic wasn't much better. Having a Secret Service driver was the best part of this job.

"Valid points all, David," Judson replied. "I'll have to defer a full response to a later date and time. Suffice it to say that the Envision-2100 board has an elaborate information and intelligence network. And yes, we are well aware of airspace restrictions and the need to file closely monitored flight plans. We've got that covered.

"Most importantly, let me put your mind at rest about a leak. There isn't one. As I alluded to a moment ago, we have our means. You'll learn a lot more once you meet the board. Assuming, of course, you accept our offer.

"To your 'why me' question, David: we've had our eyes on you for a long time. You were on our radar even before past SecState Robert Pitts recommended that POTUS designate you as the interim SecState. We were impressed with the work you did in setting up the AIFTU. We realize the Bulldog sold the concept to the Chinese and Russians, but we also know its architecture was your brainchild. And it was your idea to present it to our Cold War foes before any fireworks could erupt and start World War Three. All of this was behind the scenes. Joe Six-Pack never knew the role you played, David. But we know.

"We—the Envision-2100 board—have been watching you ever since. And we are impressed with the job you've done since your confirmation as SecState. David, we have plans for this county and its restoration as a global leader regarding the economy, the environment, and human rights. I said *a* leader, but I mean *the* leader. We want you to play an integral role, a leadership role, in those plans. To quote Forrest Gump, 'That's all I have to say about that.' At least for now.

"So what do you say, David? Can we at least take you to lunch?"

"Well, sir—Judson—how could I say no? You've piqued my curiosity. I'll see you at the heliport at eleven thirty, sharp, on Tuesday."

David spun his chair away from the desk to face a photo of his wife, Kelly. He picked up his cell phone. She'd be as intrigued by Judson's call as he was. He'd have to make it quick so he could finish his meeting with the ambassador to Mexico. In the past, the violence had been between rival cartels. Now it was starting to focus on tourists. American tourists. And it was getting medievally brutal.

3

FROM BEHIND THE F-250, Judy guided Jeremy as he backed into their campsite. "Turn to the left just a hair, and ease her back about six feet."

Following Judy's directions, Jeremy inched the Airstream into place. Then Judy stepped behind the camper, entirely outside of his line of sight. Damn. She forgot again. He pressed down on the brake, hung his head out the window, and shouted over the truck's engine, "Oh, Mrs. Richards, if you can't see me, I can't see you."

"Sorry, babe. I lost my head. Now straighten up and come on back until you hear me scream." Judy stepped to her left until Jeremy could see her in the truck's backup mirrors.

"OK, but try not to get blood on the camper." Jeremy smiled as he considered for the millionth time where the twins got their sardonic senses of humor.

When the Airstream was just the right distance from the hookups for water, electricity, and sewer, Judy held her palm up. Jeremy stopped the truck and put the transmission in park. Then the entire Richards family began a well-rehearsed choreography of campsite setup tasks. Like most RV campers, Jeremy and his family had developed a division of labor that rivaled any manufacturing company's. The routine evolved as the twins got older and began taking on more setup responsibilities.

Out of habit, Jeremy checked the bubble in the level mounted on the front of the Airstream. If the left and right sides weren't level horizontally, life inside the camper would be a lot less comfortable, but campsite number 72 had a concrete pad, so it wasn't necessary to adjust the leveling.

"Ellis, you're on deck for sewer hookup duty," he said.

"Eeeew," Ellis squealed.

Fiona covered her mouth, stifling a snort.

"I did it last time," Ellis whined. "You never make Fiona do the yucky stuff."

"Yeah, that's because I like her best." Jeremy ruffled Ellis's hair. "Fiona, unload what you can from the back of the truck. And, Ellis, don't forget to lock the drain. That campsite host in Alabama threatened to bar us from the park after it popped out last time."

Jeremy hooked up the Airstream's electrical extension cord to the campsite's thirty-amp connection box and flipped on the power switch. He then removed a water hose from a storage compartment and connected one end to a faucet and the other to a spigot underneath the camper. As he did so, Ellis retrieved a ten-foot section of collapsible plastic sewer pipe from the bumper storage and attached one end to the camper's black- and gray-water-dump connection and the other to the campsite's septic system. "It's hooked up, Dad. Now I've got to wash my hands, or we'll both catch your wife's wrath."

Jeremy grinned. Smartass.

With a thirty-gallon freshwater tank and a twenty-gallon black- and gray-water tank, it wasn't absolutely necessary to find a full-hookup campsite. They could always dry camp, using the freshwater sparingly and then dumping the wastewater at a public dump station after they left the campground. However, they had learned early on that, with three females in the family, camping was a lot more bearable if you didn't have to worry about dumping the RV's holding tanks every couple of days. Despite Judy's admonishments to conserve water, an American family of four could do a lot of flushing. So anytime they were staying longer than three days, they searched until they found a site with full hookups.

A twenty-five-foot Airstream Excella was the perfect size for a couple. When that couple had two preteens, it grew a little snug.

A tiny living area at the front of the camper held a Lilliputian-sized couch that folded out into the bed he and Judy shared. To the left—the driver's side—a swing-out table for four was mounted to the wall. The kitchen provided a three-burner propane stove and oven, a small refrigerator-freezer, a double sink, and a slide-out pantry. Three storage cabinets were mounted above the stove and sink. A bathroom, complete with a commode, a sink, and a shower the size of an airline toilet, was situated midcamper. A storage closet sat across from it. The far end of the camper housed two twin beds, each with slide-out storage below. They were separated by a narrow walkway.

As Jeremy and Ellis busied themselves with their tasks, Fiona unloaded bicycles, folding chairs, and the family fishing gear from the back of the truck. Judy readied the inside of the camper for a week's worth of close-quarters habitation. The space was cramped for a family of four, but they managed. And they loved it.

Just as Judy stepped out the door with two beers in hand, the ground shuddered. The Airstream leaped a foot into the air, and an unseen hand knocked Judy back into the camper, body-slamming her onto the floor. Pans and dishes flew out of the cabinet above the sink and bounced across the stove and countertop.

Simultaneous screams erupted from Ellis and Fiona. Then all grew still and eerily quiet.

Jeremy, stunned, raced into the camper and helped Judy up. "You OK?"

"What the fuck was that?" Judy muttered. "Were we just in our first-ever earthquake, or did you ram the truck into the Airstream?"

Jeremy put his arm over Judy's shoulders. "Well, it wasn't the truck, so I assume we just got a taste of what it's like to live on the West Coast."

Judy smoothed her hair and smiled at Jeremy. "You do realize that we are almost seven hundred miles from the coast."

As Jeremy and Judy stepped back outside, the twins picked up their toppled bicycles. People poured out of campers in surrounding sites. Plates and trays of food that had been sitting on picnic tables now littered the ground. The roof of a pop-up trailer next door had collapsed in upon itself. The ubiquitous squirrels and chipmunks had disappeared, and not a single bird was chirping.

Judy frowned and rubbed her backside. "You know my ass is still a little sore from that dribbling."

The twins sniggered. Fiona grinned and pointed at Judy. "Mom said 'ass.'"

Judy chuckled. "Watch your mouth, young lady. My butt hurts, and yours will too if you keep using that kind of language."

They all laughed.

Judy hugged Jeremy and then took charge. "Jeremy, start the fire, and I'll put the inside of the Airstream back together. We need to get supper going before it gets too dark. Besides, I'm starving."

"*Si, jefecita.*" Jeremy walked toward the back of the truck. "I'm on it. Ellis, Fiona, see if you can scrounge up some starter kindling while I get the firewood. And remember—"

"Be bear aware!" the twins shot back as they clawed the air in front of one another and, giggling hysterically, disappeared into the underbrush.

Easily accessible firewood was somewhere between scarce and nonexistent in most public campgrounds. For that reason, they always carried a supply of precut and split oak or hickory in their truck whenever they planned on having a campfire.

After the fire had burned down a bit, Jeremy placed a folding wire grill over the center of the embers. Judy came out of the camper carrying a tray loaded with brats, buns, chips, drinks, and a small boiler filled with sauerkraut. Jeremy grilled the brats and heated the sauerkraut.

When he proclaimed the dogs "ready to bark," they gathered around the dying campfire and began to eat supper.

After a few mouthfuls, Jeremy cleared his throat. "OK, let's review the plan for tomorrow. We get up at first light. At this time of the year, that's five a.m."

Fiona and Ellis looked at one another, horrified.

"Are you kidding?" Fiona moaned. "Haven't you read about that eight hours' sleep thing?"

"Yeah," Ellis chimed in. "Good luck getting Mom up at zero dark thirty."

"Yes, you two, it's god-awful early," Jeremy said. "But we want to mix and mingle with the wildlife before the other tourists start clogging up the road. I'll set up the coffee pot tonight and start it as soon as I wake up in the morning."

Judy jumped into the fray: "You ladies can fix us bagels and cheese and some fruit for breakfast. While you're doing that, I'll make sandwiches to take with us for lunch."

Oblivious to the twins' stereophonic chattering, Jeremy continued: "We should be on the road by six. It's a good fifty miles from here to Old Faithful. On park roads, that's at least an hour and a half's driving time, and we'll want to stop along the way to take photos. So we can plan on being at the geyser around nine. It erupts every thirty-five to one hundred twenty minutes. I have no idea where nine a.m. is on that cycle. We'll find out when we get to the Old Faithful Lodge gift shop."

Just then, another tremor rolled beneath them, this one a lot less violent than the bucking they had experienced earlier. It felt more like someone trying to arouse a sleeper by shaking the bed. Still a little unnerving—except for the wide-eyed, giggling, twelve-year-old twins.

"I suspect that's an aftershock from the e-ticket ride we had earlier," Judy noted. "Jeremy, why don't you break our 'no phones when we're camping rule' and check yours to see if there's any news about today's quake."

"Mom's breaking the rules," Ellis hissed to Fiona. "Can we use the phone too, Mom?"

Judy raised an eyebrow. "Not a chance, Ellis. We're looking for information, not sharing Twitter notes."

Jeremy retrieved his iPhone from its mount in the front seat of the truck and turned it on. He stopped midstride on his way back to the campfire. "Damn! They had a quake along the coast north of San Francisco that registered six point three on the Richter scale and another one, a six point eight, between Seattle and Portland. The parks-and-recreation folks decided that the Seattle-Portland quake might trigger a tsunami, so rangers evacuated the Mendicino campground just in case. The first tremor we felt must have been the aftershock from that one."

"That was no aftershock," Judy said. "If it was, I sure don't want to be around for the real deal."

"Did anyone get hurt?" Fiona asked, frowning.

"Sounds like it," Jeremy replied. "Rockslides all along Highway One, and a Luther Burbank bridge span collapsed over the One Oh One in Santa Rosa. A ruptured gas line is blazing in Petaluma, and power outages stretch from Monterey to Bodega Bay and as far east as Sacramento. It looks like we picked a good time not to go to California."

Fiona's eyes grew wide, and Ellis chewed on her bottom lip.

Judy looked from the girls to Jeremy. "OK, that's enough bad news for tonight. Turn that thing off, and let's look at the stars."

The twins gave each other a high five. "Maybe next year we could go surfing in Arizona," Ellis said to her sister with a weak smile.

Colter Bay Campground sat approximately 6,887 feet above sea level. At that altitude, in the rarefied, unpolluted, ground-light-free air, the stars seemed to explode out of the coal-black heavens. The atmosphere was so thin and distortion-free that they didn't twinkle. They burned. They stretched from horizon to horizon and seemed to go on forever.

Jeremy focused on one particular spot in the sky. Just when he thought he saw the last star, another appeared out of the darkness.

Ellis, in her folding chair, tilted her head back. "Mom, they're beautiful. Are there more here than there are in Tennessee?"

"No, you dummy," Fiona snarked. "It only looks like that because we are so high up that we're closer to them." She slid three marshmallows on her stick and reached for another one.

Judy smiled at Ellis. "Actually, baby, these are the same stars we see at home. We can see them better here because the air is clean and a lot thinner, and there aren't any streetlights or cars giving off light pollution." She pointed at the brightest star she could see. "That one is the North Star. It's really the planet Venus, but folks didn't know that when they were handing out names."

"Ha! I've got fifteen marshmallows on my stick, Fiona." Ellis elbowed her sister. "Bet you can't beat that."

Judy shook her head and grinned. "So much for an astronomy lesson." She gazed skyward again. "This is, without a doubt, the most spectacular night sky I have ever seen."

It would be the most spectacular night sky anyone in the Northern Hemisphere saw for a long, long time.

4

Foggy Bottom, Washington, DC
Two years before the day of

WITH A SECURITY GUARD and a worker from the Facilities Maintenance Department, David rode the elevator to the eighth floor of the United States Department of State's north wing and then took the stairs to its roof.

The maintenance worker unlocked the stairway door. "People don't come up here much anymore. I can't remember the last time we used the heliport," he said.

Located in what was known as the Foggy Bottom section of the nation's capital, on Northwest C Street, the Department of State housed its operations in a monstrously large complex sprawling the equivalent of two city blocks. It had taken David weeks to become even remotely familiar with the building's hallway labyrinth. Some employees spent their entire careers without seeing half of its 1.4 million square feet of office space.

The three men went up the two flights of stairs, unlocked another door, and then stepped out onto the roof of the tallest section of the building. "It's over here, sir, to your left." The facilities man motioned David toward a large yellow circle with a faded red *H* in its center.

It was one of those rare days for DC: warm, sunny, and almost cloudless. David looked to the east at Kelly Park and then south along

Constitution Avenue to get his bearings. A light, pleasant breeze blew from the northwest.

The helicopter would be flying into the wind to approach the helipad. David took out his cell phone and checked the time. It was 11:28. As he waited, he reflected on the worsening situation in Mexico and Mark Littleton's alarming comments about who might be involved. The east coast mafia? The CIA? David would have to move this up on his priority list as soon as he returned from his meeting with Ballard.

The *whup, whup, whup* of rotor blades roared overhead. Looking northwest toward the Jefferson Memorial, David saw an AgustaWestland AW160 cruising over the Tidal Basin toward him. Ten seconds later, it nosed up and settled as gently as a fourteen-thousand-pound box of moving parts could settle.

If the landing was any indicator, the pilot was good. David remembered an adage his buddies used to spout in his army days: "Either you're a world-class helicopter pilot, or you're crap on the ground."

David had no desire to be crap on the ground. That's why he had chosen Army Intelligence instead of flight school. His choice hadn't dampened his interest in aeronautics, however.

As soon as all three of the AW's wheels touched the ground, the rpm of its two Pratt & Whitney engines slowed. So did its rotor speed and the wind that was pushing David backward and playing havoc with his tie. The starboard passenger door slid open, and a man David had seen on TV but never in person jumped out. Hustling over to where David was standing, the man stuck out his hand and shouted over the engine and rotor noise, "Mr. Secretary, Judson Ballard. Let's get on board and out of this tornado."

The AW160's copilot got out and supported each of the two men as he climbed into the copter's passenger compartment. The copilot slid the door closed, significantly reducing cabin noise.

Judson slid into the forward-facing passenger seat on the port side, slipped his arms through the shoulder harness, and then glanced at

David. "It's great to meet you in person, Mr. Secretary—David," Judson said. "I've personally been looking forward to this for a long time."

"The pleasure is all mine," David replied as he fumbled with the unfamiliar harness. "I feel like I'm truly in the presence of greatness."

"Now, don't go getting all diplomatic on me, David. I'm just an old country boy." Judson chuckled and slapped David's knee. "Reminds me of something Golda Meir once told an ambassador when she was the Israeli prime minister. She said, 'Don't be so humble; you're not that great.'"

The pilot increased the throttle, eased the AW160 off the helipad, and swung its nose to the west. Seconds later, they were scooting across the Potomac and Roosevelt Island, then northwest toward Maryland.

"We're heading about fifty miles northwest of here, toward Catoctin Mountain, and the Farm, our Washington-area headquarters," Judson said. "It's about ten miles south of Camp David. We're cruising at one hundred ninety miles an hour, so we should be there in less than twenty minutes. Less time than it would take you to get to the White House from your office. We used to have an AW139, but we decided to trade up about a month ago. If I'm not mistaken, you're the first person who isn't a member of Envision-2100 to fly in it."

"You said 'we.' Does that mean this is Envision-2100's helicopter?"

"The helicopter, the Farm, and a slew of other real property assets belong to Envision-2100. It's one of those dichotomies of our organizational philosophy. We disdain the way megacorporations take advantage of gaping loopholes in government tax laws. Percentage-wise, compared to the average working citizen, those corporations pay nothing." Judson sighed. "Then we go and do the same thing. One of many, many inequalities that we—I'm talking about our government now—need to address and change. And, David, facilitating and guiding those changes is what Envision-2100 is all about."

David shifted his gaze to the right and watched the horizon below the copter whiz by from the pilot's perspective.

The AW160 sliced its way through the air at an altitude of twenty-five hundred feet, slightly east of the path set by I-270. As they flew over Frederick, Maryland, the pilot veered due north toward the heavily wooded Catoctin Mountain—or what passed for a mountain in the relatively flat Maryland countryside.

A couple of minutes later, they slowed and banked to the west as they descended onto what appeared to be either a pasture or a huge front yard. David got a glimpse of a large but rather modest two-story wooden building standing between the forest and the meadow. It looked like an old resort hotel from the late forties.

Once the copter was on the ground, the pilot reduced its engine speed, and the copilot got out. He opened the starboard passenger door as Judson unbuckled his seat belt and harness. Judson swept his hand toward the building. "Welcome to the Farm, David, formerly the Catoctin Mountain Inn."

"Nice," David replied, following Judson out of the copter.

"It's a relic of days past, for sure, but she's got good bones," Judson said. "We snatched her up during the big real estate bust, from the grandson of her original owner. The family boarded up the hotel and moved to Texas years ago. Like any empty building, it was slowly starting to disintegrate."

David and Judson headed toward the hotel.

"We renovated the interior, replaced the wiring, slapped a coat of paint on the outside, and started maintaining the grounds full time," Judson continued. "We saved a fine old landmark, got Envision-2100 a base of operations, and did so for next to nothing."

"Impressive," David said.

As they neared the hotel's main entrance, four people—three men and a woman—walked through the large double doors and onto the veranda to greet them. David recognized each face from newspaper or magazine photos or fleeting introductions at social events. It occurred to him that he had met and talked to the tall, attractive woman at the front of the line on more than one occasion.

Judson clapped David's back. "David, let me introduce you to the Envision-2100 board." He turned to face the welcoming crew. "Although he doesn't need an introduction, folks, this is David Stakley, the US secretary of state." He swept his arm toward the woman. "David, this is Melissa Gibson. I think you two have met previously. Melissa is our past president and, as is the custom with our board's executive rotation, passed the reins to me last January."

Melissa thrust her hand out to David. With a grip reflecting a passion for physical fitness and belying her external femininity, she shook his hand. "It's a pleasure to see you again, Mr. Secretary. Thank you for carving out some time to meet with us. It's an honor to have you here at the Farm."

"The honor is all mine, Melissa. Please call me David. If I'm not mistaken, my wife and I met you during a cocktail party not long ago. A fundraiser at George Washington University, as I recall."

Melissa smiled, obviously flattered by the recognition. "You have an impressive memory, David. Especially considering the number of hands you must shake each day."

His memory was less impressive than she gave him credit for. It hadn't been just any run-of-the-mill fundraiser where David had first met Melissa. She was one of five honorees who were being recognized for their contributions to both the healthcare field and humanitarian work. More than just a pretty face, Melissa Gibson was a point shy of being a medical legend.

David knew her background well. She was in her late forties and widely regarded as downright brilliant. She was a PharmD—a doctor of pharmacy—by training and had single-handedly developed the code for what came to be known as a "medical laboratory on a chip," or an MLOC.

The medical laboratory test industry fought the MLOC with everything in their arsenal, including their influence over the Food and Drug Administration, the FDA. According to news reports, Judson recognized MLOC's potential to improve medical treatment and reduce costs, especially in rural and underserved areas of the country. He brought his influence and that of the Bureau of Fiscal Service to bear on the federal approval process. The FDA approved it in record time.

Less than seven years later, Melissa had parlayed Spectral Medical into a multibillion-dollar operation. On its tenth anniversary, she took the company public. Her holdings and continued investments in the company made her one of the one-hundred-wealthiest people in the United States.

Judson nudged David down the veranda to the next person in line, a man in his early sixties. Of average height, he was dressed in a black short-sleeved Jockey T-shirt, Levi's, and leather docksiders. He had a nondescript, easy-to-forget face—until David looked into his eyes. They burned with an intensity projecting pure intelligence and a passion knocking on maniacal.

"David, this is Elton Kirby, next up for the Envision-2100 president's position and a guy who gets almost as much social media airtime as POTUS." Judson chuckled. "Elton is one of the founding members of our group and one of the first 'techno-philanthropists,' to use a term coined by Peter Diamandis in his book *Abundance*."

From the near-constant barrage of news shorts, David knew that Elton, the only African American member of the board, was a multibillionaire whose work was of enormous benefit around the globe. Like Melissa, his wealth had its genesis in software development. Using a loan from his Ugandan-born father, Elton and his future wife, Marie, had developed an artificial-intelligence, or AI, system that could gather, analyze, and store bitstream-level internet and voice-communication traffic. They subsequently sold the software, upgrades, and support to the National Security Administration (NSA) for a reputed seven billion dollars to be paid over five years.

Unlike Melissa, Elton then started one company after another without any apparent business or product-line strategy. Most notably, Elton and Marie spearheaded the invention of a radically new technique for underwater communication that eliminated the need for unwieldy, point-to-point cables, acoustic signals, and radio waves. His process mimicked the way information in the brain traveled from neuron to neuron across a synapse. Small electrical devices served as neurons and transmitted or received signals through minerals in seawater. The US Navy classified the system, dubbed the Kirby Axon, as top secret. They entered into an exclusive twenty-year agreement to lease it for use on the navy's nuclear submarine fleet.

Following that success, Elton ventured into undersea mining. Through his startup Blue Midas, Inc., he used the Kirby Axon to remotely control undersea drones. Those drones drew a variety of minerals from hydrothermal vents located thousands of meters under the Pacific Ocean. Nimble and relatively inexpensive, the drones didn't upset the seabed or generate thousands of gallons of sediment-laden wastewater, which was characteristic of legacy mining equipment. Environmentally friendly methods allowed Blue Midas to obtain exclusive mining rights to highly productive seabeds controlled by the Papua New Guinea government, creating profit for Elton and a flourishing economy for Papua New Guinea.

Elton Kirby was like a god in that tiny, dirt-poor country, David mused.

Judson continued his introduction: "Elton is also one of the most, shall we say, *outspoken* members of Envision-2100. He has a bizarre following out there who are ready to pounce on anything he says or does regardless of his intentions. But we love him."

David recalled one incident where the public pounded Elton. He had paid to have public wells constructed near a dozen villages in Uganda. Rather than garnering applause, his deed was tarnished by a vocal few who accused him of grandstanding.

David shook Elton's hand firmly. "Elton, although we've never met, I want to say how much I've grown to admire you and your efforts. Despite criticism from the peanut gallery, your work and your philanthropic efforts are outstanding."

Elton smiled graciously. "David, that's one of the nicest things anyone has ever said to me. It's easy to see how you became our secretary of state. You must have a black belt in diplomacy."

"Not at all, Elton. I tend to call them like I see them."

Gently grasping David's elbow, Judson steered him past Melissa and Judson to a familiar-looking man in his seventies who was about the same height as David, just shy of six feet. He had a head full of slate-gray, razor-cut hair, and the build of a running back.

David, this is Nelson Teal," Judson said. "Unlike Melissa and Elton, and like myself, he doesn't fall into the techno-philanthropist box. He made his money the old-fashioned way: he stole it."

The others standing on the veranda burst into laughter, including Nelson.

"I'm glad to meet you in person, David." An openly mischievous smile crept across Nelson's face. He slapped David on the shoulder. As they shook hands, David felt an instant bond spark between them.

"We've had our eye on you ever since your predecessor, Bulldog Pitts, had that cardiac meltdown. Don't go getting all swelled up or anything, but as far as I'm concerned, you are about the only Washington bureaucrat that I've seen in a long while who's worth a shit."

David chuckled. "Thank you, Nelson. I'll keep a lid on my ego; it's way too early in my career to let it boil over. Let me volley a compliment right back at you. I've read your biography, and I couldn't help being impressed with your business acumen. But the story about you and the OU cheerleaders cracked me up. Is it true?"

Nelson offered a toothy grin. "Let's just say it's based on fact. I'm not sure it was a good idea to put that out there for the whole world to see, but, what the hell, everyone who knows me knows I'll never be canonized—even if I was Catholic, which I'm not."

Another round of hearty laughter swept across the veranda.

"Besides," Nelson continued, "at this stage of my life, I've got nothing to lose. And to be honest with you, David, the cheerleader thing is a long way from the worst of my transgressions. But I'll guarantee you'll never see any of those in print." He winked.

In David's mind, Nelson Teal personified the "Will Rogers, Okie from Muskogee," "good ol' country boy" image. The cheek-to-cheek smile on his face hinted at a rare combination of honesty and humor. From reading Nelson's biography, David knew he was the sole heir to a fortune his father had grown by taking a small-town grocery store to a nationwide giant—the largest retail chain in the United States. Nelson assumed command after his father retired and expanded the business into Canada and Mexico and overseas.

Despite its financial success, the employment opportunities it provided to local populations, and the taxes it paid wherever it went, the company was seldom shown in a positive light. More often than not, it was portrayed as being just short of evil, a big company driving the mom-and-pops out of business. The older Nelson got, the more this perception bothered him, and when Judson approached him to become part of the Envision-2100 movement, he leaped at the opportunity.

David looked from Nelson to the slim, towering man standing next to him.

"Ah, here we go, David. Last but certainly not least is our token politician, champion tree hugger, and the all-around good guy of the group, Milton Freeman. Milt is a lawyer by training and keeps the board more or less in line when our conversation starts touching on the Constitution or, as you will soon see, the Federal Election Commission. Milt, direct from the Foggy Bottom section of your former stomping grounds, the secretary of state of the good ol' US of A, David Stakley."

Grasping David's hand in his massive paw, Milt said, "Mr. Secretary, let me add my thanks to your gracious acceptance to join us today."

"It's my pleasure," David replied. "And it's a pleasure to meet you, Milt. Your reputation precedes you."

Milt "the Stilt" Freeman, a popular four-term senator from Connecticut, had made an unsuccessful run for president on the Democratic ticket while David was in the army and stationed in Korea. Although relatively civil at the candidate level compared to previous campaigns, the party-level infighting was nothing short of slanderous. Even with the growing use of biometric and password-protected computerized voting machines, there were accusations of fraud and hacking, later proven to be false.

The election results were historically close. Freeman won the popular vote, but for the second time in the twenty-first century, a majority elected candidate lost the Electoral College count. The Democrats were outraged and called for nationwide strikes and protests. Freeman, who had refused to make or support any negative comments, commercials, or social media ads throughout the campaign, would have none of it. Instead, he graciously conceded to the legally elected Republican candidate. He began transitioning into the political shadows and immersing himself in his passion for protecting the environment.

Milt was the only member of the Envision-2100 board who hadn't cracked the billion-dollar barrier as far as David knew. He had married rich, and his wife, Camille, had inherited a fortune that allowed Milt to follow his political ambitions without ever having to actually practice law. It also gave Milt and Camile the freedom to devote themselves full time to their environmental protection efforts. Camile was as passionate as Milt about their various "save the planet" causes, which frequently made the news.

Milt interrupted David's thoughts: "I'm so hungry my stomach feels like my throat's been cut. Let's go inside and grab lunch. I think you'll be pleased and impressed by what you'll learn about Envision-2100, David. I'm confident you will be excited about the proposal we have in store for you. But I'm getting ahead of myself." He nodded at the door. "I hope you don't mind if we make this a working lunch. We have a lot of ground to cover, and if we're going to get you back to DC before dark, we don't have any time to waste."

"I'm fine with that," David replied.

Milt nodded. "Good. I've been drafted to facilitate our discussion and keep things on track. But as you will soon see, the rest of these folks will jump in with both feet when something touches their hot button."

With that, Milt ushered the group through the veranda door and into a new chapter in both David's life and the history of the United States.

David just didn't know that yet.

5

Salt Lake City
Two days before the day of

FOR THE SIXTH DAY IN A ROW, Dr. Roland King hunched his lean, six-foot frame over his desk at the University of Utah Seismograph Station, fixated on his array of monitors. The tracing pen on the San Andreas Fault seismic monitor twitched. Its movements had been getting stronger and more erratic on what appeared to be some yet-to-be-determined cycle. A small bounce at first, then a straight line marking no activity for seven hours. Another jump, a fraction of a second longer in duration, followed by a six-hour, forty-minute lull. Then rinse and repeat.

With each round, the cycle grew longer and the intensity, as measured by the Richter scale, got a bit stronger. There was some type of Fibonacci number pattern at play. Something he had never seen in all his years of needle watching.

He clicked his ballpoint pen repeatedly, deep in thought. If he could determine the frequency, he might be able to develop an earthquake prediction model, the holy grail of his science. That would guarantee his name on a brick at the University of California, Berkley, School of Earth and Planetary Science. However, it wasn't the allure of academic fame that kept Roland glued to his monitor this morning. There was another phenomenon at play. And it sent shivers up his spine.

This was the moment he'd been waiting for since he was thirteen and decided, thanks to his parents, that he wanted a career in seismology. While on a caravan tour of Costa Rica with his parents and older sister, he had stood on the rim of the Poás volcano's main crater and listened to his Costa Rican tour guide describe the Ring of Fire. The tour included side trips to the national park surrounding the Poás volcano, followed by a four-hour drive and an overnight stay in the district of La Fortuna in the northwestern part of the country.

In the center of La Fortuna sat the gigantic, cone-shaped Arenal Volcano and its hundreds of magma-heated springs. In 1968, after lying dormant for hundreds of years, Arenal experienced a violent, unanticipated eruption that buried several nearby villages and killed nearly one hundred inhabitants.

It was during a tour guide discussion while viewing the main Poás crater that Roland first learned about what is commonly known as the Pacific Ring of Fire. Nearly 90 percent of the world's earthquakes occur somewhere along the Ring of Fire, which extends from the Kermadec Trench, east of New Zealand, to Java, then up the coast of Asia. From there, it travels through the Aleutian Trench to Alaska and all along the west shores of North, Central, and South America.

Roland glanced at a Ring of Fire map on his wall to the right of the monitors. Nearly five hundred active and dormant volcanoes and continuously shifting tectonic plates were included. The wonderfully dangerous natural phenomenon, its aura and scientific mystery, still fascinated him.

Roland was twenty-six by the time he had earned his BS and MS and completed the coursework and research required for his PhD from the University of California, Berkeley. In retrospect, he knew that he had decided on his PhD dissertation, or at least part of it, on that tour with his family.

While pursuing his master's, Roland had convinced himself that the Ring of Fire sat atop a contiguous stream of magma, plumes of molten rock that continually rose from the earth's core and flowed through the mantle, just below the crust. He theorized that this river was confined by the oceanic and continental plates, and it lay much closer to the earth's upper mantle than previously thought. Documenting and attempting to prove this theory became an obsession that naturally evolved into the topic of his PhD dissertation. The mathematical model Roland developed to support his "rising magma plume" theory while conducting the research also led him to a serendipitous discovery. If his model was correct, it provided geometrical proof that the magma plume and concomitant changes in the earth's mantle contributed to a recently discovered, ever-increasing wobble to Earth's rotation axis.

Roland was ecstatic. So much so that he decided to incorporate both theories into his dissertation. That was a risky proposition, but if accepted, it could guarantee him a footnote in some never-to-be-read *Journal of Geophysics* article. Nerds lived for such obscure notoriety, and if there was one thing that Roland knew for sure, it was that he was the crown prince of nerds—not just an athletic body and a pretty face.

In addition to his advisor, there were four other people on Roland's PhD committee, each with theories on magma flow and tectonic plate movement that did not align with his. However, his dissertation presentation was so convincing that he received a standing ovation at its conclusion. Since UC Berkeley did not award Latin honors to graduate or doctoral students, this was as close to summa cum laude as Roland could expect. It gave him the support he needed to pursue his mission.

Roland's eyes flew between two of the four monitors attached to his desktop computer. He clicked his pen. The monitors were controlled by programs that reported measurements from remote seismic detectors.

Every time the San Andreas monitor needle had twitched over the last seventy-plus hours, the indicator on the Cascadia Subduction Zone, CSZ, moved as well. By now, they were in virtual lockstep. There appeared to be a shrinking seventy-minute-or-so separation. The CSZ activity wasn't as intense at first, but it grew stronger with each cycle. The most troubling observation was that the CSZ tremors seemed to be waking up sleeping giants. Both Mount Rainier and Mount St. Helens had started rumbling. That was not a good sign.

The CSZ started just north of Vancouver Island, in Canada, and ran almost seven hundred miles south, past Mendocino, California, making it the most extensive fault line in the Northern Hemisphere. And that was just what could be sensed and mapped by the North American Geological Society's equipment. Scientists believed that the San Andreas and CSZ were independent fault lines with no physical connections.

They were wrong.

"Cortana, expand the view on monitor two." Roland's computer responded to the voice control system. It expanded the view to include all of the remotely monitored seismic equipment in the northwest quadrant of the country. "OK, Cortana, zoom in . . . closer . . . closer." He drilled down to the seismic equipment inside Yellowstone National Park. If his seismic computer model was as accurate as he predicted, the activity at Mounts Rainier and St. Helens caused by the CSZ movement could be a prelude to something in the Wyoming calderas: the Yellowstone supervolcano. And that could be bad. That could be really, really bad.

The Yellowstone Caldera was a thirty-by-forty-mile crater created by a supervolcano eruption 640,000 years ago, give or take a few millennia. Although a significant eruption hadn't occurred there in centuries, the area surrounding the caldera, and the entire Yellowstone Plateau, was home to nearly constant minor volcanic and earthquake activity. The area just south of US Route 191, which passed less than two miles from the caldera and north of Shoshone Lake, typically experienced over one thousand earthquakes annually. Most were small, less than a magnitude 3 on the Richter scale. However, occasionally the place went crazy. In 1985 over three thousand earthquakes were recorded in fewer than four months.

It looked to Roland like this year could break that record. If things were as bad as he was beginning to suspect, the record might be broken this week. But it wasn't just earthquakes that worried him; it was the volcanic activity they could cause. Even a series of minor quakes could have a cumulative effect. A long string could start things moving in the semielastic basalt magma intrusion zone. In the section of Yellowstone that he was studying, the intrusion zone was only about three miles beneath the earth's crust.

Only the Lord knew what a 5- or 6-scale tremor might do in a relatively fragile area. It would be far more than most people expected. The Richter scale was logarithmic, based on 10. A magnitude 4 was ten times as powerful as a magnitude 3.

The volcanic explosivity index, or VEI, measured the amount of material ejected out of the volcano, how high that material was calculated to go, and how long eruptions were expected to last. Like the Richter scale, the VEI was logarithmic. Mount Vesuvius and Mount St. Helens were estimated to have a VEI of 5. The supervolcano sitting beneath the Yellowstone Caldera had an estimated VEI of 8. That potential made Yellowstone over one thousand times as powerful as the eruption that buried Pompeii under ten feet of ash and pumice in 79 AD.

Contrary to popular belief and action movie depictions, it wasn't lava that destroyed Pompeii and its neighbor Herculaneum; it was a rapid and pervasive accumulation of ash, pumice, and cinders that caused death and destruction. Things would be worse today, far worse, even in the sparsely populated Northwest. Aircraft would be unable to fly for months. Vehicle and emergency generator engines would choke on the air and grind to a stop. Rivers would be clogged, electrical grids would fail, and crops would wither and die for hundreds of miles around. And the effects on animal respiratory systems would be incalculable. Roland and numerous colleagues estimated that a full-scale eruption of the supervolcano could spread over three feet of ash within a radius extending three hundred miles from Yellowstone.

Roland caught himself clicking his ballpoint pen again and put it down. He drummed his fingers, picked up the pen, and started clicking again.

The ash and sulfur dioxide spewing into the atmosphere would slow global warming down for a few decades. Maybe it would even mitigate the self-inflicted wounds the climate change deniers were doing to themselves. But try as he might, Roland couldn't put a positive spin on what he was imagining.

Click, click. Roland dropped his pen and tore himself away from the drama unfolding on his row of computer monitors. He picked up his office phone and punched the intercom number for his supervisor and friend, Larry Ferguson. "Larry, I think the shit's about to hit the fan in Yellowstone. Maybe Mount St. Helens and Rainier as well. The needles are jumping all along the San Andreas and the Cascadia, and now things are heading east."

"Please press one to continue in English, *para continuar en Espanol pulse dos*," Larry answered in a faux computer voice.

Ignoring Larry's attempt at humor, Roland continued: "I'm going to take a road trip up to Yellowstone and see what our new ground-penetrating radar picks up around the caldera. I think there is a lot more going on than our seismic gear can show us, and it's showing a helluva lot. Do you want to tag along? We can be there in less than six hours."

The line was silent for a second, then, "I might as well. It's not like I have plans for tonight. Or a social life, for that matter."

"Great," Roland said. "I'll start packing the truck as soon as I hang up, then head home and crash for a couple of hours. How about I pick you up at your apartment at say oh five hundred tomorrow."

Larry groaned.

"Oh, come on, Larry. I've been giving the situation a lot of thought. We should discuss a plan of action if things turn out to be as bad as I'm thinking they are, what we are going to recommend, and who we're going to recommend it to. I know there's a generic evacuation plan sitting on the shelf somewhere. Probably in your office. But the thing's older than I am."

"OK, Roland, don't get your panties in a wad just yet. While you're packing up, I'll see if I can find the evacuation plan and any other what-if documents we have stashed away. And an emergency recall roster for Wyoming."

"All right, Larry, I'll see you at oh five hundred, but make that recall roster for the entire Northwest."

Roland hung up the phone and powered down his computers.

6

The Farm
Two years before the day of

DAVID STEPPED THROUGH THE VERANDA DOORS into a lobby reminiscent of grand old resort hotels like The Greenbrier or The Broadmoor. Although it wasn't nearly as large, it was just as opulent. A faint aroma of apples and cinnamon permeated the air, giving it a homey feeling despite the majesty.

"Restored to her original days of grandeur," Milt noted as the others streamed behind them into the lobby.

A long, burled-walnut reception desk with polished brass rails bordered one end of the room. Behind the counter were row after row of wooden mailboxes, each adorned with a hanging set of room keys. In the center of the room, a brightly colored Persian rug covered most of the gently worn, antique heart-of-pine floor. A brace of leather couches bracketed a long wooden coffee table, which perfectly matched the reception desk. The lobby quietly whispered wealth and luxury.

Milt guided the group toward an adjoining dining room. "There are some new fixtures, but we tried to use the original, reconditioned furnishings where possible. The main building has one hundred and twenty guest rooms. Envision-2100 members are welcome here on a first-come, first-served basis as long as it isn't reserved for special events. Like it is today."

Judson strode up beside David. "A local, semiretired couple, the Washingtons, oversee general activities. They seem to love it here, and we're thrilled at the way they take care of the place. But most of all, we can't get enough of Ms. Mattie's cooking. You'll see." His eyes twinkled.

Followed by the other board members, Milt and David entered the spacious dining room filled with several large, round tables for eight covered in spotless white linen. The table nearest the entrance had six place settings of silverware and crystal.

A spry, elderly black couple hovered just past the door, near one end of a buffet line. The woman, who must've been knocking on seventy, wore a solid black dress and a starched knee-length red apron. Her salt-and-pepper hair was pulled up into an impossibly tight bun.

The man, early to mid-seventies, about six feet tall, was fence-rail thin and stood just as straight. He had close-cropped grayish-white hair and sported a meticulously groomed beard. His dazzling-white, long-sleeved shirt was tucked neatly into black slacks. But it was his shoes that caught David's eye. Black cap-toe lace-ups whose spit shine gleamed like silver.

Milt steered David toward the couple. "David, I want you to meet Mr. and Mrs. Washington. They're the folks who run this place."

"You just call me Mattie, Mr. Secretary; everybody else do. It's an honor to meet you in person. You're the third secretary of state that I've met. Ms. Rice and Mrs. Clinton are both brilliant ladies, regardless of how you feel about their politics. From what I hear, you didn't get skipped when they passed out the brains either, and if you don't mind my saying so, you are by far the best looking of the three." She took the arm of the man standing beside her. "Mr. Secretary, this is my husband, Lucas."

Lucas thrust his hand out to David. "Watch out, Mr. Secretary. Mattie will talk your head clean off your shoulders if you give her a chance, especially if you get her started on politics or the blues."

David chuckled. "Well, Mattie, I'm a big Stevie Ray Vaughn fan myself. And I try to avoid political discussions. I get more than enough of that stuff at work."

Mattie moved to the end of the table and started removing the lids from the steaming food warmers. She waved the group forward. "Lunch is ready, Mr. Secretary, and since you are our guest, you have the honor of going first."

David scanned the buffet line. The warmers contained meatloaf, fried chicken, mashed potatoes, and green beans. There was also a medium-sized glass bowl filled with a tossed salad. At the end of the buffet sat a colossal coconut cake—David's favorite dessert. Somehow he knew that wasn't by accident. These folks did have a phenomenal inside track.

As David filled his plate, Milt leaned toward him. "Everything's fresh here. No canned or prepackaged food at all. Mattie wouldn't stand for it."

After everyone was seated, Lucas offered iced tea from a crystal pitcher dripping with condensation. Once everyone had their drinks, he placed another full pitcher on the table. He and Mattie quietly left the room, closing the doors behind them.

David politely waited for one of his hosts to start eating, even though looking at his plate made his stomach rumble. He didn't have to wait long. Elton and Melissa dove in.

Milt speared a bunch of green beans. "As I mentioned, David, I've been 'volunteered' to facilitate our discussion this afternoon. Judson tells me that you know at least a little bit about Envision-2100." Milt shoved the beans in his mouth.

David dabbed his mouth with his napkin. "I know what I've heard on the news and social media, although I have zero confidence in the validity of the sources. I did a Google search after talking to Judson last week. However, I didn't have the time to go much further than the Wikipedia page. So, basically, I don't know what I don't know."

Milt and everyone else at the table smiled at David's candid assessment. Then Elton interjected, "Why don't you give him the CliffNotes version of our background, Milt. That way, we'll all know what he knows, so we can call bullshit on any media slants he might have heard."

"Thank you for cutting straight to the chase, Elton," Milt shot back. "I'll do just that, and I'll start with Genesis.

"Way back in 2010, Warren Buffett and Bill and Melinda Gates convinced a group of billionaires to sign what came to be known as the Giving Pledge. Initially, this was a promise made by each signatory to give away at least half of his or her wealth to some charitable cause. Judson, Nelson, Elton, and several others who are now part of Envision-2100 were early adopters of this movement.

"However, at some point, a core group became somewhat disillusioned at the overall lack of direction and structure they were seeing, or instead weren't seeing. 'Disillusioned' may not be the best word to describe how they felt, but hey, I'm the one leading this discussion."

"Disenchanted, disillusioned, cynical—choose your adjective," Judson interjected. "We all know what you mean; no use trying to church it up. Buffett's Bunch—my term—had admirable intentions. But in my opinion, they were just throwing money left and right. Everyone had his own cause or charity, which is fine, but there weren't any clearly defined objectives, no end goals."

Nelson pointed a fried chicken leg at David. "As Zig Ziglar was fond of saying, 'If you aim at nothing, you will hit it every time.'"

Milt wolfed down a massive bite of meatloaf, then continued: "Everyone was acutely aware of suffering and poverty around the globe. But eventually they concluded it would be best to think globally and act locally.

"Ever since the end of the Civil War, the United States has been far and away the most generous country in the world. We follow every disaster, every famine, every political upheaval. The Lord knows we have a damn-long list of problems ourselves, and our intentions and methods are sometimes suspect at best. But at least for the time being, we are the country that the rest of the planet looks to when the crap hits the fan.

"China is trying to change its image, but they have a lot of catching up to do. And the previous administration would have totally fucked things up if they had survived for a second term, but we've almost recovered from that four-year fiasco. So, Judson decided it was time to drop back and punt, to use one of Nelson's football analogies."

Nelson looked up from his plate. "Well, Milt, you Atlantic Conference boys know a lot about punting. Let me know when your story gets around to actually running the ball."

Everyone at the table, including Milt, chuckled, impressing David with their camaraderie and the respect the group seemed to share for one another.

Milt swallowed another bite of his mashed potatoes before continuing. "Judson got a sense that some folks in the Buffett-Gates entourage shared his 'focused charity' sentiment, so he pulled a group together for a discussion dinner at his estate in Oregon." He chuckled. "You might see a 'meet while you eat' theme here. And speaking of theme, when I say he pulled a group together, I mean he had his private jet shuttle them in from all over the country.

"This core group, which included Nelson and Elton, met virtually nonstop over a three-day weekend, with discussions fueled by cases of Napa's finest and more than a few bottles of fifteen-year-old single malt. I wasn't there, but it's my understanding that there was no shortage of spirited debate. Close enough, Judson?"

Judson pointed at Milt. "That's a fair assessment, Milt. We were pretty much saying the same thing but just saying it a little differently. In the end, our consensus was uncannily close to each individual's opinion."

"And that consensus," Milt continued, "was that, as a whole, the world is a pretty fucked-up place. Regardless of any group's best intentions, the reality is that you can't make a global impact using a helter-skelter, scattergun approach. It will require a well-thought-out strategy, a laser-focused plan designed for methodical execution. And Buffett's Bunch weren't inclined to take that approach.

"So, out of that initial meeting at Judson's—which some of us refer to as the Weekend at Bernie's, if you remember that old comedy—the core Envision-2100 group was formed. They concurred on several points that would eventually come to serve as the springboard of our platform."

"Are you going to share those points, Milt?" Melissa asked, eyes twinkling.

Milt grinned. "You already know the answer to that. The first point was complete agreement that leadership by the United States would be the best, perhaps the only way, to make a lasting global impact. The second point was that although the US Constitution was the most perfectly conceived document ever developed, the government it formed had failed to allow it to evolve as it was designed to do. As a result, instead of being self-perpetuating, it had, over the years, become self-corrupting.

"Beyond these two primary areas of consensus, everyone had personal ideas of what was needed, and on the path necessary to accomplish it. That's when Elton suggested that they should formalize their objectives for the next century and lay out the milestones required to reach them. Thus, the name Envision-2100. The name stuck and eventually became the rallying cry for the group."

"It's certainly appropriate," David said. "And it's catchy."

"Glad you like it," Elton said.

"At Elton's suggestion," Milt continued, "it was decided to com-mission a team to formally and objectively evaluate the state of the state. In other words, they wanted to develop a written analysis detailing the good, the bad, and the ugly of the US government, what was work-ing and what needed to be fixed or replaced. The group empowered Judson, Nelson, and Elton to assemble a diverse panel of experts to prepare a document that they could agree to use as the cornerstone for Envision-2100's moral and philosophic compass and which would serve as Envision-2100's not-too-far-in-the-future political platform. More on that shortly."

Milt swept his hand toward Nelson. "Nelson spearheaded this effort and assembled an eclectic group of subject matter specialists to consolidate the core group's philosophies, access regional, national, and global issues, and then hammer them into a strategic plan that will be the focus of Envision-2100's energies and resources. The team included a physician, educators, retired military and law enforcement officers, social workers, civil rights activists, and representatives from various STEM disciplines—science, technology, engineering, and math."

As Milt paused to drink from a crystal glass of iced tea, David dabbed his lips with his napkin and wiped his fingers, then spread the linen back over his lap. Although he still had no idea why the board had invited him to this meeting, the group's positioning and dynamics drew him in.

Milt continued: "I served as the government, legal, and constitution expert and carried the flag for environmental causes. Nelson challenged the group to formalize its assessment and have the first draft of their plan ready for the core group's review in six months. Nelson's deadline posed a monumental challenge, but the exceptionally well-compensated and, I might add, highly motivated task force jumped on the task like a duck on a June bug."

"Nelson's Ninjas," interjected Melissa.

Milt chuckled. "Yes, that's what we called ourselves. We were sequestered here at the Farm and worked day and night seven days a week. We met every day at five to review that day's work and to discuss plans for the following day.

"Although we were remarkably close on most issues, we had to hammer out a few, especially solutions for some of the more complex problems. As we worked, it became evident that cliques were forming. As soon as that happened, Nelson broke them up. He forced us to establish new working relationships and find original approaches to problem solutions. Nelson kept us focused and always on our toes. I don't want to make him blush, but he epitomizes the concept of a leader: tireless, relentless, and just damned brilliant."

Nelson wagged a finger at Milt. "There you go, trying to canonize me again."

Milt grinned. "Didn't you just say you weren't Catholic?"

Laughter swept around the table.

"Anyway, by the end of the fourth month, we had developed a pretty decent clayman, something we could pull apart, shape, and remold piece by piece. We spent the last two months of our review period refining and wordsmithing our product, making sure it said what we as a single-minded group wanted it to say without any hint of ambiguity."

Milt motioned to Nelson. "Our new saint here compared this process to the Japanese art of sword making, the part where they forge, fold, and immerse the blade's metal in cooling water many times: *orikaeshi tanren.* When this process is complete, the metal's impurities have been removed, hammered out, and it becomes a finely honed work of art able to withstand centuries of use.

"Just like you learned in grade school, the fundamental purpose of the United States Constitution is summed up in its Preamble: 'establish Justice, insure domestic Tranquility, provide for the common defence, promote the general Welfare, and secure the Blessings of Liberty to ourselves and our Posterity.' The constitution itself is as close to perfect as any foundation of law and government ever developed. However, it was designed to be a living document, to evolve to keep pace with the times and our culture."

Judson shook his head. "Unfortunately, it's not working out that way."

Milt nodded. "As I alluded to earlier, we, through our elected representatives, weren't allowing that to happen. At least not quickly enough or to the extent necessary. You've gotta remember, we ratified the constitution in 1789, but it took another seventy-six years before it eliminated slavery and over one hundred thirty years before it gave women the right to vote. Our legal foundation and the government it supported were choking themselves. After all our work, we concluded that two fundamental issues were ripping our country apart.

"The first, and ostensibly the cause of every other problem with our government and its legal system, is an apathetic, politically ignorant citizenry." Milt stabbed his fork in the air. "The second is the ridiculously restrictive, ineffective two-party political system we have allowed to gain control over our country and our lives."

Still holding his fork but waving it like an orchestra conductor's baton, Milt reached the crescendo of his sermonette.

"Like a nuclear reactor, our political system has reached its critical mass. It's no longer responsive to the needs of our people. It's grown so big and so corrupt that it just feeds upon itself. And, like a runaway reactor, if we don't do something, and do it soon, it's going to melt down and explode. However, unlike that reactor, we don't have giant cadmium control rods that we can push into the core to stop the reaction." Milt's voice thumped with passion. "My fear, the source of all my nightmares, is that it's going to take a war or some sort of national catastrophe to bring about the constitutional changes necessary to keep our country from crashing and burning."

When Milt paused to gulp down some of his tea, David cleared his throat. "I agree with everything you've told me. I've been saying more or less the same thing for years. In the last election, well over forty percent of the people who were eligible to vote didn't bother to show up. And we were thumping ourselves on the chest with that number. Half the kids entering college have no clue who we fought during World War Two or who won the Civil War, or can't name the three branches of our government. I even saw a *Saturday Night Live* video where a fake news reporter asked some people on the street if they thought the Electoral College would get a bowl game. Half of them agreed, and the other half said they didn't follow football."

Milt sighed and shook his head as David continued: "The sad thing is, their votes count just as much as anyone's in this room. The average score on the Stanford-Binet in the United States is one hundred. That means, statistically speaking, almost one half of our voting population has a two-digit IQ. I've pretty much convinced myself that it's a good thing that we have such low voter turnout. It may sound harsh, but I'm just not sure we want someone who thinks the VP is the 'assistant president' making decisions about who should be our elected representatives.

"I'm entirely on board with what you've told me about Envision-2100 and what it's trying to accomplish. But let's cut to the chase. I can't believe you went to all of the trouble and expense to bring me up here to ask me to become part of your organization. Hell, I'm a broke-ass government employee. I couldn't even pay for the helicopter ride. I loved it, but I couldn't afford it. Besides, as I'm sure Milt knows, in my position, I am not allowed to join a political organization."

The five Envision-2100 board members exchanged glances. One by one, they turned their heads toward David. For a few seconds, silence pulsated around the table. Then Melissa laid her knife and fork on her plate.

"Mr. Secretary. David. We didn't bring you here to ask you to join Envision-2100. We brought you here to ask you to run for president of the United States."

7

Salt Lake City
Two days before the day of

ROLAND PULLED THE UNIVERSITY'S WHITE FORD ECONOLINE VAN into the parking lot in front of his supervisor's apartment building at 04:58. Larry's apartment, number 101, was on the corner of the ground floor of the brick-and-stucco two-story building.

Three long, gray, casket-like metal boxes sat in the back of the van. They contained the Seismology Department's new ground-penetrating radar equipment and two ultrasensitive seismographs. Roland had also packed his bugout gear, which included a sleeping bag, a nylon pup tent, and a three-day supply of dehydrated food. Experience told him that Larry would bring similar camping equipment and an arsenal of bear spray. He got out of the van, cut across the front lawn to Larry's apartment door, and rang the bell.

Seconds later, the door opened. Larry stumbled out wearing a backpack and carrying a bugout bag similar to Roland's.

"You know, Dr. King," Larry groaned as he tossed his gear through the side door of the van, "there aren't any state or federal laws that would've prohibited us from leaving at, oh, I don't know, say, nine or ten instead of this unholy time of day. The sun doesn't come up for at least another hour. Or so I've heard. I don't think I've ever been awake this early, at least not on purpose."

"Yeah, I know. It reminds me of my old army days." Roland climbed back into the van and settled into the vehicle's as-cheap-as-could-be-produced bucket seat.

"You've never been in the fucking army." Larry slid into the passenger seat and slammed the door. "You don't have a social life and wanted to make sure I don't, either."

Roland snorted. "Well, excuse me for interrupting your Taylor Swift sleepover with what could very well be one of the most important investigations in the history of vulcanology."

"You know, that's a pretty short list, buddy," Larry shot back. He sighed and rubbed his eyes. "At least we get to head back into the wilderness on another research boondoggle and get paid for it. It's been what? Three months now. Way too long."

"This isn't a boondoggle. And it's only been two months."

Roland backed the van out of the parking space and headed for the parking lot exit.

"OK, boss man," he continued. "We'll take the I-Fifteen to Idaho Falls. From there, we can jump on Highway Twenty and into the west entrance of Yellowstone. Depending on the traffic and construction, it should take us around six hours, assuming we stop for lunch in Idaho Falls."

"Sounds good," Larry said. "I'll set up my phone's GPS. It'll warn us if there's trouble ahead."

"There's a thermos of coffee and two travel mugs in my bag if you need a pick-me-up." Roland glanced at Larry. "That's a hint to pour me a cup, in case you didn't notice."

"You know, Roland, you'll make someone a great wife someday," Larry teased. He poured two mugs of the steaming brew, screwed the lid back on, and placed Roland's mug in the console cup holder. He rubbed his eyes again and yawned. "Well, there is at least one good thing about heading out at this god-awful time of day: there shouldn't be any traffic coming out of the city, and once we get on I-Fifteen, there won't be any until, well, ever." The I-15 was one of the least traveled interstates in the country. "We finally get to do something productive with all the new equipment. Gotta show a return on its investment. And maybe we can cobble up a research paper from whatever we find."

"Sounds like you're finally awake," Roland said dryly.

Once they got past North Salt Lake, Roland set the van's cruise control to seventy-four miles per hour. They drove all the way past Ogden before he had to put on the brakes when they stopped just south of Willard Bay State Park to relieve themselves of the coffee they'd been sipping.

They stopped at Stockman's Restaurant, off I-15 just south of Idaho Falls, for lunch. They were both hungry, and neither was in the mood for fast food. Besides, they were on official business and could put their meals on the department's expense account. After lunch, they topped off the van's gas tank and turned on US 20, which would take them all the way to West Yellowstone.

As Roland drove, Larry called the office of the Yellowstone Park rangers to confirm their arrival and let them know they would be camping in the area of the caldera on the west side, off Shoshone Lake. He also fired up an app on his iPad that, by connecting to the now nearly ubiquitous cellular network, allowed him to monitor remotely located seismographs as if he were seated in front of the computer in his office.

"Holy shit, Roland. Look at this." Larry held out the iPad so Roland could see it. An array of seismic measurement lights flashed across a map of Yellowstone. Most were yellow, but as the indicators closed in on the caldera, they changed from yellow to orange, indicating a high level of activity.

"Holy crap. What's going on in the caldera, Larry? Check the caldera!"

Larry's thumb and forefinger swept open the display. He held it up for Roland again. The five lights scattered over the actual caldera basin, atop the Yellowstone supervolcano, were bright red and blinked like strobe lights in a seventies disco. Not that Roland had ever seen a disco aside from *Staying Alive* reruns on TCM.

"Just like you suspected, buddy: this place is jumping." Larry dropped the iPad back in his lap.

There were several vehicles in a line in front of them as they neared the West Entrance park gate. As they rolled up to the checkpoint after the car in front of them moved, a tremor rocked the van, sloshing out the remains of Larry's coffee and knocking over two of the equipment crates that were stacked in the cargo bed. It only lasted a couple of seconds, and even though it wasn't necessary, it reminded them of why they were there.

"I guess you've been having a lot of those the last few days," Roland said to the ranger at the sliding office window.

"Yeah. We normally get some small quakes two or three times a month up here. But lately it's been five or six times a day. I'll tell you, it's a little unnerving, especially when we're sitting directly on top of the largest volcano in the Northern Hemisphere. I hope you guys can find out what's going on down there. I want a little warning if that thing decides to blow its top."

That would have been nice. Nice indeed.

"By the way, Roland," Larry said, "I did dig up that emergency action plan we discussed. It's at least as old as you expected, and everyone listed as a contact is long departed. However, I found a number for the Wyoming State Emergency Response Commission and the local office of Homeland Security. They have a reasonably robust website and a more current disaster plan. I downloaded key numbers to my phone just in case."

"Good." Roland drove into the park following US 191 along the Madison River. As happened every time he visited Yellowstone, he was struck by two things. One was the sheer, heart-fluttering beauty of the place. The other was the swarm of tourists and associated traffic on the road, or at least this section. Cars on both sides of the way would pull over, park, and then disgorge their cell-phone-packing passengers every time they spied a moose or elk grazing or on the edge of the water. Roland knew this practice would ease up somewhat the farther into the park they got, as the traffic dispersed and the initial novelty of seeing the animals wore off. Still, it was congested and slow going for the first four or five miles.

At the junction with US 89, they turned right, staying on 191, and headed southeast, this time loosely following the Firehole River. They passed through Whiskey Flat and then drove past the Excelsior Geyser crater and the steaming, deep-blue Grand Prismatic Spring. The wind blew from the west, spreading the rotten-egg stench of sulfur bubbling up through the water. Another fringe benefit of being a professional, government-employed seismologist: neither Roland nor Larry reacted to the smell; they had been working around these stink pits so long it barely registered.

A few miles later, they came to the entrance of the parking lot of the tourist complex that surrounded Old Faithful. Roland was starting to feel an early signal from his bladder and said to Larry, "It's only another ten miles until we turn off One Ninety-One and onto the maintenance trail that takes us into the caldera. But that coffee's ready to make an exit, if you know what I mean."

"Well, I could stand one last trip to a flushing toilet before we start sleeping in a tent and crapping in the woods," Larry replied. "While we're stopped, we may as well get a burger or something to eat. Ready-to-eat rations and canteen water are fine for about one meal, but after three or four days, I reach my limit. I didn't fight my way up the food chain to eat sticks and twigs, and that's what dehydrated stew tastes like after day one."

Roland turned off the highway and drove into the Old Faithful Inn and Visitor Center parking lot. There were cars and tour buses everywhere. He always felt a little sad every time he visited Yellowstone, Yosemite, the Grand Canyon, or any of the other natural wonders that were crawling with tourists. Deep inside, he knew he had no right to feel that way since, at times, he was a tourist too, but he couldn't shake that initial feeling.

He parked the van about one hundred meters from the Inn. Although his bladder didn't totally agree, he and Larry didn't mind walking, and the exercise would wake them up. Just as he turned off the van's engine, a huge, fire-truck-red F-250 pulled into a parking space across from them. When it stopped, two girls, carbon copies of one another, bounced out, followed by a man he assumed to be their father and a good-looking lady, whom he took to be their mother.

As the loosely assembled group started walking toward the Inn, Larry smiled at the two girls. "You must be twins."

Grinning back like little spider monkeys, the two looked at each other, and one of them pulled her head back in mock astonishment. "Wow, mister. Are you some kind of genius or something?"

The girls laughed hysterically, and Roland joined in—even though his bladder was throbbing—but the lady stopped dead in her tracks. She wasn't laughing. At all.

"Fiona, that wasn't the least bit funny! Apologize right this instant!"

"I'm sorry, sir," the young girl said, her lips trembling. An unmistakable twinkle lit her eyes. "It just jumped out."

The lady turned to Larry. "Please excuse my pair of smart alecks. They're having a hormone explosion and practicing to be teenagers."

All four of the adults laughed. The twins rolled their eyes.

Roland nodded at the F-250's license plate. "Did you guys come here all the way from Tennessee?"

The girls' father nodded. "We got here yesterday. We're camping in our RV over at Colter Bay. Name's Jeremy Richards." Jeremy shook hands with both men and introduced Judy, Fiona, and Ellis.

"Been to Yellowstone before?" Larry asked.

"It's our first trip here," Jeremy responded. "Actually, it's our first trip anywhere west of the Mississippi. Old Faithful is our last stop for the day."

Judy smiled. "We're going to wait around to watch the next eruption, and then we're heading back to our campsite for dinner under the stars. We've never seen anything like the night sky up here."

"Tomorrow, we plan to go to the falls and then just wander around the park," Jeremy added.

"There's a lot to see here if you enjoy wildlife and nature in general," Larry said. "But you might also enjoy a side trip to Jackson Hole. It's about forty miles south of Colter Bay, and the drive is beautiful, especially along the Snake River. The Hole is always packed with tourists, but they have some great restaurants if you want to have lunch. And you pass through the National Elk Refuge—although I've been through there about a hundred times and have yet to see a single elk."

"Speaking of wildlife," Jeremy said slowly, "we passed through a herd of buffalo this morning on our way up here. They were acting crazy, running back and forth and around in circles. Judy asked one of the rangers about them. The ranger said she'd lived here all her life and had never seen anything like what she had witnessed over the last four or five days. She thinks it has something to do with all the earthquakes and the increased activity around the hot springs."

Roland shared a slightly worried look with Larry but said nothing. No use in getting anyone stirred up if there wasn't a verified reason to do so. Jeremy and Judy exchanged glances, too, as if they sensed there was more to the situation than Roland and Larry were willing to admit.

Jeremy cleared his throat. "What about you guys? I noticed the University of Utah markings on your van. Are you here on official business?"

Roland nodded.

"What do you do, mister?" asked Ellis.

"We're from the Seismology Department," Roland replied.

"Oh?" Judy asked. "Well, you should have plenty of seismology to evaluate. We've felt at least ten pretty violent tremors since we arrived yesterday."

The twins grinned.

Ellis piped up: "Yeah, right after we got here, there was a big one."

Fiona jumped in: "And Mom busted her—"

A don't-even-think-about-saying-it glare from Judy stopped Fiona midsentence. Then Judy slowly shook her head and smiled apologetically. The twins giggled, and the three men hee-hawed as the group headed toward the Old Faithful Inn. They stopped at the front entrance.

"You folks enjoy the rest of your time up here," Larry said.

As the family headed toward the stone seats encircling Old Faithful, Roland called after the twins, "Young ladies, you will remember this vacation for the rest of your lives."

At the time, no one could have known how horribly accurate that statement would prove to be.

"They seemed like a nice family," Larry mused, "but Mom has her hands full with those two."

"No doubt," Roland agreed. "But I think she can handle it just fine." After their preemptive trip to the men's room, Larry and Roland joined the cafeteria food line. The queue of tourists waiting to place their orders reminded Roland that this was the height of the tourist season.

After they placed their orders and sat down, a teeth-jarring tremor violently shook the chairs beneath them. Screams and expletives in an assortment of languages exploded around them as patrons standing in line or walking to their seats stumbled and grabbed for railings or table edges. More than a few people fell to their knees.

It was only then that Roland noticed the absence of china and glassware. The Old Faithful Lodge Cafeteria was the only eating establishment in the park that used what Roland considered to be real dishes. They usually used Melmac and hard plastic "glasses," but now they were using paper plates and cups. There were no breakable items anywhere in the room. He also noticed the lack of hanging pictures or other decorations that might fall when the walls started bouncing. An absence of knickknacks was further proof that stronger-than-usual quakes had been going on for several days.

When a waiter finally appeared with their burgers and fries, the feverish buzz of anxious patrons had faded away like the tremor.

Larry lathered his fries in ketchup. "Let's eat and get out of here. This time of year, the sun doesn't go down until around twenty-one hundred hours. That should give us plenty of time to get to the caldera site and set up our equipment. I want to see if we can find out what's causing these tremors. If it's what we think it is, maybe we can convince someone somewhere to evacuate this area before it ends up being the top story on ABC News."

Roland removed the top bun and centered the lopsided tomatoes over his burger, then nudged it again, and once more for good measure. "Roger that, *mein Kapitän*. My anal sphincter is starting to tighten up a little bit. That's my body's way of telling me I may be at the wrong place at the wrong time. And it ain't failed me yet."

8

The Farm
Two years before the day of

Typically, David was unflappable, and he was seldom caught totally off guard. But Melissa's comment and her matter-of-fact way of saying it blindsided him: *We didn't bring you here to ask you to join Envision-2100. We brought you here to ask you to run for president of the United States.*

David wasn't merely surprised; he was stunned. Like someone had poked him in the chest with a cattle prod. He looked around the table at each of the Envision-2100 members. Each person stared back at him. For several heartbeats, no one moved or made a sound. Then David placed both of his trembling hands flat on the table and broke the crypt-like silence. "Jeez, folks, I . . . I don't know what to say. Talk about coming out of the blue; you caught me completely flat-footed. Did I mention I don't know what to say?"

Smiles crept around the table.

Asserting his president-of-the-board status, Judson was the first to speak: "Take a deep breath and herd your thoughts for a second, David, while I elaborate just a bit. We've shared the genesis of Envision-2100, how we came to be, and more or less who we are. And Milt has given you a thirty-thousand-foot overview of the process we used to solidify our social and political views, or at least our core beliefs. Now, as Nelson noted in his football analogy, we need someone to run the ball."

"Finally," Nelson added, "we go on the offense."

David sat ramrod straight. His adrenalin kicked in, doing the job it was designed to do. "Judson, let me interject two issues before you get started. One is that the Hatch Act of 1939 prohibits employees of the federal government at my level from engaging in political activity. Yes, I know it could always be challenged, but there would be a long, drawn-out legal slugfest that would eventually end up in the Supreme Court. That could take years to resolve. With the conservative bench we have today, and for the foreseeable future, it probably would not tilt in my—our—favor."

"Noted," Judson said. "And the second issue?"

"From my perspective, an equally prohibitive showstopper: it's public knowledge that President Sheppard is a close friend of mine, not to mention that he's still in his first term of office and he's immensely popular within his party. Yes, I know that you and everyone else in Washington are keenly aware that I don't care for the vice president. I can't stand the son of a bitch, and he spits on the ground every time he hears my name. But that's irrelevant. Somehow, I suspect that none of this comes as a surprise to you, individually or as a group."

"You're getting to know us well," Milt said, grinning. Smiles and nods of affirmation encircled the table.

Judson continued from where he had been interrupted: "We are acutely aware of everything you just said, David, but thank you for your comments. They give me a springboard for what I need to convey, which I hope will set your mind at ease and get this process moving. First of all, yes, we know about your relationship with the president and your loyalty to him as a person. We are also led to believe that loyalty does not extend to his political party. You seem to lean in their direction, at least on some matters. But you aren't rabidly supportive of either party."

"That's a fair assessment," David agreed.

Judson cleared his throat and swallowed a mouthful of iced tea. "You might recall a few years ago a religious fanatic with a history of allegedly accosting young women ran for a US Senate seat in Alabama as a Republican. One of his redneck supporters said on TV, in front of God and the entire world, 'I'd vote for a pedophile before I'd vote for a Democrat.'"

Melissa clenched her jaw, and Nelson's lips silently framed the word *asshole*.

"That single, stupid quote burned itself into the center of my brain and stuck with me all these years," Judson continued. "It encapsulates the absurdity of the straight, uncompromising party-line mentality that is eroding the fabric of our country's political system."

Judson's emotional convictions crept out in the rising tenor of his voice, but he took a deep breath and continued. "We don't see that in you, David. Your work with the Chinese and Russians in mediating the North Korean hostilities proved you were willing and able to seek out solutions that would serve both sides of an issue. And thank God that you did."

Judson met David's gaze directly, and David offered a nod, accepting his praise.

Judson leaned forward. "David, in you, we see someone who is unrestrained by the conservative or liberal party mindsets. Someone who, given the opportunity and political freedom to do so, can objectively look at all sides of an issue and then craft what we in Envision-2100 have come to call an 'eighty percent solution.' Remember that phrase while you consider all of this. It encapsulates the essence of what we have come to believe is the best course—the only course—for the survival of this nation."

"What do you mean by 'eighty percent solution'?" David asked.

"It's a simple statement of reality that neither the Democrats nor the Republicans have ever come to realize, much less accept." Judson rose from his seat and placed his hands on the back of his chair. "Regardless of your policies, regardless of your laws, regardless of the course of action we take as a nation, we can't please everyone. There will always be a ten percent fringe on the left who think we are too conservative; brown-shirted neo-Nazis who want to vacuum seal our borders and goosestep to 'The Star-Spangled Banner.' And there will always be a ten percent fringe on the right who think we want to take hard-earned money from the working class and give it to unemployed, dope-smoking baby mamas.

"No president, no political party, no one person can even come close to satisfying both of those groups at the same time." Judson threw his arms in the air. "Hell, Jesus Christ or Muhammad or Oprah couldn't do it, so we don't waste our time on either end of the sociopolitical spectrum. We focus all of our energy and resources on the remaining eighty percent. We take a common-sense, objective middle road, and we are forming a nationwide organization to represent this ideology. I'll save that part of my discussion for last. It gets a little complicated, legally speaking.

"So, back to your second and most obvious concern. President Sheppard is in his first term of office. His party loves him, and he has the highest average approval rating ever—well, since 1937. Kennedy led the pack for years with a solid seventy percent. Sheppard is knocking on seventy-two. He's the darling of the overwhelming majority of Envision-2100 members. We would be more or less content to keep him in for another four years. He's getting the country out of the quagmire created by the last administration. And keeping him in office for four more years certainly wouldn't hurt anything and would give us more time to craft our go-forward strategy.

"But here's the rub, the thing that you don't know and that we just learned the day before I called you." Judson leaned forward and pressed his palms onto the table. "Sheppard won't be around for another term."

9

Old Faithful, Yellowstone National Park
The day of

GENTLY ROLLING, SPRUCE-COVERED HILLS and a sparkling, fast-running stream surrounded the outskirts of the inn. They stood in stark and glaring contrast to the paved parking lots and walking paths that were necessary to accommodate the hordes of tourists but distracted from the park's natural beauty.

"Was it just me, or could you see Roland and Larry as regulars on *The Big Bang Theory*?" Judy mused.

"What's 'the big bang theory'?" Fiona asked Ellis.

"That's those goofy reruns with all the nerds that Mom thinks are so funny," Ellis responded.

Jeremy glanced at Judy and grinned.

"Better watch out, you two. Chances are you'll end up working for a nerd," Judy chided.

"Or marrying one. You know, like I did." Jeremy dodged an arm poke from Judy.

The foursome headed toward the Old Faithful geyser mound, which rose a few feet above the ground.

"Active geysers are extremely rare." Jeremy glanced at the brochure he carried. "According to this, there are only about one thousand on earth, and more than half of those are in Yellowstone."

Centuries of steam and mineral-laden, superhot water shooting out of the ground had left the area around Old Faithful's vent looking more like the surface of the moon than Northwest Wyoming. The landscape surrounding the geyser wasn't a pretty sight either, yet tourists flocked by the thousands to watch its clockwork eruptions. The Park Service had roped off a fifty-meter circle around the vent to prevent tourists from being scalded whenever almost eight-thousand gallons of 350-degree steam and water shot into the air. They had also built a two-foot-tall crescent-shaped concrete bench along the southeast side, close to the inn and cafeteria.

"How high does Old Faithful shoot, Dad?" Ellis asked.

Jeremy studied the brochure. "Historically, the average eruption reached a height of around a hundred and twenty feet. That's about twenty of me stacked one on top of the other."

It was a little after 5:00 p.m. when they settled on the long section of concrete seating around the geyser. At least one hundred other visitors were either sitting on the bench or milling around, waiting for Old Faithful's next performance.

Shortly before the predicted time of the eruption, a park ranger began a well-rehearsed narration. "Hello, everyone. My name is Nancy Wieser. I'm a park ranger and your host for today. Welcome to Yellowstone National Park, home of the famous Old Faithful geyser, one of the natural wonders of the world. Unlike Disneyland, what you'll see in a few minutes is the real deal, complete with water and steam that's been measured at over three hundred fifty degrees Fahrenheit. For our Canadian friends, and pretty much everyone else, that's ninety-five degrees Celsius, hot enough to cook a chicken. So when I say to keep your arms and legs inside the ride, I mean—"

A loud rumble exploded beneath their feet. Nancy Wieser toppled sideways. People on the bench bounced almost a foot into the air and slammed back down onto the concrete, only to bounce again. Those who were standing or walking around were thrown to the ground.

A mixture of surprised screams and curses erupted from the crowd. Selfie sticks sprayed into the air over a small group of identically dressed, school-age Chinese boys.

"OK, that one hurt," Ellis whimpered as she stood up, rubbing her behind.

Fiona gently touched a minor scrape on the back of her thigh. She winced. "Yeah, it was fun at first, but they're getting worse, and it's kind of scary."

Judy rifled through her purse for a bandage, spun Fiona around, tore off the wrapper, and gently pressed it over the scrape.

"Ow!" Fiona cried.

The ranger stood up, obviously trembling, and dusted off her pants. She picked up her microphone and addressed the crowd: "I . . . I think that's the worst one we've had since I've been working here. They've been getting stronger and more frequent the last few days, but the park is still open, so there is nothing to worry about." She cleared her throat and regained her composure.

Fiona gingerly touched her thigh, grumbling. "Yeah. Right. Nothing to worry about."

"As I was saying before I was rudely interrupted, Old Faithful is a cone geyser. Up until very recently, it has been erupting every forty-five to one hundred twenty minutes. However, over the last few days, the eruption intervals have been getting progressively shorter. In fact, since yesterday morning, they've been averaging—"

A mild tremor shook the area, prompting a few startled gasps and muffled screams. Jeremy grabbed Judy's arm, and Judy threw her other arm around the twins. A massive column of steam and water exploded with a deafening roar from Old Faithful's vent, drowning out shrieks from Judy and the girls. Jeremy hauled them away from the vent and the soaring column, which easily exceeded the length of a football field in height. A brisk northwesterly breeze sent the scalding water away from the spectators.

Nancy Wieser screamed into her microphone, "Ladies and gentlemen, please move back toward the parking lot. This area is closed until further notice." She herded the fleeing guests toward the viewing area exit and helped an elderly man push his wife's wheelchair toward the gate.

Jeremy and Judy muscled the twins in front of them and joined the crowd scurrying toward the parking lot. After everyone piled into the truck, Jeremy started the engine, pulled onto US 191, and began the hour-plus drive toward Colter Bay.

Due to the traffic evacuating the area surrounding Old Faithful, progress was slower than it had been during the northbound trip that morning. As they drove, Judy, assumed a no-nonsense tone. "Jeremy Richards, it's time to pull the plug on this vacation and start heading back east."

"Uh-oh," Fiona chirped in the back seat. "She used his full name."

Jeremy glanced at his wife, who was giving him a no-nonsense look to match her tone. There was no use arguing. Besides, she was right. He glanced at the truck's clock. "It's five thirty now; it will be past seven by the time we get back to the campground. And we need to fill up the truck, so let's say seven thirty before we're at the site and ready to hook up the Airstream. We could be ready to roll by eight. It'll be dark by nine. So, do we pull out right away, or do we stay the night then hit the bricks first thing in the morning?"

"You're right, that's the first question," Judy replied. "Then we need to decide which route to take out of here. Do we head due south through Jackson or southeast across the mountains?"

"Do we get a vote?" Fiona pleaded from the back seat.

"I vote we leave in the morning after breakfast," Ellis said.

"I'm with Ellis," Fiona chimed. "We didn't drive all the way out here just to stay one night. Besides, I'm starving."

"All of that is well and good, girls," Jeremy said. "However, there's a more compelling reason to try to ride out another night. It will be dark in a couple of hours. It was hairy enough pulling the camper over the mountains in broad daylight. The thought of doing it at night scares the bejesus out of me. Especially after seeing some of those dropoffs."

Courtesy of the rearview mirror, Jeremy saw the girls high-five in the back seat.

"So here's the plan," he continued. "When we get back to our campsite, we hook up the Airstream and get everything packed and ready to roll. Then we have dinner. Your mom and I'll study the map and determine our route." He glanced at Judy. "How does that sound, Sweet Tea?"

"I don't have a better idea. And the girls are right: it's been one heck of a day. We're all tired and hungry, and like you said, I don't relish the idea of dragging the Airstream through the mountains in the dark. So we have a plan."

The exit was clogged with cars, but tour bus traffic thinned out as they drove south on 191.

Jeremy had no way of knowing that to his right, between the F-250 and Shoshone Lake, was the forty-five-mile-wide Yellowstone Caldera—the cause of the quakes and geothermal activity.

Sometimes ignorance was indeed bliss.

Still more than fifty minutes away from Colter Bay, the Richards family passed the West Thumb branch of Yellowstone Lake on the northeast side of the highway. Another group of geysers bordered the West Thumb branch. They were not nearly as famous or spectacular as Old Faithful, but frequently just as active. Jeremy and Judy couldn't see the geysers as they drove—they were traveling along a road about a mile from the edge of the lake—but for the past hour, the geysers had been erupting almost continuously with ever-increasing volumes of superheated water.

The sediment areas around the Overhanging and King Geysers had tripled in size over the last hour, and the concentration of hydrogen sulfide had risen too, as evidenced by the gagging smell of rotten eggs. Most of the volcanic springs and pools in Yellowstone gave off insignificant amounts of the smelly gas. It was never enough to make a person sick, but the concentration was different for a hundred yards surrounding the West Thumb Geyser Basin. There, it was enough to make a person dead.

Heavier than air, hydrogen sulfide became explosive when combined with oxygen. It was developing into a massive, low-hanging vapor cloud that suffocated all of the ground-dwelling wildlife in the area near the West Thumb Basin. It was also converting into a naturally formed thermobaric bomb—or what the military would refer to as a fuel-air weapon, the type of violent, destructive weapon developed and used by the United States in Vietnam and later by the Soviets in Afghanistan.

The F-250 zoomed past a stone-and-wood sign next to the highway that indicated they were crossing the Continental Divide. Just before they reached another sign marking the Riddle Lake Trailhead, a small herd of about twenty or thirty buffalo burst out of the trees on the east side of the road in full gallop, charging across the highway, oblivious to oncoming traffic. Jeremy hit the brakes and pulled to the side of the road to let them pass. The twins clapped gleefully.

"Way cool! It's a stampede!" Fiona shouted.

"This is worse than what we saw earlier," Judy said, fear edging her voice. "Something's spooking them."

Jeremy tightened his grip on the steering wheel and pulled back onto the highway, his heart thudding against his ribcage. He followed US 191 out of the Yellowstone South Entrance, crossed the Snake River, and continued south along Jackson Lake.

Two other quakes shook them, one as they neared Steamboat Mountain and the other at the Jackson Lake Overlook. They were not nearly as violent as the one that sent them flying at Old Faithful, but they were starting to have a cumulative adverse effect on everyone. The twins wore tight expressions and sat quietly in the back seat, holding hands. Judy, usually cool, calm, and collected, clutched her hands together tightly in her lap, frequently glancing back at Ellis and Fiona.

Thanks to several other wildlife encounters and an increasingly heavy concentration of tourists fleeing the park, it took over two hours to reach the road leading into the Colter Bay Campground. It was seven thirty when Jeremy pulled into the convenience store located at the campground entrance. A hand-lettered sign taped to the double glass doors told would-be customers the store was "Closed Until Further Notice." Fortunately, the gas pumps were on and available for credit card purchases.

The vehicle lineup grew steadily on each side of four rows of pumps. Jeremy jockeyed the F-250 into what appeared to be the fastest-moving line. The driver of the Jeep Cherokee in front of him finished filling up his tank. He put the hose back and walked to Jeremy's window.

"There's no more E eighty-five," he said apologetically.

"No problem," Jeremy said. "I've got a flex-fuel engine."

As Jeremy raised his window, Judy chuckled. "That would usually piss you off."

"Yeah, I know. I'm just glad I can fill up with anything."

After topping off his tank with regular gasoline, Jeremy wound down Campground Road until he reached site 72. By this time of year, every RV site was typically occupied, but many were now empty, indicating the initial stages of an exodus. For the most part, the campground staff was long gone even though no official word to evacuate had gone out, and this was the height of the tourist season.

For the second time in two days, Jeremy backed the truck toward the bow of the Airstream. Following Judy's hand signals and the image on his backup camera, he positioned the truck to connect the trailer hitch. As he hooked the camper to the F-250's towing assembly, Judy and the twins began packing up everything else. Three more moderate tremors shook the area while they worked. The intervals between quakes were getting shorter now.

It was almost 21:00 by the time they were "deployment ready"—an old army term Jeremy had picked up from some Tom Clancy novel. After everyone finished a spartan, verging-on-junk-food meal of sandwiches, chips, and diet Dew, the twins took care of what little kitchen cleanup remained. They put away food trays, stashed paper plates, napkins, and empty soda cans in a trash bag, and then argued about who would take it out to the bear-proof dumpster next to the campground showers.

After Ellis, who lost the "take out the trash" argument, returned, Jeremy motioned for everyone to sit on or in front of the folding couch in the Airstream's main living area.

"OK, ladies, let's powwow about tomorrow. We will do pretty much the same thing as this morning; we'll get up at first light—"

The earth shook for several seconds, and they all grabbed hands. The refrigerator door popped open, and Judy leaped to close it before its contents came flying out. Pots and pans and dishes inside the travel-ready cabinets banged against one another.

When the shaking stopped, the twins' shoulders relaxed, but they still clung to each other.

Jeremy continued: "I'll unhook the water and electricity, raise the stabilizers, and we pull out of here. We have fruit, so if you two monkeys get hungry, you can eat a banana on the way."

Ellis rolled her eyes. Jeremy tousled her hair. "I hate that we have to cut our Yellowstone visit short," he said, "but things are getting a little shaky around here, and my imagination about what else Mother Nature might have in store for this place is running wild."

Judy sat between the twins. "I'm with your dad. All those buffalo we saw running, they were scared. They didn't know where to go or how to get there. But we didn't get to the top of the food chain by running around like a bunch of, well, like a bunch of mad cows in fur coats. We've got a plan." She turned to Jeremy. "So what is the plan, Base Hit?"

Jeremy smiled. Judy alternated between Foul Ball and Base Hit when around the twins, depending on her mood and the gravity of a given situation. She used a couple of much more descriptive monikers when they were alone. Clearly, Judy was just as spooked as the buffalo but putting on a nonchalant mask for Ellis and Fiona. He knew she had full confidence in whatever he planned to do. If she didn't, she wouldn't hesitate to privately tell him so.

He put his arm around Judy's shoulders and gave her as playful a hug as he could muster under the circumstances. "As I said, we pull out of here at zero dark thirty. We'll drive through Jackson and then head south on Highway One Ninety-One. We'll have to go through one mountain pass, but once we pass Hoback Junction and start heading southeast, the route will be mostly flat. We'll make much better time and get a helluva lot farther on a tank of gas. I figure if push comes to shove, we can get about three hundred miles from here before we run out of gas. But we'll fill up as soon as we get down to half a tank, at least once we get out of this earthquake zone."

Worries and concerns bubbled inside Jeremy like volcanic springs. He silently resolved to buy a spare gas can or two the first time they stopped to refuel. And he was glad he had topped off the Airstream's thirty-gallon freshwater tank. Things would be OK, but you couldn't be too careful, especially when looking out for your family.

"All right, ladies, let's go gaze at those Grand Teton stars one more time and then hit the hay. I'm getting tired, and it will be daybreak before you know it."

"You know, Dad," Ellis chirped, "you're starting to sound like one of those cowboys."

Fiona sniggered nervously, and all four of them piled out the door.

Jeremy led his family toward their campsite picnic table.

Five steps in, bright orange and red light burst into the northern horizon, and a searing flash lit up the entire sky. At the same instant, the ground shook violently—the strongest and most prolonged quake yet—and they stumbled forward.

A split second later, a blast of pressurized air slammed all four of them to the ground. It rocked the Airstream and whipped the trees in the surrounding forest, snapping some clean in two.

Judy, realizing the flash in the sky was a volcanic eruption, jumped to her feet and barked, "Get back in the Airstream. Now!"

At the same time, she started counting. "One Mississippi . . . two Mississippi . . . three Mississippi . . ." She ticked off seconds as everyone scrambled through the still-open door of the RV.

"Mom, why are you counting?" Fiona wailed.

Judy held her finger to her lips and continued to count until she reached fifty-five, the distance it would take sound to travel from the caldera to the campsite since they first saw the eruption flash. Then she shouted, "Put your hands over your ears and open your mouth! Hold that pose until I say otherwise!"

Usually, a command so absurd would have drawn snickers from the twins and a doubtful look from Jeremy. Not today, and especially not now. Judy's no-bullshit expression coupled with the still-resonating blast of super-pressurized air squelched any argument.

Roughly twelve seconds later, at what would be officially documented as 22:48, the loudest explosion ever heard by any living creature rocked the Airstream and everything around it.

10

The Farm
Two years before the day of

Sheppard won't be around for another term. The silence in the Farm dining room was deafening. David felt all eyes on him, as if they were awaiting his response to Judson's jolting statement.

For the second time that day, David was floored.

In many ways, he and Matt Sheppard were like brothers. Or at least David felt that way. Out of professional courtesy and respect for the rigors of the president's bewildering schedule, David never burdened Sheppard with his own issues, but the POTUS often confided in him. On occasion, he would ask David's advice on personal matters. David knew that Sheppard felt he could tell David anything and that it would be held in total confidence. Surely his good friend would have told him if he didn't plan to run for another term.

Judson's voice lowered. "It should go without saying, David, that everything I'm telling you is ultraconfidential. Only the people in this room, Sheppard's wife, and one other person—his personal physician—know the details." Judson pulled out his chair and sat down again. "You see, David, the president has been diagnosed with stage-four pancreatic cancer. He has at most twelve weeks to live."

Sadness, shock, and disbelief washed over David in nauseating waves. He leaned back. "How . . . how can that be, Judson? I met with the president last week. He was in a great mood, as effervescent as ever, and from all appearances, in perfect health. Hell, he even joked about 'pulling a Kennedy' in the White House pool with that smoking-hot press secretary of his."

Judson shook his head sadly. "He didn't know, David. He only found out the day before I called you. You know how phobic he is about the details of his private life. He doesn't trust the staff at Walter Reed, especially after the fiasco with the blatantly fake results from his predecessor's mental health exam getting splashed on the front page of the *Post*. Even that guy's staunchest supporters and his wife—especially his wife—knew he was batshit crazy. Still, he gets a glowing report from some navy O6 psychiatrist who wanted to kiss-ass his way into a flag officer promotion.

"Anyway, as I'm pretty sure you know, ever since taking office, the president has only allowed examinations by his longtime friend and personal physician, Eli Rosen, who lives in Austin, Texas." Judson reached for the pitcher of iced tea Lucas had placed in the center of the table and drained it into his glass.

"What I'm going to tell you now came directly from POTUS. He confided the details to me directly because, as you know, we, too, are good friends. More importantly, because he agrees with the things Envision-2100 stands for, the changes we are trying to bring about, and that it's time to make those changes. He also knows that, with the brief time he has remaining, we have to maximize his backing and support for our plans, or our cause will be set back for decades."

Judson went on to summarize the salient events that had unfolded during the previous several days. The president appeared to be losing weight; he had no appetite and was in near-constant back pain. Then his wife noticed, almost overnight, his eyes were starting to yellow and convinced him to call his doctor. Dr. Rosen flew into Ronald Reagan the following day, where he was picked up by the Secret Service and whisked to the White House via the secret H Street entrance. A series of quietly carried-out tests revealed an advanced stage of pancreatic cancer that had already metastasized beyond realistic treatment options.

"Rather than drag this out, I'll just cut to the chase. Sheppard learned his days were numbered, and that number was barely two digits long." Judson folded his hands and shook his head. "The president made the decision right then and there to forgo any treatment. He also decided to avoid pain medication for as long as possible so he could work out a succession plan, one that didn't include the vice president beyond the end of his current term."

He met David's gaze squarely. "He trusts the guy even less than you do—if that's possible." Judson sipped his tea. The ice was starting to melt, and the top of the glass was now mostly brownish water.

David welcomed the pause and the chance to untangle the questions whirling inside his brain. As Judson continued to sip his tea, David snatched the Montblanc pen from his shirt pocket. He jotted questions down on his napkin—until it occurred to him that it was linen, not paper. Realizing his mistake, he tucked the pen back in his pocket and looked around the table with embarrassment. No one said a word, but Elton Kirby waved his hand dismissively and mouthed, "Don't worry about it."

Oblivious to David's faux pas, Judson continued: "It was almost two in the morning before the president headed back to the White House in an armored Secret Service Tahoe. In that short trip—about ten minutes—he decided to announce the date and circumstances of his resignation within the coming week and spend the remainder of his time in office arranging the constitutionally mandated transition of power to 'that son of a bitch VP.' POTUS plans to discuss this and a lot more with you the instant you return to Washington. Don't worry, the meetings you had scheduled for tomorrow have all been rescheduled."

David raised an eyebrow. *Damn, how do they do that?*

"You'll be in the Oval Office at ten." Judson pushed his empty glass away. "As we alluded to earlier, David, we think President Sheppard is doing about as good a job as he can do within the parameters of the existing United States political system. It's that environment, parts of our constitutional infrastructure, that needs to change. We thought we could ride things out for another four years before we started the wheels turning to make those changes, but we can't. We, as Envision-2100, have to act now. I hate for this to sound the way I know it's going to come out, but the president's cancer presents us with an unprecedented opportunity to change the course of this country."

As before, Judson's passion was evident in the pitch and tone of his voice and his fierce, unbroken eye contact. But it wasn't just Judson. David felt the same intensity, something akin to a static charge, emanating from everyone in the room. Melissa's eyes narrowed, forming tiny crow's feet above her cheeks, and Nelson's ramrod posture became even straighter.

Judson seemed to be on the verge of pleading now. His right hand clenched into a fist, and he pounded the air above the table. "David, we can't let everything President Sheppard has worked for all his life die on the vine. Decent healthcare for our working citizens. Getting military-grade weapons off the street. Making peace with our North American neighbors, for Christ's sake."

Tagging on to Judson's sense of urgency, Nelson Teal interjected another sports analogy: "David, it may sound a bit macabre, but this is the pitch we've been waiting for. If we don't swing at this, and swing for the fence, we could well miss our turn at bat and leave yet another mess for our grandchildren."

"I can see that," David replied. "I don't think President Sheppard would take offense or that it would be in poor taste to capitalize on his situation. Not when it would be for the good of the country. Frankly, he would do the same thing. I'm on board with everything you've told me so far. At least conceptually. Things always get messy when you start digging into the details.

"I'm not saying that I have agreed to your offer to run for office, but I haven't entirely discounted it either. I'm still processing. So far, you've been preaching and I've been listening. Now let's throw Envision-2100's vision and these recent turn of events into the mix and map out a short-term strategy."

Elton smacked the tabletop with an open palm and grinned. "Spoken like the leader we know you are, David. Let's assume that when you leave here today, you are willing to consider our offer seriously and that you feel the same sense of urgency we do. Let's assume you have the same white-hot-fire-in-your-gut craving for fundamental changes in our government that we do. If that's the case, the first order of business would be for you to take care of whatever you must to accept the run for president. I don't know what life is like at your house, but in my case, that would involve a discussion with my wife. But whether it's her, a magic eight ball, or chicken entrails, it's damn sure the first thing that has to happen. And it has to be done as soon as you get home. Like tonight! Before you meet with POTUS tomorrow. Judson wasn't exaggerating when he said we were running against a short fuse, and it's already lit."

David nodded, acknowledging the sense of urgency apparent on every face around the table.

"Good." Elton leaned forward. "Once you've made that commitment—and in the scenario I'm describing, I'm assuming you will—POTUS will announce his decision to resign from office. Of course, he'll have to do that regardless. However, when you meet tomorrow, if you tell him you're on board, it will undoubtedly influence both his timing and the content of his resignation speech. And, as Judson said, at some point very soon he will declare his support for you and our party."

David looked from Elton to Judson and then glanced around the table at the other board members. "Our party? I hate to break your rhythm, but that's the first time anyone here has mentioned a party. Can someone elaborate before we proceed further?"

11

Yellowstone National Park, Yellowstone Caldera, 44.4123o N, 110.7232o W
The day of

AFTER LEAVING THE CAFETERIA, Roland and Larry headed toward the adjacent lot where they had parked the university's van.

"While you drive, I'll plug in the coordinates to the seismographic lab at the Caldera," Larry mused.

The lab was nothing more than eight monitors semipermanently mounted at points around the caldera's resurgent dome. Each monitor had a cellular connection linking it back to the Seismology Department's central computer at the University of Utah. This arrangement allowed the collection and recording of seismic data even if a monitor was damaged.

With Roland in the driver's seat and Larry studying data on the iPad, they traveled silently for about fifteen miles southeast on US 191 toward the caldera lab.

"Larry, heads up," Roland said.

"What?"

"Watch for the turnoff to the volcano. I always have a problem finding it. It's nothing more than a pig trail to begin with, and at this time of year, it'll be overgrown. How far out are we?"

Larry glanced at his phone. "According to the GPS, we have another ten miles or so to go before we need to start worrying about where to turn."

"Don't let me miss—"

A tremor slammed the van so hard that Roland bit his lip. "Damn!" he shouted.

Larry jumped. "Jesus H. Christ, Roland! Either you or plate tectonics are going to give me a heart attack."

Roland slowed the van down to twenty miles per hour to maintain control, but another strong tremor bounced them toward the shoulder. "Fuck, it's hard to keep this thing out of the ditch. At least it isn't raining, like the last time we were up here. We'll have to ford Spring Creek, and I don't relish doing that during a fucking monsoon. Again. By the way, did you bring the cayenne pepper?"

"Yep, I went by Costco on the way home last night and got the economy, metric-ton-sized bottle. Actually, a package of two. Plenty to spread around our tents for years to come. I'll burn a bear's nose before turning our tent into a taco drive-through for a grizzly. And I've got my bells laced into both boots. I don't wanna spook no mama bears."

Roland grinned. "I didn't wear boots. I brought my Nikes."

"Yeah, yeah," Larry shot back. "You don't have to outrun a bear. You just have to outrun me. I'm glad we got these lame-ass jokes outta the way while we're still fresh."

"Surely you haven't heard that one before."

"Don't call me Shirley, bitch."

Both men shook with laughter. *That's what good friends do*, Roland thought. *Make each other laugh.*

As Roland slowly drove along US 191, Larry alternated his gaze between his phone's GPS and the app that monitored the caldera's seismographs. "The equipment reports almost constant movement now," he said.

"Can't feel it, but maybe because we're in a moving vehicle without the best suspension system," Roland noted. The van jerked, and his seat belt tightened. He groaned. "I felt that one."

They continued on their way silently now, and then a sharp jolt reminded them that this wasn't a sightseeing trip. With rising frequency, the van bounced like a plane flying through the kind of turbulence that made passengers scream and toss drinks into the aisle or on one another. Heeding every airline pilot's advice, they kept their seat belts securely tightened across their waists.

Larry reached forward and turned on the van's radio. The university was too cheap to pay for Sirius XM, and since they were in the middle of the wilderness, they could only pick up one channel, KWYS, out of West Yellowstone.

"Every hour on the hour, KWYS Headline News. Today's edition brought to you by the good folks at Canyon Street Grill. This is Jody Martin reporting. If you're just arriving in our neck of the woods, you might have noticed that West Yellowstone is rocking and rolling. And I don't mean like with Led Zeppelin. These earthquakes have had us literally jumping the last couple of days. But just be glad you aren't in Mexico. They've had a rash of gruesome kidnappings recently. Best take your chances up here if you're a rich gringo. On the national front . . ."

When the announcer wrapped up her news report, a country-and-western tune blasted through the speakers.

Roland groaned. "For Christ's sake, Larry, country and western? You know it's been proven that your IQ drops one point for every hour you listen to that stuff."

"Sorry," Larry said, switching off the radio. "Force of habit, I guess."

After about forty minutes, Larry checked his phone again. "According to the GPS, our turn should be just ahead of where the edge of that meadow butts up to the road." He pointed out his window. "Yep, there. Some old tire tracks are heading through the field.

If I'm not mistaken, we go across Spring Creek and then about two miles through the woods to get to the clearing where the lab is set up."

"I think you're right," Roland responded. "Keep in mind that's two miles as the crow flies. It's at least two miles in one when you have to follow a cow path through a forest. But the ground doesn't look too bad. I'm glad it hasn't been raining."

Roland turned right and cautiously steered the van off the road onto a barely visible trail made by the jeeps and service vehicles that occasionally had to make their way to the caldera. After traveling just over one hundred yards, he came to a small stream, which he recognized as Spring Creek.

The rocky bed was about fifty feet wide, but he knew the water wasn't over two feet deep, so he plowed straight in. The crossing was a little rough against the waves, but nothing compared to the shaking Mother Earth had been dishing out. The van made it across the creek and over its south bank without a problem.

Larry stared out the van's passenger window. "That wasn't so bad, but are you noticing anything odd?"

"Can't say that I have. I'm concentrating on not getting the van stuck in the mud or hung up on a rock cropping. What did you see?"

"Nothing. That's just it. This place is normally teeming with wildlife: birds, deer, elk, all kinds of critters. But I haven't seen or heard anything since we pulled off the road. Not so much as a chipmunk. And there are almost always ducks on the creek's pools, especially this time of the year. Everything seems to have vamoosed."

Roland's brow furrowed. "Now that you mention it, you're right. Actually, it's creepy."

Straining to make out a path of barely visible tire ruts, Roland continued to follow the trail as it twisted through thick stands of pine and hardwood. Every few hundred yards, fallen trees had been pulled off to one side, just enough to allow a vehicle to pass. Must've been park rangers.

Larry kept his eye on the GPS, but it really wasn't necessary. Except for the service trail, there was nowhere else for the van to go.

Finally, after nearly an hour of slow, bumpy, and exhausting driving, they popped out of the forest and into a football-field-sized clearing. The university's eight seismographs, installed in porta-potty-sized, olive-drab fiberglass buildings, were arranged in a large circle inside the clearing's perimeter. They were equally spaced and resembled a space-aged version of Stonehenge.

Roland parked in the center of the seismograph circle to reduce the distance they would have to lug the three boxes of equipment packed in the rear of the van. They began their first task, setting up their two-person Marmot dome tent. The blaze-orange polyester shelter weighed less than six pounds and was assembled and staked to the ground in less than ten minutes.

After they erected the tent, Roland laid their backpacks at either side of the opening, then unrolled their sleeping bags onto the tent floor. While he was completing the housekeeping tasks, Larry circled the tent, sprinkling a generous amount of cayenne pepper about five feet from its edges. Then he placed an aerosol can of bear spray between the two sleeping bags where either man could grab it in the event one of the beasts made it across the cayenne barrier. Or when they had to go outside at night to urinate. One couldn't be too careful; an adult male grizzly could weigh over eight hundred pounds and rear up to nearly seven feet in height. One swipe from a massive paw armed with jagged four-inch claws could rip out a throat.

Once camp was ready, Larry and Roland started setting up the University of Utah's new ground-penetrating sonar-radar (GPSR) equipment. Each device consisted of an orange suitcase-sized fifty-pound fiberglass box mounted on a collapsible metal tripod about a yard off the ground. They arranged the three identical units in what they had calculated to be the center of the caldera's resurgent dome.

Roughly one hundred yards in diameter, the dome dipped inside an eroding rim, the remnant of a long, long ago mini eruption of the giant volcano below. A half mile or so underneath its surface, a series of hot-water reservoirs bubbled. Below the water, a mixture of minerals, dissolved gasses, and two-thousand-degree-Fahrenheit molten rock, called magma, protruded through the earth's mantle into the upper crust, similar to a cerebral aneurysm. It was called a magma intrusion. With each burst of seismic activity, the magma intrusion surged closer to the earth's crust, where it would eventually breach the surface and become known as lava.

As soon as the first GPSR was physically set up, Roland checked it, checked it again, and turned it on. Then he established the satellite connection and started calibrating its software. At the same time, Larry worked to unload and set up the other units. In less than an hour, they had all three devices set up. When this task was completed, Roland turned on the last GPSR's monitor and started watching the activity that was taking place literally beneath his feet.

Each unit transmitted a combination of focused electromagnetic radiation and low-frequency sound deep into the earth. Then it would collect and record the reflection, or echo, of the signals and create a digital representation of the subsurface soil composition and objects buried in the ground. Each GPSR was independently linked via satellite back to the Seismology Department's central computer, which would aggregate the signals and compile images of magma flow and volcanic activity. The images, in the form of near-real-time video, could be sent back to a GPSR monitor or a smart device like Larry's iPad. Roland stared transfixed at the computer screen.

"Image compositions are starting to pour in, and I don't like what I'm seeing. I'll tweak the contrast a little bit, but you need to confirm what I think is going on down there."

The ground rippled like water in a pond, forcing Roland to hold the sides of the GPSR to stay upright. This continued for several seconds, jarring him so violently that he began to get a headache.

"Look at this," Roland whispered, as if his voice might distract from the movement on the screen. "The bright red line at the bottom of the screen is the upper mantle, totally molten rock. The yellow area above it is the magma intrusion zone. You can see it bending along the upper and lower edges."

He tapped the screen. "That's the earth's crust floating on top of it. Every time the intrusion zone swells, it forces the brittle crust out of its way. That's what is causing the earthquakes in this area. It's like the ground is sitting on top of melting wax. And this is happening as far as the GPSR can detect in every direction."

Frowning, Larry pointed to an area near the center of the monitor that looked like a mushroom growing out of the bright red section at the bottom of the screen. "Is this what I think it is?"

"That's what I wanted you to confirm. It looks like a gigantic bubble of magma rising up through the intrusion zone. At least a half mile wide. It's coming up toward the resurgent dome, and it's coming fast. Straight at the spot where we are standing."

As they spoke, their gazes locked on the monitor, the ground shook again, violently and continuously.

"Roland, let's get the hell outta here!" Larry screamed through rattling teeth. "Leave your stuff here and get in the van. I'll call the EMS office."

Stumbling across the quivering clearing, the two men made their way to the van at near-Olympic-sprinter speed. Roland jumped behind the steering wheel and started the engine. Larry crawled into the passenger seat while punching numbers into his cell phone.

The phone rang twice before the voice of an automated attendant blared from the speaker. "You have reached the office of Douglas Kurtz, director of operations for the Wyoming Office of Homeland Security. I'm not available to take your call right now. Please—"

"Shit!" Larry barked, hitting the "end call" icon. He punched in another number, which was answered on the first ring.

"Nine One One, what's your emergency?" a husky female voice inquired.

"This is Dr. Larry Furgeson with the University of Utah Seismology Department. We are currently on-site at the Yellowstone Caldera. We have reason to believe that this thing is getting ready to blow, and blow big!"

"Sir, I don't understand what you're referring to. What's a 'calder'? And what do you mean by 'blow'? Is this some type of explosive device?"

Larry pounded the dashboard. "No, you moron! It's a fucking volcano. You need to get in touch with Homeland Security and tell them they need to activate their emergency evacuation plan for Yellowstone Park, and everything within a fifty-mile radius, for that matter."

"Sir, try to remain calm and tell me as much as you can about what is going on."

The van and its two passengers were literally dribbling across the clearing surrounding the caldera. Roland fought to keep the vehicle moving and under control.

Larry struggled to converse with the 9-1-1 operator. In sheer exasperation, he pounded the van's dash with his free hand and screamed into the phone: "We've been using the university's equipment to observe subterranean activity at the Yellowstone supervolcano. The volcano is getting ready to erupt on a massive scale. And when it goes, it will destroy this park and everything for miles around it. Now, I would like to continue our little chit-chat, but, lady, I'm scared shitless, and you've got a ton of work to do and not much time to do it. So if you don't mind, would you—"

Just then, at precisely 22:47, superheated gas, Volkswagen-sized boulders, and an enormous column of magma—now technically lava—exploded out of the ground at over four hundred miles per hour. Mercifully, Roland and Larry died instantly. Their bodies vaporized before their brains could register any pain. That was not the case for hundreds of other people in surrounding communities.

Within minutes, a plume of smoke and ash rose over twenty-four thousand feet into the air.

12

The Farm
Two years before the day of

AROUND THE TABLE, everyone sat in a state of dual apprehension, waiting for Milt to field David's request and for that first taste of Mattie Washington's famous coconut cake.

As if on cue, Milt slid into the conversation: "I'm sure we blindsided you with that one, David, and it's a subject we could spend hours discussing, but like Elton said, we have to get you back to DC before the cock crows tomorrow. Political parties are an integral part of our government. They're woven into our culture just as tightly as college football. Unless you're from Alabama, where anything else is a distant second."

Elton and Melissa laughed.

"As we alluded to earlier, our existing two-party system is at the very core of what's wrong with this country. Well, maybe not *the* core, but damn close. Plenty of discussions centered around the question of political parties. We knew we had to have a structure that would hold us together, something we could rally the eighty-percenters around."

"So why didn't you align yourselves with an existing political party?" David asked.

"I'm getting to that," Milt said. "We knew that creating a unified force was the only way to get our candidate on state and national ballots as anything other than an independent—aka a no-way-in-hell loser. At the same time, we knew that, regardless of our financial clout, we had no chance of overlaying our vision on either the Democratic or Republican platforms. They want power for power's sake. They don't give a rat's ass about what's best for this country if it doesn't fit snuggly into one of their philosophical boxes.

"So we, Envision-2100, started to cast our net in search of an existing group that we could hitch our wagon to. Did you know that, in addition to the Democrats and Republicans, there are over sixty registered political parties in this country, not including independents? At least that's the way it was when we started looking for a suitor."

Melissa twisted her head toward Milt and smiled with a faux bristle. "Now don't go getting all male chauvinist on us, Milty."

"Trust me, Melissa, I wouldn't think of it, especially with you within earshot." Milt grinned. "You get the idea, David. None of the existing parties came close to representing who we are or our vision for this country.

"We did find one group that represented almost all of our philosophies and values: the centrists. Actually, they weren't a formally established political party at all; more of a semiorganized group with a loosely written platform that just happened to match, to a tee, what we were looking for. So we started working toward getting the centrist group and our ideologies legally recognized as a political party. At the same time, we had to be careful. Some of us had learned the hard way."

"Oh?" David asked.

"I'll give you some historical context. Way back in 2011, a group of moderate politicians and wealthy donors established a coalition that was dubbed Americans Elect."

"Ah, yes," David interjected. "I recall a few discussions about that when I was in college."

"Several current members of Envision-2100 were also part of that group, myself included," Milt continued. "Although they had a few vaguely defined ideas about how to change some of the laws in this country, which I firmly believed in, their primary objective was to eliminate the two-party system we have today. They failed. And they spent over thirty-five million dollars doing so."

David nodded. "I understand there were several reasons why the Americans Elect movement tanked."

"Agreed," Milt said. "One of the key snafus was the lack of transparency concerning its source of funding. We cooed about being open and aboveboard with our philosophies and objectives, yet we refused to identify our major donors. At the time, our big-money supporters feared retaliation for daring to challenge the political machine. Still, that type of secrecy is a kiss of death when you're trying to promote the concept of an open government.

"Then there was the palatial, ultraswanky Washington, DC, headquarters and the one hundred and fifty full-time staffers. It's damned hard to sell a fiscally conservative agenda when your marble-and-walnut office building is crawling with Rolex-wearing, Bimmer-driving Harvard MBAs."

"But many of their ideas, such as an online open primary election, were brilliant," David said. "Technically feasible, way ahead of their time, but they just didn't fit into the then-current political climate."

"All true," Milt said. "But something significant emerged from the Americans Elect effort: the legal establishment of the Centrist Party in the United States. As you know, centrism, under various names, has been around for years. It's well established and successful in western Europe, notably Sweden, France, and Germany. Its time has come in the United States.

"Visualize a political spectrum." Milt laid out his napkin in the middle of the table and cocked his head. "Maybe a diamond-shaped grid is a better illustration." He shifted the napkin so its corners faced to the left and right in front of David.

"Now imagine this napkin is divided into hundreds of small squares. Each square represents an individual's stance on any given social, personal, or economic issue. It could be anything—civil rights, welfare, gun control." He tapped the napkin. "Over on the left quadrant are the liberals. Some may be on the far left, the corner of the napkin metaphorically speaking. Hell, some are way past the corner, off the table, over next to the wall. But for the purpose of my illustration, let's imagine some boundaries and assume the napkin and its imaginary grid squares capture ninety percent of the voting population. In addition to the Democrats, there are at last count over fifty established, card-carrying liberal-leaning political organizations in the US."

David wagged his finger and grinned. "Milt, you know that I minored in political science, don't you? Or did your GS-Two folks get lazy when they did my background check?"

"No, David, they are uncannily thorough. We would know you had a tattoo on your left ass cheek if you had one." Milt raised an eyebrow. "Which, by the way, you don't."

David blinked. *How the hell would they get that information?*

Milt opened his hands in a gesture of apology. "I felt the need to make sure that there was no question in your mind where Envision-2100 stands politically. And where we want our presidential candidate, hopefully you, to stand as well. So indulge me just a little longer while I attempt to verbally paint this party-platform meta image."

"I'm sorry, Milt, I just wanted to make sure you didn't think I had a brain dump when I was sworn in as secretary of state."

"Trust me, I think you are the sharpest knife in the DC drawer. Although I admit, that doesn't set the bar very high these days. But I'll speed it up a bit and get to my point."

Nelson returned to the dining room, rubbing his hands together. "Soon, cake."

"Great," Milt said as Nelson sat down again. "Now, back to the napkin. Over on the right quadrant, we have our conservatives. You know the right-hand-corner types. They fight any change of any sort. My father epitomized the image of a traditionalist. Old-fashioned, 'if it ain't broke, don't fix it,' stay-in-a-rut folks. For example, did you know that there still is an active Prohibition Party? In fact, it's the oldest existing third party in the country. Talk about political Luddites."

He tapped the top center of our napkin. "Here, we have our Libertarians. Basically, these folks oppose any government control or interference in their personal or business lives. They run the gauntlet from being mildly annoyed with government meddling to the total, off-the-table anarchist. No-government, no-rules, batshit crazies."

Milt's napkin analogy and the way he was presenting it were oddly appealing. David could visualize the transition from left to right, from long-haired hippy to blazer-clad preppie, as Milt traced his finger over the crisp white cotton cloth.

"The bottom of our napkin metaphor is home to the Statists, those who believe, as always to various degrees, the government should have significant if not total power over the economy and individual freedom. Statists generally do not trust a capitalist free market, or personal freedom to any real extent. They rely on iron-fisted central planning and have zero tolerance for what we consider lifestyle diversity. A perfect example of a far bottom corner of the napkin, the Statist system, is the former North Korean regime whose demise you helped orchestrate.

"That brings us back to the area represented by the center section of the napkin, the centrists. Everything I've been talking about for the last twenty minutes was to set the stage for a focus on Envision-2100's political ideology, who we are, our party and the party that we desperately want you to represent and take into the White House.

"In the words of Victor Hugo, 'Nothing is more powerful than an idea whose time has come.' Our time has come. That phrase may be close to worn out, but it perfectly illustrates what we believe. It's time to shake the shit out of the two-party, 'vote for who we pick for you to vote for,' back-slapping, martini-swilling system that has run this country since the Roosevelt era."

Melissa sat up straight, fire in her eyes.

Milt's passion was palpable. Not just in the tone of his voice or in the words he so carefully articulated, nor simply in his soul-piercing gaze, which locked unwaveringly on David. No, there was more. There was a dynamism. True convictions that had all but evaporated in Washington, DC, circles. But it wasn't just Milt; it radiated from everyone else in the room as they, too, sat wordlessly transfixed.

Milt's passion was contagious, and David felt the emotion swell inside himself as well. Despite his time in Washington, his bureaucratic immune system hadn't made him nearly as jaded as he had feared he was becoming.

Mattie and Lucas silently reappeared in the dining room. Lucas carried a pot of coffee and a tray of sizeable white porcelain cups. As he removed partially drank glasses of tea, he replaced each with one of the cups, which he filled with steaming obsidian coffee.

As Lucas went about his task, Mattie prepared enormous slices of the coconut cake, placing one in front of David and four of the five board members, skipping Melissa, as she removed their dinner plates. David assumed this had something to do with Melissa's exercise regime and its clearly effective, pleasing results. She looked like she belonged in an ad for Gold's Gym.

Dessert signaled they were nearing the end of their meeting.

Using his fork, Milt whacked off a chunk of icing-laden cake, wolfed it down, followed it with another, took a sip of his coffee, and continued his monologue. "President Sheppard has done a remarkable job of repairing much of the damage that his predecessor wrought with our European and Central American allies. At least our United Nations ambassador can address her peers without getting booed out of the building. The economy is starting to stabilize after the roller-coaster ride that lunatic put the stock market through for four years. And we haven't had to suffer a government shutdown since Sheppard took office.

"But we have a long way to go. When Sheppard steps down, and Vice President Phillips takes the helm, we go right back to square one. Another unstable nutjob staining the carpet in the Oval Office with his unique brand of distilled evil. We can't let that happen, David." Milt pounded the table so hard that his coffee cup rattled.

Everyone looked up from their cake; Melissa from her coffee.

Milt's voice softened. "Of course, we didn't anticipate Sheppard's demise. Like Judson said, we were all set to coast for another four years and take what we saw as a lull to get our own ducks in a row. Fortunately, thanks to Judson and the other folks in this room, we had the foresight to start organizing the Centrist Party even before Sheppard took office. There is plenty more that we wish we could do, but as Donald Rumsfeld once noted, 'You go to war with the army you have, not the army you might want.' Ready or not, David, it's time to go to war. Metaphorically speaking, of course.

"We can't wait for Phillips to fuck up what Sheppard has done and push us back ten years. The eighty percent may not know it yet, but they're ready for Envision-2100's party. They're ready to become centrist."

Melissa leaned forward, clasped her hands together, and cleared her throat. "David, a centrist almost always seeks middle ground when it relates to government control, the economy, and personal freedom. Quite simply, we don't tolerate extremes. We're liberal but not overly liberal, conservative but not too conservative," she said. "We tend to adopt the 'Golden Mean' mindset. I don't want to sound too philosophically esoteric, but Aristotle summed us up over two thousand years ago when he said—and I'm paraphrasing here—that the golden mean is the desirable middle between two extremes. For example, bravery is a virtue, but if taken too far, it's reckless. And too little is cowardice."

"Exactly right," Elton said.

Melissa nodded. "Thank you, Elton. Eighty percent of America wants that middle ground in our government, in our laws, in our economic policies. Notice I didn't say I *think* they want. I said they want. That's a fact, not an opinion. Eighty percent of Americans want a hamburger jockey to earn enough to survive, but they don't want a high school dropout to suck the financial life out of his employer.

"We believe in personal freedom while at the same time stressing what is best for the common good. It's not easy. Too many times, government and business take the path of least resistance. They emphasize one at the expense of the other or totally ignore the other. I suppose it's human nature, but our philosophy is based on a constant quest for checks and balances, dissension, and compromise. These things have to be done consciously and overtly. There just isn't room for emotionalism or gut reaction when it comes to making our laws and running our country. Nor should there be. We've seen way too much of that, especially during the previous administration. But you know that. You saw that lunatic nuke a pissant country into the Stone Age. Well, in their case, further back. What he did worked out for us but at the expense of well over two million people. It could just as easily have gone the other way. Washington, New York, San Francisco, and a dozen other of our cities could have ended up as massive dark spots that glow at night. We can't let that happen again.

"Like Milt said, for the past three years, we have been working hard to build the Centrist Party. We've spent a ton of money getting it established in every state, getting it legally registered by the Federal Election Commission, and promoting its ideologies to the public.

"Of course, we've used every marketing trick known to Wall Street to focus on our eighty percent target group. We even picked our party color by combining red and blue. Purple, that's our color. We are both red and blue, Republican and Democrat. We are too conservative for the Democrats and too liberal for the Republicans—just like the eighty percent of Americans we represent. We certainly could've used a couple more years to grind off the edges, but in reality, we're ready to go."

"Here, here." Judson thumped the table.

"All we need is a candidate," Melissa said. "A face with a brain. A little experience but not politically tainted. Not a sinner, but not a saint. We've conducted thorough research, a personality analysis, and plenty of background checking. And you know what, David? You're our man. We know you're the one. Now, what do we have to do to make you realize that?"

13

Joyce King was a little more than an hour away from the end of her shift as a 9-1-1 operator. She worked for the Idaho Falls Department of Emergency Communications, or IFDEC as it was proudly and prominently stitched on the breast-pocket patch of her blue uniform shirt.

The IFDEC was a multijurisdictional agency that served dozens of geographically dispersed communities in western Wyoming and eastern Idaho. None of the cities in its service area could afford their own 9-1-1 services, even Jackson Hole, with its collection of out-of-state millionaires. For this reason, fifteen years ago, the Idaho Falls City Council established the IFDEC as a public service coalition. It was funded by a combination of federal grants and dues from surrounding municipalities.

"Sir, are you still there?" Joyce spoke into her microphone-earpiece assembly, her husky voice tired and drawn from a long shift. She had been with the IFDEC for just over a year and was the most junior of the three operators on her shift. Like the others, she loved her job and thrived on the near-constant adrenaline she got dealing with the "front end" of an emergency. There was no such thing as a dull day at the IFDEC.

She focused intently on the four computer monitors on her new New World Enterprise Computer-Aided Dispatch, or CAD, work-station.

The monitor on her left showed a map that automatically zoomed in on an electronic pin indicating the caller's location. Thanks to a government-funded program that had added powerful, advanced cell towers in hundreds of previously underserved areas nationwide, and new satellite communication interfaces, cell phones could now be used and traced in virtually every square mile of North America. The CAD system used triangulated signal information to calculate incredibly accurate, real-time caller locations. This particular call had originated northwest of Shoshone Lake, more or less in the middle of Yellowstone National Park.

Joyce moved the wheel on her mouse and zoomed in. Another pin appeared indicating the location of the Yellowstone Caldera. "Sir, can you hear me?" she repeated. She shifted her focus to another monitor, which reflected first-responder locations and information correspond-ing to the caller's physical location. There was no answer. Joyce tried once more. "Sir, if you can hear me, please tell me about your situation."

No reply.

The first-responder monitor indicated there was a fire station at the National Park Service headquarters next to West Thumb Lake, about six miles from the caldera location. Joyce clicked the link on the screen, which automatically dialed the station's landline. Seconds later, an automated message blared from her computer speaker: "The num-ber you have dialed cannot be reached. Please hang up and try again." Joyce clicked end call on the screen and tried again. After getting the same results, she scrolled over the map until another fire station appeared on the screen: the Hebgen Basin Fire District located outside the park entrance in West Yellowstone. She clicked on its number and was rewarded with a ringing sound. No answer.

Ten rings later, Joyce clicked on the emergency radio reference icon and scrolled down a list of repeater locations until she found the

Yellowstone West Net, frequency 166.8750. As the phone continued to ring, she keyed her radio mic. "Hebgen Basin Fire Station, this is IFDEC, over."

Two other station operators hummed in the background: "Nine One One, what's your emergency?"

While holding the radio mic, Joyce stood up to peer over the sound-dampening walls, which created the operators' cubicles. The man in the cubicle next to hers pounded furiously on his keyboard. His monitor was zoomed in on the same area as Joyce's.

Joyce raised her mic to her mouth. "Hebgen Fire Station, can you read me? Come in. Over."

Nothing but static—and then a surge of background noise. Wailing sirens and the roar of engines from fire trucks and ambulances. And screams.

"IFDEC, this is Hebgen Mobile," a response crackled, barely audible over the background chaos. "All hell's breaking loose. There was an eight point six earthquake. Then the volcano blew. Either that or the Ruskies missed and planted a nuke in the park. There was a terrible explosion. About half of the people that were outside are deaf. We're scrambling all units and heading for the west entrance, Highway One Niner One, over."

"Roger, Hebgen Mobile. How can we help? Over."

"We need every first responder within a fifty-mile radius. And while you're at it, the National Guard. And they better bring body bags. Fucking boulders are falling everywhere. There's an enormous cloud of smoke and ash moving up into the sky and, from what I can see, in all directions. It's starting to blot out what little sunlight is left. It's almost dark now. I can barely see the taillights on the unit in front of—" Silence.

"Hebgen Mobile, come in, over. Hebgen Mobile, can you hear me?" Joyce frowned. The radio was dead. That meant whatever had happened was bad, but Joyce had no idea how bad—or how historically significant the eruption would be for its intensity and its capacity for destruction.

Glancing from one monitor to another, hands alternating between clicking her mouse and dancing across the keyboard, Joyce somehow tuned out the nonessential noise and commotion that was all around her.

Then, out of nowhere, she recalled reading an article in *National Geographic* during a lull in a late-night shift. The story was about the dormant Yellowstone volcano, but as a lead-in, the author recounted in horrifying detail the destruction that thing was capable of dishing out.

Approximately seventy-five thousand years earlier, the Toba super-volcano in Sumatra, Indonesia, exploded in what scientists considered to be the single most massive eruption on Earth, thousands of times more powerful than any before or since. Vulcanologists estimated that the Toba eruption had a volcanic explosivity index of 8.

Some theories postulated that the ash cloud created by the Toba eruption settled over the globe like snow, causing a "volcanic winter" that lasted over six years and resulted in a global cooling period of nearly one thousand years. Researchers estimated that the amount of material in the ash cloud greatly exceeded 2,500 cubic kilometers. Reviews of mitochondrial DNA pointed to a link between the Toba eruption and a bottleneck in the evolution of *Homo sapiens.*

Scientists believed the event came dangerously close to causing the extinction of human life.

On Sunday afternoon, August 26, 1883, a semi-active volcano situated on the Indonesian island of Krakatoa erupted and then col-lapsed into the bubbling caldera that still exists today. It was the largest, deadliest, and most destructive volcanic event in recorded history. More than thirty-six thousand people died as a result of heat from the blast and from the tsunamis caused by the collapse of the volcano below sea level.

The Krakatoa explosion was estimated to have generated a blast whose sound exceeded three hundred decibels, loud enough to be heard over three thousand miles away and to rupture the eardrums of sailors on the decks of ships forty miles from the island. Just two hundred decibels generated enough energy to vibrate the human body apart; three hundred would cause it to explode.

Krakatoa, with an estimated VEI of 6, wasn't classified as a super-volcano; Yellowstone was—even if Joyce didn't realize it yet.

Suddenly the room—the entire building—shook violently. Coffee sloshed out of the cup on Joyce's workstation, and every picture on every wall crashed to the floor. Joyce staggered and grabbed the side of her desk to keep from falling.

"Whoa, Nelly," she blurted above the ruckus. "That might explain why we lost the Hebgen Mobile connection."

By now, icons and warning lights flashed from every monitor on every operator's workstation in the EFDEC control room. Despite the apparent chaos, Joyce and her associates had things more or less under control. The EMS supervisor had joined the fray, and everyone was following the emergency action protocols that had been developed over the years and refined with every quarterly drill. There actually was an evacuation-and-response plan specific to earthquakes and volcanic eruptions. However, no one had imagined the scope of the disaster that was at that very moment unfolding ninety miles away. It was literally unimaginable.

Physically and mentally exhausted, Joyce collapsed in her chair and stared at the explosion of activity on her monitors. She had dealt with traffic accidents, fires, and the occasional domestic dispute. Although rare in Idaho Falls, she had even responded to a couple of murders over the years. But nothing, absolutely nothing, came close to the sense of overwhelming fear and helplessness that washed over her now.

For the first time in her career, she felt sick to her stomach with pure, unadulterated fear.

14

The Farm
Two years before the day of

"**THE BALL IS IN YOUR COURT,** David. We need a decision." Melissa folded her hands on the table.

David sat up ramrod straight in his chair and placed both of his hands on the table. He looked from left to right, locking eyes with each individual board member. No one spoke, at least not verbally. But every single person's eyes burned with a blowtorch intensity that conveyed distilled passion and commitment for what they believed in. And in what they were trying to do.

David tried to gain control of the thoughts synapsing through his brain and then decided just to let his frontal lobe and the amygdala fight it out. Controlled, rational decision-making versus his raging emotions. This semiconscious mental exercise always seemed to work.

Finally, he broke the silence: "I know I haven't given enough thought and introspection to what I'm about to say, and if you knew me on a personal level, you would know that's not my style. I don't make decisions based on passion or gut feel. But right now, I'm just a point shy of being overwhelmed by what you've been telling me. I'm honored beyond comprehension. At the same time, my left brain is throwing up glaring caution lights and sirens. This may be one of those times when the analytical me needs to be subordinate to the emotional me.

"Let me be clear, I totally bought into what Envision-2100 and the Centrist movement represent. I just haven't convinced myself that I'm the best person for the job, that I've earned or deserve the trust you are placing in me.

"Conversely, I've got a damn-good sense for the other players. I'm just as disgusted as anyone in this room at what the Democrats and Republicans can offer up as candidates when President Sheppard steps down. And you and everyone else in DC know how I feel about Vice President Phillips. If he runs, and he will, and if he's elected, I'll resign. Of course, I wouldn't have to. He'll fire me on his way to the Oval Office as soon as he's sworn in.

"I don't know who's winning the left-brain, right-brain battle raging inside my head right now. So, Melissa, in answer to your question, I'm convinced. I still need to discuss everything with my wife. From day one of our marriage, we've made major decisions together. Hell, we debate whether to have our eggs scrambled or fried, for Christ's sake. And nothing we've discussed in the past comes anywhere close to being as life-altering as this. I don't anticipate her having issues with whatever I decide, but win or lose, our lives will never be the same again.

"I do have a couple of practical questions. There is the issue of finance. Personal finance. The instant I announce my decision to run for office, I'll have to resign as secretary of state. Kelly will need to resign from her job as well. She's a GS-Thirteen research analyst with the General Services Administration." David laughed. "Of course, you all knew that. Anyway, we have developed a habit of eating, sometimes two meals a day."

"Only two?" Melissa asked.

"Plus coffee. Lots of coffee," David said. "Like I told Judson earlier, my salary is just a rounding error compared to most Envision-2100 members. It's a matter of public record, so you shouldn't have had to waste any intelligence-gathering energy on it. As one of twenty-one Level One government officials, I make two hundred ten thousand seven hundred dollars annually. And Kelly, as a GS-Thirteen—"

Judson raised his hand with an exaggerated flourish. "Your financial situation was the second or third item we discussed when we chose you as our candidate. We want to set up a trust fund that will provide you with twice your combined salary, plus incidental personal expenses from the time you resign your current job until you are elected, take office, and start drawing a POTUS salary. If, God forbid, you aren't elected, we'll continue to pay your salary for a minimum of one year."

Milt chimed in: "Our lawyers have done their homework and have already drawn up an agreement. That arrangement is perfectly legal. In fact, our PR team wants to disclose this to the public on day one as part of our complete transparency policy. If nothing else, we learned that lesson from the Americans Elect funding fiasco."

Judson nodded. "Well, David, here we are. We know that today has been a shocker for you, and no one expects you to decide until you have had time to process the discussion and our proposal with Kelly. Unfortunately, the fuse is burning. President Sheppard is literally living on borrowed time. You have a scheduled meeting with him tomorrow. I would ask that you make it your personal deadline for a go, no-go decision."

"I have to agree," David replied. "I'll call Kelly on my way back to DC and let her know we're going out to dinner. She loves the Comus Inn at Sugarloaf Mountain, so if I can get reservations, I'll surprise her. Lord knows she will be surprised."

"David, let us take care of making the reservation. I can almost guarantee you that it won't be a problem. You have way too much thinking to do without worrying about making dinner reservations. In fact, let us free up a little more of your time. Rather than flying you back to your office this afternoon, why don't we shoot you straight to your house in Germantown. You have plenty of room on the back side of your farm to land the copter. Hell, our guy could almost put the AW160 on your front porch if he had to. That would save you at least an hour's drive and a ton of commuter stress. Plus, imagine the message that kind of entrance will send to your wife—and neighbors, for that matter. We'll make things right with the sheriff and the FAA if need be. Or at least ask for forgiveness. That will give you and Kelly more time to have dinner. And more time for you to do whatever you have to do to convince her that she would make an unbelievable First Lady. Then we'll pick you up from home in the morning and fly you to the Truman Building in plenty of time to make your ten o'clock meeting with POTUS. What do you think, David?"

"I'll tell you, Judson, a guy could get accustomed to this kind of treatment." David leaned back. This would shock the hell of Kelly. He couldn't wait to see her face. "All right, that sounds like a plan."

With an exaggerated flourish, Judson slapped the table in front of him. "Great! Now let's get you in the air."

15

Colter Bay Campground, Grand Teton National Park
The evening of the day of

EVEN INSIDE THE AIRSTREAM with the door closed and their hands over their ears, the sound was so loud that it vibrated the fluid in Jeremy's inner ear, causing a wave of nausea to sweep over him. From the collective strained look on their faces, Judy and the twins seemed to be experiencing the same sensation.

Then, just as quickly as the explosive pressure had come, there was silence.

Judy's voice, controlled but commanding, broke that silence: "Girls get in the truck. We're getting out of here."

Jeremy, already moving out the door, sprinted around to the side of the Airstream. He visually double-checked the trailer hitch and towing assembly. They didn't have time to waste, but they didn't want their refuge on wheels to disconnect itself the first time they made a sharp turn.

He climbed behind the wheel, started the engine, and leaned forward. An eerie red glow illuminated the darkening sky to the north. Judy and the twins were staring at it as well, transfixed. No one said a word.

Blinding white and blue bolts of lightning ripped open the twilight every few seconds. The tempo of the dazzling light show seemed to increase with every new burst of electrical energy. The instantaneous rise in pressure and thirty-six-thousand-degree heat from each flash caused a sonic shockwave, thunder, reaching a near-constant crescendo. Jeremy could barely hear the twins' screams.

Between the shockwaves, Judy noted, "It's a unique phenomenon referred to as volcanic lightning. It's caused by static electricity generated by the ejecta that's flying out of what will soon be a mountain."

When Jeremy turned on the truck's headlights, a peculiar sight appeared. It seemed to be snowing. Except it wasn't snow. Fine grains of glittery black something fell on the windshield. Only it wasn't falling; it was actually angling toward them from the north. At the same time, tiny seed-sized pebbles peppered the F-250 and everything around it.

"It's the ash and lava fragments from the pyroclastic flow," Judy said. She continued to stare out the window, hypnotized.

"What?" Jeremy shouted, trying to be heard over the continuous roar of thunder.

Judy turned away from the window, her face pale. "The pyroclastic flow. The volcano erupted, more likely exploded, and that stuff is probably the outer edge of the cloud. At least I hope it's the outer edge. A volcanic eruption spits out millions of tons of ash at over four hundred miles an hour in the form of what they call a pyroclastic current or cloud."

"How do you know all this shit?" Jeremy asked as he maneuvered the truck and twenty-five feet of trailer around a log blocking the pine-straw trail serving as the campground road.

"I took an elective in geophysics. Now get us the fuck out of here."

Jeremy glanced in his rearview mirror. With their seat belts snuggly fastened, Ellis and Fiona held hands and looked at each other fearfully, communicating as only those with duplicate chromosomes could do.

Judy gripped her door handle and Jeremy's knee as the truck bounced along. "We're just getting started. It'll be like one of those California wildfires, only it's not a cloud of smoke, it's a cloud of ash and pumice. See those sparkles on the windshield? That's not glitter.

It's flecks of silica. Glass. If we swallow it or breathe it in, we're in big trouble.

"Do you remember Mount Vesuvius and Pompeii in 79 AD? It wasn't lava that buried the city, it was ash. Hot ash, about five hundred seventy degrees Fahrenheit. Not that many years ago, scientists thought the victims were asphyxiated by the ash and noxious gas. But recent studies indicated that most died instantly from the heat retained by the cinders. They went into almost immediate rigor mortis, frozen for all time in their last physical position. Well, not frozen, but you know what I mean."

Jeremy glanced at Judy. "Really, you're cracking a joke now, for Christ's sake? Don't ever give me your wrong-place, wrong-time jab again." They each managed a smile. A weak smile, but a smile.

Just then, a deafening, heart-stopping bang shattered the conversation. Twin screams burst from the back seat. Judy's hand flew to her mouth.

A rock, roughly the size of a softball, bounced off the F-250's hood. Other stones—some smaller, some larger, one massive—descended from the sky, flying through the beams cast out by their headlights. Most of the larger rocks had a dim red glow. It was like being in the center of a meteor shower, only it was scary, not pretty. Smoke and steam floated off the rocks after they struck the ground. The larger ones buried themselves into the layer of mulch that covered the ground. Flickers of flames sprang up around their edges and lit up the forest floor.

They would soon turn into a raging inferno.

Jeremy tore off the campground trail and onto Colter Bay Village Road, speeding past the check-in office and convenience store. He silently gave thanks that he had had the foresight to fill up the truck that afternoon. At the Colter Bay Campground entrance stop sign, he turned right onto John D. Rockefeller Jr. Parkway, driving south.

By now, the heavier particulates from the pyroclastic cloud were giving way to finer ash. It fell lightly at first, like the initial part of a winter's snow, and then increased in intensity. By the time they reached Pilgrim Creek, it had covered the road.

Jeremy flicked on his fog lights and low beams to see better, but even this trick gave him less than fifty feet of visibility, and it was getting progressively worse. He was making twenty miles an hour but knew that speed wouldn't last long. At mile five, just before the Jackson Lake Lodge entrance, a smoldering boulder roughly the size of a Volvo slammed squarely into the center of the right-hand lane. Sparks and dust flew in all directions from its impact.

"Jesus fucking Christ!" Judy blurted in horror.

The twins screamed, and Jeremy swerved to the left to avoid crashing into the massive projectile. He put the F-250 in four-wheel drive and eased around it, barely. As he pulled back into the right-hand lane, another RV, a Greyhound-bus-sized Class A, blasted out of the lodge entrance, turned right, and headed south.

Whoever was behind the wheel was driving too fast. Way too fast for near-blackout conditions. In a matter of seconds, Jeremy lost sight of the Class A's taillights. He looked down at his instrument panel and turned on his flashers, mumbling, "I should have done that an hour ago."

The falling ash grew thicker. Even though the earth seemed to be flying apart at the seams, Judy maintained her composure—but not without effort. She squeezed the armrest with her right hand and clenched her jaw as she stared transfixed at what little she could see of the road. She'd never make it as a horror film star.

The twins were uncharacteristically quiet, not screaming and out of control like most twelve-year-olds. Maybe they were scared speechless.

Jeremy broke the silence: "We're a good forty miles from where I thought the caldera was. I was hoping we could get ahead of the cloud. It seems to be blowing almost due east, and we're heading almost due south. Even at the snail's pace I have to drive, I thought we could avoid most of the stuff."

Judy shook her head. "The problem is the eruption sent ejecta well into the stratosphere. The air currents up there flow at different speeds and different directions depending on the altitude. Most likely, the material fanned out in every direction, like the head of a giant mushroom. Most of it will eventually fall to the east, but we're talking about years, maybe even decades. If it makes you feel any better, we are probably on the light side of the cloud, which initially blew out to the west."

"You know, that's one of the things I love about you, Judy." Jeremy grinned. "You may be a treasure chest of useless information, but at least you always try to find the bright side of every situation. Right now, I'm looking for the cloud around your silver lining. And I could use a little company."

Ellis piped up in the back seat: "You know, I don't get this conversation."

"Yeah," Fiona added. "What the hell are you talking about?"

"Watch your mouth, young lady," Judy said, looking over her shoulder. "You're lucky we didn't leave you behind when we had the chance."

Everyone laughed. Jeremy hoped it wouldn't be their last.

They continued their tedious, *über*cautious trek southward, gradually slowing as the ash snow intensified. Four times, vehicles came speeding up from behind and flew around them. A pickup with dual rear wheels, a Jeep, and two cars. The same pattern of insane driving appeared on the interstate every time there was torrential rainfall. Drivers who could barely see past the hoods of their cars, screaming down the hammer lane, half the time without headlights. Invariably, they were the ones that ran off embankments or rammed into the back of semis when the six o'clock news had its obligatory video clips about the storm.

At mile nine from their departure, as the truck approached the bridge over Pacific Creek, Jeremy saw the Class A RV that had sped past them earlier. It was upside down in the center of the creek. Its taillights cast a blurry glow in the falling ash as its rear tires continued to slowly spin. Bluish smoke drifted up from the bottom of the engine compartment.

Jeremy pulled onto the right shoulder. He put the F-250 in Park but left the engine running and the lights on. He turned to Judy. "I'm going down there."

"Yeah, I figured you would," Judy replied. She took a terry-cloth towel from her door pocket and handed it to Jeremy. "Wrap this around your mouth and nose. None of us need to breathe in that stuff. This will help keep it out. When you get to the creek, hold your breath, take it off and wet it, then put it back on. That will help even more."

Appreciating Judy's clinical savvy and her concern more than ever, Jeremy put the towel over his nose and tied it behind his head. He grabbed a flashlight from the glove compartment, opened the driver's door, and stepped out into the silently falling ash storm. Grains of pumice stung his eyes, and the distinct smell of sulfur burned his nose. Hell's version of air conditioning.

He walked to the front of the F-250, and staying within the glow cast by the truck's headlights, he started down the slope toward the creek and the overturned RV. The RV's door was on the passenger side, which now faced the road. The stream wasn't terribly deep, and even with the vehicle stuck nose-first in the center of the flowing water, it was only partially submerged. Jeremy shone his flashlight through the passenger window and jumped backward.

The passenger, apparently a plumpish female, had slammed into the windshield, knocking it out of the cockpit. The windshield and most of the person's skull dangled out the front of the RV. Her body lay half in and half out of the passenger compartment. A stump where her right shoulder should have been poked through her "Yellowstone National Park" T-shirt.

The driver had fared no better. He had been thrown against the steering wheel, shearing off the rim and thrusting the post through his upper chest. There was blood everywhere, even the ceiling.

Jeremy assumed, correctly, that neither had been wearing a seat belt.

The smell of gasoline was almost overpowering. Jeremy, gagging from the combined stench of fuel and death, instinctively realized two things: there was nothing else he could do, and he needed to get away from the smoking engine immediately. He turned and retraced his path up the creek bank. When he made it back to the truck, he got inside and, before anyone had a chance to ask any questions, said, "There was no one inside. I guess someone else picked them up after they wrecked."

Judy locked eyes with Jeremy. Her intense expression told him that she knew he was lying.

16

The Farm
Two years before the day of

DAVID AND HIS ENVISION-2100 board-member hosts got up from the table and, as a group, headed toward the foyer. Mattie and Lucas materialized from the dining room's side door. Lucas held a small white cardboard box tied together by a length of red ribbon, with a little bow at the top. They intercepted the group.

Mattie, ignoring the others, went straight for David and offered him her hand. "Mr. Secretary, I can't tell you what a pleasure it has been to make your acquaintance. I hope you come back up here real soon and let me cook for you again." Taking the box from Lucas, she handed it to David. "Here, Mr. Secretary. Take the rest of this coconut cake home for you and your wife. I've heard it's your favorite."

After shaking her hand, David accepted the box, shook hands with Lucas, and gave them a sincere smile. "Thank you so much. This is very sweet and thoughtful. What you hear is correct, it's my absolute favorite dessert. I think your meatloaf may be my new favorite main course. I've got a feeling I'm going to be back up this way shortly. Maybe next time I can sample some of that fried chicken."

"You do just that, Mr. Secretary. For now, I think your chariot awaits." Mattie and Lucas turned and started back into the dining room. In the background, the *whup, whup* of the approaching copter let everyone know David's ride was about to land.

As the group stepped outside, the AW160 nosed up slightly and dropped onto the Farm's front-yard helipad. The main rotor continued turning as the engine slowed but didn't stop. The copilot climbed out and opened the passenger door.

Judson shook David's hand and raised his voice to be heard over the engine noise: "I'll be looking forward to your call after you and Kelly have talked tonight. So let me know, one way or the other. Don't worry about calling late. I won't sleep until I hear from you anyway. The copter will pick you up at seven in the morning. Enjoy your dinner and give my best to Kelly . . . Mr. President." Judson grinned.

The other four shook David's hand and slapped him on his back for luck. Elated but apprehensive, David turned and walked to his multimillion-dollar ride home. As he climbed in, he looked back and waved to his new colleagues. Today bubbled up the list of the most exciting things that had ever happened in his life.

David strapped himself into the flight harness and put on the headphones next to his seat as the copilot slid the passenger door closed. Twenty seconds later, the pilot simultaneously pulled up on the collective, twisted the throttle, and pushed forward, gently, on the cyclic. The AW160 lifted off the ground, and as the pilot applied pressure to the left pedal, sped off to the south.

The copilot's voice came over David's headphones: "Your back yard is about forty-five miles from here. Even fighting the headwind, we should have you there in about fifteen minutes—less time than it would take you to get from your office to your car in the Truman Building parking deck."

Keying his mic, David shot back, "That's for sure. By the way, is it OK for me to make a cellphone call while we're in the air? I don't want to get the FCC on your case."

"Making a call is no problem, Mr. Secretary. This bird is equipped with Wi-Fi, so just leave that on and switch off your cellular. The ghost of Steve Jobs will take it from there. The person's caller ID will show 'Envision-2100,' but other than that, you'll never know the difference."

"Thanks," David replied as he paired his iPhone with the AW160's Bluetooth signal. He gave Siri a command to "call Kelly," and seconds later, with a quizzical lilt to her voice, she answered, "Kelly Stakley."

"Hey, babe, it's your husband. Are you home yet?"

"David? My caller ID says Envision-2100. It sounds like you're in a laundromat or a car wash somewhere. Are you still with Judson Ballard and his cronies?"

"I was, but now I'm . . . well . . . just go into the back yard when the windows start to rattle."

"What? I'm in the kitchen, looking into the back yard."

"We have dinner reservations at the Comus in an hour. And, honey, we have a lot to talk about."

"The Comus? Well. It sounds like we're celebrating something. I can't wear slacks to the Comus. I have to change and slap on a coat of war paint. We can't have the secretary of state's main squeeze looking like she just got off work and drove for nearly an hour in Beltway traffic.

Now, what's this about our windows starting to—what? Oh my God!" Kelly's voice was drowned out by the low-pitched, ever-increasing sound of the helicopter cycling from her phone through his, along with the loud rattle of vibrating kitchen dishes. She stepped outside just as the helicopter touched down in the back yard.

The copilot opened the passenger door, and David stepped out. He thanked the copilot and ducked below the whirling rotor blades. Walking in military quick time, he made a bee line for his wife.

"Shit. You bought a helicopter?" Kelly shouted. "A lot of people would have just called an Uber. But no, not you. I can't wait to see that on our Visa bill."

David laughed, kissed Kelly, and put his arm across her shoulders. They walked toward the house. "I told you we have a lot to talk about."

"Let's start with what's in the box." Kelly nodded at the package David carried.

"This? This is dessert. Maybe the most delicious coconut cake I've ever had. I'll put it on the table, and we can eat it when we get home from the Comus."

"That sounds like a plan. Now enough with the chit-chat. What's going on? Where have you been all day? And how did we end up with a helicopter in our back yard?"

They stepped into the house, and David put the gift-wrapped cake on the food prep island in the middle of the kitchen. He turned to Kelly, placed both of his hands on her shoulders, and looked at her with an uncharacteristically stern expression. "Kelly, they want me to run for president of the United States."

Kelly burst out laughing. "Right."

David tightened his grip on her shoulders. "I'm serious. They want me to run for president."

Kelly, stunned, flinched backward. "Jeez, David." Her voice trembled. "Wow . . . I . . . I don't know what to say. First the helicopter and then this. What other surprises are going to pop out of the box?"

"Well, I do have a one-on-one meeting with the president in the morning, but other than those surprises, it's been a relatively quiet day."

David offered a slightly worried but happy smile. "Let's go upstairs, get dressed, and go to dinner. I'll synopsize my discussion with Judson and the Envision-2100 board. We have a lot to talk about. Then we have to make the most significant decision we've ever made. Ever."

After a quick shower, David put on a pair of tan slacks, a blue pin-stripe shirt, black loafers, and a blue Brooks Brothers linen jacket. He would skip the tie tonight. As Kelly sat in front of her dresser mirror, putting on her obligatory, never-leave-the-house-without-it cherry-red lipstick, David headed down the stairs to get his car keys.

The front doorbell rang.

"This is a lousy time for drop-ins." David studied the small camera monitor State Department Security had installed on the hallway wall next to the front door. A large white male with a close-cropped military-style haircut and dressed in an impeccably tailored black suit stood on the porch. A slight bulge protruded from the upper left side of his jacket.

David pressed a microphone button on the speaker mounted to the left of the door. "May I help you?"

The man held up a small, opened leather case containing a photo and company identification card. "Mr. Secretary, my name is Charles Crum. I'm a security specialist with Blackwater Associates. Mr. Judson Ballard, on behalf of Envision-2100, has engaged my company to provide escort and protection services for you and Mrs. Stakley from now until further notice. I'm here to drive you and Mrs. Stakley to the Comus Inn, with your permission of course, and return you home after you have dinner. I would be honored if you would grant me that privilege."

David opened the door and assessed the man. "Mr. Ballard is just chock-full of surprises. Do you mind if I get a closer look at your identification, Mr. Crum?"

"Not at all, Mr. Secretary." Charles Crum handed the case to David through the partly opened door.

David took the case and carefully studied the ID. At the same time, he completed his visual assessment: not huge, maybe six two, not an ounce of body fat. David's military and martial arts training instinctively told him that the guy could handle himself.

After comparing the man's face with that in the photo, and to the best of his ability making sure the ID hadn't been forged, he handed it back. "Thank you, Mr. Crum. Would you like to come in while I clear things with my wife?"

"If you don't mind, Mr. Secretary, I'll just wait next to the car."

Parked in the driveway was an absolutely stunning black Mercedes Maybach.

"If you insist, Mr. Crum. Do you go by Charlie?"

"No, sir. Just Charles."

David didn't miss the fact that "Charles" hadn't smiled or really changed facial expressions at all during their short conversation. "That's fine, Charles. Unless there is some major snafu, we will be out in just a minute," David said as he started easing the door closed.

"Yes, sir." Charles shifted slightly toward the Maybach. When David closed the door entirely, he checked the monitor. Only then did Charles turn his back on David.

"Never turn your back on the king," David mused. Charles Crum was former SEAL or Delta. One or the other, for sure.

Kelly came down the stairs, adjusting her earrings. "Who was that?"

"That, my dear, is our escort-slash-bodyguard for the evening, and depending on how our discussion goes, he and his ilk may be lurking around for the next several weeks. I'm pretty darn sure we won't get mugged tonight. Now, if you're ready, let's go marvel at what German comfort and engineering are all about."

Tilting her head, Kelly gave her husband a what-are-you-talking-about look—until he opened the door.

17

The city of West Yellowstone, Montana
23:30 the day of

THE **IFDEC** CONTROL ROOM WAS IN TOTAL, albeit controlled, chaos. Every phone on every desk was ringing, and each string of "hold" lights blinked incessantly.

Joyce paid no attention to the fact that her shift had ended two hours ago, as she and her counterparts continued to answer a continuous stream of telephone calls and coordinate the growing list of first- and second-tier emergency responders. At the same time, her IFDEC supervisor began executing the steps laid out in the Idaho section of the Bureau of Homeland Security's Emergency Action Plan, EAP.

Much of the emergency effort was directed toward US Route 20, the one and only paved road leading out of West Yellowstone. Utter pandemonium covered every inch of it. Traffic was headlight to taillight heading west out of the city toward the Idaho state line, twenty miles away.

The official resident population of West Yellowstone fluctuated around fourteen hundred. This time of year, another five or six hundred tourists were staying in the hotels and private RV parks. There was a daily pilgrimage into the park every morning after breakfast, a lull from ten until three, and then a returning stream in the late afternoon. The local sheriff estimated there were around five hundred vehicles, between the locals and visitors, in and around the city at any given time.

Tonight, every civilian car, truck, and motorcycle that would run was westbound. Virtually no one was planning to ride this thing out. It would be years before they found the bodies of those who tried.

Thanks to almost zero visibility and insane driving, the wrecks started before the fleeing caravan could even get past the city limits. All north- and southbound streets intersected with 20 as it snaked east and west through the center of town, forcing traffic to merge into a single artery. Even in the middle of the day, it would have been challenging to get so many vehicles on to a sole road, heading in the same direction, without pileups. At midnight, with ash-induced blackout conditions and panic-crazed drivers, it was literally impossible.

To compound the problem, the combination of violent earthquakes and red-hot boulders falling out of the sky had disrupted all electrical power within a thirty-mile, and growing, radius around the caldera. The city's gas main had also ruptured, igniting its spewing vapor into a raging tower of blue flame in the center of, ironically, Firehole Avenue.

Everyone in Northwest Montana knew about the sleeping giant that lay beneath the Yellowstone Caldera. Everyone knew there was always the chance that one day the reputed supervolcano could erupt on an unimaginable scale—but no one actually believed it would. After all, it had been over six hundred thousand years, according to people who were supposed to know those things, since its last major eruption. That was well over four hundred thousand years before the first *Homo sapiens* made his appearance somewhere in East Africa.

People had simply learned to live with this remote possibility of disaster, even laugh and joke about it. They wouldn't be joking about it any longer. Not the survivors.

Rescue ambulances were called first and dispatched, followed by the various fire departments her computer flashed on its monitor.

Joyce started with the units situated north and east along the US 20 corridor. Unfortunately, there weren't many. One inside the

Caribou-Targhee National Forest and one in St. Anthony. All the rest were located nearby in Idaho Falls. Each time she connected with a station's emergency operator, she had to explain why they needed to dispatch their units, all of their units, to a location, in Idaho Falls's case, ninety miles away. She keyed her mic, mentally forcing herself to remain calm and directive as she reached out to stations closer to the caldera. "Hebgen Mobile, Canyon Village, anyone, come in!"

Nothing.

The Hebgen Basin Fire District rescue vehicle driver had pleaded for her to dispatch all units within a fifty-mile radius. But there just weren't any. It was no exaggeration to say that West Yellowstone lay smack dab in the middle of nowhere. For that reason, it would be hours before National Guard units from Bozeman or Idaho Falls would begin to make their way to West Yellowstone or the northern entrance at Gardiner.

But there was another option. A section of the EAP was dedicated to the eventuality of a volcanic eruption, specifically with the Yellowstone supervolcano.

Joyce stood up and looked over the top of her cubical wall toward her supervisor. "Russell, when you can get free for a sec," she shouted while motioning with her hand.

The supervisor glanced in her direction, said something to the operator he had been talking to, then dashed over to Joyce's cubicle.

"What'ya got, Joyce?"

"I can't raise any responders north of Big Springs, not even the volunteer FDs. I think it's time to activate section two of the EAP. Worse case, we piss off your boss and send the snow removal boys on a wild goose chase. I'm not seeing a best-case right now."

"I agree! Keep doing what you're doing, and I'll activate the next phase."

Someone on the planning committee had had the foresight to stipulate that second-wave responders include snow removal teams that were already organized within every city and county in the three-state region. These teams were to arm themselves with the snowplow equipment that usually sat idle from April through October. This strategy, initially labeled as ridiculous during the summer months, would save more lives and prove to be more useful than any other single initiative.

The regional director of the Idaho DHS arrived at the makeshift command post at around 01:15 on what would unofficially become known as "the day after the day of."

He jumped directly into the fray and started working through his section of the EAP by calling the FAA office in Salt Lake City. At 01:35 Yellowstone and Jackson Hole Airports were closed to all traffic. By that time, shutting down departing air traffic was beyond just a precaution. It was a matter of "if you try to take off, you will die." This didn't stop a nationally known Alabama lawyer from going berserk when the pilots of his brand-new Citation CJ4 refused to meet him and his girlfriend at the Jackson Hole Airport to fly them back to Birmingham.

Within two hours, the FAA had rerouted all flights within an area of the northwest United States extending east past Casper, Wyoming; south to Provo, Utah; and west to Boise, Idaho. The area would remain off-limits to air traffic for weeks, until late-summer weather fronts disseminated the still-rising column of ash, the prevailing jet streams forcing ash as far east as Philadelphia and along the North Carolina coast.

By the end of the day after the eruption, highways within a twenty-five-mile radius of what had previously been the Yellowstone Caldera, and what in just six days would be sixteen-thousand-foot-tall Mount Shoshone, were buried in almost ten feet of ash and pumice.

Working around the clock for the first three days, snowplow teams were able to keep the three main arteries, US Routes 20, 191, and 14, more or less drivable south past Jackson Hole, east to Wapiti, and north to Big Sky. Driving within that almost sixty-five-mile circle was virtually impossible after the first twenty-four hours following the eruption. And the closer you got to the epicenter, the less likely it was that you would return.

Using a technique learned and refined during the winter months, snowplow drivers cleared the path by pushing the ash to both sides of the road. They were followed by front-end loaders, which would scoop up the sometimes still-smoldering ejecta and load it into an endless stream of dump trucks. The trucks hauled the ash to previously identified ravines and washed-out gullies.

In the months to come, this practice would present its own set of problems and environmental issues. But on a battlefield, every soldier knew you had to "clear the airway, stop the bleeding," and then "protect the wound." These units were on the front line and working like madmen to clear the airway and save their patient, metaphorically speaking. They would let someone else worry about cleaning up the mess.

Meanwhile, back at the IFDEC, Joyce and her team were going through their daily shift-turnover routine. Only today wasn't routine. Not even close. Every member of the next shift had shown up early, and every member of Joyce's team offered to stay late. However, the regional director would have none of that.

"Wrap up your turnover report and then go home," he ordered. "It's a fact that the second day of a disaster is the worst. Everyone comes off their adrenalin high and starts to crash and burn. We can't have that. I want the current shift to go home, get some rest, and be ready for a fresh start tomorrow. Now, finish up and get out of here!"

...

Martin Driggs sat at his desk at ABC affiliate KIFI polishing copy sheets for the early-morning news. The talking-head newscast team would roll in at four thirty to begin their daily makeup routine and to review the summary of national and local events he had gleaned throughout the night from the Associated Press wire service. They would bitch and whine like two-year-olds if his electronic copy sheets weren't polished up, double spaced, and available on the iPads on the anchor desk.

Martin was just biding his time at KIFI, waiting for a chance to move up the investigative reporting ladder. Maybe at a larger station in Seattle or Portland or, if he struck newsperson gold, Sacramento or San Francisco. He thought of California as the promised land.

As he assembled what in just a few hours would become the early-morning news, he listened, sort of, to the scanner that occupied one corner of his desk. It continuously squawked with police, fire, and 9-1-1 department radio chatter. One of Martin's duties was to monitor the scanner and alert KIFI's standby news team if there was a wreck, a fire, or, if they got fortunate, a murder within their catchment area. He had been doing this for so long that his brain tuned most of the radio traffic out as merely background noise. Not tonight.

As his fingers nursed what he initially thought would be the morning's headline story from his iMac's keyboard, he heard the tone of one IFDEC operator's voice move up a couple of octaves.

Usually, each member of the 9-1-1 team worked diligently to maintain a calm, detached, almost perfunctory radio demeanor. They sometimes sounded bored as they responded to mothers calling to report a missing child, or the wife of a suspected heart attack victim.

This woman was undoubtedly under control, but Martin could detect a not-so-subtle sense of urgency in her voice. Then he heard keywords that caused him to stop what he was doing and pick up his phone.

"Idaho Falls, this is Hebgen Basin Fire District, Mobile One. There has been a major earthquake and an explosion like nothing I've ever heard before."

"Hebgen Fire, Idaho Falls, what's your twenty?"

"We're rolling out of West Yellowstone, heading east toward the park entrance. I think the volcano has erupted. It's like the sky is on fire. It's lit up as far as I can see."

"Roger Hebgen Fire, do you require assistance?"

"Hell yes, we need assistance! We need every first responder within a fifty-mile radius. And while you're at it, the National Guard. And they better bring body bags. Fucking boulders are falling everywhere.

There is an enormous cloud of smoke and ash moving up into the sky and, from what I can see, in all directions. It's starting to blot out what little sunlight is left. It's almost dark now. I can barely see the taillights on the unit in front of . . ."

Then, for a few seconds, until it picked up another radio signal, the scanner was silent.

Martin realized he had overheard what might very well be the beginning of the most earth-shattering disaster—he brushed aside his mental pun—that modern man had ever witnessed. He forgot the half-cobbled news summary on his iMac and barked, "Siri, call the KIFI News Response Team driver."

18

Germantown, Maryland
Two years before the day of

David held their front door open for Kelly. She stepped outside, focused on the Mercedes. "Wow, nice ride. Beats the hell out of my Prius."

Charles, who had been simultaneously watching the road and the front of David's house, walked to the passenger side of the car and opened the rear door.

"Kelly, this is Mr. Crum. Charles. He'll be watching out for us tonight," David said.

Kelly smiled and thrust out her hand. "It's a pleasure to meet you, Mr. Crum. May I call you Charles?"

"Yes, Mrs. Stakley, Charles is just fine." Charles shook Kelly's hand.

Kelly nodded at the car. "I was just admiring the Maybach. Is this the V-twelve version of the S650?"

"Yes, it's the six-liter V-twelve, six hundred twenty-one horse-power," Charles replied casually. "She will get you there in style and, if need be, quickly."

David followed Kelly into the back seat. "My wife is something of a car buff. Especially the ones we can't afford." He fastened his seat belt. "Tell me, Charles: SEAL? Ranger? Marine?"

"Army Special Forces, Mr. Secretary, eight years."

"I sensed it was one of our more elite branches. So, Charles, what all are you cleared to tell me?"

Charles glanced over his shoulder and pulled onto the street. "I am cleared to respond to any question you ask that I have an answer to. I am not cleared to volunteer anything."

"I gotcha, Charles. I came from an Army Intel background myself. So does the Maybach belong to Envision-2100?"

"No, sir. They lease both it and me from Blackwater."

"Interesting, and I guess not surprising. I suspect that the group wants to keep their big-dollar asset inventory as skinny as possible. I assume you know how to get to the Comus Inn?"

"Yes, sir. Twenty-Three Nine Hundred Old Hundred Road. We should be there in about twenty minutes."

David and Kelly sank into the luxury of the Maybach's impossibly soft leather back seats. David leaned closer to Kelly and lowered his voice. "Can I be so bold as to assume you've been thinking about what I told you?"

"You can assume I haven't been thinking of anything else," Kelly whispered back. "On the one hand, I am, to put it ever so conservatively, surprised. You have never expressed any interest in running for anything. Or at least not to me. And I thought I was privy to just about everything that was going on up there." Kelly playfully poked the side of David's head. "And then you come flying into our back yard in a frigging helicopter and tell me a bunch of rich kids wants you to run for the most powerful office. In. The. World."

David gave her a guilty-as-charged smile.

"On the other hand," Kelly continued, "you are without a doubt the smartest, most politically adroit man I've ever known or read about. So, if I come at it from that angle, it makes me wonder why it took them so long to give you the nod. But what's with the raging sense of urgency? Matt Sheppard is one of the most popular presidents we've had in the last twenty years; he's doing an admirable job and can still run for another term. What am I missing?"

"Well, to the first question, thank you!" David leaned across the Maybach's enormous back seat and pecked Kelly on her cheek. She smiled sweetly and put her hand on David's knee.

"It's always nice to know that my wife thinks I've got at least a little bit of walking-around sense. And I guess some of the Bulldog's political skills rubbed off on me. At least I haven't been fired yet. Now back to your question about the urgency and why me and why now."

Despite his confidence in the privacy afforded by the Mercedes's back seat and Charles's discretion, David put his arm around Kelly's shoulder, drew her face closer to his, and began speaking in a conversational whisper. He told her about the president's recent cancer diagnosis and his expected imminent demise.

Kelly's eyes welled up as the news sank in. She had been a fierce supporter during President Sheppard's election and had grown to admire the man after he took office. Kelly wasn't a party loyalist and, like David, had zero use for Vice President Phillips, but she worshipped the president and what he had accomplished over the last few years.

David sat up straight and looked out the window. The countryside outside Germantown surrounding the meandering path of the Potomac River and up into Sugarloaf Mountain was a montage of hardwood forest and meticulously maintained farms and horse stables.

They drove past a monastery. The Aung Yadana Monastery, a Myanmar Buddhist temple, was hidden among the oaks and pines just north of Comus Road. Most of the real estate in the area had been snatched up years earlier by Senior Executive Service employees and the staff of government contractors and was now obscenely expensive.

The neatly laid-out pastures and tree-lined farms would typically have made the drive from Kelly and David's house a pleasant and relaxing break from their pressure-cooker jobs in DC However, tonight they paid scant attention to whatever lay outside the Mercedes's passenger windows. Kelly was still rebounding from the news David had shared.

"Kelly," David said softly, "I have a meeting with President Sheppard at ten o'clock tomorrow morning. He wants to discuss his condition and his decision to resign immediately with me face-to—"

"We're here, Mr. Secretary," Charles announced.

Charles maneuvered the car to the front of a long, wooden former farmhouse with a muted red metal roof. What was now the Comus Inn had originally been the Johnson-Wolfe Farm, whose construction dated back to 1862. In 2002 a group of local investors bought the building complex and restored it as a fine-dining restaurant.

As soon as the Mercedes stopped, a black male dressed exactly like Charles opened the door on David's side.

"Good evening, Mr. Secretary. Welcome to the Comus Inn. My name is Lawrence Smith. I'm Mr. Crum's associate and will be working alongside him as a part of your security team. The restaurant is expecting you, and your table is waiting."

Except for his skin color, Lawrence was a physically exact copy of Charles. Both were an inch or so over six feet, devoid of body fat, and immaculately dressed in perfectly tailored black wool suits.

Blackwater must get a volume discount on custom-made clothes, David thought as he helped Kelly out of the Maybach's back seat.

"Let me guess, Lawrence: Special Forces?" David asked.

"No, sir. Marine Recon."

David glanced at Kelly and grinned. "You know, I almost wish someone would try to mug us tonight."

Lawrence led David and Kelly up the porch steps and into the inn's reception area. A beaming, twentysomething hostess stepped out from behind the reservation podium. "Welcome, Mr. Secretary. It's good to see you again. We have a table already set up for you on the back corner of the veranda."

David and Kelly followed the bubbly hostess as she snaked through the main dining room to a long, somewhat narrow room at the back of the inn.

Six tables with place settings for four aligned the floor-to-ceiling windows of the room, with its unobstructed view of Sugarloaf Mountain. Three couples and two parties of four were already seated. The hostess ushered David and Kelly toward the last table, tucked away in the far corner.

As they made their way to their designated table, people from two of the other tables greeted David, who stopped and shook hands with them and their dinner companions. It was getting harder and harder for David and Kelly to share an intimate night on the town. Soon it would be impossible.

When they arrived at the table, a young male wearing a white shirt, black slacks, a black bow tie, and a burgundy vest, with a burgundy napkin draped across his left arm, glided up behind Kelly. As he seated Kelly, the hostess announced, "Mr. and Mrs. Stakley, this is Chris. He will be your attendant this evening. If there is anything you need or anything that any of us can do to make your experience here perfect, and we mean perfect, please let Chris know."

"Thank you, Madison," Chris said. "I'll take good care of them from here on."

As Madison left, Chris turned to David and Kelly. "Before we begin, I need to let you know that Mr. Elton Kirby and his associates are taking care of everything tonight. He has even suggested the menu, the wine, and dessert—if they meet with your approval. Of course, you are more than welcome to make your own choices, but his instructions are to make sure you are nothing short of impressed."

David looked at Kelly and then turned back to Chris. "Since there's nothing on the menu that we don't love, and since Elton and his posse never fail to amaze me, I think as long as it's agreeable with my wife, we'll follow his suggestions for dinner. Except for dessert. We have dessert waiting for us when we get home."

Kelly offered a nod of approval. "That sounds fantastic, Chris. At least that's one less decision we have to struggle with tonight."

"In that case, let me start you off with the wine that Mr. Kirby selected."

Chris nodded at another attendant standing near the veranda entrance, who picked up a tray with wine and glasses. Chris turned his attention back to David and Kelly. "The wine is a 2018 Bordeaux from Domaine de Chevalier, Grand Cru Pessac."

The assistant gently placed a long-stemmed crystal glass in front of Kelly, then David.

"We were able to get a single case of this a year ago." Chris opened the bottle. "We only offer it to special guests, and only then for special occasions. It's unbelievable, but don't fall in love with it. I'm afraid that after this bottle the 2018 batch is gone."

He poured a small amount of wine into David's glass and said simply, "Sir."

David swirled the pour and took a tiny sip. He let it roll across his tongue, then pursed his lips and breathed in slightly through his mouth. David was no sommelier but knew what he liked. This was smooth with just a hint of what he recognized as oak and cherry. "This is incredible."

"Perfect," Chris said as the assistant filled Kelly's glass. "I guarantee you will also be impressed with the dinner selection. Mr. Kirby has suggested the Chef's Tasting, a seven-course dinner featuring cuisine made to order by our executive chef. It's only available three nights a week, and each night, he prepares a different combination of dishes."

"Thank you, Chris," David replied. "It looks like we are in your hands for the next hour or so."

As Chris left to begin their dinner service, David shifted his chair closer to Kelly. "As I was saying before we had to get out of the car, I have a one-on-one meeting with the president in the morning. According to Judson, Matt wants to personally let me know about his condition and his plans to resign immediately. Judson said he also wants to ask me to run for POTUS and to pledge his support for my doing so, and on the Centrist Party ticket."

David moved his glass to the right, then reached out and lightly placed his hand over his wife's.

"Kelly, this whole thing is unprecedented on so many levels. But we have to decide tonight. I have to be ready to give the president a thumbs-up or -down when I meet with him in the morning. If I say no, the case is closed. We go about our lives and our careers as if nothing ever happened. We drive to the grocery store, buy clothes off the rack, and eat at Cheeburger Cheeburger, just like we've been doing for the last five years. However, if I say yes, our lives are turned upside down. Win or lose, things will never be the same.

"The campaign will be intense. Every word either of us says and every move we make will be splashed on CNN and FOX, taken out of context, analyzed by a dozen talking heads, and tucked away for future reference. Right now, I'm as happy as a monkey with a peanut machine. I love the life we're living, and I'm not the least bit sure that I want to change it. On the other hand . . ." David's voice trailed off, and he locked a conflicted gaze on Kelly's eyes.

Just then, Chris and his assistant appeared. Chris placed two small plates, each containing a sliver of farmer's bread, two oval slices of duck sausage, and a dollop of scrambled eggs and truffles in front of his guests. As he did so, his assistant poured a splash of wine into each glass.

"Your appetizers, like everything you will be served tonight, were made from scratch today. The eggs and the duck are free-range from right here on our farm. The only thing that isn't local is the wheat in the bread and the truffles, which we import from a small estate in France. Bon appétit."

Chris and his assistant made a hasty retreat.

Kelly leaned forward. "David, there are three hundred million people in this country, give or take a few hundred thousand illegals. I'm not going to sit here and let you talk yourself out of an opportunity that ninety percent of them have fantasized about. Not once have you shared any political aspirations with me, and now this drops in your lap. You've got to swing at this one, honey. And if you swing and miss, so what? How many times have I heard you quote Theodore Roosevelt? 'Who, at the worst, if he fails, at least he fails while daring greatly, so that his place shall never be with those cold and timid souls who neither knew victory nor defeat.'

"And don't worry your pretty little head about me or changing our lifestyle. We're in things together. Remember that 'for better or worse' thing? Besides, nothing would please me more than to see you slam-dunk Jim Phillips. This could well be our one and only chance to keep him and his posse of lunatics out of the White House.

"Now, eat your duck, drink some wine, and let's talk about how we're going to pay our mortgage while you're running for office."

David smiled and squeezed Kelly's hand. He was well attuned to that tone of voice. Argument or resistance was fruitless. Besides, he genuinely wanted his wife not just to support him but to be entirely on board with his unspoken decision to go for the gold. He had been vocalizing his own subconscious fears. She wasn't afraid of a damn thing.

"Thanks, sweetheart! You can't imagine how much what you just said means to me. Oh, by the way, I hadn't got around to telling you that Envision-2100 will pay both of us a generous stipend during the campaign and for quite some time afterward in the event I'm not elected."

"Well jeez, David, that puts this decision squarely into a no-brainer category. Now, Mr. President, let's enjoy this feast. This is the best wine I've ever had."

David relayed details of his meeting with Envision-2100, and for the rest of the meal, they discussed some of the countless tasks that lay before them. A tingle of anticipation and excitement prickled David's skin.

After they had finished the last course, Chris brought each of them a china mug, not the dainty little cups that David was expecting in a restaurant like the Comus. As he poured steaming hot coffee from a polished silver pot, David commented, "So, Chris, you aren't going to tell me that you guys grow your own coffee beans, are you?"

"No, sir. This is Community Club, from New Orleans, the same brand you can get at Safeway. The chef says he has tried them all, and you can spend a lot more for Starbucks, Seattle's Best, or some Whole Foods foo-foo variety, but you can't get anything any better. He pairs the blend to the meal, just like he does the wine."

David sipped his coffee. "The guy knows what he's doing. It's delicious. Not too strong and not the least bit bitter." He smiled at Chris. "Now, if you'll bring us our check, we will get out of your hair."

"Everything has been taken care of, Mr. Secretary, including the gratuity. It's been our pleasure to serve you and Mrs. Stakley. I hope we have exceeded your expectations."

"Indeed, you have, Chris," Kelly interjected. "Personally, this was the nicest dining experience I've ever had."

As they got up to leave, David noticed Lawrence sitting at a small table situated beside the veranda entrance. Lawrence stood up the instant that David got out of his chair. He scanned the other diners as the Stakleys made their way out of the room. When David and Kelly drew near his post, Lawrence joined them. He walked two steps in front and, as the hostess opened the restaurant entrance, led them outside, where Charles was waiting, holding the rear passenger door open.

Once David and Kelly were in the car, Charles slipped behind the wheel and Lawrence climbed into the front passenger seat.

"I take it you two have been working as a team all evening," David said.

"Yes, sir," Lawrence replied. "Charles dropped me off on his way to your house. Whenever possible, we follow that method: at least one advance scout and at least one escort. Unless you tell us otherwise, we'll be your 'in public' shadow for the foreseeable future. Except when we're driving you somewhere, you'll most likely never see us. But Charles and I, or one of our associates, will be close at hand anytime you are outside your home or office."

Fifteen minutes later, they arrived home. Charles stopped the Mercedes at the front entrance, and Lawrence escorted the couple to the door. He handed David two small cell phones. "We ask that you accept these communication and tracking devices. One for each of you. If you ever need Charles or me, or our backup team, just enter two one zero zero. It will automatically call the dispatcher at Blackwater HQ, indicate your location, and connect you to the appropriate SO—security operator. It's encrypted, so even if its signal is intercepted or monitored, your conversation and location can't be understood or tracked."

"Thank you, Lawrence." David took the phones and unlocked the front door of his home with an electronic cipher key. "I've got about a million questions, but they can wait. Right now, I've got to prepare for a meeting, and I have another call to make."

Lawrence nodded. "Good night, Mr. Secretary, Mrs. Stakley. I hope you enjoyed the evening. It has been a pleasure."

"The pleasure is ours, Lawrence. Enjoy the rest of your evening." Kelly stepped inside.

"Good night, Lawrence. We appreciate what you and Charles are doing for us." David shook Lawrence's hand and followed Kelly inside, locking the door.

David found Kelly in the kitchen. As he opened the box of coconut cake Mattie had made for him, Kelly popped a Starbucks pod into their Keurig.

"We've got to get some of that Community Club coffee. That stuff was delicious." Kelly's remarks sounded somewhat offhand, as if her mind was elsewhere. "What's this phone call you were telling Lawrence you have to make this evening?"

David sliced the cake and slid the slices onto dessert plates, which he laid on the kitchen's breakfast table. "I promised Judson I would call him with a decision, one way or the other, after you and I had a chance to talk." David pulled Kelly's chair back as she walked to the table with their coffee. After they were both seated, he got out his iPhone.

"Are we going to eat our cake first, David?" Kelly quizzed with just a tiny hint that they were breaching her rules of cellphone etiquette.

"No, we can eat while we are talking. This shouldn't take long, and I want to get it behind me before either of us changes our mind. Sort of like when Hernán Cortés and his fleet landed in Veracruz. He ordered his men to burn their boats so they could get about the task of conquering Mexico and wouldn't be trying to find an excuse to go back to Spain."

"You read too much, David," Kelly remarked with her dry humor. "Wow! This cake is scrumptious. Forget the presidency. Let's hire that lady and open a bakery."

David raised his phone. "Siri, call Judson Ballard, on speaker."

A pleasing, yet also somewhat creepy, voice responded: "Calling Judson Ballard, mobile, on speaker."

Taking advantage of a three-ring pause, David and Kelly munched bites of cake. As they were sipping their coffee, Judson's voice rang out.

"If my caller ID is accurate, this is the future president of the United States."

"And his wife," David instantly replied.

"An unexpected surprise, Kelly. I look forward to meeting you in the flesh, and hopefully in the very, very near future. I've heard a lot about you."

"All good, I hope," Kelly responded.

"Well, of course. In fact, I can't wait to see if you really do have wings and a halo. So, David, you haven't actually said you were in the game."

"First of all, Judson, thank you for everything you have done for me today, from the flying limousine to what turned out to be the most fantastic dinner we have ever had. You've made Kelly and me feel exceptional, so thank you from the very bottom of our hearts.

"Yes, we discussed my candidacy. Not so much the details but what it means and how it will impact our lives. To say that we are both apprehensive would be to state the glaringly obvious. But to answer your question: yes. You, Envision-2100, and the Centrist Party have got themselves a presidential candidate."

"That's without a doubt the best news I've had in a long time, David. You shouldn't worry about the details. Not tonight. We've already started pulling a team together to handle those, starting tomorrow. But it's getting late, you have a meeting in the Oval Office in the morning, and I have a long list of stuff to do running through my brain. Let's plan to talk tomorrow after your meeting with POTUS."

19

Grand Teton National Park
The evening of the day of

JEREMY PULLED THE TRUCK BACK onto the highway. Even with his fog lights, the visibility extended only thirty or forty feet beyond the hood. Both he and Judy stared straight ahead. Clutching the wheel in a sub-conscious death grip, he eased forward, driving barely ten miles an hour. He switched on the wipers, and ash smeared across the windshield.

"Oops, bad move," he said. "No wipers. The ash is bad enough, but if I leave them on, the pumice will scratch the glass, and visibility will go from bad to worse."

"Now I wish I'd sprung for the radar guidance option when I bought this thing," Judy added.

Right after they crossed the bridge over Pacific Creek, Jeremy spotted a massive lump in the middle of the left lane. It was the lifeless body of a buffalo. Another lump appeared next to the road a few yards in front of the truck, on their right.

The F-250's headlights revealed dark stains on the pavement coming from the animals' nostrils. Jeremy realized that, as Judy had warned earlier, the beasts had been running, blinded and terrified, as glass-like particles in the ash cloud shredded the inside of their lungs.

"Oh my God, Mom! Did you see that poor buffalo?" Ellis wailed.

Fiona chimed in: "He's dead in the ditch. And there's another one over here. Dad, are we going to die like that?"

Still maneuvering the truck through the ever-increasing rain of ash and pumice, Jeremy tried to restore some semblance of calm despite his own nauseating sense of dread. He glanced at Judy. "We're going to be OK, ladies. Help me keep an eye on what's going on in front of us. It's almost impossible to see where we're going. The road has practically disappeared. I'm trying to drive where I think it is. I need everyone to focus. If you see something, say something. Don't assume I see it. I'd rather have a scream in my ear than a bear on our hood."

"Or a Volvo," Judy added.

They crept along for another hour, barely moving the needle on the speedometer.

Off to the right, Jeremy made out the entrance to the Snake River Overlook. They had passed this heavily visited spot when they had first driven up US 191 in the opposite direction on their way to Colter Bay. The view of the Snake River and the valley it formed as it flowed south was unquestionably one of the most beautiful sights in the park. Normally. Tonight, it was invisible, marked only by the highway cutouts leading into a parking lot.

As they slowly drew closer to the entrance, Fiona announced, "I've gotta pee."

"For once, your timing is perfect," Judy replied. "Let's pull over, Jeremy. I could stand a comfort stop myself."

As Jeremy eased the truck and trailer off the road, Judy continued, "Girls, here's the deal. After we're stopped, I'll get out and open the door of the Airstream. Once I have it open, hold your breath, run after me, and get inside. We will each wet a towel and make a mask, like your dad did when he went down to the creek.

"Once everyone has their mask on, we'll all go outside together. I don't want to take a chance of any of us getting separated and losing our way in this mess. We'll squat and pee on our way back to the truck, so we don't need to worry about flushing the Airstream toilet. We have to conserve every drop of water possible. Any questions?"

The girls shook their heads.

Leaving the engine running, Jeremy grabbed his flashlight and pulled on his towel mask. "Wait up, Judy. I'll come around to your side of the truck and hold the light for you and the girls. Probably not necessary, but as you said, it's best to be on the safe side."

"We're gonna be on the wet side if you don't hurry," Fiona moaned.

Opening his door as little as possible, Jeremy slid out of the truck and dashed around the front end to Judy's door. He eased it open and shone the light back toward the entrance of the Airstream. Although it was only about twelve feet away, it was barely visible through the falling muck.

For the first time since they had bought the Airstream, Jeremy and Judy had failed to lock it when they were packing up. And for once, this turned out to be a blessing. Judy put on her towel mask and got out of the truck, forgetting to grab the keys. She ran to the front of the trailer, jerked the door handle, and scrambled inside.

Jeremy turned to the girls. "Ellis, you go first, and as soon as you're inside, I'll send your sister." Ellis took a deep breath, and when her dad gave her a nod, she took off. Three seconds later, he gave the order to Fiona: "OK, go!" With all three women safely inside the RV, Jeremy closed the truck door, tightened his own towel mask, turned to face the left rear wheel, and urinated.

After relieving himself and making sure the truck was OK and still running, Jeremy walked back to the Airstream and joined Judy and the twins inside.

As the women soaked hand towels and fitted them around their necks, Jeremy pulled a plastic Walmart bag from the counter underneath the sink. He pulled out four apples from a mesh bag hanging on a wall hook and snatched his family's hiking canteens. Then he went to the rear bedroom and pulled a case off one of the pillows.

When he returned, Judy and the twins had finished donning their towel masks and were making their way outside to pee. Once they'd finished and everyone was back in the truck, Jeremy opened the driver's door and tossed the food and canteens onto the storage console. He then reached down to the lower left side of the dash and tugged back on the hood latch.

From her position in the passenger seat, Judy gave Jeremy a puzzled look. "Is something wrong with the truck?"

"Well, let's see. The sky seems to be falling, the ground takes a leap every five minutes, and we can't see more than twenty feet in front of us," Jeremy replied. "Other than that, things are peachy. But it dawned on me that if this stuff makes it hard for us to breathe, it's doing the same thing to the truck"—he held up the pillowcase—"so I'm making it a mask."

Taking the pillowcase by its open end, Jeremy stretched it over the F-250's air filter, then knotted the bottom to keep it tight and away from the engine block. He then closed the hood and got back into the truck.

"So, for the benefit of those of us who aren't mechanics, elaborate . . . smartass," Judy said.

"I more or less added another external filter to keep the ash from clogging up the air intake, or at least keep it from getting any worse than it already is. If air can't get into the intake manifold, the engine chokes and dies. If the engine chokes and dies, well, you get the picture. Anyway, the pillowcase will keep the ash out for a little longer. At least until the stuff sticks to it as well. Then we replace the dirty one with the one from your side of the bed."

"I'm impressed that you still have your sense of humor, but I'm glad you do. It will help keep our minds off the shitstorm we're in." Judy glanced into the back seat. "Oops, pardon my French, girls. I guess I owe you one, but wait until you turn eighteen to collect."

Everyone chuckled.

Jeremy put the truck in gear and slowly, carefully pulled back onto US 191. They continued south at a rate that barely registered on the speedometer. At least they were moving away from the volcano. Surely either they would get out from under the ash cloud soon or seasonal winds would blow it off them, toward the mountains to their east.

Jeremy simply couldn't comprehend the size and scope of the disaster that loomed over him and his family. Sometimes ignorance was bliss.

With the day's excitement, Jeremy's body had dumped a load of adrenaline, and he knew he was starting to physically crash and burn. He glanced in the rearview mirror. The twins were sitting up but slumped together, fast asleep. He glanced at his wife. Judy's eyes fell closed, her head bobbed, and her eyes popped open again. Not alert, but awake and doing her best to help watch the road.

They would have to stop soon and get a couple of hours of sleep. But visions of a rooftop in Pompeii collapsing from the weight of five feet of pumice kept him going. At least for a little longer. They crept through the Moran Entrance on the southern border of the park. Jeremy knew there was a ranger station somewhere off to his left, but he couldn't see the building, and there were no lights or activity. Of course there wouldn't be: the rangers were long gone, or so he hoped for their sake.

After inching along for another hour, they came to an intersection. Jeremy had memorized the map, which wasn't all that difficult given the absence of towns and roads in this area. US Route 287/26 to his left would take them over the mountains and almost due east. Continuing on US 191, to his right, would take them southwest toward Jackson Hole, forty miles away. Going through Jackson Hole would be the safest choice.

Jeremy turned right.

The ash kept falling, but Judy was the first to notice that there seemed to be less of the course-grained pumice peppering the truck. "It looks like either the deep-earth ejecta is tapering off or we are finally moving out of the heavy stuff. This is almost all ash. Just an observation; I don't know if that's good or bad."

"Yeah, me neither, but it's reassuring to know that you're awake enough to notice. I'm telling you, babe, we've been up and going for a long time. That plus the shear stress is starting to kick my ass. I can barely keep my eyes open. The Elk Ranch Flats Turnout shouldn't be too much farther down the road." Jeremy yawned, then shook his head. "When we get there, I'm going to pull in the parking lot and get some sleep."

"Totally agree. I'd offer to drive, but I can barely make vowel sounds. It will be daylight in a couple of hours. It won't make much difference, visibility-wise, but a couple of hours of sleep will help keep us between the ditches."

The falling ash seemed to grow thicker as they continued. Jeremy recalled that this section of 191 was reasonably straight. This was a blessing since, in his current state of exhaustion, he was nowhere near vigilant enough to negotiate the hairpin turns and switchbacks he would have encountered on the eastern route had they turned left at the Moran Entrance.

Despite the relative safety of this section of the highway, they passed several wrecked and abandoned vehicles. Jeremy stayed in what he thought was the middle of the road. The lines had long since disappeared, buried under what he estimated to be ten inches of ash—and growing deeper every second.

He had lost his sense of time, but finally, after what seemed like hours, Judy pointed out a sign: Elk Ranch Flats Turnout, 500 feet. It was barely visible even though it was mounted less than twenty feet from the side of the highway. Regardless, it lifted their spirits, even if only a little bit. At least they could get some sleep, and once the sun came up, see what daylight would bring. Jeremy subconsciously increased the speed of the truck.

Ten minutes later, the turnout entrance appeared on the right. Jeremy eased the F-250 into the turnout's abandoned parking lot. He really couldn't tell if anyone else was parked there or not. He couldn't see another vehicle, but he didn't hit anything, so as far as he was concerned, they were home free.

After pulling forward a short distance, Jeremy stopped, put the transmission in park, and killed the engine.

"Well, it's not near as nice as Motel 6," he said to Judy, "but it will do for now." She was already sound asleep.

Reaching to the left side of his seat, Jeremy pulled up on a lever and angled the seat back to an almost prone position. He couldn't go all the way back without bumping Fiona's knees, which he feared would wake her up.

As Jeremy manipulated the seat, his right hand brushed against the butt of the .357 Magnum revolver that he kept tucked in a holster wedged next to the front console. Although neither he nor Judy was a gun enthusiast, by any stretch of the imagination, they both felt safer keeping one in each of their vehicles and at home. This decision came after burglars had murdered a young father in their neighborhood, then proceeded to brutally rape and repeatedly stab his wife and daughter. Despite their mutual misgivings, they bought three pistols and enrolled the twins in a firearms safety and training course.

This morning Jeremy wasn't worried about criminals or raging grizzlies, but for some reason, he did feel reassured. As it would turn out, his instincts were amazingly accurate.

20

Germantown, Maryland
Two years before the day of

DAVID OPENED HIS EYES and looked at the clock next to his bed. It was five thirty. He never needed an alarm clock. Apparently, he was genetically wired to wake up within minutes of the time he set in his consciousness before he went to sleep. Something about his circadian rhythm. Kelly did not suffer from this affliction. Each night she would set the alarm to go off after he planned to get up. She was like that: always thoughtful and always thinking of him first.

As he put on the robe he kept draped over a bedpost, and slipped on the houseshoes sitting next to his side of their California king, David mentally mapped out his plans for the day.

The first order of business was his meeting with the POTUS. He wasn't really sure what to expect, despite Judson's assurances. He had grown about as close to the president as you could get to someone in that position. Yet the man was sick, most likely in a lot of pain, and very possibly on the fringes of medication-induced confusion and an altered mental state.

Then again, he could be perfectly normal, from a psychological perspective. Or as normal as you could be when you were standing toe-to-toe with the Grim Reaper. David had to prepare himself for either eventuality.

As he started down the stairs to the kitchen for his first cup of coffee, the alarm clock started its opening notes, softly at first, then increasing in tone and tempo. That would be enough to rouse Kelly out of what was almost a coma. She loved to sleep. Years earlier, David had learned that life was a whole lot better if you weren't anywhere in her vicinity for the first thirty minutes or so after she woke up.

David made his way to the kitchen and hit the brew button on their Keurig. As was his practice, he had placed the Columbian Blend pod and his favorite cup in the machine the night before. He then walked to the front door and went outside to try to retrieve the day's copy of the *Post* from wherever the delivery girl had thrown it as she whizzed past their house. He went back inside and laid the paper on the kitchen table. Typically he would have read most of it while he sipped his first cup of coffee. But not today. He would leave it there for Kelly while he got dressed and cleared his mind for his meeting with the POTUS.

David took his cup from its place on the Keurig, put in a fresh pod for Kelly, and started back toward the bedroom. Kelly was stumbling down the stairs as he headed up. She groggily mumbled, "Good morning, dear," as he moved aside to let her pass.

It would be another fifteen minutes before she was ready to have a decent conversation. This was one of those mutual idiosyncrasies they had learned about each other early in their marriage.

David put on a white Brooks Brothers shirt, a navy-blue Hart Schaffner Marx suit, and a red tie with old-style blue and gray stripes. He then slipped on his black Allen Edmonds oxfords, completing what was pretty much his Washington, DC, uniform. He didn't vary his standard office dress very much except for a different color or pattern of his always bright but conservative tie. He went downstairs intending to retrieve his briefcase off the desk in his home office but then remembered he had left it in his real office in the Truman Building.

He returned to the kitchen and walked up behind Kelly's chair, put his hands on her shoulders, bent down, and kissed her cheek. "Good morning, gorgeous. Any earth-shattering headlines in the news this morning?"

Kelly looked up from her newspaper and mustered an early-morning smile as David slipped another pod in the coffee maker. "Just the usual rhetoric from the ayatollah du jour, another singer that's fucking everyone in LA, and a suspicious plane crash in Venezuela," Kelly replied. "Business as usual. Things sure have calmed down since your old boss scrapped North Korea off the map and we got in bed with Russia and China. Oh, there was an article about Mark Littleton and the situation in the Mexican Yucatán Peninsula."

"Don't tell me there's been another kidnapping."

"Yep, some advertising exec's wife. And things didn't go so well. The Policia Federal Ministerial is reaching out to Mark to have the FBI assist with their investigation."

"Well, despite my confidence in Mark, I'm going to have to get involved in that mess ASAP. On the bright side, the Asian Independent Free Trade Union has turned out to be a real plum," David said. "It's starting to turn a profit, which means the United States, Korea, Russia, China, and our other shareholders are making money. The remaining North Koreans are happier than they have been in decades, and the three-nation arms race has tapered off to a walk. Now we can focus on feeding the planet's eight billion bellies. And a couple million other global issues."

Kelly folded the paper, stood up, and gave David an I'm-awake-now-and-you're-looking-damn-good kiss. "Well, honey, you can take credit for a good ninety percent of the AIFTU's success since it was your brainchild. That's evidenced by the fact that you've got a pack of heavy hitters begging you to run for president, not the other way around."

"You sweet talker, you!" David grinned. "I may have to tell the pilot not to get over ten thousand feet, or my head will explode. Of course, we will barely top two thousand between here and DC, so I guess I'm safe."

Just a few minutes later, as they were finishing their coffee and after David had wolfed down two bananas and a toasted bagel with cream cheese, the windows and kitchen dishes started to rattle.

David glanced at his Apple Watch. It was 6:55. Through the kitchen window, he saw the AW160 glide in from the east, pivot, and drift down, tail wheel first, in his back yard. "It looks like my taxi is here. I hope the neighbors aren't trying to sleep in. I'll call you later today and let you know how things went with President Sheppard. Despite what Judson has told me, I am a little apprehensive. He could always change his mind about supporting me. Hell, he could be out of his mind by now, even though, according to Judson, he's not going to do chemo. I guess I'll have to wait and—"

"Hush, David. Get your tight ass out the door, meet with the POTUS, and start thinking about who we'll invite to the inauguration."

David started for the door, then turned around, kissed Kelly, and headed outside. She laughed and smacked him on his butt.

It was only a twenty-six-mile flight from David's house in Germantown to the State Department headquarters in the Harry S. Truman Federal Building in the Foggy Bottom section of Washington, DC. The offices wouldn't officially open and support staff wouldn't arrive until nine, but a maintenance and security skeleton crew worked twenty-four seven. As soon as they were airborne, David called the security office to let them know he was inbound and to have someone open the helipad access door on the roof. He was only mildly surprised to learn that the AW160 copilot had already made the call and had provided precise approach directions and landing times.

It was almost eight o'clock by the time David made it through the labyrinth of the Truman Building's hallways and to his office on the seventh floor. A small trash can was turned upside down on the center of his spotless desk. He and all senior State Department officers used this simple approach to ensure there were no loose or unaccounted-for documents available to prying eyes.

As he removed the trash can and unlocked his desk, Trish, his administrative assistant, tapped on the frame of his open door. She entered the office carrying a cup of steaming coffee in one hand and a folder in the other. "Good morning, Mr. Secretary. I trust you had a nice visit with Mr. Ballard and the Envision-2100 folks. You've upped your game when it comes to rubbing shoulders."

Trish set the coffee on David's desk, then handed him a green manila folder and a sealed white envelope with TOP SECRET stamped across its front and back. "Here is yesterday's PDB and a couple of documents that need your review and signature." Trish placed both items in the center of David's desk.

The PDB, or the *President's Daily Brief,* was a top-secret document prepared by the director of National Intelligence and provided to the POTUS, select senior officials, and Secretary-level cabinet posts. It summarized ultraclassified intelligence and information about covert operations directed by the CIA and other US and foreign agencies.

The PDB was first produced at the direction of President John F. Kennedy in 1961 and made available to every subsequent president. The previous POTUS had the reading comprehension and attention span of a fifth-grader. Much to the chagrin of the administrative staff, he found the PDB boring and a waste of time.

Immediately upon his election, President Sheppard began receiving the PDB electronically every day, and following his inauguration, via a face-to-face meeting six days a week.

David scooted his chair a little closer to his desk and broke the seal of the white envelope containing the PDB. "Thank you, Trish, I should have just enough time to scan the PDB and sign whatever you've got stashed in the Green Folder before I have to leave to meet with the POTUS. If I didn't know you were as efficient as you are, I might be tempted to ask if you have my transportation arranged. But I know better, right?"

"What? You have a meeting with the president this morning?" Trish asked, feigning surprise. She smiled. "Yes, sir, the driver will be here to escort you to the car at nine o'clock. That should get you to the House in time to hang around outside the Oval Office before your ten o'clock meeting with President Sheppard. Oh, I've already told the driver, but the chief of staff asked that you come in through the bathroom window." Trish sounded puzzled.

"Ah, of course," David said. To "come in through the bathroom window" was code among insiders to use the lesser-known H Street entrance to the White House. The phrase was from an old Beatles song written by Paul McCartney. That entrance had been used for years by the Secret Service to steer clandestine visitors, or those the POTUS wished to shield from public exposure, to what was known as the "back door" of the White House. An inconspicuous but discreetly guarded alley off H Street wound between other federal buildings until it ended at the East Wing of the chief executive's headquarters. President Sheppard would want to keep his meeting with David on the down-low, at least for now.

"Sir?" Trish questioned.

"Never mind, Trish. Thanks for the coffee. Let me know when the driver gets here. It's easy to lose track of time when I'm reading the PDB."

"Yes, Mr. Secretary." Trish left the office, softly closing the door behind her. Thirty minutes later, she buzzed David on his intercom. "Sir, the driver is here and ready whenever you are."

21

Station KIFI, Idaho Falls, Idaho
22:48 the day of

THE KIFI NEWS TEAM SIX DRIVER paused the game of solitaire on his office computer and answered his phone on the second ring. "KIFI Dispatch, Kevin speaking."

"Kevin, this is Martin. Throw the camera and all your shit in the satellite van. There's a story breaking in Yellowstone, and it could be huge. We need to go to the West Yellowstone entrance. If we hurry, we might just beat the crew from Bozeman. Pick me up in front of the station. I have to grab a mic. Oh, and don't forget your badge."

"I've got it around my neck, Scoop. I'll be out front in thirty seconds."

Martin hit the "end call" icon on his phone, snatched his mic from its place on the wall, and stuffed them both into a canvas KIFI travel bag he kept under his desk. Moving as if his feet were on fire, he headed for the door leading to the station's parking lot. He smiled at Kevin's use of his nickname, "Scoop." If this thing was anywhere near as big as he thought it was going to be based on what he'd heard on the scanner, it could get his foot in the door with some of the West Coast stations.

Martin knew that he should call Micca Corbin, the station manager, and update her on what was without a doubt the biggest breaking news story since ever. But she'd be sound asleep at this time of night;

otherwise, she would have already called him for a sitrep. Knowing her overachieving, type A personality, he suspected her alarm clock would go off between five and five thirty. That meant she would be blissfully unaware that nature had decided to wake up one of the only two super-volcanoes on the planet from its 650 million year nap. And she would be pissed!

On the other hand, if he had called her when he got his first sniff of the story, she would most likely have brought in KIFI's reporting A team and he would have been relegated to watching the story break from his apartment. No, he would wait until he and Kevin were past the point of no return, when they were far enough up the road that the bitch would have to let them run with the ball.

It was a gamble he was willing to take. The worst case: Corbin would fire him from his dead-end cub-reporter job at a pissant television station, in a one-horse town, in fucking Idaho. But if he pulled this thing off, like he knew he was going to, he could leapfrog straight from being a nobody to the twenty-first century Walter Cronkite.

Martin got to the parking lot just as Kevin pulled in. He jumped in the van, put his bag between his feet, and fastened his seat belt. "Drive it like you stole it, Kevin," he growled. "For once, we're gonna be the first on the scene."

"You got it, Scoop," Kevin shot back. "Just hang on and don't scream."

Kevin screeched out of the lot toward US 20 North. As he slowed without stopping at the first stop sign, Martin switched on the van's scanner. There was hardly a break in the radio traffic. Having been monitoring KIFI's scanner for over a year, Martin had learned to identify not only sources of communication, such as the Idaho Falls Police Department, but also many individual dispatchers, at least those on his shift.

At this time of night, there was usually very little chatter. Just the occasional 10-66, suspicious person, or 10-70, prowler, coming from the old female sherrif's department dispatcher. Martin had never seen her but had formed his own mental image of a chunky, bleached-blonde Marlboro smoker sitting behind a battered old radio with a tall aluminum microphone on a vinyl-covered ledge in front of her.

Probably nothing like that at all. Over time Martin had formed a different mental picture for each of the regulars, and since they never used their own, he had given them names. The third shift operator at the sherrif's department was Shirley. And she was busy tonight.

There was almost no traffic on US 20 at this time of night, and with every on-duty law enforcement officer glued to their radios, Kevin was able to drive like the NASCAR racer he fantasized of being.

"OK, Kevin, I'm trying not to scream, but damn! You do realize we're not wearing helmets, and this thing doesn't have roll bars."

Not taking his eye off the road, Kevin replied jokingly, "You said we wanted to be first on the scene, we're gonna be first on the scene. Now quit nagging. If I'd wanted a wife, I would've ordered one from Amazon."

One hour and twenty minutes later, after passing through the Caribou-Targhee National Forest, the pair started seeing grains of ash and pumice falling through the beams of the van's headlights. Just a smattering at first but getting noticeably thicker the farther north they drove. As they neared the intersection of US Route 20 and Idaho 87, the ashfall grew thick enough to seriously interfere with their visibility, and Kevin had to slow down well below the speed limit.

It was here that they also started seeing the first of what would turn out to be a long string of vehicles heading in the opposite direction, each covered with a thick layer of glittery ash—and each with a shell-shocked look on the driver's face when it was illuminated by the van's headlights. Martin assumed they were fleeing the eruption.

By the time they crossed into Montana from Idaho, the visibility was so poor that, despite the road being straight and flat, the van barely managed twenty miles an hour. By now, there was virtually no westbound traffic. Apparently, everyone who could have had evacuated the town of West Yellowstone. A sign just past the state line marker proclaimed, "Yellowstone National Park, 10 miles."

As they crept east toward the park entrance, Martin saw a red-or-ange glow on the horizon, even though it was hours before sunrise. Still-smoking boulders appeared every few hundred feet, as well as wrecked and abandoned cars and trucks. One late-model, jacked-up Jeep had managed to run off the road and hit dead center on a sign that read, "Entering Motor Vehicle Restricted Area." Ironic. If he and Kevin hadn't been in such a rush to get closer to the volcano, they would have stopped and filmed the wreckage. It would have made a catchy side note on the early-morning news.

Martin looked at his watch. It was 2:48 a.m. He figured they couldn't be over a couple of miles from the edge of West Yellowstone. Time to call the station manager, wake her ass up, and let her know that her newest star reporter was two miles west of a story that would have KIFI on national—no, international—headline news.

Martin dug his company cell phone out of the travel bag sitting between his feet. "Siri, call Micca Corbin, mobile." A second later, a familiar robotic voice responded: "Calling Micca Corbin, mobile."

Four rings later, a surprisingly alert-sounding voice blared, "This is Micca. Go!"

Martin had never had an opportunity to call his boss's boss before, and for just a second, he was taken aback by the sharp manner in which she answered the phone. But he wasn't surprised. He got cold chills every time he encountered the woman. He had always thought she was a bitter, calculating shrew with a pot full of dead-daddy money. Oh well, maybe she'd warm up to him now. "Ms. Corbin, this is Martin Driggs, from the station."

"That's great, Driggs. Did you butt-dial me, or is the station on fire?"

"No, ma'am, neither of those. I called to tell you that, apparently, the Yellowstone supervolcano blew its top."

"Well, hang up the phone and get our news team up there immediately. And tell the lead reporter to call me as soon as they're on the road."

"Yeah, well, that's the thing, Ms. Corbin. We is the news team, and we is on the road, and from the looks of things, we is going to be the first and onliest television crew on the scene, at least for a while."

There was an uncomfortable pause. Martin pictured Micca Corbin scowling as she collected her thoughts.

"OK, smart-ass, but don't you fuck this up," she snapped. "Start the satellite uplink as soon as you find something worth looking at. And round up a couple of Skoal-spitting locals to interview. A little hometown color is always fun to watch."

"Will do, boss lady, but that might be tough. From where we are right now, it looks like the town is deserted. We'll drive as far as we can toward the volcano and see what we can find on our way."

"OK, Driggs, and call me every half hour until I can—"

The cellphone connection died. Martin looked at his phone. There were no green signal bars, which meant that the cell towers in this area weren't working. He made a mental note to dig the satellite phone out of the back of the van as soon as they stopped and raised the communication dish.

Nothing moved as Kevin eased the van into the outskirts of town, crossing Iris Street and rolling past the Rustic RV Campground entrance. Rocks the size of trash cans had peppered the street, creating a driving obstacle course. "They don't pay me enough to do this shit!" he muttered as he swerved left, then right, trying to miss one bolder after another. "The first couple were kind of fun, but this is fucked up big time!"

Martin paid scarce attention to what was now an endless string of obscenities spewing from his driver.

Even in the almost nonexistent visibility provided by the van's headlights through the ashfall blizzard, gaping holes appeared in the buildings on the left and right sides of the street. Every window in all the shops and houses had been blown out. Not a single pane of glass remained.

It was 3:27 when they finally reached the corner of Town Park. There, US Route 20 intersected Route 191, which ran north toward Bozeman, Montana. The ashfall was impossibly heavy now. Straining headlights revealed enormous smoking boulders and other forms of debris sprinkled all over the ground. The dash-mounted GPS indicated that they were only three miles from the official park entrance.

Kevin stopped the van. "Looks like we are at the end of the road, Scoop."

"You're right, Kev. I'm surprised we made it this far. Since we've got what's left of the road to ourselves, let's set up here. If you'll raise the dish pole and make a satellite link, I'll set up the lights and fire up the generator."

"Will do." Kevin unsnapped his seat belt. "But first I'm going to break open the hazmat kit we keep in the back of the van. I know there are some surgical masks in there as well as a few plastic decon suits. We'll need all the protection we can wrap around us once we go outside."

Ten minutes later, wearing full-body white plastic coveralls and blue surgical masks, the two men opened the side door of the KIFI News Team van and went outside.

22

Washington, DC
Two years before the day of

David climbed into the back seat of the imposing black Chevy Suburban that served as the secretary of state's official vehicle.

After the driver took his seat, David watched him go through a "preflight" routine. He radioed the Secret Service control center and let them know the SecState was on board and that they were en route to the "House." He gave them the code for the predetermined course they would follow from the Truman Building to the nondescript alley entrance between Fifteenth Street NW and Vermont.

When they stopped at the first of three security checkpoints on White House grounds, a guard checked the driver's and David's identification cards and compared their names to a visitor manifest. While she was doing this, another guard used a long pole with mirrors attached to one end to look underneath the Suburban. Once the security team was satisfied that the SUV contained who it was supposed to be transporting and that it wasn't concealing any explosives, they waved the driver through the checkpoint gate. The vehicle maneuvered around to the West Wing entrance, next to the vice president's office.

David got out of the Suburban and walked to the small, "authorized staff only" entrance, where he was required to pass through a metal detector and issued a personalized Secretary of State White House visitor pass. A White House intern then escorted him down the hall, past the Roosevelt Room, to the outer office of the president's secretary.

"Good morning, Mr. Secretary. It's good to see you again," cooed the most powerful administrative assistant on the planet, without getting out of her chair.

"And you as well, Lizbeth," David replied. "I trust my timing is good."

"Just about perfect, Mr. Secretary. The president is on the phone but should be with you in just a few minutes. Please have a seat, and I'll let him know you're here."

David sat down on one of the straight-backed chairs on either side of the main entrance. Lizbeth sat in front of the two computer monitors on her desk and clicked her mouse. He knew that would turn on one of the lamps that were mounted above a bookcase recessed into the wall in the Oval Office, to the left of a portrait of Abraham Lincoln. This discreetly let the POTUS know a scheduled visitor had arrived.

Four minutes later, the small door leading into the secretary's office opened and President Sheppard, ignoring long-established introduction protocol, came out and greeted his friend. "Mr. Secretary—David— thank you for coming on such short notice. Please come in. We have a lot to discuss. Lizbeth, would you order us a pot of coffee and a tray of whatever breakfast pastries Antoine has to offer. Then, after they are delivered, no interruptions until I say so. No intercom, no taps on the door, nothing. And kill the video-voice recorder."

"Yes, Mr. President," Lizbeth replied, already calling the kitchen.

The president ushered David into the Oval Office and motioned for him to sit on one of the two couches that faced each other across a small coffee table. The couches flanked the presidential seal embedded in the floor in the center of the room, and in front of the president's massive wooden desk.

The POTUS sat down on one end of the couch, directly in front of David. "Well, if my sources are correct, and I know they are, you spent most of the day yesterday with my oldest friend and confidant, Judson Ballard, and the other members of the Envision-2100 board."

"Yes, sir. It was, without a doubt, the most intense day of my life. And, Mr. President, if you don't mind me crawling right on top of the elephant in the room, I can't express in words the grief I felt when I learned of your situation."

"My situation? No use spouting those diplomatic euphemisms with me, David. I remember the Bulldog telling the story of a construction foreman who was doing some work at a Catholic hospital. The Mother Superior was rapping his knuckles about the language his men were using on the job. After she dressed him up one side and down the other, he sheepishly says, 'Come on, Sister, the boys just call a spade a spade.' But the nun replies, 'Yes, but most of the time, they call a spade a fucking shovel.' No use tiptoeing around it, David. I'm dying. There. We've got that nasty pachyderm behind us. Now we can get on with the business I called you here to discuss."

There was a serene look on the president's face.

"Judson and I have been planning for this day for a long time. Well, not me and not my cancer. I'm speaking figuratively now. Despite being the poster child for my political party for the past forty years, I've come to realize just how flawed our two-party system is. This country was founded on the concept of democratically elected representation. But we don't represent the people. A two-party system, our system, shoehorns them into diametrically opposed political extremes. In reality, our process boils the field of pampered, wealthy candidates down to a single pair who represent not the voters but the financial interests of the power brokers who put them in office. Our system forces ninety percent of the voters to cast ballots not for their candidate of choice but against the other one. I know because I'm a product of that machine.

"You don't have to search far and wide to find the perfect example of what I'm talking about. I guess you can call it a good bad-example. Just look at the election that put the previous administration into power. You had a card-carrying moron eke out an Electoral College victory over a generally despised opponent who rode a political-correctness horse to the party finish line. Most people didn't vote for the winner, they voted against the loser. Inadvertently, I guess, we forced the American voter to choose what they thought was the lesser of two evils.

"Man, that turned out to be a joke. As just one result of that fiasco, I've had to spend the last three years trying to clean up the economic damage caused by the wake of an ignorant, out-of-control narcissist running roughshod over the constitution and the rights of the people who put his ass in office. And just to remind you and everyone else, it was less than a majority of the people. Plus being forced to suture the wounds the arrogant clown inflicted on literally all of our allies while kissing some twenty-first century tsar's ass. Hell, it's a wonder I was able to accomplish anything other than fix what that sociopath broke."

The president gazed wistfully at the massive wooden desk at the far end of the Oval Office, the symbol of his position. David sensed a feeling of relief and melancholy.

"I'm sorry, David. I haven't been able to vent like that in years. It's a relief to finally be able to get things off my chest and not worry about having my comments splashed across the front page of the *Post*. More importantly, I treasure having you as a friend. Someone I can open up to besides my wife, especially as I head into the home stretch of this life. You can't imagine the comfort I get from knowing I can always be brutally honest with you and Judson."

With a tap on the door, Lizbeth entered the office, escorting a white-jacketed steward pushing a small serving cart.

The steward nodded. "Good morning, Mr. President, Mr. Secretary. I have your coffee and a selection of breakfast pastries right out of the oven."

"Thank you very much, Jacob," President Sheppard said sincerely. "Just put the cart here to Secretary Stakley's right, and we'll take it from there."

"Yes, sir." Jacob positioned the cart as the president had requested; then he and Lizbeth hurriedly exited the Oval Office.

President Sheppard picked up one of the coffee mugs, dropped in two cubes of sugar using a small pair of tongs lying next to a sterling-silver bowl, filled the cup with steaming coffee, then handed it to David. "Here you go, my friend. Help yourself to the goodies." The president poured his own coffee and loaded a small plate with two cheese Danish. "You may have to watch your schoolboy figure, but I don't."

Placing his plate on the coffee table and sipping his coffee, the POTUS eased back onto the couch. "Judson may not have told you that our succession discussions started several years ago. Many Americans in what President Richard Nixon called the 'silent majority' have grown increasingly disillusioned with partisan politics in this country.

"Envision-2100 didn't formally exist when I ran for office, but I did get a healthy dose of financial and moral support from Judson and some of the others. In fact, if it hadn't been for him and his social network, I would never have been elected. I owe them a debt I will never be able to repay.

"It wasn't long after I was elected that Judson and I started laying out a strategy to make some changes that we both knew were long overdue but that we knew would never be taken up by either Republican or Democrat party hardliners. However, our political instincts, along with a couple dozen statistically significant surveys, told us that a good seventy to eighty percent of mainstream Americans were chomping at the bit to change directions. Or it might be more accurate to say alter the country's course. So we set out to do just that.

"Judson established Envision-2100 and started actively recruiting the A-team players you met yesterday, as well as other socially enlightened political moderates who had the means to bankroll a nationwide movement. He didn't set out to exclude anyone based on personal wealth, just the opposite. However, we both knew that realistically it would require people of power and substance, like our Founding Fathers—Jefferson, Madison, Hamilton, and Washinton—to finance a party that could take on the Republicans and Democrats. After all, efforts like this had failed in the past.

"H. Ross Perot and his Reform Party only managed to garner eight percent of the popular vote when he tried in 1996. But Perot wasn't aiming at America's center of mass. Truth be known, he was to the political right of Richard Nixon. Although I did incorporate some of his philosophies into my modus operandi. Perot once said, 'The activist is not the man who says the river is dirty. The activist is the man who cleans up the river.' And everyday operations in the White House are based on his observation 'If you see a snake, just kill it—don't appoint a committee on snakes.'"

A smile split David's face as he visualized a wizened Perot spouting one of his famous Texas aphorisms.

The president, now on a roll, paused just long enough to splash a bit more coffee into his and David's cups. "But I digress, David. My point is our river has gotten filthy, and we have to clean it up. But it will take people with more than just thoughts and prayers to get it done. It's going to take a lot of that green stuff to get us over the hump. Then we—well, you and yours—can sit around the campfire and sing 'Kumbaya' for another hundred years.

"The instant that Judson chartered Envision-2100 and formed its core members, he initiated two critical projects. The first was to establish a viable political party for the candidates that Envision-2100 would offer up for sacrifice. I bought into the plan from day one. But I had to do so under the radar. I had my own newly elected administration to lead. And as I'm sure Judson shared with you, I was confident we had eight years to get the country back on track, or in today's vernacular, to position it to become America two point oh. Regardless, setting the stage for a new party and subliminally softening up its perceived near-left and near-right opposition would prove to make the Labours of Hercules look like a day at the beach, at least from my somewhat paranoid perspective. And, David, always remember: just because you're paranoid doesn't mean they aren't out to get you."

David nodded and laughed at the president's attempt to lighten the mood even in one of the worst personal situations imaginable. *And that, boys and girls, is why he's the POTUS*, David thought, smiling.

"Establishing a political party at the national level can be an arduous, time-consuming effort. It's fraught with opportunities for endless delays, starting with the requirement to register with the Federal Election Commission," the president continued. "That's why the Envision-2100 Political Coalition task force elected to hitch on to the already-established Centrist Party. No one was infatuated with the name, and it did wear a faint stain of failure, but it was in place with some degree of name recognition. And it did represent, in the minds of those knowledgable in such things, the eighty-percenters—the voters we wanted to win over.

"So Envision-2100 adopted the Centrist moniker, the color purple, and the owl as its mascot. The consultants convinced the board that you've got to have a mascot. I'm sure they spent a not-so-small fortune coming up with that caricature. But hey, that kind of money is just a rounding error for those folks. And now we have a symbol that will hopefully be around at least as long as that elephant and donkey. Settling on a name and cartoon icon was the simple part of this project. They also had to hammer out a party platform to lay out its fundamental principles, beliefs, and sociopolitical values.

"I'm greatly oversimplifying the work that went into this component and its significance. Both are just too complicated to do justice to in the time we have to discuss. Suffice it to say, no single task or set of activities was more important than developing the Centrist foundation. This would become what our constituents rallied around. Their battle cry. Fortunately, Milt Freeman had orchestrated the development and formalization of most of what became the Centrist credo shortly after Envision-2100 was created."

"Yes," David interjected. "Nelson Teal and Elton Kirby shared tales of a marathon session they and some of their fellow Envision-2100 members had at the Farm putting that manifesto together."

That comment seemed to fan the flame for the POTUS. He set his cup on the coffee table, leaned forward, and locked eyes with David. With renewed passion, the president said, "They came up with an absolutely brilliant set of ideas for some fundamental changes, enhancements to our constitution. And, David, you are being allowed to implement what they have architected. A chance to slap a coat of paint on what is unarguably the most perfect governance document ever created. When fully implemented, these changes will have an impact equal to the Thirteenth Amendment's—and, I fear, will be just as challenging to push through Congress.

"Imagine, David, if you pull this whole thing off, and I have all the confidence in the world that you will, your place in history will be secured right alongside Abraham Lincoln's." The president sipped his coffee while peering at David across the top of his cup.

David was stunned. He fought to control his pulse and maintain a sense of composure. "I'm feeling a little overwhelmed, Mr. President. I think the gravity of the whole situation just punched me in the gut."

"It'll pass, my friend." The POTUS smiled and took a bite of his Danish. "Then the adrenalin will kick in, and you'll be back in the hammer lane. Now to continue my story.

"The next essential project was the search for a candidate that everyone could agree on who could and would represent the ideals that formed the foundation of the Centrist Party. Actually, this effort ran parallel with the FEC's registration effort. You would be surprised to learn just how shallow the pool of viable, qualified people is once you start factoring in all of the attributes we were looking for in a candidate. You might say the pool didn't have a deep end."

David smiled and nodded, once again impressed by the president's ability to maintain his sense of wit and humor.

"You will notice my use of 'we' rather than 'they.' By the time the Envision-2100 Presidential Candidate Selection Team got into full swing, I was committed to the cause. I couldn't come out and admit it publicly, of course; I had to keep my beliefs and support under wraps. But secretly, I had defected into what would become the Centrist camp. I felt a little guilty and disingenuous after riding my party's ticket into the White House. And I still had to wear a loyalist mask, thinking I had another five years in office. At times, I almost felt like a turncoat.

"Surprisingly, however, I had so many diplomatic relations and domestic policy snafus from the previous administration to mend that those partisan politics weren't a factor for the first two years. And by the time I had things back on course, well, here we are.

"In retrospect, this charade worked for the best. While I worked on healing the wounds my predecessor had inflicted on every faction that disagreed with his lunacy, I was able to plow the ground for the Centrists without raising the suspicion or ire of almost anyone. The policies, the endless executive orders that spewed from Sixteen Hundred Pennsylvania Avenue, were so loathsome that I could do no wrong. I felt like John the Baptist.

"In Luke, the Bible says that John was to 'go before the Lord to prepare his ways, to give knowledge of salvation to his people in the forgiveness of their sins.' Yes, I know, I may be tooting my own self-righteous horn here, but the analogy is spot on: I was preparing the way for the messiah."

David blushed.

"And while I was surreptitiously setting up a political chessboard, the Envision-2100 Candidate Selection Team was scouring the land for the perfect man or woman for what is, or what should be if done correctly, the most demanding job on the planet. After they slimmed down the list of potential candidates, they took a genuinely scientific, structured approach to ranking the names.

"Back in the midfifties, the RAND Corporation came up with a process called the Delphi technique, or the Delphi method, depending on whether you went to MIT or Caltech. To try to explain something that is way above my head: it's basically a forecasting system. It uses a panel of subject matter experts to assign assessment values to whatever is being evaluated and then goes through an iterative repetition of steps to select a logically best choice. And, David, you'll embarrass me if you ask for any more detail than I just gave you. I'm smart enough to understand when someone explains but not smart enough to elaborate on my own."

"Don't worry, Mr. President," David replied. "I'm intimately familiar with the process. In fact, it's on the top shelf of the State Department toolbox. Our teams use it all the time when evaluating treaties, sanction options, those sorts of things."

"Somehow I knew you'd be up to speed on that little trick." The president grinned. "Anyway, there was no small amount of discussion around political experience. In the end, it was decided that we didn't want a career politician as our first choice for POTUS. For the VP, perhaps, but not POTUS. The team was looking for someone with at least some degree of name recognition but did not want to go to the congressional, state legislature, or gubernatorial bullpen for our first candidate. There were too many opportunities for regional bias and corruption.

"So, after months of effort, after screening hundreds of potential nominees, and after thousands of hours of investigative work, do you know what they found?"

"No, sir," David replied.

"The ideal candidate was right under our collective noses. You, David! Our squeaky-clean, confirmed-by-a-landslide secretary of state, blissfully slaving away in the Harry S. Truman Building, flying hither and yon with your own brand of shuttle diplomacy, and number four on the presidential line of succession list. As soon as your name bubbled to the top of the list and everyone on the Envision-2100 board and its candidate selection committee agreed—and by the way, they did so unanimously—Judson reached out to you. The rest, as we like to say, is history.

"Now that you have that bit of background and have heard first-hand about my rather grim situation, we can move on to the 'where do we go from here' discussion. There are a couple of things we need to do that we need to do in sequence and that we need to do ASAP. And as you might suspect, I have a plan."

23

The town of West Yellowstone, Montana
The morning after the day of

THE STIFFENED PLASTIC COVERALLS the two newsmen wore were officially known as Level D personal protective equipment, or PPE. It was designed to give the wearer some protection against chemical splashes and to keep airborne contaminants off skin and clothing.

With the drawstrings of the hoodies pulled tight around their foreheads and faces, Martin and Kevin looked like set extras on a sci-fi flick. The surgical masks covering their mouths and noses and the protective goggles contributed to the effect, as well as making it impossible to identify them.

Martin didn't like that one bit. Once they were powered up and transmitting in real time, he wanted everyone to see his face and remember his name.

As Kevin unlocked the clamps securing the telescoping pole that held the basketball-goal-sized satellite dish to the roof of the van, Martin drug a tripod-mounted set of spotlights out of the back. The things weren't all that heavy, but they were bulky and hard to maneuver, especially while wading through ten inches of slippery ash and grit.

After managing to unfold the tripod and aiming the lights in what he thought was the direction of the park entrance, he pulled their electrical cord to the back of the van. He plugged the cable into a small, gasoline-powered Honda generator and pressed its starter switch. The motor turned over several times but didn't start.

"Shit," Martin muttered through his mask. The generators were supposed to start the first time every time. "Fucking Japs!" Then he remembered he had to turn the fuel control from off to on. He twisted the lever to its vertical position and pressed the ignition switch again; the engine started immediately.

Walking back to the lights, he pressed the on-off switch, and twin beams of brilliant light exploded forward. But the ashfall was so thick, even the powerful halogen bulbs couldn't penetrate beyond fifty feet.

Kevin approached and pointed over his shoulder at the erected satellite dish. "We're all hooked up, Scoop." His voice was muffled by the protective mask. "I fired up the sat phone in case you want to call Ms. Corbin before we start broadcasting."

"Yeah, I guess I'd better call the bitch first. Otherwise, she'll have a level-four hissy fit. Besides, she can prep the station and make sure the early-morning manager knows to let us interrupt whatever episode of *The Andy Griffith Show* they're airing."

Martin took the phone, which also had a Wi-Fi connection to the satellite uplink computer, and punched in Micca Corbin's number. This time she answered on the second ring.

"OK, Driggs, are you on-site? I've got everyone here at the station on standby. Let's get on the air before the folks from Bozeman get down there."

"We are as close as we can get to the volcano, Ms. Corbin, which is about thirty miles as the crow flies. The road is utterly impassable."

"What? Speak up, Driggs. I can't hear you."

"I'm wearing a mask—to keep the ash out." Martin spoke louder, and he smiled at the thought of making Corbin strain to understand what he was saying. "There's an ash blizzard, and it's still dark. We can't see more than thirty feet in front of us. We can see a creepy-as-shit glow due east of where we are standing and assume that's the volcano.

"Oh, and every ten minutes or so, there's an earthquake. Most are relatively mild, but we had one a while back that would have knocked our light set over if Kevin hadn't been there to catch it. It's getting pretty damn hairy, Ms. Corbin, but to answer your next question: yes, we are ready to start broadcasting as soon as someone gives us the green light."

"All right, Driggs, put your earphone in and gear up. BHB-Squared just rolled in and plopped her cute butt on the anchor chair. She will break in with a news alert in about ten seconds. Get ready to be famous, Driggs."

Martin clicked off the sat phone and hooked a small headphone around the back of his ear. As he did so, he laughed out loud at the station manager's use of the early-morning news anchor's station nickname, BHB2: bubble-headed bleach blonde, from the old Don Henley song "Dirty Laundry." Couldn't be more apropos. But, damn, she was hot.

"We interrupt our regularly scheduled program to bring you this breaking news alert!" BBH2's voice blasted through his headphone. "This is Hannah Brooks, KIFI News Team Six. We have just learned that the long-anticipated eruption of the Yellowstone supervolcano is happening as we speak. KIFI's Martin Driggs is on-site and broadcasting live. Martin, can you hear me?"

Standing in front of the tripod-mounted light set, Martin pulled down the hoodie of his PPE suit and removed his goggles so viewers could see and remember his face. He didn't remove the surgical mask that was keeping the muck out of his mouth. He might have been vain and desperate for recognition, but he wasn't stupid.

Swiftly, the gritty, sparkly grains began to sting his eyes, causing tears to well up. It would only be a matter of minutes before he had to put the goggles back on. Maybe he could do it dramatically, something for visual effect.

Squinting through tears, Martin saw the camera's green light flick on. They were broadcasting. Holding up his mic like some kind of magic wand, Martin took his first step into newscaster history.

"This is Martin Driggs, broadcasting live from the outskirts of West Yellowstone, Montana. We are about a mile from the entrance to Yellowstone National Park and about twenty-five air miles from what scientists call the caldera, better known as the Yellowstone supervolcano. It has been over six hundred thousand years since the supervolcano last erupted, but it appears that the dormant period came to a climactic end around eleven o'clock last night.

"We can't get any closer to its physical location due to the thousands of rocks and boulders that are scattered everywhere, making it impossible to proceed any farther east on Highway Twenty. Besides, that doesn't seem like it would be a good idea. As you can see, the air is thick with ash caused by the eruption.

"If my partner can zoom the camera in the direction of Shoshone Lake, you can see a fiery glow on the horizon. That's from molten rock, not the sunrise."

At that very instant, a violent tremor slammed the light set to the ground. Both Martin and Kevin dropped down on one knee.

Martin, still holding his mic and looking toward the camera, scrambled to set the lights back up. "Oh, I forgot to mention the earthquakes. They are getting stronger and more frequent."

Hannah broke into his narrative. "Martin, how about the citizens of West Yellowstone? And the city itself. What can you tell us?"

"Hannah, we haven't seen a living soul since we arrived. It appears that the entire town has been evacuated. Based on the traffic we encountered coming in, they are headed into Idaho or south toward Utah. And it's a good thing too. There are fires everywhere, and the ash is about twelve inches deep where we are standing right now. Some of the roofs on the buildings that are still standing are starting to sag or have caved in. I don't know how much longer we can stay here. We can barely breathe."

Hannah continued: "We have learned that units of the Montana National Guard are mobilizing and should be heading to your location. Martin, have you seen any first responders since your arrival?"

"No, we haven't seen anyone else. In fact, we haven't seen any signs of life of any kind. No dogs, no birds, nothing."

A burst of light flooded the sky in the direction of the caldera, followed by a deafening explosion sharper, louder, and more bone-jarring than anything Martin or Kevin had ever experienced.

"Hannah, I believe there has been another eruption. It sounded like a hydrogen bomb, and the sky appears to be on fire."

As Martin spoke, red-hot rocks and pebbles started to rain down, trailing streams of smoke as they fell. A marble-sized cinder hit the side of Kevin's right leg and burned through the plastic of his PPE suit.

Kevin danced in shock and pain. "Oww! Som ov'a bich. Thas erts." His mask muffled his screams and more or less disguised whatever he was trying to say. He switched the camera to his left shoulder and swatted his leg with his right hand, but he never dropped the camera or even stopped recording.

"That's it for now, Hannah. We've got to pull back a couple of miles. We'll be back as soon as we are in a safer location. This is Martin Driggs, Station KIFI, back to you, Hannah."

Kevin switched off the camera, and as they started throwing their equipment back into the van, Micca Corbin's voice blared out of Martin's earphone.

"Stay your ass right there, Driggs! We've gone national. The only coverage of the biggest story of the century. Every affiliate in the Northwest will have crews up there by sunup. Don't you dare lose our spot!"

"We hear you, Ms. Corbin. We're not going to lose our spot, but we're damn sure going to change it! Since you're in the station and watched the broadcast, you undoubtedly heard me tell the whole world that we *can't fucking breath*! Fire and brimstone are raining down all around us. Kevin just got a hole burned in his leg, for Christ's sake."

Regaining some of his composure, Martin continued: "We're heading back west on Highway Twenty until we are at least out of this meteor shower. I have no idea how long that will take because I have no idea how far this 'falling chunks of stuff' extends. As soon as we quit hearing rocks hit the van, we will stop and set up again. Besides, it will give our bloodthirsty viewers even more drama—and keep Kevin and me not dead."

"Well, you go ahead and move, you pussy. But when you get back here, you and I are going to have a little chat. And not in a good way."

"I'll keep that in mind, Your Highness, but I'm telling you, that's not at the top of my list of shit to worry about right now."

24

Washington, DC; the White House
Two years before the day of

THE POTUS PUT DOWN HIS PLATE with its half-eaten Danish, leaned forward, and looked fiercely into David's eyes.

"I've given the steps we need to take and the sequence we need to take them in a lot of thought over the last twenty-four hours. As they say, timing is everything. We want to send a shockwave across the political landscape. Or better yet, a tsunami. In fact, that's the perfect metaphor. We'll knock 'em down with my first announcement, and then, just as they are starting to get on their feet, *boom*, we'll hit again, and then one more time for good measure. Within the span of half an hour, we will have made the most unconventional, most aggressive opening gambit ever seen on a US political chessboard."

"I hate to say it, Mr. President, but I never really learned to play chess. I remember how to move the pieces, but that's about it. So it would probably be best if you didn't rely too heavily on a board game as an example of our strategy."

"Good point, David. Thanks for sharing that with me, since I was all set to talk about the Ruy Lopez, the Italian, and Caro-Kann as followup moves. I'll be a little less oblique from here on out.

"So the first step is for me to set up a press conference and announce my condition and my decision to resign immediately. I'm afraid this needs to be done within the next few days. The Grim Reaper could knock on my door at any time.

"Equally concerning are the medications. I'm shying away from the pain meds, at least the opioids. They make me constipated, and when I'm constipated, I'm really grouchy. The chemo drugs are even worse. There is a yard-long list of mental side effects those things can cause, everything from raging panic attacks to depression. The last thing this country needs is a suicidal president who can't shit."

Despite his best efforts, David laughed at the president's macabre joke.

"My point is that I need to get out of the Oval Office before I'm dead or crazy. When I first started mapping out my exit strategy, I thought it would be best if you submitted your resignation and announced your plan to run for office as the first step. Then I put myself in your shoes and realized that would require a superhuman leap of faith. Although clinically impossible, there would always be the prospect that I could hang on for another year or so and decide not to resign. You would be out of a job, and you would have shown your hand to Jim Phillips."

"I understand, Mr. President, and I'm totally on board with your sense of urgency. However, with all due respect, I have to disagree on the sequence you just laid out. You are correct that it will take significant trust and commitment on my part to take that first step. But Kelly and I've made our decision. We know there are risks involved. We plan to do whatever is legally and morally necessary to win this thing or die trying.

"Today is Tuesday. I'll write my letter of resignation this afternoon, then gather key members of my team together and let them know of my plans. I owe them at least that much. They are loyal and the most dedicated collection of government employees I've ever encountered. Of course, I'll swear them to secrecy, at least until word hits the streets. And I won't mention your illness or your intentions. This will be like tossing a pebble in the DC pond. Without a doubt, there will be ripples, but they'll flatten out by the weekend. But your announcement will be like a belly-flop. It'll splash water everywhere and might even create a couple of puddles on the beach."

The president sat back, looked up at the ceiling for a moment, and pursed his lips in a half smile, half smirk before turning his gaze back to David.

"That's an interesting image you've painted, David. And since what you're suggesting was my first inclination before I overthought it, I agree on your approach. I'm going to enjoy sitting back and watching this first petal unfold and listening to the vice president's reaction."

"Yes, sir, that'll be entertaining. I'll formally submit my resignation and announce my plan to run for office on Thursday. That will allow the dust to settle down over Friday and the weekend. It will also give Judson time to start getting the Centrist campaign machine moving. I suspect they are already 'standing in the door,' to use an old Airborne term, just waiting for a name to plug into their media blitz."

The president picked up his cup and took a sip of his still-hot coffee. "That being the case, I will plan on having my resignation press conference Monday afternoon. I don't mean 'plan' in the classical, Oval Office sense of the word. No one, except the two people in this office right now and Judson, who has some strings to pull behind the curtain, will know what I intend to do until I tell my press secretary on Monday morning. We will catch Jim Phillips completely flat-footed. But you'll need that jump out of the starting gate. Despite being a world-class douchebag, the man's no dummy."

Pointing toward the desk in front of the Oval Office's bay windows, the POTUS continued: "Once he is in that chair, he'll start pulling out every dirty trick he and his soon-to-be-assembled team of slimeballs have at their disposal. And trust me, David, he knows them all.

"That brings me to the next and final point that I wanted to make this morning: your running mate. This is something else I've given considerable thought to and discussed with Milt and Judson. As you know, when the Envision-2100 team was casting their net for a presidential candidate, they purposely steered away from career politicians.

However, you don't want to completely divorce yourself from the establishment, at least not the mainstream. The radical Left or Right, yes, and the old-school career politicians, but not those who represent capable, bipartisan, objective leadership. Make that tripartisan now that you're in the mix."

"You're generally at least one step ahead of me, Mr. President, but not this time. I've been winnowing a list of possible VP candidates in my head and came to pretty much the same conclusion. Some but not too much name recognition. Experienced but not jaded. Willing to take a stand but not die on a hill for a lost cause.

"I've tried to run this thing out mentally through, with Phillips in the game, what is bound to be a nasty campaign and well into the first one hundred days in office. That's an arbitrary benchmark, but I think it's reflective of how aggressive the POTUS is coming out of the chute and the potential driving their agenda. And long-term success. FDR pushed an astounding seventy-six bills through Congress and signed ninety-nine executive orders in his first one hundred days. And none of the EOs were revoked.

"As I worked my way through my self-compiled list, I kept coming back to one name: Texas Senator Mia Lopez. She ran and won as a Democrat in a historically red state. She is about as conservative a Democrat as you'll find, which may account for her swinging fifty-two percent of the popular vote. Admittedly, her opponent was a pathological liar and reeked of corruption, but she did change the leopard's spots. And she is a she.

"Could we swing her? I don't know. We have a cordial relationship, but I don't know her on a personal basis. I do like what I've seen of her professionally. She's not afraid to back off of a stance if someone on either side of the aisle makes a logical case for doing so. And she's gained a reputation for herding hardliners to a compromise. We could do a lot worse. Assuming she would be willing to be reborn as a Centrist."

The president leaned back, shifted his gaze toward the portrait of Washington hanging over the fireplace, and nodded in contemplative agreement.

"I admire your thought process, David. I agree that the one-hundred-day benchmark, albeit, as you say, a bit arbitrary, is as good as anything else we've got. And it does seem to be a predictor of success. Not necessarily popularity, but you'll have to learn to get over that concept anyway.

"Mia Lopez would be a damn-good choice. In fact, I'm thrilled that she bubbled to the top of your candidate list. I do know her personally, and now that you've brought her name up, I can't think of a better candidate. If it's OK with you, and if I'm still around, I'll reach out to her the day after my announcement hits the streets. But before I do, you might want to bounce the idea off Judson and Milt. I don't see either of them having an objection, but it would keep them from wasting Envision-2100 resources if they agree on her as your running mate. Besides, it's a courtesy and sends an 'I'm in charge but haven't forgotten who brought me to the dance' message to those guys.

"So, David, we've both got resignation letters to write, and I've got a photo op scheduled in the Rose Garden. Funny, it could be one of the last ones I will ever do. If you don't have any burning questions, I'll let you head back to Foggy Bottom."

The president stood up and thrust out his hand.

As the two friends shook hands, David replied, "As always, Mr. President, thank you for your counsel and, most importantly, your confidence. It looks like it's time to shake things up in this town."

25

Grand Teton National Park
The morning after the day of

Fiona's shriek shattered the muffled silence and jerked Jeremy out of his pitifully shallow sleep. It cut to his core, like fingernails scraping on a blackboard. He jerked up straight from his semireclined position in the driver's seat and spun around to face a cacophony of screams.

Ellis and Fiona were both looking out the left passenger window, their faces contorted in fear. Judy bolted upright too, her eyes reflecting the fact that she was now in fight-or-flight mode, but not fear.

A face was pressed against the rear passenger-side window, like a kid window-shopping at Macy's. Only this wasn't a kid, and this damn sure wasn't Macy's.

The sun had risen less than an hour earlier, giving the air the soft gray glow of impossibly heavy morning fog. The visibility was better than it had been the night before, but barely so. Ash continued to fall just as heavily as it had been doing. Everything was covered in a smothering blanket of the stuff for as far as Jeremy could see, which, despite the radiance from the filtered sunlight, wasn't over thirty feet.

The man whose face was pressed against the wind—Jeremy could tell it was a man by the figure's size and hulking demeanor—had pulled a T-shirt over his head and torn two half-dollar-sized holes in it to peer through. The shirt, the skin around the man's eyes, and his clothes were covered in black, glittering ash. He was so close to the truck that Jeremy couldn't judge how tall he was, but his arms and shoulders made him out to be well over six feet and thickly muscled.

Three or four steps behind the man moved another smaller, shadowy, ghostlike figure. The cantaloupe-sized bumps inside a two-sizes-too-small Harley Davidson pullover indicated this was the man's female companion. She had a bandanna wrapped over her nose and tied in the back, train-robber style. Her hair was stuffed inside a biker do-rag.

The man rapped on the window with the knuckles of his hamlike left hand.

"Hey, mister, we need to hitch a ride," the man hollered through the closed window. "My bike choked up in all of this shit. Me and my old lady are stranded."

Jeremy felt a wave of compassion—until he saw the tire jack handle clenched in the man's right fist. Compassion was replaced by alarm.

"We're heading south, toward Jackson Hole," Jeremy shouted through the closed window. "If you put that club down, you can ride in the back of the truck until we get out of this mess." He started the F-250's engine.

"Sure, mister, but how about we ride in your trailer? Get us out of the volcano dirt."

"That's not going to happen," Jeremy shouted back. "We're leaving now. If you want a ride, throw your jack handle down and climb in the back." He put the truck in M1 and started slowly moving forward.

"OK, motherfucker, you win, but you've gotta stop sometime!" the man screamed. He and his "old lady" clambered into the bed of the F-250.

Watching the pair through his rearview mirror, Jeremy didn't miss the fact that the man was still holding on to what was potentially a deadly weapon. He didn't say anything to Judy or the twins, who were watching through the back window.

The F-250 continued rolling as the man and woman crawled over the truck's tailgate and into its bed, moving forward as far as the rack of bicycles and toolbox allowed. They settled under a tarp Jeremy had used to cover their firewood supply.

As he maneuvered slowly back onto US 191, Jeremy kept his eyes on what he hoped was the middle of the ash-covered road. "We'll drive as far as we can, but at some point, we'll have to take a potty break. I'm not even going to try to pull over. I'll just stop, and we all get out and do our business. We'll just have to play it by ear with those two."

Jeremy caught Judy's eye. He reached between his seat and the center console for the .357 Magnum. Judy nodded slowly. He laid the gun next to his right hip so that either of them could grab it if, heaven forbid, the need arose. The pistol was a five-shot revolver. The first two rounds in the gun's cylinder were loaded with CCI shotshells, each of which fired 150 pellets of birdshot instead of a solid projectile.

Years earlier, when they first decided to purchase a firearm, Jeremy and Judy had jointly decided they wanted the protection. But even if push came to shove, they would try to avoid killing an attacker if at all possible. For that reason, they planned to pepper an assailant with birdshot rather than blast a hole in his chest the first time they squeezed the trigger. This strategy did not sit well with their die-hard Second Amendment friends, but Jeremy and Judy were more comfortable with this approach.

The visibility was much better now that the sun was out. Jeremy could make out rough shapes up to thirty feet in front of the truck, and he had a better sense of where the highway shoulders were. There wasn't much, if any, difference in the volume of ash that continued to fall. It had accumulated significantly since they had pulled over for what pitifully little sleep they had been able to get. A good ten-to-twelve-inch-thick glittery black mat now covered the road and ground for as far as he could see. Tree branches sagged under its still increasing weight. Many had broken and fallen to the ground. These were evidenced now only by swollen mounds on an otherwise smooth surface.

Despite the increased visibility, Jeremy still wasn't able to drive over ten miles an hour. The F-250's four-wheel drive was able to push the truck forward, but Jeremy knew it would only be a matter of time before the ever-accumulating ash would grind them to a stop.

Please, God, let us make it to some kind of shelter in Jackson Hole before that happened.

The truck's GPS had stopped working. Jeremy suspected this was due either to the layer of ash covering its roof-mounted receiver or the amount of material in the air, blocking satellite signal reception. Most likely, both. Regardless, he had only a vague idea of where they were and how much farther they had to go before they reached anything resembling a city.

As he pondered the question, they crept by another park sign next to the road: Snake River Overlook, 500 feet. If memory served him well, this would put them roughly thirty miles from Jackson Hole. The road would be flat and about as straight as it got in this part of the country. Jeremy drove on, hoping to get at least another hour farther south before they had to stop for a bathroom break. And to change out the makeshift filter he had put on the F-250's air intake.

Just as they passed the first overlook turnoff, Judy pointed out lights in the distance. "Jeremy, look over to the right. Looks like a stranded vehicle."

The vehicle—one of the trendy BMW SUVs that was so popular with young professionals—had stopped partially off the road, its emergency blinkers flashing. When the slowly moving F-250 was about sixty feet from the BMW, a man and woman got out. The woman was holding a small child in her arms. Jeremy guessed the kid to be less than a year old. Once out of the SUV, the man started waving his arms above his head.

Jeremy eased the truck up next to the BMW, and Judy lowered her window a crack to talk to the couple. They didn't need any more ash drifting into the truck.

Stepping closer to the passenger door, the man said, "Thank God you stopped. We've been stranded here for hours. We're the Tanners, from Duluth, Minnesota. I'm Brandon, this is my wife, Sophie, and our son, Hunter."

Jeremy and Judy locked eyes. Jeremy nodded. Judy unlocked her door and opened it halfway. "We'll do formal introductions later. Put Hunter in the back seat with our twins. You and your wife can get under the tarp in the back of the truck. Be careful climbing in. We picked up another couple a while back. Bikers. They're under the tarp, probably asleep."

"Asleep! How the hell we gonna sleep?" the man roared, sticking his head out from under the ash-covered tarp. "There's four bicycles back here. There ain't room for anyone else."

Jeremy partially opened the driver's door, leaned out, and shouted back, "Throw the bicycles overboard and make room. But do it while we're moving. Even with four-wheel drive, I don't know how much longer we'll be able to push through this stuff."

As Jeremy shifted the transmission back into M1, Sophie handed Hunter to Judy.

Cursing for all to hear, the biker got out from under the tarp and tossed one of the four bicycles over the side of the truck as Sophie and Brandon climbed in over the tailgate.

"Well, grab a bicycle, Brandon from Minnesota," the biker growled as he tossed another bike off the side of the truck.

Brandon did as he was told, first one bike and then the last, as the F-250 slowly muscled its way forward, its obscenely wide all-terrain tires slipping in twelve inches of powdery pumice.

From his side mirrors, Jeremy watched Sophie pull one side of the tarp up and slip into the semiprotective shelter it provided from the falling cinders. She held it up high enough to allow Brandon to crawl in next to her.

"Close the door, sweetie," the biker chick twittered. "You're getting the floor all yucky."

Openly leering at Sophie, the biker added, "Yeah, we might as well get cozy. Looks like we're gonna be here awhile."

26

Washington, DC; the Harry S. Truman Federal Building
Two years before the day of

It was scarcely a mile's drive back to his office in the Truman Building, even following the least circuitous route from the White House. Yet thanks to a combination of DC traffic and never-ending road repairs, the trip took almost twenty minutes. David didn't mind, though. Getting behind the wheel gave him a little uninterrupted time to mentally compose the letter he had to write.

He entered through his office's side door to avoid any impromptu visitors who might be waiting for him in the reception area. Once inside, he woke up his computer by moving its mouse. He then clicked on an icon that caused Trish's workstation to ding and changed a symbol on both their screens from red to green. This let her know David was back in his office and she could come in if necessary.

Thirty seconds later, there was a muted tap on the door. Trish opened the door and slipped inside, gently closing it behind her. "Welcome back, Mr. Secretary. Here's a list of people who have been trying to get in touch with you this morning." Trish handed David a sheet of paper. "I've taken the liberty of organizing them according to what I think will be your sense of urgency."

David glanced at the list and then laid it on his desk. "You've got some kind of superpower, Trish. But today these folks are all going to have to wait a little longer. Go grab a steno pad. We've got a fire to light."

"A steno pad? Mr. Secretary, you do realize we're a quarter of the way into the twenty-first century. I've never seen an actual steno pad. I've heard the term, maybe from my grandfather."

"Yeah, I guess I forgot. You learned your trade after the days of voice recognition and cursive handwriting. Just get your iPad, transfer our phones to the switchboard operator, and hurry back."

As Trish scurried away, David sat down at the small conference table in the center of his office, a somewhat casual departure from his usual, more formal working position behind his desk. When Trish returned seconds later, David motioned for her to sit down across from him.

"Trish, I know we've discussed some extremely sensitive material before, but nothing—and I mean nothing—comes close to what I'm going to share with you now. My saying that may be a bit insulting, especially given your security clearance, and if so, I apologize."

"Mr. Secretary, I can't imagine anything you might say that would insult me," Trish said.

"I'm obligated to ask you to treat everything we discuss in this meeting just like it was top-secret sensitive compartmented information. It isn't officially classified SCI simply because we don't have time to go through normal channels. Again, forgive me for asking, but can you swear that what you are about to hear will not leave this room until I release it?"

"I assure you that I will treat whatever we discuss as a matter of national security."

"Thank you, Trish. I knew you would and that you would understand my caution. And it is a matter of national security. This coming Thursday, I will announce my resignation as the United States secretary of state."

It was a good thing Trish wasn't trying to take shorthand. She would have broken her pencil. A stunned expression flooded her face as if someone had punched her in the stomach.

David continued, anticipating his next words to be a knockout blow to her senses. "And I'll announce my intention to run for president in the next election."

Trish's jaw dropped.

"So let's compose a letter to the POTUS," David said. He proceeded to dictate to his shell-shocked administrative assistant. When he was finished dictating his gratitude for the opportunity to serve and his regard for the president, he leaned back in his chair.

Trish closed the cover on her iPad. "My head's spinning, Mr. Secretary. I hope the last two shockers are all you have for today. I don't think I can handle anything else."

"You're safe for now, Trish. Once you print my letter on State Department letterhead, I'll sign it and we will send it by courier to the POTUS. Any other time, I would have hand-carried it, but he knows it's on the way. And he knows what it says. He'll call me on my cell once he receives it.

"As soon as I get his call, I would like you to set up an emergency close-hold meeting in my conference room." He tore off a sheet on his yellow legal pad and handed it to Trish. "Just the staff on this list. It might be wise to send a group text and tell them to be on standby, just in case someone has plans to leave early."

Scarcely twenty minutes later, Trish tapped on David's door and came in with his letter of resignation. David signed it in the painstakingly precise brush script he had mastered in grammar school. After making copies of the signed document, Trish placed it in a white nine-by-twelve envelope stamped POTUS EYES ONLY, sealed it, and gave it to the waiting courier.

Back in his office, David texted Kelly: "It's done. Plan on submitting your own letter as soon as word hits the streets. I'll be home for dinner at the regular time tonight. This may be our last chance to have a regular meal for a while."

David meant his last statement to be hyperbole; it wasn't. Not by a long shot.

27

The town of West Yellowstone, Montana
The morning after the day of

"LET'S GET OUT OF HERE, Scoop!" Kevin jerked open the driver's door and leaped into the van. "It's raining fire and brimstone. I'm not sure what brimstone is, but I do know my leg hurts like hell and there's a hole in my PPE. Protective my ass!"

"It's sulfur," Martin said, climbing into the passenger side and buckling his seat belt.

"Huh?" Kevin slammed the van into drive and started rolling as an increasing number of smoldering pebbles dropped from the sky, peppering the van and covering the ground all around them.

"Sulphur. Brimstone is burning sulfur. You know, an element. The symbol S. Atomic number sixteen."

"I'm a driver, Einstein. You don't have to have a degree in chemical engineering to make this thing go forward when you want it to go forward and to stop when you want it to stop."

"Well, make it go forward faster, then. It sounds like hail hitting a tin roof in here."

In the glow from the van's headlights, they could see that some of the projectiles were beginning to exceed the category of "pebble."

Martin studied a paper map; the GPS was on the blink. "Let's head north on One Ninety-One until we run out of this meteor shower.

We know there is nothing to see heading west on Twenty. If we get on One Ninety-One, we can still put some distance between us and the volcano, and we might be able to intercept the teams from KTVM or KBZK on their way down here. We were first on the scene, and I don't mind rubbing their noses in that little fact. Besides, KBZK is a CBS affiliate, and a public display of beating them to the punch just might get us out of hot water with the ice queen."

"Aye, Captain. Setting a course north," Kevin responded in a pitiful George Takei imitation.

They had driven about ten miles when the van's GPS started working again. Martin assumed this was the result of accumulated ash blowing off the receiver and that they might actually be on the outer fringes of the cloud. And they seemed to be far enough away from the eruption to be out of danger from falling rocks. The GPS indicated they were about thirty miles from the caldera and just south of a bridge where US 191 crossed over Cougar Creek.

"There's a pull-off just ahead at the bridge," Martin said. "Let's stop there and set up again."

Ash continued to fall and accumulate in drifts as Kevin raised the satellite dish. A slight breeze blew from west to east, which, if Kevin's prayers were answered, would start pushing the cloud away from their location.

In the distance, the volcano rumbled, occasionally increasing to an ear-splitting roar. Each explosive clap was accompanied by violent tremors powerful enough to bounce the van sideways. Even though the rock bombardment had slacked off, they were still in danger. To the east, the sun was peeking through pines, its light competing with the red-orange glow in the sky above what had been the caldera.

As the sun climbed over the tree-studded horizon, Martin spied the outline of a tall, perfectly shaped cone to the southeast. It was hard to see through the polluted air, but it appeared to be a mountain.

One that hadn't been there before.

What Martin didn't know, couldn't have known, was that one of the tectonic shifts caused the caldera to collapse and fall into itself and its magma intrusion zone deep below the surface. In an instant, it went from caldera to supervolcano, releasing billions of tons of pressure and molten rock through the earth's upper crust. It was this explosive eruption of lava that formed a gigantic—and growing—mountain whose core was belching ash and bedrock thousands of feet into the air.

In less than a week, this pile of still-smoking volcanic ash and rock would rise to 16,530 feet, towering over Alaska's Mount Bona. It would eventually be named Mount Shoshone, after the nearby lake and Native American tribes originally indigenous to the area.

As soon as Kevin raised the satellite antenna into position, he started the generator and pressed auto seek on a control panel. The dish rotated, tilted upward, and in seconds locked onto a communication satellite twenty-two thousand miles above.

While Kevin was once again getting their equipment ready to begin broadcasting, Martin tried to make himself presentable. He pushed back the hood of his PPE and removed his goggles, but his eyes began to sting the instant he did so. He would hold off on the surgical mask until he actually started speaking into his microphone. As before, he wanted his audience to recognize his face, but he didn't want to look too fresh. He had to elicit some empathy, but he didn't want to choke to death doing so.

Just when he found his presentation sweet spot, the sound of approaching engines roared above the volcano's rumbling. Stepping into the center of the highway, Martin looked north toward the noise.

At this location, US 191 ran straight as an arrow, slicing through the pine-and-hardwood forest without being hindered by hills or curves. If the ash weren't falling, Martin would have had an unobstructed view for miles. But through the dense layer of ash, the sun was still struggling to turn the night into dawn. The glow of headlights, lots of them, pushed through the cloud of ash.

Perfect timing, Martin thought. "Kevin, bring the camera over here. I think the army's coming. Get them and the highway in the background behind me, and let's get on the air."

"Got it, Scoop," Kevin said, moving the camera. "Ready in three, two, one."

When the camera's green light came on, Martin snatched the surgical mask off his mouth and started talking.

"Hello again. This is Martin Driggs, KIFI, reporting live just outside Yellowstone National Park. Earlier this morning we brought you the story of what appears to be the eruption of the Yellowstone supervolcano. I say 'appears to be' because no one has been able to get close enough to verify that to be the case. However, as you can see, the air is so thick you can almost slice it, the landscape is starting to look like the surface of the moon, and in the distance you can see the outline of Wyoming's newest mountain."

Kevin panned the camera to the east and, using its telescopic lens, zoomed in on the ominous, glowing shape on the horizon. He then pointed the camera back toward Martin and the approaching convey.

"We believe the fabled Yellowstone Caldera, which sat above the long-dormant volcano, literally blew its top shortly before midnight. That cataclysmic event was responsible for most of the damage we've seen. However, the volcano is still active and extremely dangerous. In fact, we had to retreat from our original broadcast location due to falling chunks of rock and spewing lava."

Martin knew he was taking a bit of literary license with his use of "spewing lava," but it was a technicality. He was painting a mental image for his viewers. Besides, the overwhelming majority wouldn't know the difference.

Making a quarter turn to his right so that Kevin could still keep his face and torso in the foreground, Martin pointed up the highway, toward the line of vehicles inching their way in his direction. "It looks like we are about to get some company."

An olive-drab—better known as OD green—five-ton truck with an eleven-foot snowplow lumbered its way down the highway, pushing a path through the accumulated ash and creating a four-foot-high drift on the right-hand side of the road. Two Humvees followed two vehicle lengths behind the truck, then three two-and-a-half-ton trucks, the US Army's fabled deuce-and-a-half, and finally, two white-and-blue buses with Cline Tours painted on the sides, all spaced precisely the same distance apart.

The truck with the snowplow pulled up alongside the KIFI van and stopped, bringing the rest of the convoy to a halt. After the first Humvee stopped, someone on its passenger side, wearing a military-standard-issue protective mask and a battle dress uniform, which the army called a BDU, started walking toward Martin.

Kevin focused the camera on Martin and the approaching soldier.

Martin strode to meet the BDU-clad figure. "Martin Driggs, KIFI News. Are you with the Montana National Guard?"

"I'm Major Lynette Kohler, Eighty-Third WMD Civil Support Team, headquartered outside Bozeman. We're an advance party here to provide medical assistance and to support evacuation efforts."

The protective mask and its rubberized hood completely covered her face and head, muffling her voice and making it almost incomprehensible. However, Martin could not help noticing that even the bulky BDUs could not hide an exceptionally well-constructed woman. *Hmmm. This might prove interesting.* He switched off his mic. "Do I call you Lynette or Lynn?"

"You can call me Major, Mr. Driggs. Where are you two from, how long have you been here, and what is your assessment of the situation from a disaster perspective?"

Martin slid his surgical mask and goggles back on. "ABC affiliates out of Idaho Falls. Got here last night. Made it as far as West Yellowstone and started broadcasting live from there. Then the thing blew its top again, and we left. We've been here for less than an hour."

"Your assessment?" the major repeated.

"Shit, Major, this is ground zero, the biggest natural disaster in our lifetime, maybe ever." Martin pointed toward the smoking mountain. "That wasn't there yesterday morning. Your convoy won't make it much farther south, but if you don't mind, we'll tag along."

"You can fall in behind my Humvee. Just make sure your driver watches our cat's eyes and keeps proper convey distance. We don't need anyone getting rear-ended during all of this."

Martin recalled one of his army buddies telling him that the taillights on military vehicles were equipped with two small red bulbs. At night, if a driver could see both of the red lamps on the vehicle in front, they were too close and needed to back off until only a single red blur was visible. This amazingly simple technique, which had been around since WWII, helped prevent rear-end collisions.

"Yes, ma'am," Martin replied, "we'll keep an eye on your rear." He couldn't see the glare coming from Major Kohler, but he could sense it.

"A couple of other things," Major Kohler said sharply. "First of all, don't go poking that microphone in front of any of my troops. If you feel the need to interview anyone, talk to me first. Also, like I said, we're an advance party. The governor has already declared a state of emergency and is mobilizing an MP company and a battalion of combat engineers. They should start rolling in here in a few hours. The governor will be coming with them and could very well place the region under a state of martial law. If she does, your invitation to join the convoy may be off the table.

"Finally, the word is that President Stakley may be coming out later. Not sure when or even if, for that matter. I'm just telling you because that will bring about a whole new ballgame, security-wise. Since the airspace is shut down over three states, he can't do the normal flyover, and I seriously doubt that the Secret Service will drive him too close to this stuff. This is a dangerous and fluid situation. They won't put the POTUS's life at risk for a photo op.

"So, Mr. Driggs, it looks like you are at the right place at the perfect time for a news reporter."

Yes, it certainly did. Martin smiled at the major—for more reason than one.

"Saddle up!" Major Kholer barked into the radio microphone set attached to the collar of her BDU blouse. "Let's see if we can get a little closer to the action."

28

SECRETARY OF STATE STAKLEY RESIGNS, Announces Intention to Run for President.

The news exploded within every media agency and across the internet. At President Sheppard's direction, White House Press Secretary Preston Woods orchestrated first a leak and then the official announcement at a hastily arranged briefing.

From the front row in the briefing room, a *Post* reporter caught the press secretary's eye. "Besides announcing his candidacy, did Secretary Stakley give any other reason for his sudden resignation? Is there a rift between President Sheppard and Mr. Stakley?"

Using this first question as an opportunity to take control and set the tone for the briefing, Preston calmly replied, "Ladies and gentlemen, please, only one question at a time. No, the secretary did not give a reason for his resignation other than his intention to run for office." He pointed to a tall brunette in the third row. "Darlene."

"Thank you, Preston. It's common knowledge that President Sheppard and Secretary Stakley are close personal friends. What was the president's reaction to the resignation?"

"The president hasn't made an official announcement, nor have we had an opportunity to discuss the situation in any detail. I take it he was just as surprised as everyone else," Preston said. "Josh."

"Thanks, Preston. The SecState is a key cabinet post. Has the president given any clues to who he may be looking at to replace Mr. Stakley and when he plans to do so?"

"Josh, were you just not paying attention?" Preston replied jovially.

Laughter rippled through the room, and from the left, someone chided, "He's with the *Times*, Preston. They're required to have a short attention span."

"In answer to your question, Josh—rather, questions—the president hasn't had time to discuss Secretary Stakley's replacement with any of his advisory staff," Preston continued. "I'm sure he is doing so as we speak, and that information will be forthcoming. But I don't have anything to share at this time."

For the next fifteen minutes, the press secretary shared what scant details he had about the situation. Over the previous three years, White House briefings had been cordial and informative. Nothing like the contentious bickering prevalent in the last administration. They reflected President Sheppard's style: respectful and open.

Glancing at the Brady Room's wall clock, Preston said, "Fran, you have the last question."

A stocky, early-forties black female armed with a pen and spiral notebook peered at the press secretary over her bifocals.

"Thank you, Preston. I was beginning to think you were going to skip me. There has been no shortage of formally announced candidates in the last three campaigns. However, President Sheppard has earned one of the highest approval ratings on record. Has he ever, even privately, voiced concern about a challenger, from either party, at this stage of his political career?"

"Fran, you know the president. He's never been one to strut around or to display any degree of overconfidence. I personally think he sees the potential in everyone, and as such, he would tend to take any opponent seriously, especially someone with David Stakley's reputation and qualifications, if that's where you are going with that question."

"That's precisely what I was asking, Preston. Along that line, to the best of my knowledge, Secretary Stakley, like his predecessor, has never formally acknowledged membership in any political party. On the heels of his announcement, will he do so now, or do you see him running as an independent?"

"That's an excellent question, Fran. There is nothing in his letter of resignation that indicates his intentions. So the answer at this time is, I don't know. Ladies and gentlemen, that concludes today's briefing. Thank you for your time."

Press Secretary Preston closed his notebook, left the briefing room, and walked back to his office. It was tucked into a corner of the West Wing, directly across from the Cabinet Room, and only a few steps down the corridor from the Oval Office.

Minutes later, there was a tap on his open office door, and President Sheppard walked in. The press secretary stood up, but the president motioned for him to sit back down.

Maybe it was his imagination, but Preston thought he detected a slight yellowish tint on the president's face. Perhaps it was just the light in his office. Maybe the POTUS was experimenting with makeup or some type of tanning lotion. No, he wouldn't be caught dead doing anything like that. Not President Sheppard.

But there was also something else. The president almost seemed to be moving in slow motion. He looked tired. The spring was missing from his step, and his eyes looked dull and listless. Preston couldn't put his finger on it, but something was akilter.

The POTUS pulled a chair away from the small conference table, moved it close to Preston's desk, and sat down. "Well, how did it go, Preston? Were they civil, or did they go into a feeding frenzy? You can never tell with the press once they smell blood."

"As well as could be expected, Mr. President. Especially considering we didn't have much information to share, except for announcing the secretary's resignation itself. They were pretty constrained. They should have a field day writing their own speculations around the announcement. Some of them never let a lot of facts get in the way of a good story. Especially CNN and the *New York Times*."

"We'll let 'em simmer for a couple of days," President Sheppard replied. "A little wild-ass conjecture makes good press, and the public loves it. We'll let the rumor embers smolder over the weekend. Now I have another short-fuse mission for you.

"Tomorrow afternoon, I want you to schedule a special press briefing for Monday morning. You can let it be known that it will be my dog-and-pony show. If Vice President Phillips, or anyone else for that matter, asks what it's going to be about, you can tell him you don't know. That should be easy because you don't know and I'm not going to tell you.

"I want you to schedule it in the Rose Garden. You'll invite foreign as well as domestic press, so we'll need more space than we have in the Brady Room.

"I know I don't have to tell you how to do your job, but my message to you is that I want this one to get maximum exposure. I want every major news agency that's still in business to be here. Take it from there and plan accordingly. Any questions, Preston?"

"No, Mr. President. I'll take it from here."

With an uncharacteristically weak smile, the POTUS muttered, "Thank you." He turned and left Preston's office.

...

At the end of the corridor, President Sheppard turned left and walked through his administrative assistant's office, stopping in front of her desk. Unlike every other person in Washington would have done, she adhered to the president's order from day one and didn't stand up.

"Lizbeth, two things. First, Preston is going to schedule me to do a press conference Monday morning. I have a boatload of crap on my calendar that day. Cancel everything. I also want you to schedule a meeting for myself and Senator Mia Lopez for early Monday afternoon. Better yet, make it lunch, just me and her, in my dining room. If she's not in town, we can do a phone call or secure Skype. But I suspect that if you get in touch with her today, she will arrange to be here Monday."

"Yes, Mr. President. Will that be all?"

"No, Lizbeth." The POTUS turned and headed toward the side door to his office. "Clear my calendar for the rest of today and all weekend. And don't schedule me for anything past Monday unless I say otherwise."

"Yes, Mr. President." Lizbeth's voice trailed behind him as he closed his office door.

29

"Dad, I gotta pee," Ellis moaned.

Despite well over twelve inches of volcanic ash on the road and poor visibility, the F-250 continued to bulldoze its way forward, albeit slowly. Although they had been moving for almost two hours since picking up Brandon and Sophie, they had only traveled a little over five miles.

Nevertheless, Jeremy knew they needed a bathroom break, and he needed to change out the pillowcase covering the engine's air filter. "OK, ladies, the Glacier View Turnout is just ahead. We'll stop there. Stay with your mom, do your business, and then get back in the truck."

"You don't have to tell me twice," Fiona said. "Not with those two goons in the back."

A few minutes later, Jeremy stopped the truck but, as before, didn't turn off the engine. Once the transmission was in park, he attached the pistol's holster to the left side of his belt, with Judy quietly watching. Grabbing the clean pillowcase from the space between him and Judy, he popped the truck's hood latch and got out.

At the same time, Judy got out on the passenger side. "Ellis, hand Hunter to me, and you girls get out on this side." Hoisting Hunter over her left shoulder, she shepherded the twins out of the truck and toward the edge of the road, continually glancing back at the truck. They disappeared into the ash-thick air.

As Jeremy replaced the clogged pillowcase covering the air filter with a clean one, he heard the truck door slam. Good. That meant Judy and the kids were back from their pee break. He closed the hood and took the opportunity to urinate.

"What the . . . Get your hands off me!" Judy snarled.

Jeremy zipped up his pants and tore around the front of the truck to the passenger side.

The biker stood by the rear cab door, clutching Judy in his massive left hand, his tire-tool weapon in his right. "Hold this bitch, Rose," he growled, shoving Judy toward his "old lady," standing slightly behind and to his left.

He turned to Jeremy. "We're gonna be needing your truck, hill-billy. You drive like old people fuck. Me and Rose can make better time if we don't have to stop every ten minutes so the women can make peepee. You and your pretty little wife, those two in the back and their snot-nosed shit machine, you can wait here. We'll keep the two brats for insurance. Once we get clear of this shit storm, we'll send somebody back for you."

Rose dug her fingernails into Judy's arms.

"Let me go, you slut!" Judy growled with no hint of fear.

"Smack her in the face, Snake," Rose screamed. "That'll shut her up."

Brandon and Sophie clambered out the back of the truck, alarm on their faces. Brandon crouched behind the tailgate, a few feet behind Snake, and motioned for Sophie to get back.

Ellis and Fiona pressed their faces to the window, clearly terri-fied.

"Take your bitch and get over there," Snake barked at Jeremy. "Brandon from Minnesota, get your little larva outta the truck and go stand with these two. We'll add Miss Sophie to our insurance policy. Go! I ain't got all day."

Brandon glared at Snake and clenched his fists.

Judy twisted violently to her right, shot her left arm forward, then slammed her elbow back straight into the bridge of Rose's nose. With a soft, almost inaudible crunch, blood gushed down the biker chick's face.

"I'll murder you, bitch!" Rose screamed, cupping her hand over her now oddly angled nose.

Snake raised his right hand up and across his chest, clearly preparing to smash Judy's face with the tire iron.

At the same time, Jeremy pulled the .357 out of its holster and, in one smooth, well-practiced move, cocked the hammer back, pointed the pistol toward Snake's stomach, and pulled the trigger.

The explosion was deafening.

One hundred fifty pellets burst out of the gun's two-inch barrel and burned their way into the flesh in a pie-plate-sized pattern around Snake's navel. The combination of the pistol's short barrel, the low-mass birdshot, and the distance between Jeremy and Snake kept the pellets from penetrating more than an inch into his fleshy belly.

Snake screamed like a banshee. He dropped the tire iron and fell to the ground, clutching his stomach. Rose cupped her hand over her still-bleeding nose and knelt on one knee beside him, placing her free hand on his shoulder. "You didn't have to shoot him!" she cried.

"Brandon, you and Sophie get in the back seat with the twins," Jeremy ordered. "We're leaving now." He opened the passenger door and ushered a still-steaming Judy inside.

"What about us? You can't leave us here. We'll suffocate in this stuff!" Rose wailed. Then, standing up, she started for the truck. "Take me with you."

Jeremy got behind the wheel, put the truck in gear, and started driving. Sophie, Brandon, and the twins looked out the rear window and watched as Rose stumbled forward a few feet, then stopped and started back toward Snake.

"Wow! Dad popped a cap in his ass," Ellis whispered to Fiona.

"Those idiots," Judy fumed. She twisted around, facing the twins for a second, then turned back around and stared out the windshield. "Yes. Yes, he did."

30

The White House
Two years before the day of

President Sheppard stared through the windows behind his desk in the Oval Office, lost in thought.

"Ready, sir?" Press Secretary Preston asked.

President Sheppard turned and nodded. Then he, Vice President Phillips, and the chief of staff followed the press secretary out the rear door of the Oval Office, turned left, and walked along the West Colonnade to the entrance to the White House Rose Garden.

Despite scant advance notice, the chairs on the lawn's briefing area were packed with cellphone-wielding reporters, and in the back and along each side, cameramen. There was literally standing room only.

The press secretary walked through the double doors first, took two steps, stopped, and stood at semiattention, then announced, "Ladies and gentlemen, the President of the United States."

The crowd rose as the press secretary moved to the left, the vice president to the right. The president stepped to the lectern in the center, empty-handed, his face uncharacteristically grim. "Please, take your seats," he said brusquely.

As the press members took their seats, President Sheppard grasped the lectern with both hands. He took a deep, audible breath and looked slowly from his left to his right at those sitting in the front row. "My fellow Americans, I know today's press conference comes without a lot of notice and even less fanfare. That was my intent, the reasons for which you will learn in the next few minutes.

"The information I must share with you today came the same way to me, as a total and complete surprise. Only my wife and five other people are aware of what I'm going to announce. Not my chief of staff, not Vice President Phillips, and not the news agencies that are broadcasting this conference.

"You, the American people, the people who put me in office, deserve to be the first to know. And you deserve to hear it straight from the source. Unfiltered, without political commentary, and without pulling any punches."

Silence. Almost as one, the crowd stopped taking notes and focused on the POTUS.

"Actually, I have two announcements. I've been struggling over when and how to make the second ever since I learned of the first. I made the decision to announce both literally the second I stepped in front of the camera and looked, figuratively speaking, at three hundred million American citizens."

The president straightened his stance, tightened his grip on the lectern, and gazed across the crowd of anxious reporters. "First, and perhaps the least important of the two. Last week, I learned that I have stage-four pancreatic cancer."

The room erupted into a cacophony of shocked murmurs and clicking cellphone cameras. Anticipating this reaction, the POTUS paused for a few seconds. Then he raised his hands in a nonverbal request for silence.

"This is a particularly virulent strain of cancer. Mine is totally incurable. In fact, it has advanced to the point that it is untreatable. I have, at best, only a few weeks to live."

Stunned silence, stifled gasps, and welling eyes swept across the press corps and most of the administrative staff.

The vice president showed no emotion.

"On July 4, 1939, Lou Gehrig, perhaps the greatest first baseman to have ever played the game, addressed a sold-out crowd in Yankee Stadium. There is no way I can better convey what I feel than by quoting the Iron Horse.

"Lou had been diagnosed with amyotrophic lateral sclerosis, ALS, or, as it came to be known, Lou Gehrig's disease, a horribly destructive, incurable disorder that is always fatal. His condition had been front-page news. On that day, standing behind a microphone that had been set up near the pitcher's mound, Lou, ever a pillar of strength and courage, addressed the crowd with these words: 'Fans, for the past two weeks you have been reading about the bad break I got. Yet today I consider myself the luckiest man on the face of this earth.' He went on to heap praise on his parents, his teammates, his wife, and even his bitter rivals, the New York Giants. Then he ended his illustrious career and brought tears to the eyes of everyone in the stadium when he stated, 'So I close in saying that I may have had a tough break, but I have an awful lot to live for.'

"That about sums up my first and, as I said, the least important announcement. I'm dying. We're all going to die. But I'm here to tell you that, like Lou Gehrig, I'll be going out as the luckiest man on earth. So today I'm announcing my resignation as the president of the United States of America. My term of office will officially end at midnight tomorrow."

There was complete silence, but only for a heartbeat. Then pandemonium broke loose. Hands shot into the air, and an unorchestrated chorus of questions erupted.

Again, the president raised his hands, asking for silence. "As I said, ladies and gentlemen, I have a second announcement to make, and in my opinion, it is the most important of the two. I would ask that you hold your questions until the end. I don't want to bog us down in a Q and A just yet.

"As most of you know, last Thursday I received a letter of resignation from our secretary of state, David Stakley. David and I have been close friends for several years. He has done an absolutely remarkable job as secretary of state, and I've grown to respect and admire him in that role. His resignation took this nation's political leadership totally by surprise and will leave a gaping hole in the State Department and our diplomatic mission.

"What you don't know is that David's letter also stated his intention to run for this office in the next general election."

Once again, an audible gasp swept over the Rose Garden. The packed crowd of reporters stood up almost in unison. Hands shot into the air, signaling a tsunami of questions.

But the POTUS continued: "There is some logic behind my decision to combine these two announcements. Part of it is to downplay the significance of my own resignation. Mostly, however, it is to publically announce my unequivocal support for David Stakley as your next president of the United States of America."

31

The White House
Monday afternoon, two years before the day of

IT WAS AMAZING. In less time than it took for the president to respond to his press secretary's prescribed ten postbriefing questions and to walk back into the West Wing, the world knew. Every major television news channel across the planet and millions of internet pop-up apps exploded.

"We interrupt this broadcast to bring you this breaking headline. The president of the United States has announced that, due to the sudden onset of a terminal illness, he is resigning from office effective midnight tomorrow. Stay tuned for our special report on this and related details."

After several minutes of news reporter chaos, President Sheppard had stepped back from the lectern and relinquished control to his press secretary, signaling the end of the briefing. The president and his entourage had then walked back through the double doors and into the West Wing corridor leading to the president's secretary's office.

"Gentlemen," the POTUS began, "I know your heads are exploding with questions, and we can block out time to meet this afternoon and discuss. However, right now I have another task that requires my immediate attention. Lizbeth will set up a meeting with each of you within the hour." Without waiting for a response, the president turned and walked toward the secretary's entrance to the Oval Office. "Lizbeth, could you step in here for a second?"

She quickly rose from her chair and followed him, closing the door behind her.

"Well, Lizbeth, I guess that's one way to start a Monday." The president slowly eased into the leather chair behind his aircraft-sized desk.

"Mr. President, I simply don't know what to say. I'm shocked, I'm sad, and I'm stunned. On the other hand, that was the most spiritually uplifting resignation speech I've ever heard."

"Thank you, Lizbeth, but in the words of Robert Frost, I have 'miles to go before I sleep.' And I'm going to need your help on those last few miles. Let's start by getting Senator Mia Lopez on the phone. If she's in session or otherwise can't talk, you can schedule for later, but I need to speak with her today."

"Yes, Mr. President." Lizbeth started back to her office, then turned to face the POTUS. With her eyes brimming, she blurted, "I'll say it one more time, then you won't hear it again from me: I am so very sorry. It has been and will always be an honor to serve you. Now let me run Senator Lopez down for you."

As she walked away, the president said, "Thank you, Lizbeth. It is I who is honored to have you on my staff."

When she closed the door, President Sheppard swiveled his chair to face the small wooden table sitting in front of the window behind his desk.

Four framed photos adorned one side of the table. One frame held a picture of him and his wife taken years ago during a visit to Glacier National Park. Although bundled in a dazzling white ski suit, she was radiant, outshining even the surrounding ice pack. Another photo was of his oldest son standing proud in his army dress blues. It was taken after he had graduated from his Officer Advanced Course, one month before he shipped out with his company to help quell the conflict that had just started in Iran. The president picked up the frame and gazed wistfully at his son's photo. A lump rose in his throat.

"Mr. President," Lizbeth said over the intercom, "I have Senator Lopez on line one."

Sheppard turned away from the photo and cleared his throat. He picked up the receiver. "Senator Lopez, thank you for taking my call. I hope I'm not interrupting anything too terribly important."

"Not at all, Mr. President. Actually, it's a welcome reprieve from an office full of drug manufacturer lobbyists. Besides, it's an honor to hear from you. I've never had the president of the United States call little ol' me before."

Sheppard chuckled. "Their loss, Mia. I have a matter of quite some importance that I want you to consider. Can I assume that you either saw or heard about my announcements today?"

"Mr. President, I can't tell you how sorry I am to learn of your cancer. It breaks my heart. I feel for you, your family, and, most of all, for our country. But in answer to your question: yes, sir. My news app has been pretty much exploding all morning. I actually had to turn the buzzer off so I could get through a staff meeting. Of course, everyone else's were going off. It sounded like springtime in a den of Texas rattlesnakes."

"Thank you, Mia. I would have my press secretary sign you up to deliver my eulogy," the POTUS quipped, "except I intend to leave instructions to have a very private, family-only ceremony.

"The reason I'm calling has to do with David Stakley. As you know, he has resigned his position as secretary of state and has declared his intention to run for this office in the next election. He will run on what will be a revitalized Centrist Party ticket. You also know he has my total and complete support. Hell, he would have my vote, too, except I won't be around to cast it.

"What hasn't been announced is that David has the support of an influential group of politically active philanthropists. I'm sure you are familiar with Envision-2100, especially since several of their more notable members hail from the Lone Star State." The president leaned forward, placing his elbow on the table, anticipating what he knew would be the senator's response.

"Yes, sir, I'm very familiar with Envision-2100. They've always been relatively low-key, from what I've seen. But I know for a fact that they have privately funded several help-those-who-help-themselves educational and employment initiatives in Texas and elsewhere. They call it Bootstrap."

"That's right, Mia. And Bootstrap is just one of their give-back-to-the-people programs. I mention Envision-2100 because I wanted you to know that the Stakley campaign won't be forced to spend a lot of time and effort on fundraising. Not only has Envision-2100 pledged their financial and political support, they actually actively recruited David to run for office."

"I'm getting the picture, Mr. President. I know Secretary Stakley, although not on a personal level, and like most Americans, I'm keenly aware of his diplomatic success in dealing with the situation in what was North Korea. I've also been extremely impressed with him in his role as SecState. Finally, based on what you're telling me, which of course I did not know, it sounds like he is coming into the arena with a commanding financial and, given your announcement, political support base.

"What I'm not seeing, Mr. President, is how any of this entitles me to a personal phone call from you less than an hour after what is without a doubt the most important day in your career. How could I possibly deserve that level of attention?"

"That's one of the things I admire about you, Senator Lopez. No pussyfooting around. You cut right to the chase. The reason I called, and the reason I called so urgently, is that David, myself, and the entire board of Envision-2100 would like for you, Mia Lopez, to be the next vice president of the United States."

The POTUS paused to let his words sink in.

Finally Mia broke the silence: "Mr. President, I don't know what to say. Talk about a surprise. This morning, like any other morning, I get up, have a cup of coffee, eat a muffin, go to the office. Then an hour later find out that our president has terminal cancer, is resigning from office, and wants me to run for vice president in a campaign whose existence I only learned about three days ago. Are you kidding me? Hell yes, I'll run!"

President Sheppard chuckled, charmed by the senator's candor and sharp-tongued Texas wit.

"Actually, sir," Senator Lopez continued, "I need to recover my composure and let this sink in before I commit to getting on a horse I can't ride. I hope you weren't expecting an answer this morning."

"Not at all, Mia. Take as much time as you need, as long as you don't need much time."

The POTUS pleased himself with his own jocularity, especially given the gravity of the time and situation. "David will be calling to ask you himself as soon as I let him know we've talked. I wanted to be the first to reach out to you, if for no other reason than to assure you first-hand that David's campaign will have my unconditional endorsement. I'll call him as soon as we hang up. I suspect you will hear from him before lunch, so give some prayerful consideration to this offer, Mia."

"Thank you, Mr. President. Believe me, I will."

"No, thank you, Senator. I hope to talk to you again soon. Goodbye."

The president hung up the phone and turned again to face the four photos on the table behind him. He picked up one of his son. "Well, son, it won't be long before I see you again. I've missed you so much. I love you, Matthew."

He set the frame back down on the table, swiveled his chair around, grabbed his telephone, and punched in David Stakley's mobile number. He could have used the digital assistant that was now incorporated into his desk phone, but something about that disembodied, soulless voice gave him the creeps. Besides, despite the NSA's assurances to the contrary, he wasn't totally sure that someone deep in the bowels of Fort Meade wasn't listening to his conversations when he used that robotic bitch.

Stakley answered on the second ring. "Good morning, Mr. President. I just saw the clip of your announcement. It was exceptionally moving, sir. Of course, it's all over the news channels now. You caught the pundits off guard, so now they're all over the board with their post-briefing analyses. How did the vice president take it?"

"I haven't talked to him yet, David. I promised I'd meet with him later today, but first I wanted to get back to my office and call Mia Lopez. I just got off the phone with her. As you might imagine, she seemed surprised. And if I read the inflections in her voice correctly, she was more than a little flattered. I didn't press her for an answer. I told her to think the offer over and that she should look for your call later today. Actually, I told her to expect a call before lunch."

"That will happen as soon as I hang up the phone," David replied. "I know you don't like for someone to gush, but let me say one last time how much I appreciate everything you've done for me over the years. And that's a long list, Mr. President. Thank you."

"It was my pleasure, David. I appreciate the level of professionalism you have displayed before and after becoming SecState. I am equally appreciative of your devotion and loyalty. I know a lot of people don't hold those traits in such high esteem these days, but, believe me, I do. I better let you go so you can take care of lining up your running mate. Good luck, and let me know how things go.

"Oh, and, David, don't hesitate to let me know if there's anything within my power that I can do to help you succeed with what lies before you. Now I can't put it off any longer; I have to meet with Jim Phillips and let him tell me what a turncoat asshole I am. Talk to you later."

The president gently placed the phone back in its cradle, took a deep breath, and, with a sigh, pushed himself off his chair.

Before he had fully straightened, his heart stopped beating.

The most powerful person on earth saw a blinding flash of light, and then everything went black.

Lizbeth found him an hour later, swallowed up in his huge leather chair, a faint smile etched forever on his face.

32

US Route 191 approximately ten miles north of Jackson Hole
The day after the day of

JEREMY HAD BEEN INCHING the F-250 forward at an agonizingly slow pace for over five hours, stopping every hour to change out the cloth he was using to cover the truck's air filter. Each time, he was amazed that the engine was able to keep running, yet it did, despite over an inch of gunk caked around the air intake. The F-250 just kept bulldozing its way forward.

Finally, the ever-growing blanket of ash was too much. Even in four-wheel drive, and with the transmission in low, the truck could not push forward. It ground to a stop approximately half a mile past a road sign indicating the Craig Thomas Visitor Center was located to their west.

"I'm afraid this is the end of the line, folks," Jeremy announced. "Unless someone has a better suggestion, we have to hole up here and wait for the National Guard or the Park Service or someone to rescue us."

From the center of the back seat, Sophie, who was cradling Hunter in her lap, spoke up. "We might as well face the facts: there's a real good chance we could be trapped here for days, maybe longer."

Brandon, sitting to Sophie's right, on the passenger side, added, "I agree. The situation is what it is. It would be best for us to plan for the worst and hope for the best."

Jeremy looked at Fiona, sitting on the driver's side of the back seat, through his rearview mirror and then at Ellis sitting between him and Judy. Their eyes welled up in apprehension and accumulating fear.

Judy glanced at the twins with concern. "OK, folks, everyone gets out of the truck and into the Airstream. We can take stock of our situation and come up with some sort of action plan. This stuff will stop falling eventually, and we just have to ride it out until it does."

Judy pulled her makeshift mask over her mouth and nose and reached for the truck door. "Give me a few seconds to unlock the Airstream, and then everyone can come inside. But put on your mask first and keep it on until you get inside." She closed the door and started toward the RV.

"Jeremy, are you concerned that Snake might find us while we're stopped?" Brandon asked as he wrapped a towel around his face.

"Sure, that thought crossed my mind as soon as we ground to a halt. Just one more thing on my list of shit to worry about, but I've got five more rounds in my three fifty-seven, and four of them aren't birdshot. Plus, even if he feels like walking, he and his hog of a girlfriend will have to slug through a good ten miles of volcano dirt to reach us. We'll deal with that if it happens. Our first order of business is to assess the mess we're in and how we're going to survive as a group until someone shows up to dig us out. Now, let's go see if Judy has things all cozy for us."

Jeremy stepped out of the truck and helped Fiona out of the back seat as Brandon, Sophie, and Hunter crawled out the passenger side. Trudging through a foot of ash, they made their way back to the Airstream and, as Judy held the door open as little as possible, went inside.

Judy, Sophie, and Brandon wedged themselves onto the couch. Ellis and Fiona took a squirming Hunter and plopped onto one of the twin beds at the back of the camper. All seemed to feel a sense of relief at getting out of the truck. Among the adults there was also a sense of dread that this might not be the worst to come.

From the rear of the RV, Fiona consoled a whining Hunter. "Don't be scared, little man," she said. "Our dad has things under control."

"Yuck!" Ellis pointed at Hunter's diaper. "He's not scared. The kid needs an oil change."

Both twins burst out laughing. Sophie wiggled out from between Judy and Brandon and changed Hunter's diaper.

Jeremy took a small folding chair from its storage space next to the door, opened it up, and sat down between the stove and refrigerator, facing the couch. "I think we all knew it was only a matter of time before we were forced to stop. I was hoping we would either run out from under the ash cloud or make it into Jackson Hole first. But that didn't pan out, and here we are. Like it or not, we're stuck here until emergency responders find us."

"That could be days from now," Sophie noted. She held up Hunter's neatly folded dirty diaper. "In the meantime, what do I do with this?"

"That's a good question, Sophie. We've got a stash of bags below the sink. For now, just wrap it up in one of those, and we can bury it outside later. We need to make a field latrine anyway, and that can be our first deposit. But that brings up a housekeeping point. Since we don't know how long we'll be holed up here, you need to think about diaper substitutes, unless you've got a lot more in your bag than I suspect you have."

"You're right." Judy turned to the twins. "Ladies, grab a spare sheet out of the cabinet over the bed and start making some old-fashioned diapers. It's time to get back to the basics."

Sensing a break in the discussion, Jeremy picked up where he had left off: "It would be suicide for any of us to try to hike out of here. Hell, it was hard enough just to walk from the truck back here. Maybe if we had snowshoes and could see more than a hundred feet. But right now, we don't and we can't. I've been thinking about what we'd need to do when we got to where we are now. Let's assume the worst-case scenario, that we'll be stuck here for ten days or longer. We've got thirty gallons of fresh water in the holding tank, and the Snake River should be less than one hundred meters west of here. That should be enough.

"The refrigerator is designed to run on propane and a trickle of current from our storage batteries for a while. I don't know for exactly how long. There are eggs, sandwich meat, frozen hamburger patties, and hot dogs in the fridge. There's also a little milk. We should have enough to last for several days if we ration. We should eat cold food first. We'll save the milk for Hunter. We have two tanks of propane that are almost full. Even accounting for the fridge and stove, that should last for weeks. The Airstream has two twelve-volt storage batteries that are charged when the truck engine is running or by its roof-mounted solar panel.

"Now herein lies a problem. The solar panel is covered with ash. Who knows how much? Somehow, we have to get up there with a broom and sweep it off every few hours. Even then, there won't be enough sunlight penetrating the cloud to generate much more than a trickle charge. Still, we have to try. Worst case, we start the truck every few hours and let it charge the batteries. Since we've driven less than forty miles and at less than twenty miles an hour, the gas tank should be almost full."

"Dad," Ellis blurted, "if you took the screen off the inside of the skylight, Fiona or I could open the cover, crawl up through the opening, and get on the roof, then use the broom to sweep it off like you said."

Jeremy turned to face his daughters crouched on the bed, leaning into the conversation. "That's a great idea, Ellis. I'm sure your mother doesn't relish the thought of you getting up on the roof, but I'm afraid we don't have many other options. And even your mom is too big to get through the opening." He shrugged at Judy apologetically. "No offense, honey."

Judy playfully punched his shoulder and fired back, "None taken, Foul Ball. But I'm adding that comment to the list."

"Now back to my survival assessment," Jeremy said. "We've got camp food—Spam, canned tuna, pork and beans, and my personal favorite, corned beef hash. We also have a couple loaves of bread, chips, and a relatively large bag of rice. The bottom line is that, even though there are seven of us, with a reasonable amount of discipline we should be able to survive for quite some time. So, unless someone has a better idea, I'm going to ask Judy and Sophie to take charge of our food and water supply."

Sophie waved her hand in the air. "Speaking of water, I suggest everyone take advantage of the great outdoors when you have to use the bathroom. Those chemical toilets are convenient, but they get down-right nasty if you don't flush them every time. And when you do, there goes our freshwater supply."

Jeremy gave Sophie a thumbs-up. "That's a good point, Sophie, and it reminds me to mention that when you do need water, you will need to turn on the pump. There is an on-off switch above the stove. The pump runs off our storage battery. There are also lights next to the switch. They indicate the level of charge on our batteries and how much water is left in the freshwater tank. We need to check this a couple of times a day, and if the battery level indicator turns yellow, we'll have to sweep off the solar panel or run the truck's engine long enough to charge everything.

"Last but not least, we need to talk about security. One adult needs to be in the front seat of the truck at all times to keep an eye out for rescue parties. It would really ruin my day to think that a ranger or a sheriff's deputy drove by looking for survivors and missed seeing us. And in this stuff, that could happen.

"I think we need to pull watch from six a.m. until around six p.m. each day, in the daylight. With these conditions, I don't foresee search parties out after dark. They won't want to lose any of their own people looking for survivors who may or may not exist. That means each one of the five of us will be responsible for manning the cab for three hours a day. Three hours is a pretty long time to sit and stay alert, so I suggest we take one-and-a-half-hour shifts. Any objections?"

"I don't have any objections," Brandon said. "That's a good plan. Actually, everything you've said makes good survival sense. I would also recommend that whoever is on watch have your pistol readily available. I'm not too worried about that psycho finding us, but stranger things have happened. And he and his girlfriend will be pissed, big time."

"Good idea, Brandon. Will you and Sophie be able to use a gun if push comes to shove?" Jeremy asked.

"We don't have a problem at all," Sophie replied. "You didn't ask, and we didn't volunteer any personal information about ourselves, but there are a couple of things you should know. Brandon is a detective in the Duluth PD, and I'm an assistant DA. We met when I was leading the prosecution on a murder trial. Brandon had arrested the suspect, and I was interviewing him as the arresting officer in preparation for court. So the answer to your question is an unqualified yes.

"Brandon typically has a sidearm on his hip except when he's in the shower. And in my business, with the objects of my affection, I always have one within arm's reach. With that said, I'll volunteer for the first shift. It's right at the hour, so the three of you can decide among yourselves who will be next in the barrel and come relieve me when the time comes."

Sophie stood up, pulled her makeshift mask back over her nose and mouth, and, still holding Hunter in one arm, started for the Airstream's door.

Brandon's eyes followed his wife. "Soph, if you see anything or need to get our attention, just get down on that horn, and we'll come running."

"Will do. I'll give it short blasts if there is some kind of danger and long ones if I see a rescue party. Now I'm outta here. I'll see one of you in an hour and a half."

With that, Sophie handed Hunter to Brandon, gave each of them a kiss, took the pistol from Jeremy, and went out the door.

33

Washington, DC
Tuesday morning, two years before the day of

The World Is Stunned, Then Saddened by the News from the White House.

That headline and hundreds just like it adorned the front page of newspapers across the nation and around the world on Tuesday morning.

As the new POTUS, Jim Phillips sat behind his desk in the Oval Office with his secure phone pressed to his ear, complaining to the caller on the other end. He angrily tossed his copy of the *Washington Post* to the floor.

First, President Matt Sheppard had announced that he had been diagnosed with terminal cancer, then he shared his resignation as POTUS, and then, in his most profound declaration, he let it be known that he endorsed David Stakley, not his VP, Jim Phillips, in the upcoming presidential election.

Finally, less than two hours following these precedent-shattering proclamations, the president was found dead, the victim of a massive myocardial infarction. All of this in one day, a day already being called Gray Monday.

Complete and utter chaos consumed the White House.

In a hastily convened ceremony that had taken place at nine o'clock the previous night in the Diplomatic Reception Room of the White House, Vice President Jim Phillips had been sworn in as president of the United States by the chief justice of the Supreme Court. It was a struggle to put on his game face and appear to mourn the loss of President Sheppard throughout the proceedings.

Internally he was seething. Thoughts of revenge raged through his mind as he spoke in somber tones with a wistful, melancholy expression plastered on his face. If nothing else, he was a master of deceit, a trait for which he was well known and which, among his opponents, had garnered him the nickname "Smoke and Mirrors" Phillips.

Now, Phillips spoke into his phone with a hushed voice bubbling with hatred.

"That deceitful son of a bitch stabbed me square in the back. Sheppard didn't say a word about being sick, much less terminal. And adding insult to injury, he pledged his support to that dipshit Stakley. Somebody on this staff knew what was going on, and, by God, I'm going to find out who they are and make their lives miserable."

On the other end of the line, a male voice spoke with a heavy Brooklyn accent: "Just gimme the word, Mr. President; he'll never see it coming. But we need to move fast. Now that he's an official candidate, the Secret Service will be crawling around him like ants at a picnic. What do you want we should do?"

"Nothing just yet. I don't want the guy whacked. That'll just make him a martyr. Better to find a way to make him drop out of the race. I'll circle back with you between now and this time tomorrow.

"In the meantime, put a tail on him and his wife, but back off if you see the boys in black Tahoes snooping around. I don't want to do anything that even appears to be threatening. Keep your burner phone within reach and go somewhere secluded for the next twenty-four hours. We don't want anyone overhearing even a snippet of our conversation."

"Will do, Mr. President. I'll be waiting on your call."

After that phone call, the new POTUS met with his chief of staff over breakfast to begin discussing plans for President Sheppard's funeral and President Phillips's transition into the office of chief executive.

"Mr. President," the chief of staff asked, smoothing her hair, "I know we are all still in shock, but have you given any consideration to who you might nominate as vice president? You know, of course, that your nominee must be confirmed by a majority of both houses of Congress."

"Yes, I know, and that is one of the reasons I don't plan to nominate anyone, at least not now. I've got to focus all of our energy and resources on the next election. It's too close to stir up the shit-slinging pot and make any more enemies than I already have by chasing after someone to fill a do-nothing job.

"I'll let a name for the new VP come out of the national convention process," Phillips continued. "It's just around the corner. If something happens to me, the constitutional order of succession takes over, and the Speaker of the House takes the reins just as fast as I did when Sheppard checked out. This 'let the pot simmer' strategy was set before you or I were even born. Between the assassination of JFK on November 22, 1963, and January 20, 1965, President Johnson didn't have a VP. Say what you like about that old crook, he was a politician's politician.

"I want you to focus on arranging Sheppard's funeral. Once we get him in the ground and an appropriate number of days of mourning have passed, we'll throw ourselves into the business of getting me formally elected as the next POTUS. This succession thing is all well and good, but you know, it's just not the same.

"Oh, and get your little staffer monkeys started on some emotional, heartfelt words for Sheppard's funeral. And start drafting my acceptance speech for the national convention. I want tears and cheers, respectively. Now, let's get to work." President Phillips pushed back his chair, not giving the CoS time to finish her breakfast.

"Yes, Mr. President, I'm on it," the CoS replied. A look of distaste flickered across her face.

Bitch, Phillips thought. He'd replace her ass as soon as he could get his head above water.

An hour later, President Phillips's intercom buzzed. "Yes, Lizbeth." The POTUS swiveled around in his chair, the one he'd had delivered from his old office this morning. He wasn't about to conduct business from Sheppard's stool.

"Mr. President, the chief of staff is on line one."

Picking up the handset from his desk, President Phillips snapped, "Let me guess: you have questions about the eulogy I need to deliver."

"No, sir, I don't have any questions, but I do have news. I just spoke with President Sheppard's wife. She says there won't be a funeral. According to her, he didn't want one. And he didn't want to be buried in Arlington. His last wishes were that he be cremated and his ashes, along with those of his son Matthew, be scattered over Bodega Bay by his wife, his two sons, David and Kelly Stakley, and some minister friend of the family. No public ceremony, no fanfare, and absolutely no news coverage whatsoever.

"I tried to reason with her and suggested a public remembrance ceremony of some kind. But she was adamant, and fiercely so. She flat-out refused to discuss any other options."

"What's your take? Would it help if I called her?"

"No, sir. In fact, it would inflame her. I don't know what's going on, but she was verging on hostile when I tried to discuss other options. I've never seen her like this."

Phillips slammed the phone down. "Shit!" The guy was dead and still managing to stiff-arm him.

34

"**Senator Lopez's office.** This is Tammy. How may I direct your call?"

"Tammy, this is David Stakley. I believe Senator Lopez is expecting my call."

"Yes, sir, she is. If you hold for just a second, I'll let her know you're on the line."

"Thank you, Tammy. I'll hold."

Seconds later, a firm, feminine voice with a hint of Texas twang purred in David's ear.

"Good morning, Mr. Secretary, rather, David. Or, better yet, Mr. President. With everything that has happened the last few days, I'm not sure what to call you."

Laughter burst in David's ear. He smiled and spun his chair to face the window. "If it's OK with you, Senator, let's go with 'David' and 'Mia,' respectively. I just spoke with President Sheppard, and he told me I'd better call you before you changed your mind about hitching on to my wagon. I've always respected his council and decided it would behoove me to continue that trend and to call and make things official."

"I'm thrilled and excited, but pretty darn apprehensive," Mia responded.

"Well, Senator, let's make it official. I would be honored if you would join me—no, partner with me—in my bid for the presidency. I know you have a lot going on with that healthcare bill, but quite frankly, I think you would have a more significant impact at the executive level."

"You don't have to sell me, David. President Sheppard has already plowed that ground. From what he told me about Envision-2100's support, we wouldn't be spinning our wheels scraping for funding. We could actually focus on policy development and communicating our vision to America. I'm ready, David, and if you tell me this is the official green light, I'll prepare my own announcement. I don't know how much more news this town can take, but we might as well push the limit."

"The green flag has officially dropped, Mia. As of this minute, on this day, the race is on. Our next step will be a kick-off meeting with Envision-2100 leadership and the campaign team they have already started to assemble. Milt Freeman has been designated as the point man and will most likely assume the role of campaign manager. He's a brilliant tactician and political strategist. Plus, he and others in that group have already done a lot of work on what will become the Centrist Party foundation and our campaign platform. You and I just need to grind the burrs off and sell it to the voting public."

As they were speaking, Tammy's voice rose in the background: "Senator, forgive me for interrupting, but I thought you would want me to, especially since you're talking to Secretary Stakley. We just received a security alert. The Secret Service announced that President Sheppard passed away. Apparently, his assistant found him less than an hour ago. They haven't officially announced it to the public yet, but that will happen any minute now."

"Oh my God, David, did you hear that?" Mia asked.

Although he had been mentally preparing himself for the inevitable, Tammy's announcement stunned David. Like a boxer expecting a short left jab but then getting nailed by an uppercut from the right.

"David?"

"Yes, I heard." David paused to let his emotions settle. "After our meeting last week, I guess deep down inside, I knew it was imminent. That doesn't numb the shock the least bit. We have a lot more to discuss, but I think it best we press the pause button for now. I suspect the hoard of press locusts will be descending soon, and I need to cobble up a statement.

"I suggest you hold off on your announcement until after the dust settles from this latest event, not to trivialize anything by using such a casual term. But President Sheppard knew it was coming, and he was at peace with the eventuality. We don't want your decision to be lost in a news aftershock. I'll circle back to you before the end of the week, and we can pick up where we left off.

"I don't want to sound like some heartless opportunist, but we need to capitalize on the president's and my relationship and his pledge of support. And we need to do so before Phillips starts dumping his poison in the well. The fuse is burning, Mia. I'll call you in a day or two. You and I need to meet with the Envision-2100 team and start hammering out the platform I mentioned. I'll ask Milt to round up the team, and we can meet at their Maryland Shangri-La. If you aren't busy the night before, you can have dinner with Kelly and me and stay the night at our house. We can get to know one another on a more personal basis. I'll arrange our transportation the next morning. Trust me, you'll be surprised and impressed."

"That sounds like a plan, David," Mia said. "I'll take your advice and hold off on my own announcement until we have our first strategy session with Milt and Company. Just say when on dinner and the sleepover. There is nothing on my calendar that can't be delayed until after the governor appoints my replacement."

"OK, Vice President Lopez, I'll call you in a couple of days."

David eased the phone into its cradle, then leaned back in his chair, momentarily gazing but not seeing. His thoughts roared across his consciousness until, a heartbeat later, he got them and his physical self under control.

That evening, as David and Kelly sat in their living room watching CNN, President Sheppard's wife called.

The caller ID flashed ******0000, which David knew was an unspoofable mask to disguise the POTUS's personal number.

Jim Phillips's code would have been 0001, indicating his relative position in the line of succession to the office of president. Up until last week, David's mask had been 0004. In a rare display of compassion, Phillips had not directed that his mask be changed the minute he found out the POTUS had died.

Seeing David's expression change from curiosity to concern, Kelly grabbed the remote and muted the TV.

"David Stakley. Nancy, is that you?"

"Yes, David, it's me."

David detected a slight quiver in her voice.

"As you can imagine, we are all in a state of shock. Thank heavens my secretary is here with us. Condolences have been pouring in, but I'm in no mood, nor state of mind, to deal with an endless barrage of phone calls. Not right now. I did take a call from Matt's chief of staff earlier today. She offered to help with funeral arrangements and burial at Arlington. I'm sure Jim Phillips directed her to do so. I mean, David, Matt's body is still at Walter Reed, and the man is pressuring me to start making funeral arrangements.

"You know, they wanted to do an autopsy to rule out foul play. I said absolutely not. The man had terminal cancer. I refused to let some slice-happy pathologist make a name for himself by dissecting my husband. Matt had directed that his vital organs be donated, but by the time Lizbeth found him and medics responded, it was too late for that. You know organs have to be harvested quickly once the heart stops beating or they become unusable for transplant."

The First Lady was starting to ramble, most likely the result of a combination of shock and sedatives. David let her do so. During times of intense grief, it was good therapy. He remembered an old saying, "Grief shared is grief diminished."

"Nancy, I know it sounds a little trite, but I am so very, very sorry. Kelly and I are still in shock. You know that if there is anything either of us can do to help you get through this, all you have to do is ask."

"Well, David, there is something. When our son Matthew was killed in Iran, Matt decided that he wanted to be cremated and for his and Matthew's ashes to be scattered over Bodega Bay. This is way out of the norm for a president, or for a vice president, for that matter. In fact, Nelson Rockefeller is the only one who has ever been cremated. And Matt demanded that he not have a funeral.

"I think something snapped inside him when Matthew was killed. But that doesn't matter. I intend to carry out his wishes, and that is precisely what I told the chief of staff to pass along to Jim Phillips. We are having a private celebration of Matt's life. Just me, my two sons, and Judson Ballard. Matt also wanted you and Kelly to be there, if that's not too much to ask. Matt spelled his request out very explicitly in his will. My husband treasured the friendships he had with you and Judson."

"I know, Nancy. I've lost a friend. And a mentor. But even more than that, our country has lost a truly remarkable leader. Matt was a good man."

"Thank you, David. That means a lot to me. Not just because your words are so poetic. It's because they're sincere. I know you are unbelievably busy getting your own campaign kicked off and that Matt's death and his last request is probably catching you unprepared, but if you could somehow find a way to help me get through the next few days, I would be eternally grateful."

"Say no more, Nancy. It will be an honor and a privilege for Kelly and me to be with you and your sons. And you shouldn't feel the least bit guilty about asking. Actually, President Sheppard shared his wishes with me a long time ago in one of our late-night powwows. There was no small amount of Scotch involved, but I committed myself then, and I stand behind that commitment now."

"I appreciate that so much, David. I will have my secretary make the necessary arrangements and accommodations. Judson has pledged to fly us out on his private jet, so we don't have to grovel to Jim Phillips for the use of Air Force One. We'll stay for two nights and then fly back. By then, our personal belongings will have been packed up, we can move back to the ranch, and I can start the next chapter of my life. We all know that's how it's going to be at some point—either me without him or him without me.

"Forgive me. I'm getting all melancholic, and that's the last thing I want or need to be doing. Thank you again, David. This means so much to me. I'll let you get back to what's left of your evening."

35

The Farm
The beginning of the Stakley campaign, eighteen months before the day of

DAVID POURED ANOTHER CUP of coffee at the buffet table and surveyed the conference room on the ground floor of the main building at the Farm. Once, many decades ago, the space had been used for weekly dances, plays, and semiannual balls hosted by the Catoctin Inn's owners. Now, the center of the room held an enormous, round wooden table. The table had a history too, according to Nelson Teal.

Nelson had donated the table. Initially dubbed "King Arthur" by Envision-2100 members and later referred to as merely "Arthur," the table was constructed from two gigantic walnut trees. Nelson had salvaged them from the aftermath of an F5 tornado, which had laid waste to a small city in Benton County, Arkansas. Siloam Springs, his hometown. The trees had been milled for the sole purpose of building the table, which Nelson had designed himself. The wood was shipped to the farm, cut on-site, and then assembled section by section inside the former ballroom. Not a single nail or screw was used in its construction, just wooden dowels and tongue-and-groove joints.

Arthur was built like a ship in a bottle and could never be removed without completely destroying it. The table dripped with symbolism.

David took his mug over to Arthur and slipped into a chair beside Mia. Also sitting around the table were three Envision-2100 board members, Judson, Melissa, and Milt; three members at large; and a small team from the nationally recognized public relations and political consulting firm Watkins & Evans.

A voice-activated microphone was strategically placed in front of each attendee. In addition to slightly amplifying their conversation, the microphones were wirelessly connected to the Farm's computer network and to Microsoft Word and its voice recognition application. As participants spoke, their names and presentations were converted to text and displayed on four seventy-inch monitors, one mounted on each wall of the conference room.

In this manner, the entire verbiage of every meeting was recorded for online access by any Envision-2100 member. This process was at the insistence of David and Milt and part of their open-meeting, full-disclosure campaign strategy.

Milt leaned toward his mic. "I've been nominated to serve as the chairperson for David and Mia's campaign, and in that capacity, I want to officially open up our first strategy session. All proceedings will be recorded, transcribed, and made part of the permanent record.

"We, the Board of Trustees and various nominees from our general membership, have conducted a great deal of preliminary work on our strategy and presidential campaign platform. Each of you received a copy of this effort in advance. I trust you have read it.

"The points covered in that document, and everything we do between now and the time our platform is ratified, will be referred to as a 'clayman.' To grossly paraphrase Yogi Bera, nothing is final until it's final. Over the next couple of days, we'll start reshaping the clayman. Our objective is to have a presentable draft by the end of this weeklong conference. Once we have completed that onerous task, we will begin developing an eight-year strategic plan with associated goals, milestones, and checkpoints. All of this will be presented to the citizens of the United States.

"In the two hundred plus years that our country has been a country, that kind of detailed planning has never been done, much less made publically available. So we will make that one of our plan's initial objectives. Now, before we start getting our hands dirty, I would like to ask David, the next president of the United States—"

Applause thundered around the table. Milt raised his hands and joined the revelry. "David, it looks like the place is on fire."

David grinned and waved. "Thank you, everyone. Thank you."

"I'm going to ask David to kick things off and say a few words about how he wants us to run this campaign. Anything he wants us to do and, equally important, not to do. President Stakley."

Milt swept his hand toward David.

David leaned toward his mic. "Thank you, Milt. I'll share what I suspect I'll frequently be saying over the next several months. As my wife, Kelly, reminds me daily, I'm being given an honor that most people only dream about. I can't put into words what that means to me, so I won't waste our valuable time together by doing so. I will say that I'm both humbled and thrilled by the opportunity. And I will never, ever do anything, at least not intentionally, to bring disgrace upon that honor."

David paused for a couple of heartbeats, then looked directly at Melissa. "Now. Melissa has already made it clear that it is Envision-2100's policy to be open and aboveboard in everything we do. I want to take that a quantum leap further. This will be the most upbeat and positive campaign ever waged in the twenty-first century. It is my plan, my desire, to set the example for how elected, or even nominated, representatives should conduct themselves from this point forward.

"In every ad, every debate, every interview, we will avoid making any, and I mean any, negative comments about our rivals, their party, or anything they did or failed to do in the past. Of course, we'll be forced to highlight the changes we want to bring to our constitution and what has spawned the need to do so. But we will do that from an opportunity, 'set the stage for our future' perspective.

"We will not take the bait if our opponents attack or slander us during debates, in the press, or on social media. And we damn sure won't say anything negative about them. Mia and I have discussed this in detail. Both of us have been sickened by this kind of conduct in the past. The name-calling and mudslinging may have been acceptable, even expected behaviors in the past, but they have no place in my campaign, period.

"And here are a couple of other things that I believe are long overdue. I ask that you keep them in the back of your mind as we begin working on our campaign and expanding upon the work already done by Envision-2100 on the Centrist platform.

"I firmly believe that we need to rein in some of the elitist privileges currently enjoyed by members of Congress. Literally every American I have discussed this with feels the same. For example, members of Congress should receive healthcare under our current Medicare program. Let them enjoy the same coverage as forty-five percent of the population. I'll go into much greater detail on my vision for healthcare coverage later. But I would like to see that as an early-on objective on our strategic plan timeline. Hell, that alone might win us the popular vote.

"I also want us to address term limits. That is touched on in the Envision-2100 clayman, but I want it to be top-of-mind starting today. I'm thinking two six-year terms for the Senate and three two-year terms for the House with a requirement for each to sit out a minimum of one term before being considered for reelection. We can flesh the numbers out once we start getting into the weeds on this. But we need limits.

"Yes, I know: in theory, term limits should come from the ballot box, but we know how effective that has been. Historically, ninety-three percent of incumbents are voted right back into office each election cycle. I would like to think that's because they are doing their job of representation and deserving of such support. But again, history seems to prove otherwise.

"I hope what I just said are the only examples of dictatorial rhetoric I will ever subject you to. However, it had to be said, and sometimes, as Judson has told me on previous occasions, you can't 'church it up.' Now, before I toss the floor back to Milt, I want to allow Mia to add her *dos pesos* to this preamble."

Raucous applause and cheers filled the room.

Mia smiled. "Thank you, David. I'll begin by making a small linguistic correction. That should be *dos centavos* rather than *dos pesos*. Although if we include the effects of Mexican and US inflation, your example may be more accurate. I won't add a great deal to what David has said as it relates to establishing the foundation of our political agenda. There may be a few things that we see differently, but after hours of spirited discussion, I'll be darned if I know what they are. I'll make a note of two things I would ask that you keep in mind beginning with today's discussions and planning—and forevermore, as far as that goes.

"First, I made it crystal clear when I agreed to be David's running mate that I expect the position of vice president to be more than a political potted plant. In the past, the VP has served as little more than window dressing for the president, occasionally casting a tiebreaker vote in the Senate. That has not been my way of doing business, nor will it be when we are elected. I plan to be heavily involved in policymaking.

"Years ago, President George W. Bush asked Dick Cheney to become his running mate. Cheney made the same demand. He performed more like a chief operating officer than a second-in-command figurehead. That was my request, and David has agreed.

"By the way, since 1789, there have been two hundred sixty-eight of them—tie-breaking votes, that is."

Appreciative laughter rippled across the room.

David smiled and nodded. "Mia said that I agreed. She should have said that I *wholeheartedly* agreed."

Mia beamed at David, then turned her attention back to the group. "In agreeing to run for vice president, I became only the third female from a major political party to seek this position. That's following Geraldine Ferraro, a Democrat, in 1984; and Sarah Palin, a Republican, in 2008. If I have to tell you that they both lost, you may be in the wrong meeting."

Mia's barb drew even more laughter from the group.

David leaned back and grinned. He'd made the right choice. Clearly, the lady had a sense of humor. It would serve her and their party well in the months to come.

Mia continued: "Despite being the gender majority, fifty point eight percent female versus forty-nine point two percent male, we have a pretty weak track record when it comes to leadership in business, politics, and professional football. Even in this enlightened group, there's only me, Melissa, and the lady who runs the kitchen. I'm a long way from one of those screaming feminists you see on the news, but I do feel like I'm becoming the political poster child for half the population of the United States. That's an opportunity, and one we need to capitalize on.

"The other asset that I bring to our campaign is my Hispanic heritage. Latinos are the largest ethnic minority in this country, representing seventeen point eight percent of the population. Statistically speaking, just those two facts—my being Hispanic and a female—should tilt the needle in our direction.

"I mention these two blindingly obvious facts to emphasize the need for including a tightly focused advertising and voter registration effort as part of our campaign strategy. I know this won't escape the attention of our partners from Watkins and Evans, but doing my due diligence"—Mia pointed at the monitor facing her—"means getting it plastered on that screen."

Applause exploded around the room, and Melissa shouted, "You go, girl!"

Milt stood up. "Thank you, David and Mia, for sharing those words of inspiration and guidance. Now, folks, it's time to do what we came here to do."

…

For the remainder of the week, the team worked twelve to fourteen hours a day refining the clayman materials into the Centrist platform and campaign strategies. Even when they weren't working, they talked about working.

Milt made sure there was nothing to distract the team. From 7:00 a.m. to 9:00 p.m., both cellular and internet access was blocked. Technically, it was illegal to block cellular access, or even to have the equipment to do so. However, no one seemed to know the details of this FCC regulation. Or if they did, they either didn't care or acquiesced to the perception that their mission justified this esoteric infraction.

Oddly enough, at least in the world of politics, even this slight deviation from the letter of the law troubled David. He had sworn to run a "clean machine." That was his story, and he, by God, was gonna stick to it.

By the end of the third day, the team agreed that what started as their clayman had been shaped, reshaped, and wordsmithed into a manifesto that reflected the core values of their vision for the Centrist Party. They were convinced that what they had developed would serve the citizens of the United States well into the twenty-second century.

Despite their convictions and their confidence in the Stakley-Lopez ticket, they knew they were facing an Omaha Beach–grade uphill battle. They were planning to dramatically change the underlying principles, the very fabric, of the United States Constitution, the document and the legal framework that had held the nation together for over two hundred years. Everyone knew the time had come for the amendments they had developed. In fact, they were long overdue.

As the third day drew to a close and that struggle become a hard reality, Milt stood up to verbalize the concern creeping onto everyone's faces. "We all know the American people, at least the sixty-one percent who bother to vote, can be a politically entrenched lot. Everyone in this room knows, and should fear, the sociopolitical magnitude of the crusade we are preparing to launch. But I need to accentuate this even more. It will take a cataclysmic event to bring about the forum for legislation necessary to make the amendments envisioned in our Centrist platform."

Milt paused and looked around the room. "Folks, that forum must be a constitutional convention. And, David, you'll have to know when to pull the trigger. You might want to start praying for an act of God."

36

Mexico, the Yucatán Peninsula
Sometime in the nineties

Two men sat at a small, white, wrought-iron table next to the pool of a house about forty kilometers south of Cancún, near the city of Puerto Morelos. The larger of the pair clutched an ice-cold Modelo, his third, in his catcher's mitt of a hand. The other, much smaller man sipped from a glass of Perrier.

They were quietly celebrating the success of the partnership they had entered a year earlier, as well as the horrific reputation it had earned among the *federales* and their criminal counterparts all along the Yucatán Peninsula. They were professional kidnappers and extortionists who now focused exclusively on rich *norteamericanos*.

Although they always worked as a two-man team, the authorities didn't know that. They were referred to on the street by the singular moniker "El Choppo."

The name came from their modus operandi. From day one, their strategy had been to put the fear of God into their victim's significant other by including a severed fingertip along with their demands for ransom. They would also convincingly tell the victim they had implanted a heat-fusing chip at the top of his or her spine that could be ignited remotely if either of them was reported to the police.

Despite the frequency of abductions and the demands of outrageously large sums of money, their grisly intimidation techniques were so successful that the pair never came close to actual apprehension. But the whispered legend of El Choppo, and the gut-wrenching fear it inspired, was starting to draw the attention of Mexican authorities as well as others north of the border.

...

Arturo Flores was born and raised in Mérida, the capital of the Mexican state of Yucatán, where both his mother and father were tenured professors at the Universidad del Mayab Escuela de Medicina.

Growing up as the only child in an academic, upper-class family, Arturo learned early on the benefits of education and exposure to the arts and science. In addition to his native Spanish, he spoke fluent English and acceptable French.

Arturo was exceptionally bright. When tested during his first year of secondary school, his IQ registered in the 150 to 160 range. Naturally, his parents expected him to follow in their footsteps and attend medical school. However, Arturo wasn't the least bit interested in comforting the sick. As he entered his teens, with their inevitable testosterone-induced changes, he discovered what began as a curiosity and then blossomed into a raging, all-consuming passion: he liked to hurt things.

At first, it was relatively harmless: pulling the wings off the ubiquitous June bugs that swarmed the tomato plants in his parent's garden or squirting lighter fluid on a hapless green snake, then watching it writhe in agony when he set it on fire.

As he got older, he started trapping agoutis, the small Mexican rodents that looked like an overgrown squirrel. They would make amazingly loud screaming sounds when he nailed their feet to a board, sliced them with a razor, then used pliers to pull strips of skin from their living bodies. It was after graduating to stray dogs and cats that he decided he wanted to become a veterinarian.

Masking their disappointment at his decision not to attend medical school, Arturo's parents agreed to pay his tuition with the stipulation that he study at the Universidad Autónoma de Yucatán, UADY, which was less than twenty kilometers from their home. UADY was just fine with Arturo. He could live at home and not have to worry about cleaning an apartment or cooking or buying his own clothes.

Physically, Arturo wasn't unattractive. In fact, he was incredibly nondescript. A little above average height with a slim, teetering-on-muscular build, Arturo was eerily easy to forget. He was not the party type and really wasn't into girls, or boys, for that matter. At eighteen, Arturo had never tasted alcohol, didn't smoke, and was still a virgin with no desire to change that status. He was the polar opposite of the image of a male college freshman.

He enjoyed his chemistry and pharmacology classes and absolutely loved anatomy, especially the dissection labs. But it was during his fourth year, when he and his fellow students were able to practice what they had learned on living, breathing pets and farm animals, that he realized he had made the right career choice.

During their internships, each student was required to assist staff veterinarians in the school's free clinic. Following the "see one, do one, teach one," practice long associated with veterinary and medical schools, Arturo was soon allowed to perform procedures on his own, without supervision.

It didn't take him long to begin diluting or totally withholding anesthesia when he clipped dog ears and tails. Or his favorite procedure, neutering. Their screams of pain brought the same sensation that rock-and-roll or heavy-metal music gave an average person: a quickening of the pulse and waves of pure, albeit fleeting, pleasure.

It was during one of the commencement speeches, shortly before being confirmed as "Doctor Flores," that he heard a comment he would take to heart and that would set him on a course that would change his life forever. Before sending the graduating class out into the real world, one of UADY's professors challenged them to "apply their education and academic calling to fulfill their lives by realizing their individual passion."

Arturo had only one passion, one burning desire, and he decided at once to begin his quest for a profession that would allow him to apply his training and live out that passion.

He would stumble across his calling much sooner than he expected.

Arturo and Hector were introduced to one another virtually, while each was visiting the fiercely secure chatroom Wet Work Wanted—WWW—deep inside what was referred to as the "darknet." As was common among those who frequented WWW and most other darknet sites, Arturo and Hector danced around getting to know one another for weeks before finally connecting.

Hector lived in Cancún, the famous resort city, roughly 270 kilometers south of Mérida, where he worked as a part-time tour guide.

"Part-time" was something of a misnomer. He trolled just outside the Cancún airport's arrival-passenger customs and baggage-claim area throughout the day, timing his rounds to coincide with international flights. When he wasn't at the airport trying to hustle tourists into signing up for tours to Chichen Itza or Tulum, he was working the lobby of the big hotels doing the same. It was a living, but only barely so.

His physical appearance didn't help much, not in the tourist trade. He was a tall, brutish-looking man whose ill-fitting clothes highlighted thick, construction-work-hardened muscles. The scarred knuckles on his callused hands suggested a lifetime of bar fights and beatings. Hector was well aware of his intimidating appearance and had recently decided to try his hand at the dangerous but lucrative kidnapping-and-extortion trade.

Following Arturo and Hector's darknet *tête-à-tête*, they met face-to-face at Cenote Dzitnup, a picturesque but touristy natural-spring-water-filled cavern about ten kilometers south of

Valladolid, the halfway point between Mérida and Cancun. They hit it off immediately; a Laurel and Hardy–looking but far-from-comedic pair.

Hector reiterated what they had been discussing for weeks. He needed a partner to help break into the tourist-abduction-and-extortion business. He elaborated on the business model they had gingerly discussed in the WWW chatroom. They would stalk the airport, bars, and upscale hotels for Brits, Europeans, or gringos who had that filthy-rich look about them. Once they identified a suitable couple, they would stake out their movements. Then, once they identified a pattern to the couple's actions and a location, he and Arturo, working as a team, would grab the female, throw her into a black-market van, and start the ransom process.

After hearing the details of Hector's partnership proposal, Arturo responded, "I like your strategy, *mi amigo*, but if you don't mind, I have just a couple of suggestions. First, we need to demand payment in bitcoins. A bitcoin account is completely untraceable, and so is everything associated with it: purchases, transfers, withdrawals, everything. And ten or eleven thousand dollars is peanuts. We need to hit these rich fuckers up for at least a hundred grand, maybe more. We can demand a deposit up front, and thanks to being able to hide behind bitcoin security, we can give them a little longer, *un poco*, to scrounge up enough to make it worth our while.

"Unbelievably, even obscenely wealthy people, especially Americans, don't have money that is just lying around. They have it invested in stocks or mutual funds or stashed away in annuities. That means we need to give them a little extra time to scratch it up if we want to make *el dinero grande*. But not too much time. We don't want them getting over the shock of what they are going through and bringing in the *federales*.

"That brings me to another change I want to make in our future modus operandi, what I call the 'horror factor.' Since our initial discussion, I've studied the accounts of hundreds of kidnapping cases. Most of the successful ones, at least from the banditos' perspective, were for small potatoes, or they ended up with a body in a ditch with nothing to show for the effort or with the nappers getting caught and thrown way the fuck back in prison—or here in Mexico, executed. The reason in ninety percent of the unsuccessful cases is that the nappers were too soft or gave the family too much time to collect the ransom. If they snatched a drug lord's kid, *zap*, no more napper.

"We're going to do things differently from the get-go. We're going to instill absolute terror in their hearts, unimaginable shock and pure, unadulterated horror, before they realize what is happening. I've given this concept a lot of thought, and I've come up with a plan that will make your worst nightmare look like a bedtime story.

"Rather than just snatching the woman and then trying to contact the *hombre*, we grab 'em both at the same time. You're a fucking gorilla, so unless we stumble upon the ghost of Bruce Lee, you shouldn't have any problem putting the guy in a bear hug and throwing his ass in the van. I'll do the same with the *chica*.

"Now here is where we put the fear of God in our guests."

37

US Route 191 approximately ten miles north of Jackson Hole
Five days after the day of

THINGS WERE CLOSE TO UNBEARABLE in the Airstream.

This time of year, the daytime heat in Southwest Wyoming was always in the low to mid-nineties. Four adults, two near-adult-sized teenage girls, and a year-old baby cooped inside a twenty-five-foot aluminum tube with virtually no ventilation were almost more than was humanly tolerable. Throw a lack of water and diapers into the mix, and you soon had an environment ripe for explosive tempers.

Jeremy had anticipated this eventuality. He set aside regularly scheduled times for the adults to discuss their predicament. His intention was to remind his fellow cellmates of the need to focus on anything other than their situation.

Jeremy and Brandon opened out the Airstream's awning to create at least a semiprotected space outside the RV. Although they positioned its roof at its steepest angle to keep the ash from accumulating, someone still had to pound the underside every few hours. Ash built up like snow underneath the steep roof of a Swiss chalet. Even though the space under the awning was only about four feet wide, it did afford them some degree of airflow, and the tasks involved in keeping it open exercised both their minds and bodies.

Using an army entrenching shovel that Jeremy kept in the truck's toolbox, they continually cleared a path through the mounding ash between their latrine and the F-250.

Trudging through fourteen inches of the dry ash covering the ground was physically exhausting. Jeremy fashioned a pair of snowshoes from two baking sheets they kept in the Airstream's kitchen oven and trudged down to the Snake River for fresh water. The continuously falling ash had choked the winding, slow-moving stream into a sticky, black bog. Still, after five days of living like chickens in a coop, despair was starting to set in.

Then it began to rain.

The rain turned the ash into volcanic mud. Moving became virtually impossible. However, they had no choice. They had to keep the path to the truck and their latrine area open, and so they did. Hour after agonizing hour, everyone but Hunter took turns shoveling the accumulating mud out from under the awning and out of the two paths.

The blade on the entrenching tool was less than a quarter of the size of a standard shovel, about five inches by six inches. This meant that whoever was using it could pick up little more than a double handful of the soggy ash with each scoop. The good news was that a small amount wasn't all that heavy, so even the twins could do the necessary work without physically exhausting themselves.

At around five thirty, after four days of captivity, Judy jerked open the door of the Airstream and stepped outside. She screamed.

In an instant, Jeremy bounced off the couch and headed toward her, a mixture of fear and bewilderment masking his face. "What's wrong, Judy? Are you all right?"

"Nothing. Nothing's wrong!" Judy shouted. Sweeping one hand toward the horizon and grabbing Jeremy's arm with the other, she gleefully blurted, "It's stopped! The ash isn't falling anymore."

By now, Sophie, Brandon, and the twins were all trying to squeeze out the door, making it look like a circus clown car. Everyone started laughing and hugging.

Then Judy, regaining her composure, calmly told the group, "I suspect the front that brought all this rain is pushing the volcanic cloud toward the east. You can see the sky already getting a little brighter out toward the west. Not much, but enough to notice."

"Well, it's enough for a celebration," Jeremy said. "Back inside! This calls for a round of Jack Daniels."

"Oh boy, Fiona," Ellis cried, clapping her hands and bouncing up and down. "It's adult-beverage time!"

"Not quite," Jeremy interjected. "But I'll let you two split one of the Cokes."

Everyone slept a little better when they went to bed that night.

Shortly after he began his watch the next day, Jeremy saw the faint glow of headlights piercing the mixture of morning fog and the slowly dispersing ash. He couldn't think of a single time in his life when he had been more excited, and as the lights inched their way closer, he felt the first waves of relief washing away all of his other thoughts.

Snapping out of his newfound state of euphoria, Jeremy started pressing, then pounding the truck's horn.

It was Sophie's turn at shoveling, and she was going through the perfunctory motions of scraping and tossing ash sludge, which she noticed, as the day got warmer, was starting to develop a slight crust. She dropped the entrenching tool the instant she heard the blaring horn. She would later recall it as the most melodic, sweetest sound she had ever heard.

Once again, the Airstream took on the appearance of a clown car as Brandon, Judy, and the twins, with Fiona carrying Hunter, poured out the door. They stood cheering and hugging each other as the first Wyoming National Guard double-bladed road grader, followed by a string of deuce-and-a-half cargo trucks slowly became visible through the haze.

Jeremy continued to blast away on the horn until the driver of the road grader blinked her lights, acknowledging the group's presence.

As the convoy moved forward, the grader pushed up four-foot-high walls of ash and sludge on either side of the road. This unstable mass immediately started to spill back onto the edges of the highway. But someone on the WNG disaster-planning team had anticipated this situation. A second grader, about ten meters behind the first, pushed the spillover farther off the road, allowing the trucks to move virtually unimpeded.

Thirty minutes later, the convoy commander and a Humvee bearing the red cross insignia of a military medic vehicle drew up next to the evacuees. The grader moved past the F-250, then stopped.

"Did you folks call Triple A?" called a grinning captain as he trudged through the muck toward the clearly exuberant group.

Sophie was the first to reach their rescue party's company commander. She threw her arms around him, laid her head on his chest, and gave him a bear hug. The twins, followed by the rest of the cheering group, were right on her heels and literally mobbed the captain, barely giving him a chance to speak.

"I'm Captain Bailey, One Thirty-Third Engineer Company, Wyoming National Guard," he said, smiling. "It appears you folks could use a little roadside assistance."

"That and a shower." Judy, too, hugged Captain Bailey, joining Sophie in her display of sheer exuberance.

Captain Bailey switched to a more serious demeanor. "We're on a search-and-recovery mission. We've been looking for survivors, such as yourselves, but unfortunately, you're the first that we've found. Alive, that is. And we are just about as far as we can go in this stuff.

"You've probably noticed, once the volcanic ash gets wet and the air warms, it basically turns into concrete. The volcanologists down at the University of Utah, in Salt Lake City, warned us that after this rain and heat, everything in roughly a seventy-mile radius from the Yellowstone Caldera would essentially become the world's largest parking lot. So we've got to get you out of here. As I said, we're on a search-and-recovery mission. The search means we're tasked with finding people, and the recovery means we have to return them or their remains to a safe zone.

"I have been explicitly ordered not to waste time and resources trying to salvage RVs or other vehicles. That means you'll have to abandon that Airstream. However, if we can unhitch your truck and drag it out into the cleared section of the highway, you should be able to drive it down One Ninety-One and past the area blanketed by fallout. That will free my unit up enough to get a little farther up the road before this stuff turns into asphalt. Otherwise, you will all have to load up into one of my two Humvees, and we'll drive you to our staging area in Hoback."

Jeremy locked eyes with Judy. She nodded, and Jeremy turned back to the captain. "We'll dig out the back and unhitch immediately and worry about getting the Airstream later. Or not, depending on how this stuff sets. Right now, we need to get out of here."

"It's getting a little ripe in here," Judy added.

"OK, let's get these things disconnected." Motioning to a private first class waiting by the vehicles, Captain Bailey ordered, "Private Flinn, give these folks a hand and let's get 'em headed south."

"Oh, FYI, Captain," Jeremy added, "we had to leave a man and woman in a parking lot several miles north of here. I don't think you will make it that far, and I don't think they would still be alive even if you did and were able to find them. But I felt like I needed to warn you. How and why we came to abandon them is a long story, and I'll be glad to fill out a report when we make it back to wherever we're going, but now you know."

"We'll keep an eye out for them, but I don't think we'll be able to bust through the ash fallout much farther."

As Jeremy unhitched the F-250 from the Airstream, Brandon and PFC Flinn unwound a section of steel cable from a winch mounted on the front of one of the two-and-a-half-ton trucks and connected it to tow hooks on the F-250.

Jeremy got behind the wheel of the F-250, started its engine, and put it in gear. At the same time, PFC Flinn activated the winch, which slowly pulled the truck away from the Airstream through the mounds of slushy ash and onto the recently cleared highway. Within minutes the truck was free and ready to roll. Judy shooed the twins into their assigned seats as Sophie, holding Hunter, climbed in as well.

Brandon unhooked the cable, and he and PFC Flinn dutifully rewound it onto the winch. While they were doing so, Captain Bailey retrieved a bright red, five-gallon plastic container of gas from a carrier mounted on the back of his Humvee. He placed the fuel into the bed of the F-250.

"A little gift from Uncle Sam. This should be more than enough to get you past the fallout radius. Stay on One Ninety-One until the road splits north of Hoback. Then take Eighty-Nine all the way to Ogden. Thanks to the volcano cloud pattern and the jet streams, the path will be clear as soon as you cross the gap twenty miles south of Jackson Hole."

"Thanks for everything, Captain," Jeremy replied.

"That's my job, sir. By the way, the president has declared most of Wyoming, the western sections of the Dakotas, Nebraska, and northern Colorado a national disaster. The NRO hasn't been able to use regular satellite imagery due to the cloud."

With a puzzled look, Jeremy asked, "NRO?"

"Yeah, sorry, that's the National Reconnaissance Office, which is part of NSA, the National Security Administration, or as we call it, 'No Say Anything.' Anyway, they had to revert to some of their spooky tricks, like the NROL-50 reconnaissance satellite. That stuff is so ultraclassified that they wouldn't even release the images to the convoy commander. They will get real-time, turn-by-turn directions as they make their way toward Yellowstone. That's all you folks need to know.

"Now, you best get on your way. My guys and I have a mission to complete, and as we say in the military, the mission isn't everything, it's the only thing." Captain Bailey slapped the rear window, giving the northwestern US signal to get moving.

Thanks to the pair of double-bladed army snow plows and what was at least a lull in the ashfall, Jeremy was able to drive almost twenty miles an hour on the straight sections of US 191. In less than an hour, the group entered what had once been a tourist mecca, Jackson Hole. Now the area was comprised of dark two-story lumps—buildings caving in from the weight of a five-foot blanket of gray-black volcanic sputum.

Roughly fifteen miles out of Jackson Hole, they passed through a gap in the mountains that had allowed centuries of passage from the plains of Southwest Wyoming through the Tetons and into the Snake River valley.

Just south of that gap, the fallen ash vanished. Just like that. The road in front of the little group was as clear as if nothing had happened. But only a few hundred yards behind them, mounds of pumice were pushed to either side of the road.

"Captain Bailey wasn't exaggerating when he told us about the jet-stream effect on the volcano cloud," Brandon mused, looking out the window. "It looks like we will be in for clear sailing, at least for a while."

Just north of Hoback, the road split into US 191, which veered southeast, and US 89, which headed southwest following the Snake River and its load of ash. Jeremy stayed on 89 as it meandered through Logan and Ogden before ending in Salt Lake City. Along the way, they joined the swelling ranks of tourists and residents fleeing the fury of the formally dormant Yellowstone supervolcano.

Refugees were easy to spot. Their cars and trucks were still covered in crusty blankets of gray and black.

"The scene reminds me of *The Grapes of Wrath*," Judy said. "The John Steinbeck novel about the Joad family who fled their repossessed farm in the Oklahoma Dust Bowl. They headed for the 'promised land,' California."

Jeremy nodded. He knew the story. The movie starring Henry Fonda was one of Judy's all-time favorites and always made her cry.

After seeing scores of No Vacancy signs on the small-town hotels along US 89, Judy pulled out her recharged iPhone and found a Holiday

Inn Express on the outskirts of Farmington, just north of Salt Lake City.

After everyone had what may well have been record-breaking showers, the group drove to the Costa Vida Mexican restaurant. Brandon, Sophie, and Hunter would be flying out the next day, and a celebratory dinner was in order. As everyone stuffed themselves on sizzling fajitas and homemade tacos, Sophie broached what was clearly an elephant in the room.

"If you two don't mind my doing so, I'm going to put on my lawyer slash prosecutor hat and give you some unsolicited, pro bono legal advice. I wouldn't say a word—*nada*—about the incident that happened when we were running from the eruption. First of all, it was purely self-defense. That animal was getting ready to crack open Judy's head. Secondly, your pistol was loaded with shotshells, not technically lethal rounds of ammo. In fact, they are downright humane compared to hollow points.

"Lastly, and most importantly, you only wounded the guy. I could go on and on, but trust me, there's not a DA in the country that would waste time trying to prosecute that case, even if the guy died, and they somehow found his sorry ass, which according to Captain Bradley, they most likely won't."

"She's right," Brandon added. "You probably saved Judy's life, and God only knows what he was planning to do with Sophie and the twins once he had the three of us out of the way. This is a perfect example of when it's wise to let sleeping dogs lie."

"I appreciate your advice," Jeremy replied. "That's pretty much the course of action I had planned to follow. Or I suppose 'nonaction' would be a better term. But it's always good to have your decision legitimized. Especially by a pair of law enforcement experts."

After dinner, everyone lingered, reminiscing about the events of the last several days and discussing plans for the future. The next morning, Sophie, Brandon, and Hunter would take a hotel shuttle to the airport and fly back to Duluth. Judy, Jeremy, and the twins would run the F-250 through a car wash and begin their trek to Nashville. Everyone hugged one another, sent and accepted Facebook friend requests, and vowed to get together again on a more relaxing vacation.

Four years later, almost to the day, in one of those tragic twists of irony, Jeremy learned that Brandon had been killed when a drug bust got out of control.

38

The Farm
Unveiling of the Centrist/Stakley-Lopez campaign platform, eighteen months before the day of

THE MOOD WAS OPTIMISTIC, almost festive, as the Centrist Party planning committee gathered for the final day of the conference. Select members of the press had been invited to the Farm conference room for the unveiling of the party platform and objectives.

David, who had been chatting with Judson, walked over to where Mia was already sitting and sat down next to her. "It warms my heart to see someone who may be more obsessed with punctuality than I am," he whispered.

"I may have a touch of OCD, but right now, I think my adrenal glands are running full tilt," Mia replied.

David scanned the reporters standing on one side of the room. "The press was warned beforehand that this would be an informational conference only, not a question-and-answer session and absolutely not a traditional press conference. Milt is eager to start some campaign buzz, but he doesn't want to turn our meeting into a circus. At this stage of the game, I agree wholeheartedly."

Mia nodded. "Yeah, the old warhorse is a master at campaign publicity. I'm glad he's on our side."

Milt stood to the right of the enormous monitor that was suspended from the conference room ceiling, a few feet from its equally disproportionately large table, Arthur. A summary of the Centrist Party platform's preamble was projected on the screen, a single slide encapsulating its purpose, objectives, and justification for existence.

Looking over at David, Milt raised his eyebrows in an are-you-ready-to-get-started expression. David nodded and gave him a thumbs-up.

Milt stepped up to the mic. "Good morning, everyone. I trust you all had a good night's sleep and that you are well rested and ready for this last day of our retreat, seven days that could well prove to be one of the most critical workweeks in our country's history." He pointed to the monitor. "Now I'm proud to present you with the synopsis of our beliefs, our core values, and the strategy we will follow to make David Stakley and Mia Lopez the next president and vice president of the United States of America."

Milt left-clicked the button on a wireless presentation remote, and a PowerPoint heading appeared on the screen.

Summarized Preamble of the Centrist Party Platform and the Stakley-Lopez Presidential Campaign

"The following slides share the basic tenets of our party and serve as the foundation for the Centrist platform, which, in turn, sets forth our strategy, our plan, to move this great country forward. Away from the extremes of the Left or Right and toward common ground. Toward the ideals, the hopes and dreams shared by the overwhelming majority of our people. Not just the loudest, the true middle class."

Milt proceeded to click through a series of slides, one for each tenet, and read them aloud, but giving his audience time to read them as well, visually reinforcing the message.

The Centrist Party platform sets forth the principles that will unite all Americans around a common belief that we are stronger, more productive, and happier when we work and live together. Truly one nation, indivisible, with liberty and justice for all.

We believe the Constitution of the United States is the most effective governing document ever developed by humankind and that it was designed to be self-perpetuating and able to adapt to the needs of its citizens and legal residents.

We believe in taking a moderate stance on all political, social, and economic issues and a negotiated, common-sense approach when addressing local, national, and global problems.

We believe in the complete separation of church and state and that our government, laws, and elected officials are not to be influenced by any religion, institution, or foreign power.

We believe in participatory government and in the power of an engaged citizenry.

We believe that citizenship is a right that must be sought after, earned, and cherished and should not be bestowed simply by the geographic location of one's birth.

We believe the United States is and must always be a democratic republic, that no elected or appointed official has the right to remain in office for life, and that all such officials must be held to high moral and ethical standards.

We believe in the power of the free market, international trade, and capitalism.

We believe in the sanctity of our borders while simultaneously developing and nurturing political and unrestricted trade relationships with other countries.

We believe that the United States must maintain the most powerful military on the planet but that we are not a global police agency. We will not, once engaged, wage drawn-out conflicts, nor will we attempt to win the "hearts and minds" of our foes.

We believe that every citizen and permanent resident has a right to receive quality healthcare. Still, this right must not be squandered through the inappropriate use of any substance or behavior.

We believe that every mentally stable, law-abiding citizen has the right to keep and bear legally procured, non-military-grade arms and ammunition.

We believe that every adult resident has an obligation to work and contribute to society to the best of his or her ability. We do not believe that anyone has the right to expect support from our government or our citizenry if he or she is not willing to do so.

We believe we must eliminate our dependence on fossil fuels, develop a nationwide uninterruptable power grid, and achieve a zero-carbon footprint by the end of the twenty-first century.

Milt turned his attention back to his audience. "As soon as David Stakley is sworn in as POTUS, we'll begin working on the two most fundamental and radical changes to our constitution in over two hundred years. The first thing we must do is repeal and replace the Fourteenth Amendment."

An audible gasp swept the room, followed by muted murmurs among members of the press and others who were not part of the working committee.

Milt clicked the remote, and another slide appeared on the screen.

Eliminate Birthright Citizenship

To obtain citizenship in the United States, one must

- apply for such on or after his or her 17th birthday;
- serve a minimum of 2 years in the military, law enforcement, or another federally approved service organization; and
- pass the same citizenship exam currently required of naturalized citizens.

"As you can imagine, this will be by far the most contentious of the amendments we hope to pull through Congress. But it will also have the greatest across-the-board impact on the future of our country. We passionately believe that apathy and political ignorance lie at the very core of many of the issues we face. This modification will go a long way toward ensuring we have a far more engaged citizenry willing to actively participate in their government, not just sit idly on the sidelines waiting for someone else to steer the ship.

"Over the next hour, we will discuss how this, in concert with other sweeping changes, will serve to alleviate the most egregious and growing problems threatening the safety and well-being of our people. We'll get to those problems and their solutions shortly.

"But first, let me point out my use of 'pull through Congress' as opposed to 'push through.' I hope this subtle shift in semantics sends the subliminal message it is intended to send. A long-standing management maxim states that you lead from the front. The traits central to pull, versus push, leadership include empowerment and collaboration, thoughtful problem analysis, and engagement. That's precisely what we want to foster in our citizens.

"Now, as those of you who just joined us recover from the birthright citizenship shocker, I'm going to ask Elton to review the second and third constitutional changes we hope to enact. Then Nelson will walk us through some of the details of how these changes will dramatically improve our election process, reduce if not eliminate illegal immigration, and save lives. Elton, you have the helm."

"Thank you, Milt." Elton strode to the front of the room. "I guess in this day and age, 'you have the remote' may be more appropriate." Smiles lit up the room.

"Regardless of where you stand on the issue, everyone in this room knows we have long had a gun violence crisis in this county," Elton began. "We have three hundred sixty-one more murders per one hundred thousand residents than Japan. The most gun deaths, homicides, of any industrialized country on the planet. Yet, over the past fifty years, we have done virtually nothing to get any semblance of control over this situation. This is long overdue.

"Our party prides itself on finding the middle ground, a balance, on every issue. That sweet spot lies somewhere between 'thoughts and prayers' and complete firearms confiscation. The change to the Second Amendment that we propose will get us closer to reasonable, intelligent gun control than ever before." As he spoke, Elton pressed the remote, and another slide appeared on the screen, line by line.

Modify the Second Amendment such that

1. only citizens may purchase/own/carry firearms;
2. all firearms must be registered in a federal database;
3. a background investigation must be completed before allowing item 1 above;
4. the prospective owner must complete basic firearm safety and user training;
5. a ballistic test must be performed, with the results entered into the item 2 database; and
6. no automatic or military-grade weapons/enabling modifications, large-capacity magazines, or armor-piercing ammunition may be privately owned.

Using the remote's laser, Elton pointed to the screen. "Pay special attention to item one. As Milt mentioned earlier, these changes have been designed to build one upon the other. To use an overused word but still a brilliant concept, they are synergistic. When combined, as we intend to do, the result is greater than the sum of the individual parts. When fully implemented, these modifications to our constitution will make this country far safer, our government more efficient and responsive, and our citizens more engaged than ever imagined.

"However, I have to disagree with one of Milt's previous statements, at least a little. He said that our recommended requirements for citizenship would be the most contentious amendment we will attempt to ratify. I, on the other hand, believe the one you are looking at, the vaunted right to bear arms, is the most revered constitutional privilege held by our fellow Americans, at least by an extremely vocal minority.

"A survey conducted by Pew Research two years ago indicated that nearly forty-seven percent of American households owned at least one gun. That comes to over three hundred ninety-five million guns, or, for you numbers freaks, one point three two guns for every man, woman, child, and zygote in the continental United States. Over three percent of the US population owns between eight and one hundred forty guns, even though last year alone, over forty-two thousand Americans were killed by guns, and we're on track to break that record this year. The NRA and their little weeny cultists will lose their shit when they hear what we are going to propose.

"We aren't suggesting that guns be outlawed or confiscated. We just want to see common-sense registration and controls. You know, like with planes, trains, and automobiles. Oh, and by law-abiding, sane adults."

Elton's tenor crept up. David knew that getting control of gun violence was Elton's passion. His fifteen-year-old granddaughter had been gunned down by her clinically depressed biology teacher, slaughtered, along with four of her classmates, as she sat in her third-period class.

"Thanks, Elton," Milt said. "In the interest of time, I'm going to ask that you move us along to the next recommended constitutional change, though I damn sure don't want to diminish the importance of a more enlightened approach to the right to bear arms. If we can prevent just one school shooting or one senseless workplace massacre, we will have succeeded. And we know we will do a lot better than that."

David admired Milt's ability to strike a balance between not dampening the mood in the room and emphasizing the importance of the Second Amendment change while keeping the overall presentation on track. Not an easy task.

Milt stepped back to the mic and continued: "We have another monumental change to review. I know David is raring to let the press know how these new laws will put an end to our illegal immigration problem, without pissing off our neighbors to the south, and save a boatload of money at the same time."

Elton clicked the remote and brought up the next slide. "I appreciate you keeping me on target, Milt. You're right: I am a bit zealous about that subject, and that passion can sometimes get me in the mud. But I promise to stick to the script during the remainder of my allotted time."

Implement Term and Age Limits

For all federal elected/appointed positions:

• President/Vice President	2 four-year terms
• House of Representatives	3 consecutive two-year terms
• Senate	3 consecutive six-year terms
• Supreme Court	12 years total service

Note: Representatives and Senators can be reelected after sitting out 1 term. No one may remain in office beyond the age of 80.

"Our recommendation for term limits will be a lot more palatable among the voting public. The overwhelming majority of those surveyed are not in favor of career politicians," Elton said. "Oddly, however, that doesn't square with the fact that historically we put ninety-three percent of incumbents right back into office every single time they run for office. I can only explain that through a combination of name recognition, voter apathy, and pure laziness. Most people just don't take the time and effort to study the issues and learn where other candidates stand on them.

"Some people will say we already have term limits: the voting booth. Sadly, that simply isn't true. And unless impeached and removed from office for high crimes and misdemeanors, which has only happened once in the history of our country, a Supreme Court justice can serve until death or resignation.

"The notion of term and age limits is one of those not-so-rare situations where the voting public is on one side of the fence and our elected officials on the other. Even though service caps make perfect sense, we expect an out-and-out congressional dog fight when this legislation finally comes up for discussion.

"But its time has come. Actually, it has passed. And that's why the people of the United States need a common-sense party, and that's why we need David Stakley and Mia Lopez in the White House."

Everyone in the room applauded. Almost as one, everyone stood up, cheering and whistling.

"Thank you, Elton," Milt said as folks started to settle back into their seats. "Great wrap-up to a timely message. Now let's take a fifteen-minute break, test the Farm's plumbing, and refill our coffee cups. Even you fitness freaks don't want to miss out on the goodies Mattie made for us. When we come back, the next president of the United States will present some of the initiatives we have planned, which are dependent on the revisions you just heard and which, over time, will tie it all together."

39

Germantown, Maryland
Near the end of the first campaign strategy session, eighteen months before the day of

KELLY FINISHED PUTTING ON her obligatory deep-red lipstick. That was the only makeup-related vanity she allowed herself, at least when going out during the day. She sometimes got a bit more aggressive for a special occasion in the evening.

David and Mia had been gone for most of the week, but they would return home later in the afternoon. Kelly was planning a special dinner to celebrate David's arrival. She missed him terribly when he was away for any length of time. Despite having been married for nearly five years, she still liked to surprise him with little gifts or his favorite food.

And sometimes a trip to Victoria's Secret was in order.

Tonight she would focus mostly on food and wine. The dessert course would depend on how tired David was when he got home. That didn't mean she wouldn't be at the top of her game in the looks department. So before going to Safeway, Kelly would make her Barbie rounds for a manicure and pedicure and to freshen up the lowlights in her hair.

Kelly did some mental gymnastics and calculated that she could drive downtown, get her hair and nails done, and then swing by Sabai Simply Thai for a bowl of their red-curry noodle soup.

Eating the stuff was like taking a swig of molten steel, but, damn, it was good. Then off to the market for bone-in pork chops and sweet potatoes. If things went as planned, she should be home in plenty of time to brine the chops, get the potatoes in the oven, and have a drink ready for David when he walked through the door. It sure beat working. She took her car keys off their designated hook and headed for the side entrance to the garage.

...

Arturo grew increasingly impatient as he sat for the third day in a row in the white cargo van he had purchased in Atlanta. He had paid cash for the Ford Econoline, to a dubious dealer who was the associate of an acquaintance from Mexico, creating a sufficiently convoluted transaction trail.

Hector sat behind the wheel, drumming his fingers impatiently, ready to roll at a moment's notice.

That evening, they drove north along the east coast on I-95. On the way, Hector stole a license plate from a delivery truck parked at South of the Border, the garish rest stop near Dillon, South Carolina. The stolen plate and two new magnetic signs bearing the name "BBB Accredited Construction" now adorned the van.

Following a near-disastrous snatch that resulted in scars on his face and a kick to his groin that still ached, Arturo decided to trade the stun gun for a less hazardous means of subduing his victims. It wasn't as much fun—his victims didn't squirm, they just went limp—but it was more efficient.

After some fairly intense research, layered on top of his veterinary and chemistry laboratory experience, Arturo decided to use trichloromethane, aka chloroform, as the base for an incapacitating formula. Even in small doses, chloroform alone could daze or knock out land animals. Arturo determined that the effects of this mixture would be dramatically enhanced if administered as an aerosol. He was at a loss as to how this could be done until one afternoon, while shopping for ibuprofen in the *farmacia* of the Cancún Walmart, the solution literally fell off the shelf and into his cart: Vicks nasal spray. Not the medicine itself, the bottle.

This morning, as he sat in the passenger seat, scanning every vehicle that passed the innocuous-looking van, Arturo absentmindedly fingered the Vicks bottle tucked inside his shirt pocket.

"Heads up, ke-mo sah-bee!" Hector screeched. "The chicken's flown the coop."

Where did Hector come up with that shit? Arturo shook his head and zeroed in on the Stakley chick's Prius as she drove past the parked van.

Hector started the van, allowed another car to pass, and then pulled onto the street, maintaining a distance of about fifty meters behind the Prius. Arturo admired Hector's skill. He had to keep the vehicle he was following in view while trying not to be conspicuous. Stoplights and traffic circles were always problematic. He had to continually adjust his speed to avoid being stopped or cut off by other vehicles. But he had become something of an expert at tailing his prey.

Hector chuckled. "Mrs. Stakley's obliviously a safe driver. That makes following her almost easy."

...

Kelly drove down Clopper Road, turned left onto Kingsview Village Avenue, and then right into the parking lot in front of Four Seasons Nail and Spa.

In an attempt to avoid getting dings on her new Prius if someone should carelessly open the door of his car, she pulled into a parking spot on the outskirts of the lot, the back end of her car facing the spa. She didn't mind walking a little farther, especially in such beautiful weather. The extra steps added to her goal of twelve thousand a day and went a long way toward keeping her fit and trim. Besides, she was a few minutes early for her ten o'clock appointment.

She unconsciously checked her reflection in the rearview mirror, fluffed her hair, got out of her car, and headed for the spa's entrance, remotely locking the car door as she walked.

…

"It's almost like she wants to get snatched," Hector said as he parked the van in an empty space on the driver's side of the Prius.

"Well, my Cro-Magnon friend, our first lucky break in three days," Arturo noted with a toothy grin. "I suspect it'll be a while before she comes out of there, but I'm going to go ahead and open the side door and get in place, just to be on the safe side."

Arturo got out of the van and slid open the passenger-side cargo door. He then walked to the back of the truck, opened the left rear door, and turned on a laptop mounted on a portable table. With the laptop's camera set to selfie mode, he was able to view everything behind him while pretending to work on some imaginary BBB Accredited Construction task.

As he proceeded with this charade, he reviewed his plans for the snatch for the hundredth time. When Mrs. Stakley left the spa and started walking back to her car, he would pretend to complete his work. He would close the rear door, being careful to do so as she slipped between the van and the Prius to get to her driver's-side door. He would fall in behind her, and just as she drew even with the cargo door, he would call out her name.

That was a funny thing about human nature. Even in a strange or threatening situation, Arturo knew he could get someone to drop her guard, if only for a second or two, simply by calling her name. Mrs. Stakely would turn to see who had recognized her, and then Arturo would strike. He would have his Vicks bottle of sleepy juice ready, and the instant she turned, he would give her a full-on facial.

And just like with his test animals, she would be startled and inhale involuntarily.

For the next hour and a half, Arturo kept his eyes glued to the laptop's monitor. As he waited, Arturo reflected on his encounter with the gringo from DC. He and Hector would receive $500,000 for the snatch, $100,000 up front and the balance when they were instructed to release the Stakley woman. The man gave precise details on how they were to conduct her abduction, what they were to do and, more specifically, what they were not to do.

They were instructed to subdue the woman, remove the tip of her ring finger—their signature terror tactic—and then place her digit and wedding ring into a Ziploc bag provided by the gringo. They would then enclose this ghoulish package in a manila envelope. The packet, which contained a sealed letter, was addressed to David Stakley in Germantown, Maryland.

Arturo had no earthly idea of how the gringo, or the people he worked for, knew their tactics, but they damn sure knew. That scared Arturo. But his fright paled in comparison to the warning the man provided about what would happen to him, Hector, and their closest relatives if any additional harm came to the Stakley woman.

The people the gringo worked for wanted Stakley to drop out of the presidential campaign, but they didn't wish to bring about a groundswell of public sentiment about his poor kidnapped wife, which might end up helping him get elected.

Arturo and Hector were to hold her until Stakley publicly announced his withdrawal. Then they would release her, without additional harm, in some podunk town in West Virginia. Hector would be castrated if he touched her as he had done with their previous victims. And Arturo would have both of his legs amputated at the knees by a twelve-gauge shotgun.

Arturo had zero doubt that the man and his employers would follow through with their threat. This scared the coon dog shit out of him.

Finally, Mrs. Stakely came out of the spa. She smiled as she checked herself out in the reflection of a storefront mirror, touched the back of her hair, and started walking toward her Prius.

"Game on, *tonto*," Arturo called to Hector. He chuckled. Payback for Hector's "ke-mo sah-bee" crack since *tonto* was Spanish for "fool." Arturo knew Hector would never catch the humor from that double entendre, but he thought it was hilarious.

"Watch my six. Here she comes."

Kelly walked at the brisk pace of someone who had a lot more to do before heading home. As she passed the Hispanic man at the rear of some business vehicle, she pressed a button on her car key, unlocking the Prius.

...

Arturo eased the rear door closed, then reached inside his shirt pocket for the Vicks inhaler. He unscrewed the already-loosened tip, dropped it back into his pocket, and held the bottle in his right hand.

When the lady was parallel to his shoulders, and he was out of her peripheral vision, Arturo stepped behind and to her right. One more step and she would be in position.

Arturo pointed the inhaler at the back of her head and called, "Kelly Stakley!"

The woman hesitated for a split second and then turned toward the voice.

A blinding flash of light and searing pain shot through Arturo's head when the leather-wrapped blackjack smashed into his skull just behind his right ear.

Then, nothing.

...

Charles Crum wrapped a muscled arm around Arturo's neck, catching him not so gently as his knees buckled and he crumpled toward the ground, a trickle of blood leaking from inside his ear.

"Good morning, Mrs. Stakley," Charles said as he dragged Arturo's limp body toward the van's cargo door.

From the driver's seat, Hector saw the split-second scene unfold in the rearview mirror. Knowing in a heartbeat that things had gone horribly wrong, he bolted out of the van to go to Arturo's aid.

Small holes appeared between Hector's thick black eyebrows as two subsonic twenty-two-caliber bullets punched their way through bone and into his brainstem, causing flaccid paralysis and instant death.

The pops from the pistol in Lawrence's hand were barely audible. That is precisely why those who have to perform close-up wet work—on either side of the law—favor subsonic ammunition.

"Mrs. Stakley, please turn around and walk to your car," Charles said in an even but commanding voice. "Don't look back. The less you see, the better. Get in your car, lock the doors, and start the engine. Wait five minutes, then pull out as you usually would and go about your business. Mr. Smith and I have a little cleanup to do, but we'll be finished and have you covered by the time you leave. Don't say anything to anyone about what you've seen. Except for Mr. Stakely, of course. He will get a full report by the end of the day."

A slightly delayed fight-or-flight reaction sent wave after wave of nauseating fear washing over Kelly as she realized what had just happened. Her hand shook violently as she struggled to open her car door. Once inside, she grabbed the steering wheel, trying to regain self-control. The physical reaction lasted only a few seconds before another, more cerebral fear kicked in.

"He can't tell David," Kelly murmured to herself. "That'll derail everything." Kelly opened the car door and scurried back to the van.

Charles was just sliding the side door closed when he saw her. "Mrs. Stakley, please get back in your car. We have to get out of here."

Although visibly shaken, Kelly was rapidly regaining her composure, focusing on another objective.

"Mr. Crum, you can't say anything to David! Not now! I know him better than anyone alive, and I know exactly what his reaction will be. If he thinks for a second that someone tried to hurt me, he'll renounce his candidacy."

Charles reached forward, gingerly grasped Kelly's shoulders, and started steering her back toward her Prius. "Please, Mrs. Stakley, we've got to leave and leave now. I hear what you're saying, but I have to make a report."

Quickly scanning the parking lot and assuming a casual air, Charles kept talking as he ushered Kelly back to her car. "Get in and plug the secure phone I gave you into the USB port. Start the engine. This will launch a modified version of Apple CarPlay. Then leave, driving slow and safe, like nothing happened. As soon as I get back to our vehicle, I'll call Mr. Ballard, explain what happened, pass along your request, and ask him to call you ASAP. That's the best I can do, Mrs. Stakley. Now, we've got to go."

Gaining some degree of composure, Kelly slid into the driver's seat and fumbled with her purse before dragging out the Blackwater phone. "I'm sorry I lost it, Mr. Crum. I'm OK now," she said firmly as she connected the phone to one of the Prius's USB ports and started the engine. "Let's go."

"Yes, ma'am," Charles replied as he closed the car door and started toward the Tahoe, which Lawrence was pulling out of its parking space.

Minutes later, as Kelly maneuvered down Clopper Road, the phone rang through the car's speaker system. Pressing a button on the steering wheel, Kelly blurted, "Judson, is that you?"

"Yes, Kelly, it's me. I just got off the phone with your security team leader. He explained what happened and your request not to tell David, or at least to keep a lid on it for the time being."

"Judson, we have to. Like I told Mr. Crum, if David hears what happened, he'll drop out of the race. When it comes to himself, he's the bravest person I have ever known. But if he thinks for one second that I am in any real danger, he'll flip out. Besides, it doesn't matter. It's over. Nothing happened. Well, not to me anyway. It will serve no purpose to tell him anything. At least not now. After the election, I'll confess." Kelly clenched the steering wheel, consciously trying to control her post-traumatic jitters.

"I agree with you, Kelly," Judson unexpectedly concurred. "What neither you nor David knew was that over the last few days, our sources picked up some underground chatter that had us spooked. Nothing specific as it relates to how or when, but more than enough for us to up our game. I'm sure you didn't pick up on it, but we actually doubled the number of spooks on your security team.

"We also have reason to believe that Jim Phillips is somehow involved. Again, nothing in concrete, just some troubling correlations."

Kelly smacked the steering wheel with her right hand. "Shit! David can't stand the guy, but it never occurred to me that he would sink to this level."

"Well, like I said, we don't have anything we can build a case on. Just rumblings. But still . . . OK, back to your suggestion. Let's do this. I will send you today's security report via encrypted email. You hold on to it until you are comfortable sharing it with David. Just give me a heads-up before you do. I don't want to be blindsided if he doesn't like the fact that we hid it from him."

"Thank you, Judson. I'll tell him the day following the election, as soon as the results are in, one way or the other. Oh, and don't worry about how he'll take it. He would do the same thing if he were in your shoes. Now that I have that worry behind me, I need to get to the market. Thank you again, Judson. We're doing what's best for David. And for the cause."

40

The Farm
The end of the Stakley-Lopez campaign strategy session, eighteen months
before the day of

EXACTLY FIFTEEN MINUTES after Milt announced a break in the presentation summarizing the party platform and objectives, everyone was back in their seats.

"Ready to go, David?" Milt asked.

David nodded, and Milt returned to the right-hand side of the monitor.

"What you've seen this morning is an assemblage of concepts that we've been working on to some degree for years. During the past several months, we used them to develop the framework of a strategy and a long-range plan that will take our country, its people, and our government from being the greatest nation on earth to a new, previously unimaginable level. There simply aren't words for it. We may have to add to the inflection of 'good.' Maybe good, better, best, 'besteriest.'"

A few smiles and a smattering of laughter rippled across the room.

"OK, I get it," Milt quipped. "I'll stick to politics and constitutional law. I don't want to put any comedians out of a job."

That self-deprecating jab resulted in a round of applause.

"But speaking of constitutional law, I want to wrap up this morning's discussion and lead into David's remarks by making what I believe is a crucial caveat surrounding our campaign strategy. Despite the healing balm that our late president, Matthew Sheppard, was able to spread over Washington, DC, I see no way for David Stakley and our party to overcome the bipartisan bickering and self-serving politicians in a manner that will allow the amendments we have presented to be passed. It's simply not going to happen in the current political environment. Not even in two terms of office.

"The route used to pass the existing twenty-seven amendments—a two-thirds vote in each chamber of Congress and subsequent ratification by three-fourths of the states—is virtually impossible.

"The other way is by calling for a constitutional convention. We've only had one in the entire history of our country, and that was in 1787. Today, since we have an existing constitution, we could call for a convention as specified under its Article Five. This has never been done. And in my opinion, the only thing that will bring such a gathering about is a direct military assault on the United States or a disaster, natural or manmade, of biblical proportions."

Milt paused and looked around the room. There wasn't a sound as everyone reflected on the magnitude of what he had just said.

Nelson Teal raised his hand and broke the silence: "Milt, you're a damn good attorney and a nationally known expert on constitutional law. A lot of the people in the room may have heard of this type of convention, but few if any of us really understand its significance. Maybe you could give us a Campbell's Soup overview. And by that, I mean condensed, short, and as sweet as you can make it."

"Ah, thank you, Nelson. Never use four words when two will do. You know, you'd starve as a lawyer. But yes, you have a valid point. As specified in Article Five, a constitutional convention can be called if two-thirds of state legislatures—that's thirty-four states—apply for amendments. Their applications remain in effect unless they are rescinded.

"Over the years, there have been numerous campaigns to call for an Article Five convention over issues such as the Balanced Budget Act and term limits. Currently, there are twenty-eight states with existing Article Five applications, just six away from the required thirty-four, but that's a big six.

"I firmly believe that it's going to take an Article Five convention to make the changes we've presented today. I'm also convinced that it'll be a monumental task to bring the other states on board. Not impossible, but not easy, even with our group's leadership and influence. Especially for those western holdouts, California, Oregon, and Washington and a couple of their eastern counterparts, like New York and Virginia.

"There are those—and I'm one of them—who say an Article Five convention could be a dangerous process. Our constitution isn't perfect. That's why we have twenty-seven amendments today. However, it has served us pretty darn well for over two hundred years. An uncontrolled convention could change all of that and threaten our fundamental rights and freedoms.

"The biggest problem is a constitutional convention has no rules. Even how states would choose delegates and thus how our citizens would be represented isn't specified. The list of potential problems goes on.

"So we find ourselves in a dilemma. To effect the changes we envision will require an Article Five convention, but that process itself could be like a runaway nuclear reactor and result in a constitutional meltdown. Like so many things, it all boils down to leadership. We need to develop a clearly defined set of rules, have those rules ratified, and then, and only then, proceed.

"Equally important, we should only go down that road after we have the leadership in place to keep us out of the metaphorical ditch. And I believe—no, I know—that leadership comes in the form of David Stakley and Mia Lopez."

The room resounded with applause and shouts of agreement.

Raising his hands to acknowledge the ovation and to restore order, Milt continued: "Now, David will wrap things up by describing a couple of the initiatives that are dependent on the changes we are going to work toward. David."

David strode forward and, with a beaming smile, shook Milt's hand. "Thank you, Milt." He faced the delegates. "And I thank each and every person in this room for your participation and support, even if today was your first day here at the Farm. It's been an intense but staggeringly productive week.

"I have the honor of closing this week's campaign strategy session. But I feel obligated to remind each of you of what you already know. This is just the beginning of a long, uphill struggle. Now it's up to us, Envision-2100, and our fledgling Centrist Party to coalesce around what we laid out today. We've got to mount a 'get out the vote' crusade like this country has never seen, keeping in mind, this will be a marathon, not a sprint. The voter will be our salvation.

"However, there is a dichotomy to what I just said. On one hand, the average American citizen is where we should find our greatest strength. Conversely, therein lies the fundamental weakness that is plaguing our country: political and historical ignorance and raging voter apathy. These are the festering, malignant issues that our recommended modifications to the Fourteenth Amendment will change.

"Citizenship, or at least US citizenship, has all but lost its luster. It no longer means anything to the average Walmart shopper. We have an entire generation, *more* than one, who have never voted. People who can't name the attorney general, or give you a blank stare when you talk about the Soviet Union or the Berlin Wall.

"Our redesigned and updated Fourteenth Amendment will bring the ideal of citizenship back to life. It will be something to strive for. A goal. Obtaining it will be an achievement.

"The reward from such a change can't be overstated. You will have a sense of pride in having served your country. And you will have a more significant say in how your government operates.

"Today most of our citizens, regardless of their party affiliation, have a feeling of bureaucratic helplessness. And that helplessness breeds a sensation of hopelessness. It becomes a cycle that feeds upon itself. It grows and spreads like an infection. It's killing the spirit that made the United States the greatest nation on earth. We've got to stop it before we find ourselves slipping down the slope toward mediocrity. The one-two combination of our Fourteenth Amendment change and the implementation of term limits will be the first and most crucial step in that direction.

"Legal residents—I'll get to legal versus illegal immigration in a few minutes—legal residents who chose not to pursue citizenship will still enjoy most of the rights and privileges, just not all of them. Like the right to vote, or bear arms, or hold federal office. And there may well be tax advantages afforded our citizens. We will have to see how that shakes out legally.

"It will take time for some of these changes to work their way into our population. For example, everyone born before the change becomes law will be grandfathered in as a citizen. Those born on or after that date must meet the service-and-testing requirements. We've got to start somewhere.

"This brings me to the point I want to make about immigration. We must make a distinction between legal and illegal immigration. We have long had a serious problem with illegal immigration. We wholeheartedly welcome those who enter our country legally, and especially those who, after doing so, seek citizenship. We cannot and will not tolerate those who enter illegally.

"A logical and appropriate question may be, How will the constitutional changes we are proposing stop the flow of illegal immigrants when every effort we have tried in the past has failed so miserably? Not only have they failed, but they've wasted billions of taxpayer dollars doing so. The eyesore of a partially completed wall along our southern border is a perfect example of this folly.

"Immediately after making the Fourteenth Amendment change, we will enact a federal law that requires every human in the United States, regardless of age or mental status, to be issued a federal ID. This

FID will be based on a unique DNA sequence that will be encrypted and blockchain protected. The FID will identify its bearer as being a legal resident, or a citizen, or a visitor slash tourist, or a visitor with a work permit such as an H-1B or an H-2A, et cetera.

"'So what?' you might say. 'You've got an FID. How will that eliminate illegal residence?' This same law will require that you have an FID to get a job of any kind, to receive any nonemergent healthcare or medical treatment, to get a driver's license, to vote, or even to purchase, own, or lease real property, such as a house or car. You will also have to provide your FID to travel by plane, bus, train, or any public transportation. And we've already stated that you must be a citizen to possess a firearm.

"Oh, and perhaps most importantly, you will need an FID to receive any government assistance of any kind, period.

"I'll use that last statement to wrap things up. More to come, but for now, go back to your districts, ignite your local voter-registration movements, but be positive." David was amped up by his own enthusiasm. He swept his gaze around the room, managing to lock eyes with each person sitting around the table. "Even though one side can't field a single viable candidate, and the other, thanks to our late, great president Sheppard, has been body-slammed to the bottom of the polls, don't trash-talk either party. We're going to run a clean campaign, let the facts speak for themselves, and, by God, we're gonna win this thing."

The applause was deafening as everyone in the room shot to their feet.

Beaming, David raised both fists high above his head.

...

The copter flight back to Germantown was smooth and amazingly quick as the pilot, wanting to show off a bit for David, pushed the AW160 to just a few knots below its max speed. David and Mia, at the insistence of the Blackwater team, flew back on separate aircraft. This was standard procedure for officially designated candidates and senior members of the executive branch.

After the copter touched down, David reached forward and shook the pilot's hand, saying, "This thing's amazing, and so are your flying skills. But I thought you were going to peel the paint off those last few miles."

As soon as the copilot slid the passenger door open, David climbed out, shook his hand, and trotted toward Kelly, who was waiting a safe distance away from the still-whirling blades.

"Welcome home, baby—I mean, Mr. President. How was the retreat?"

"Unbelievable. I'm pumped! You look incredible. How did things go here?"

"Oh, just a typical day in the life of a wife in the presidential-candidate fast lane. I'm sure nothing near as interesting as what you've been doing."

David shot her a quizzical tell-me-more look as they entered the house.

41

All across the United States
The Centrist convention, four months before the November election, eleven months before the day of

OVER THREE DAYS OF INTENSE DEBATE, David watched the Centrist National Convention, the CNC, unfold in a manner unlike anything ever staged by a United States political party.

Traditionally, Republicans and Democrats selected a host city, then descended on it like a swarm of flies. These events were more akin to a carnival than a forum to formally select and announce their candidates for the highest office in the most powerful country in the world. Even though their picks had been known for months beforehand, the RNC and the DNC had devolved into loud, rowdy displays of hype and bravado.

Not so the CNC. The occasion was designed and conducted in a distributed, hub-and-spoke virtual format, with smallish centers located in every state, Washington, DC, and Puerto Rico linked electronically, via the internet.

Anyone over the age of eighteen was allowed to physically attend the CNC at any of these locations or by internet access. Remote participants were required to log in to the Centrist Party website and provide basic demographic information and any federally recognized voter-registration identification, such as a driver's license, passport, or state-issued ID number.

Each registrant also had to agree to allow his computer's media access control, or MAC, address to be collected as part of the process. This allowed some, albeit slight, degree of control and security when conducting attendee opinion surveys.

Adhering to David's insistence that the campaign be squeaky clean and free of any attacks on other candidates, CNC delegates focused their speeches and presentations on the positive aspects of their party's strategy. Although considerable attention was paid to national issues that required corrective action and changes in policy, not a single negative comment was made about any of the other candidates.

Instead, David and Mia focused on the Centrist platform and how the implementation of those principles would work to solidify the United States' position as, quite simply, the greatest nation on earth.

In support of this theme, significant energy and attention were devoted to the need to get every legal citizen registered to the polls on Election Day. Historically, less than 60 percent of eligible voters actually cast a ballot.

The Stakley-Lopez campaign was dependent upon high voter turnout and getting a majority of the ordinarily complacent population to take a stand. They were relying on the right-leaning liberals and left-leaning conservatives to coalesce around the Centrist common-sense, middle-ground approach to governance.

Although David and Mia were the only CNC candidates in this election cycle, they still went through a traditional recommendation process.

On the second day of the convention, a nationally known and well-respected delegate from Florida delivered the nomination remotely, to thousands of internet attendees across the country. Seconds later, computer "tally boards" started whirring as the yeas were counted and posted on monitors in each state.

The results were staggering. If these counts were indicative of what could be expected in November, David, Mia, and the Centrist Party were set to make history.

David and Mia were back-to-back speakers on the third and final day of the convention. As was appropriate, Mia's remarks opened the session. She thanked her Texas constituents, her peers in the Senate, and current and future members of the Centrist Party. Then she ripped into a blistering, emotion-rousing call for "every US citizen with two X chromosomes to get off their butts, get their neighbors off their butts, and vote."

Mia focused on the accomplishments women had made since the Nineteenth Amendment was passed in 1919 and that, in terms of gender equality, they were "just hitting their stride." She went on to say that the pro-life, pro-choice debate still raged on.

Most mature, clinically aware adults would agree, a universally accepted definition of when life begins would never, ever come to pass. Mia stated that, as with almost all issues, the Centrist Party would "stake its flag" at a place that seemed to be the most scientifically and morally acceptable to the majority of the population.

She personally felt comfortable defining this point somewhere after fertilization, around twelve hours following a sperm cell's surviving an upstream swim and nuzzling itself inside a much larger oocyte, and several days before week twenty-one, when a fetus had a chance, albeit minute, of surviving outside the womb.

She stated that for the past couple of years, laboratories could pinpoint, within hours, when this time would be for any individual fetus. Mia noted that currently, and for the foreseeable future, it was each state's decision where, along the fertilization-to-birth continuum, to draw the line on when life began. She was a staunch advocate of women's rights but found late-term, anything after week twenty, abortion reprehensible, regardless of state or Supreme Court positions.

When Mia concluded her combined acceptance speech, lecture, and sermon, every attendee in every convention center was on their feet, slamming their hands together. The "like" counters on CNC monitors were spinning so fast they were just a blur.

Finally, after an appreciative yet humble period, Mia raised her hands and asked for order to be restored. "Ladies and gentlemen, we are indeed blessed to find ourselves at a point in history that allows us to revitalize our great country. To alter its course and direction. We have before us the opportunity to be part of that process, to play an active role. Not just to read about it in years to come, but to look back and tell our children's children, 'I was part of that. I helped make it happen.'

"It's as if every one of us is sitting behind a monitor at the Kennedy Space Center on July 16, 1969. You may not be strapped atop that Saturn rocket, you may not get a ticker-tape parade, but by the grace of God, you are part of this great adventure.

"I am truly honored and take great pleasure in introducing you to our mission commander, the next president of the United States, Mr. David Stakley!"

As the cheering crowd rose, a beaming David strode confidently across the stage toward Mia. Smiling while looking at the cameras and the cheering crowd, he waved and let the applause, the near pandamonium, continue for a few heartbeats. Then he turned and shook Mia's hand. "Thank you, Mia. That was an inspiring, motivating speech, and an unbelievable introduction. It makes me wish I had gone to the Navy Flight School instead of Airborne. Neil Armstrong was always one of my heroes."

He turned to the crowd. "My fellow Americans, it is indeed an honor to accept the nomination as the Centrist Party candidate, your candidate, for the next president of the United States. To be cut from the herd and, keeping with Mia's inspiring moon-launch metaphor, to be selected to lead our nation in its 'giant leap' forward.

"As I shared with some of you, I have rarely, and by that I mean never, used a speechwriter. However, I did acquiesce to the suggestions of my campaign manager and agree to have our folks prepare a few talking points for my address today. Yet, after listening to Mia, I've decided to put those aside and save 'em for another day. What I'm going to say today is about as ad hoc as I get. Not entirely impromptu, but darn close.

"Last night during our press corp meet-and-greet a nationally known columnist for the *Wall Street Journal*, Douglas Kellogg, asked the question that every financial type in every company in every city always asks: 'How are you going to pay for it?'

"We do have several initiatives in our strategic plan that will require new funding. Our vision for a federal identification system and a national gun registration and database are two such examples. Both of these are new initiatives. Each will cost a substantial amount of money to develop, implement, and maintain. Neither, even when combined, will come close to costing as much as we wasted on that thankfully aborted attempt to build an ineffective barrier—the wall—along our southern border not that many years ago. That fiasco, the eyesore that can be seen from space, serves only as a good bad-example.

"However, this doesn't answer that standard CFO question, so let me give just two examples of policies that I plan to initiate during the first thirty days I'm in office. The first, in addition to providing a substantial sum of divertable revenue, also helps alleviate our illegal immigration problem.

"Currently, state and federal governments provide over twelve billion dollars in subsidies each and every year to illegal immigrants. They, and 'they' is 'we,' shell out twenty-two billion in food stamps, three billion on Medicaid, thirteen billion for education, and, get this, nearly ninety billion dollars on welfare and social services. I'm no math whiz, but these add up to just north of a hundred and twenty-five billion dollars. Every. Single. Year.

"The vast majority of Americans, our party, and I personally are empathetic when it comes to the plight of those less fortunate than ourselves. We are compassionate to a fault. But the keyword here is 'illegal.' We will do everything within our power to provide aid and comfort to those who enter our country legally. However, we cannot and will not spend another dime supporting, caring for, or educating invaders. And that's exactly what anyone who enters our country illegally is.

"I already have an executive order to immediately halt these expenditures drafted up and ready for my signature. I'll sign it within forty-eight hours of being sworn in as president. That single item, the stroke of that pen, will itself pay for the development, implementation, and support of our FID system and our firearm registration database. It will leave enough money left over to begin the design of a national power grid, another of my pet projects.

A less lucrative and perhaps equally, if not more, controversial option we have on our drawing board is a federally managed national lottery. Modeled loosely around the EU's EuroMillions transnational lottery, we estimate that the United States, with its population of three hundred and twenty million, will net, that's after payoffs and expenses, over ten billion dollars a year. That money will be congressionally earmarked to help fund several national initiatives we have identified, which are designed to place the United States back into the world's technological and social driver's seat.

"What I have just said will be made available, word for word, on the Centrist Party website no later than close of business tomorrow for all to see, along with our strategic plan and information about the projects I've touched on or alluded to. I'll close by mentioning those that I feel are the most important, the most urgent, and the most progressive.

"If you think about it for just a few seconds, you will realize that Americans live by the grace of electricity. Just a few hours' disruption at our homes is an inconvenience, but a regional or statewide outage can be devastating. A nationwide shutdown would be a disaster, the stuff of science-fiction novels.

"Very few of us understand how fragile our power distribution grid is and, as such, how vulnerable we are. And this is just from conditions posed by a natural disaster, or as happened in the Midwest only a few years ago, when a local overload effectively shut down the entire grid in four states and part of Canada.

"If that's not bad enough, the threat of an intentional nuclear electromagnetic pulse, or EMP, strike would literally cripple our nation. The Department of Defense estimates that a medium-sized fission weapon detonated between two hundred fifty and three hundred miles above the state of Kansas could destroy much of the electrical infrastructure across the continental United States. We are literally living under the sword of Damocles. We've got to build a redundant, shielded national electrical grid. I don't want to sound cliché, but this is a national disaster waiting to happen.

"While we are rebuilding the electrical grid, we will install a nationwide internet backbone with sufficient bandwidth and speed to carry us into the next century and which is upgradable even beyond that date. As with the electrical grid, our internet backbone will be what our techies call 'massively redundant,' including NSA-level hardware and encryption security. It will also include physical connections for our neighbors in Canada and Mexico.

"Again, following the path blazed by JFK, I will challenge our government and private industries to work together to eliminate our use of fossil fuels and the internal combustion engine by the end of the next decade. This may well be my most ambitious goal. It would also be one of the noblest achievements in human history.

"We will not just participate; we will take the lead in combating human-accelerated climate change. We will take the lead in stem cell research and genetics. We will begin the development of a plan to transition to digital, perhaps eventually a global, currency. This will require a previously unimaginable paradigm shift. But so did the cell phone and thousands of other innovations whose time had come. We will be the foundation and lead the establishment of a North American Union, along with our staunchest allies and trade partners, Canada and Mexico.

"The keyword here is 'lead.' Change and social evolution are inevitable. We can fight it and die, accept it and survive, or lead it and prosper. And by God, we are going to lead!"

The applause was deafening. The giant monitors flashed images of CNC centers across the country. They were all the same. People were on their feet, clapping and hugging each other. The excitement and pure joy were nothing short of electric. Their time had come.

David raised his hands to still the applause and continued: "Finally—and by finally, I don't mean to imply that is all; I just want to acknowledge that I know it's time for me to close and for all of us to go home, back to our districts, our neighborhoods, and start working to turn our vision into reality. But in closing, allow me to share one last inspirational thought. In 1968, then-Senator Robert Kennedy paraphrased a quote from the author George Bernard Shaw. 'Some men see things as they are and ask why; I dream of things that never were and ask why not.' Ladies and gentlemen, thank you and good night."

42

All across the United States
Eight months before the day of

THE OTHER TWO PARTIES HELD their national conventions during July and August in the traditional manner. The party of incumbent President Phillips met in Baltimore, and the party of soon-to-be-nominated Sheila McCray met in Las Vegas. As usual, there were placards, music, and endless speeches hyping their candidates and deriding the opposition. There were also protests and riots. Ironically, neither of the delegations focused much of their vitriol on the Stakley-Lopez campaign. They mainly went after each other.

Sheila McCray and her running partner, Tyrone Brown, had emerged out of a field of twenty-four other nominees. Most analysts attributed the wide playing field to a lack of party unity and the absence of a robust platform or political agenda. If the party had a strategic plan, it wasn't communicated to the voting public. The result was, at best, a fractionated mob mostly held together by their disdain for President Phillips. This may have blunted their effectiveness, but it didn't dampen their ferocity.

Following the two mainstream conventions, both parties came out swinging at each other.

Sitting in the meeting room of the Maryland Centrist campaign office, his eyes glued on one of four seventy-inch HDTV monitors, each displaying a different national news channel, David barked, "Siri, Facetime Mia Lopez."

Seconds later, a picture-in-a-picture screen appeared on all four monitors.

"*Hola, señor Presidente!* Oops, there I go, getting ahead of myself again. Let me start all over. Good afternoon, David."

"And good afternoon to you as well. You're forgiven. Actually, I'm kind of getting used to it. And you know what? I like it!

I suspect this may be something of a rhetorical question, but are you watching Fox News? Or CNN? Jim Phillips just called Sheila McCray a damn liar on national TV."

"Yep, I just saw the interview. McCray may take a few liberties with the truth, but being called a liar by President Phillips is like being called ugly by a toad."

David chuckled. "I can't get enough of your Texas aphorisms. Of course, now I can't unsee that image. We'll let 'em fight it out. They'll be after us soon enough, but their little feud will give us more time to get our owls in a row, so to speak."

"Now look at who's spouting aphorisms," Mia replied, smiling.

"Well, I didn't mean to totally derail your afternoon, Mia, but I wanted to make sure you didn't miss the little catfight. I'll call you later tonight and we can review our next move. David out!"

As David had noted, both the Phillips and McCray campaign staff were paying only scant attention to the Stakley-Lopez Centrist ticket, blowing them off as just another doomed third-party, Ross Perot–style lost cause. That is, until the first poll numbers following their respective conventions hit the press and social media.

The results stunned both of the established party campaigns. President Phillips held the lead but not nearly by the margin traditionally associated with an incumbent—even one so arrogant and polarizing. And the McCray-Brown camp was in near panic. The sheer number of candidates in the fray before the convention would splinter their effort, at least initially. They had expected the resulting factions to regroup and coalesce immediately following McCray's nomination, but this wasn't happening. In fact, they were in second place, but only by a Saran Wrap–thin margin.

Things were starting to unravel on the traditional fronts.

Meanwhile, David, Mia, and their rapidly swelling army of supporters were ecstatic. Their level of voter popularity had never been experienced by an independent party. And they continued to chip away at the establishment. But these gains weren't coming as the result of happenstance. The Centrist movement was on fire.

Working independently, David and Mia covered five or more rallies in major cities each week, hitting every state, Puerto Rico, and DC before the election. In addition, they made multiple stops in California, Texas, Florida, and the industrial sections of the country.

Kelly proved to be an exceptional campaign asset in her own right. She also worked independently, stumping colleges and universities coast to coast, always urging students to get registered, get involved, and get out the vote.

The results were staggering. Most mainstream Americans had long grown weary of shit-slinging politicians. They ravenously welcomed the energetic, upbeat Stakley-Lopez style. The evidential majority were vociferously amenable to the Centrist platform and ideals. Even the suggestion of national service as a prerequisite to citizenship went over better than anticipated. In fact, most people who were already citizens or who would be grandfathered in thought it was an excellent idea for their children and their children's children.

By the end of September, the Stakley-Lopez campaign had moved to within a few points of President Phillips. Although not totally out of the running, McCray-Brown slipped into an increasingly distant third. If the always-dubious polls were anywhere near reliable, swing voters from both major parties were defecting in droves.

But David and Mia and the campaign team did not allow their success to lure them into complacency. Just the opposite. Every increase in the polls seemed to double the intensity of their effort. The same held true for Centrist supporters. It had become a movement. And oddly, the more vicious the attacks from the Phillips camp, the larger and stronger the Stakley-Lopez crusade became. By the first of November, statistics and artificial intelligence algorithms discerned a virtual tie.

Then came the Tuesday after the first Monday in November, Election Day. The American people were ready for a leader capable of taking their country from "great" to "greatest." The Stakley-Lopez ticket found itself squarely in the center of "the right people at the right place at the right time."

And so, it came to pass that the Wednesday edition of the few remaining printed newspapers all across America carried their version of the *New York Times* headline declaring, Stakley-Lopez Win by a Landslide! President Phillips Refuses to Concede, Demands Recount despite Underwhelming Performance.

43

The White House
The day of

The secure phone on the nightstand next to David's side of the bed blared an earsplitting ring shortly after midnight.

David was instantly awake. Kelly didn't move. It would take more than two rings on a phone to wake her at this time of night. He swept his phone off the nightstand. "POTUS here."

"Mr. President, Major Cain, duty officer. Sir, we have a situation!"

David sat up. "Major Cain, I'm awake, sober, and alert. Go!"

"Sir, seismographic stations in Utah and Montana indicate there was an enormous explosion in the northwest corner of Wyoming around twenty-two hundred forty-seven hours. Their calculations point to an area known as the Yellowstone Caldera."

"The Yellowstone supervolcano." David swung his legs over the side of the bed.

"Yes, sir. NRO satellites have confirmed an eruption with a plume of over twenty-five kilometers. The team at the University of Utah estimates a volcanic explosivity index of seven or eight. They say right now it's classified somewhere between a supercolossal and a megacolossal eruption.

"The folks at UT are comparing the Yellowstone eruption to Krakatoa, which exploded in 1883. When it did, it produced the loudest sound ever heard on earth. Its sound waves traveled around the world four times and could be heard three thousand miles away. Yellowstone is roughly seventeen hundred miles from Washington. The speed of sound is seven hundred sixty-seven miles per—"

"So the boom we heard a while ago was from the eruption?"

"Yes, Mr. President, and there may be a couple more on the way. Right now, my team has the FAA duty officer on the line. They are shutting down airspace in the northwest quadrant immediately. Plans call for NOAA to calculate plume drift and to work with the FAA so they can close airspace as necessary when it moves east. And it's going to be necessary, and it's going to be big."

For a fleeting second, David realized that he had never given any consideration to how, and especially how closely, government organizations worked together. Here was the National Oceanic and Atmospheric Administration, NOAA, working tongue-in-groove with the Federal Aviation Administration, the FAA. He pushed the thought aside. "Roger that, Major Cain. If this thing is as serious as they're leading us to believe, we need to get in front of the action. I need for you to do some things neither one of us has done before."

"Just say the word, Mr. President."

"OK, first of all, I need to get as close to the front line as possible without putting anyone else at risk. And the ball needs to start rolling the instant we hang up."

"Clear, sir. Are you authorizing me to alert the Air Force One team?"

"Negative, Major. Too slow and too many moving parts to get me there during the time frame I envision. I want you to scramble one of the F-15s sitting on the tarmac at Andrews. They'll want to fly as a pair, and that's fine. I have a pressure suit sized and ready in the Andrews squad room.

"As I recall, the F-15G has a ferry range of three thousand miles and change. So even if we have to swing south then north to avoid the plume, we should be in good shape. But you don't need to worry about all that. Just give the scramble order, my destination, and that I want to be wheels up in sixty mikes. They will take it from there.

"I need Marine One on the front lawn in fifteen minutes with orders to get me to the Andrews flight deck in time to get me suited up and strapped in the number two seat before the jockey lights his Pratt and Whitneys. I know all of this is tight, but that's why we pay you the big bucks, Major Cain. But wait, there's more."

Kelly rubbed her eyes and sat up. Looking appropriately puzzled, she opened her mouth to speak, but David held up his hand. She flopped back down on her pillow.

David continued: "I want you to alert the secretary of defense and the secretary of homeland security. Tell the SecDef I want him to convene the National Security Council. I'll call the vice president when I'm on my way to Andrews, tell her what I know, and direct her to ride herd on the NSC. I'll also give her your name as a temporary point of contact.

"Depending on feedback from NOAA and the NRO, the chairman of the Joint Chiefs of Staff will most likely want to go to DEFCON Four. They'll want to let Iran know that we know that they know what's going on. We may be distracted by Mother Nature, but we can still turn Tehran into a slag heap if they fuck with us."

"Roger that, sir! Based on the images the NRO is releasing, it looks like military airspace in Wyoming, the Dakotas, and points east could be compromised, if not crippled, when the volcano's plume starts spreading. SAC will be forced to relocate our B-52 and B-2 launch sites. The LGM-30 Minuteman silos may be less at risk. They could probably punch right through atmospheric ash.

"But our friends on the Persian Gulf may not know that. They may see this as an opportunity to launch a strike in retaliation for that spanking we gave them two years ago. A shift to DEFCON Four, or Three, will get everyone's attention.

"That brings me to the subject of where we want to put you on the ground once we get you out west."

"Yes, I was thinking the same thing," David said. "Airports anywhere near Yellowstone will be shut down. Bozeman may be north and west enough to keeps its doors open, but like an old friend of mine likes to say about flying, even when you're there, you're not there. That means at least a two- or three-hour convoy to West Yellowstone."

"Don't take this the wrong way, Mr. President, but I'm way ahead of you on this. The Secret Service guys will be all over my ass if they find out that I told you what I'm about to say. The F-15 model G is carrier ready, meaning it has the beefed-up suspension necessary to land on US aircraft carriers. The F-15 drivers are navy pilots who have already logged carrier landings. What that means is that any of those jockeys can put a model G down on a straight stretch of two-lane highway.

"Officially they need a minimum of four thousand feet to land empty. And you'll be close to empty after a one-hour Mach two ride. They can take off in less than one thousand feet, so getting them out will be no big deal. I'm checking the map as we speak. There's a nine-mile stretch of Highway Two Eighty-Seven northwest of Yellowstone that, once cleared, will work just fine if you're feeling lucky."

"Luck has never been my strong suit," David said. "Things just seem to work themselves out. But one thing I've learned is that nothing makes a decision easier than a lack of options. Make it happen, Major!

"Now I've got to get dressed and ready to catch my ride on Marine One. And it looks like I have about an hour's worth of explaining to do in five minutes to a very perplexed looking wife. Did I mention she's not a morning person?"

44

Andrews Air Force Base and points west
The day of

MARINE ONE TOUCHED DOWN on the lawn of the White House directly south of the main entrance.

As soon as it did, with its engines running and rotors spinning, David dashed to the port-side door surrounded by four puzzled third-shift Secret Service agents. They would be briefed on his zero-dark-thirty departure later.

It was less than eleven miles, as the presidential helicopter flies, from the White House to the Andrews Air Force Base Rapid Response hangar. That barely gave David enough time to call the vice president. "Mia, we've got our first executive branch crisis. And guess what? I need you to run with the ball for the next several hours while I take an e-ticket ride to Yellowstone National Park. Or as close as I can get to it." David gave the vice president an overview of the situation and orders to coordinate the NSC and to contact the White House duty officer, Major Cain, for additional details.

As Marine One touched down near the RR hangar, a small group of military personnel, three of whom were dressed in flight suits, came out to greet him.

"Welcome to Andrews, Mr. President. I'm flight leader for today's mission. Commander Davis, call sign Redtail Three. This is Lieutenant

Commander Fenster and Lieutenant Commander Pruitt, call signs Tabasco and Cornflakes, respectively."

After shaking Commander Davis's hand, David did the same with Fenster and Pruitt, then smiled and said, "It looks like you've got the major food groups covered."

David turned his attention back to the flight leader. "Redtail Three, Commander Davis? Why does that sound familiar?"

"I'm Benjamin O. Davis the Third. My great-grandfather was Benjamin O. Davis Junior. He was one of the original Tuskegee Airmen. He used the call sign Redtail Two during the Second World War. He advanced to four-star general before he retired. I tell folks that I can fly a lot faster than he did but not near as far."

"Well, you're still young, Commander. Now, let's get me out of here and see what that thing will do," David said.

Twenty minutes later, David was suited up and strapped into the weapons systems officer seat behind Commander Davis.

As Redtail Three maneuvered the eighty-thousand-plus pound, thirty-two-million-dollar F-15G into takeoff position at the north end of the main runway, he spoke into his flight helmet microphone. "Mr. President, we've been cleared for afterburner takeoff and unrestricted climb out of here. We're going to stand this bird on its tail, so you might want to hold on to the handles in front of your seat."

Commander Davis stopped the plane at the end of the runway, pressed the brakes, and pushed the throttle forward. The sound was deafening as the two recently upgraded Pratt & Whitney turbofan engines poured out over twenty-five thousand pounds of thrust each. Pressing hard on the F-15's brakes, Redtail Three set the throttles at 50 percent until the engines stabilized. When the whine settled into a continuous hum, he pushed the throttle forward.

"Here we go, sir. Hold on."

David expected to be pushed back into his seat when the jet reached its takeoff speed and lifted off the runway, but he wasn't prepared to be body-slammed.

As the F-15 went from zero to two hundred knots in less than five seconds, he was pinned to the back of his seat. Then the afterburners kicked in, and the plane rocketed into a near-vertical ascent. David fought off a wave of nausea.

The F-15G reached its cruising altitude of sixty thousand feet in a little over two minutes. According to the FAA and NOAA, and supported by real-time images provided by NRO satellites, the volcano's fan-shaped plume had reached eighty thousand feet. Aided by the southern edge of the west-to-east jetstream, it was spreading across central Wyoming and southern Montana at sixty miles per hour.

That was good news for David and his flight team. They were cruising at a little over twice the speed of sound, Mach 2.3, or 1,764 miles per hour. At that rate, they could swing south, avoiding the plume, which was, relative to the F-15, moving slowly eastward, and still be at the recommended landing site in less than an hour.

David tried to focus on what he planned to say and do once they were on the ground. Naturally, he wanted to provide some level of comfort to survivors and those suffering from the disaster. And motivation to the National Guard and first responders. But primarily, he had to carry the flag without disrupting rescue efforts or otherwise getting in the way.

Redtail Three's voice exploded in his earphone, derailing his thoughts: "Mr. President, can you see that glow at the peak of that mountain on our starboard side?"

"Yes, I see it, Commander. It's pretty hard to miss," David replied.

"Well, sir, that mountain wasn't there yesterday."

45

US Route 191 north of what was the city of West Yellowstone
The morning after the day of

THE EASTERN SKY GLOWED AN EERIE REDDISH ORANGE and cast shapeless, ghostly shadows through the falling ash.

"Change of plans, Driggs," Major Kohler shouted over anew and increasingly ominous rumbling. "I told you the situation was fluid. And it just got more so. A lot more. My convoy is going to head west on Highway Two Eighty-Seven. We'll pull back from here and head out past Hebgen Lake and into Montana. We've received orders to rendezvous with a VIP.

"We'll provide security and convoy him back to this area, or as close as we think we can get without putting anyone in danger. I can't imagine how things could get any worse, but the volcanologists at the University of Utah haven't ruled it out. And I've been warned that this guy better not get hurt on my watch.

"Anyway, climb back into your van and stay a cat's-eyes distance behind my Hummer. Or as you so cleverly stated, watch my rear. You're coming with us."

Maybe it was his imagination, but for a second, Martin thought he detected the hint of a smile behind Major Kohler's mask. "Hold on, Major. The action is here. What if we don't want to tag along with your convoy?"

"I'm sorry, Driggs. Apparently, I gave you the impression that you had a choice. You don't. As I predicted, the governors of Wyoming and Montana have designated the eruption as a disaster. And, just as I suspected, they have imposed martial law. Guess what Driggs, until a higher-ranking officer shows up, I'm the only sheriff in town. But if it makes you feel any better, you're less than thirty minutes away from being famous. World famous."

"How's that, Major Kohler? Yeah, we were first on the scene, but within an hour, reporters will be on this place like flies on . . . well, you know the old saying."

They headed toward their respective vehicles.

"Wrong again, Driggs," Major Kohler said. "Every road within a fifty-mile radius is either impassable or closed to everything except emergency and military vehicles. And civilian airspace has been totally shut down. So your competition can't even get close. But that's not your news reporter pot of gold, you lucky son of a bitch."

"Really? Then what is my pot of gold?"

"You are about to meet and probably get an exclusive interview with the most powerful man in the world."

"Nick Saban is coming out here?"

"No, you moron. We're going to pick up the pres-o-dent and give him an up-close and personal tour of what's left of Northwest Wyoming."

"President Stakley?"

"Nothing gets by you, does it, Driggs? Yes, President Stakley. Now saddle up and let's get out of here. We can't be late for this gig. Besides, we've been tasked with cleaning up a stretch of Highway Two Eighty-Seven along the Madison River so they can land without crashing into some redneck's abandoned pickup."

"Serendipitous," Martin muttered as he scurried toward the KIFI van. "All those years of scut work, and the biggest scoop ever lands squarely in my lap. Well, like they say, better lucky than good."

46

US Route 287; not the end of the world, but you can see it from there
The morning after the day of

FIGHTING CRAMPS IN HIS LEGS and severe pain in the small of his back, David concluded that the old air force saying was spot-on: the F-15 was built for speed, not comfort.

Even at this time of year and at this latitude, it was still too dark to see anything more than the orange-red glow coating the mountain in the distance.

At the direction of the NRO's geostationary spy satellites one hundred twenty-five miles above, Commander Davis was giving the volcano and its noxious plume a respectfully wide berth. They had reduced their airspeed from Mach 2 to .5 as they passed over the Grand Tetons and turned north toward what they hoped was at least a mile-long section of debris-free pavement. The F-15 slowed even more as they started their descent, in an impossibly steep approach, in what David thought was total darkness.

Then Redtail Three turned on the jet's powerful landing lights, and the president of the United States almost shit his pants.

David recalled a navy fighter jockey once telling him that even the most experienced carrier pilot feels a chill when he's hurtling toward a little patch of tarmac heaving up and down and pitching left and right in the middle of the ocean. But a carrier has a tailhook that can take an

F-15G from 150 to zero miles per hour in less than five hundred feet; there was no such hook on a highway.

US 287 wasn't moving, but it was narrow and bumpy, and even the combination of headlights from a short line of National Guard trucks and Humvees and the F-15's landing lights barely illuminated their runway.

None of this seemed to bother Redtail Three. He didn't hesitate or waver in his approach. And he didn't say a word, which David thought was a little creepy given their situation. Apparently, the man's heart was pumping ice water.

At what David estimated to be a half mile away from the semi-illuminated highway, the commander lowered his flaps and increased his angle of descent. David realized that Redtail Three was going to simulate a carrier landing. He remembered reading somewhere that a pilot makes well over two hundred corrections to his approach during the eighteen seconds he is in "the groove."

When executed correctly, the plane hits the deck at around thirteen feet per second. When it's not done correctly, the carrier captain writes a letter to the pilot's next of kin.

David thought that Redtail Three was coming in hot. He wasn't. But the F-15 slammed down hard on the highway. So hard that David wondered if the impact had broken his coccyx. He was sure the jet's seats were designed to absorb the effects of this kind of landing, but, damn, his tailbone hurt.

Redtail Three still had one more surprise in his pilot's bag of physical abuse tricks. As soon as all three wheels touched the pavement, he popped the F-15's drag chute. The law of physics kicked in, and David's body continued forward at the speed the jet had been traveling and squeezed so hard against his harness he thought his eyes were going to pop out.

Once the F-15 had come to a stop almost a half mile up the highway, Commander Davis raised the canopy. David crawled down a makeshift ladder and onto the bed of a National Guard truck.

As soon as he jumped from the truck to the ground, a major dressed in BDUs walked over, rendered a crisp salute, and greeted him. "Major Kohler, Mr. President. Welcome to Montana."

Not twenty feet behind the major stood two men, obviously a reporter and his cameraman, both dressed in what used to be white protective overalls. Amazing. There he was, on the fringes of what could be the largest natural disaster in recorded history, in the middle of no-damn-where, and out popped a reporter.

"Mr. President," Major Kohler continued, "my team has been dispatched to provide security and escort services until our main force arrives."

"Thank you, Major. I'm afraid you're stuck with me for a few hours. I've ordered the Guard to secure a perimeter around the volcano, but that no one is to venture inside until the area is deemed safe. And it looks like you'll have to make that determination. In the interim, take me as close to that glowing mountain as we can get so I can do a firsthand assessment."

"Yes, sir! We're ready when you are."

The reporter took two steps forward and spoke into his microphone: "Mr. President, Martin Driggs, station KIFI. Most of the country is waking up to the news that we've just experienced the most massive volcano eruption in recorded history. And it's still erupting. Yet here you are, less than four hours later. Your visit and mode of transportation are unprecedented. How do you respond to the situation and your decision to make such a risky journey?"

"You don't waste any time, do you, Mr. Driggs? Martin. My heart's still pounding from that landing, and you're already hitting me with multiple-choice questions. But what the hell, I'd do the same thing if I were you.

"Rather than answer your 'risky journey' question, I'll quote a parable I heard a long time ago that stuck with me. A wise man once posed a question to a group of his followers. 'Which of you men, if you had one hundred sheep and lost one of them, wouldn't leave the ninety-nine in the wilderness and go after the one that was lost, until he found it?' I don't presume to be looking for the lost or endangered. But in my role, I damn sure won't be sitting in DC watching on TV.

"I can't really respond to the situation until I can actually see what's happened. And with Major Kohler and her team's assistance, I plan to start that process right now. In fact, if the major doesn't mind, you and your sidekick can tag along and document what Mother Nature has done to us." David turned his attention to Major Kohler. "Major, it'll be sunup in less than an hour. I'd like to be as close as we can get to the volcano when that happens. Let's hit the bricks."

Less than an hour later, David, a beguiled National Guard major, a cub reporter, and their eclectic convoy of military trucks and Humvees stopped on the north shore of the Grayling Arm of Hebgen Lake. They were still thirty-five air miles from what was now the largest active volcano on the face of the earth—and that was as close as they were going to get.

David and his convoy focused on the east as sunlight started spilling across what had once been a lush string of forest at the feet of the western side of the Rocky Mountains. Now, a course, gray-black material that looked like sand covered every square inch of everything, mile after mile.

Steam and smoke rose in hundreds of columns in all directions. The upper branches of taller trees smoldered, while the flames of lower-lying vegetation had been snuffed out as accumulating ash deprived them of oxygen.

Dotting the landscape were thousands upon thousands of ash-blanketed boulders, some as large as the major's Humvee. To say the area looked like the lunar landscape would be inaccurate. It lacked the craters that pitted the surface of the moon. There was no sign of life. Nothing moved. The usually ubiquitous flocks of geese were nowhere to be seen. Not a single bird in the sky.

David didn't know that the plume of ash and smoke had fanned out north and south, and mounting layers of ash crept toward South

Dakota and Northwest Nebraska. Most of central Wyoming and southern Montana had already accumulated over six inches of the suffocating grit.

All along the cloud's expanding path, cattle and wildlife died, gasping for air, then choking on their thickening saliva. Hydroelectric plants were starting to automatically shut themselves down when their sensors detected a drastic change in water viscosity. Sections of I-90 and I-25 were closed and would remain so for days to come.

Months later, David would receive a Homeland Security disaster assessment that estimated that over fifty thousand lives had been lost or unaccounted for during the first seventy-two hours following the eruption. In the months immediately following the eruption, corn, wheat, and other crops were decimated across much of South Dakota, Nebraska, Iowa, and Minnesota. This drove grain prices up across the United States and generated food shortages across the globe.

However, the following year grain production in these same states hit record highs. This was due to high concentrations of nutrients such as phosphates, nitrates, and potassium found in the particular type of ash, basalt based, belched out by what was now Mount Shoshone.

Although the long-term environmental effects of the eruption wouldn't be fully understood for decades, its first-year impact caused scientists the world over to scratch their heads in confusion. Initially, the cloud resulted in a reduction of the earth's average temperature by over fifteen degrees Fahrenheit. But it also reduced the average rainfall in the Amazon and central Africa by nearly 50 percent. This, in combination with the lack of sunshine resulting in cold weather, caused crop failures across the globe.

However, due to the massive amount of carbon dioxide, which was also released into the atmosphere, not only didn't the cloud stop global warming, it actually increased it in the years following the eruption. By post-Shoshone year three, the average temperature had recovered, and by year five had risen by two degrees Fahrenheit.

After a six-hour damage assessment, and David's first army ration lunch in years, it was time to get the POTUS to Bozeman, where Air Force One and a swarm of Secret Service agents were not so patiently waiting.

Leaving the main body of her convoy at their Hebgen Lake outpost to continue to search for survivors, Major Kohler and the KIFI news team retreated up US 287. The route the convoy had initially taken down US 191 would have been the least circuitous, but it had vanished.

The POTUS convoy was met just south of Ennis by the governor of Montana, a contingency of National Guard soldiers, and a Secret Service security team.

When the convoy stopped, several members of Major Kohler's team, carrying their weapons, got out of their vehicles and flanked the Humvee carrying the POTUS to provide security. After they did so, David dismounted and started toward the governor and his entourage. But after taking only a few steps, he turned around and walked back to where Major Kohler and the KIFI team were standing as they observed the VIP exchange.

Major Kohler snapped to rigid attention, rendering a salute as the POTUS approached. David returned the salute and then thrust out his hand.

"Major, I can't thank you enough for your assistance. I know you're obliged to say you were just doing your duty, but I appreciate you, your soldiers, and all that you do to keep our country safe."

Then turning to Martin and Kevin and shaking their hands, David continued his praise: "And you two, the luckiest news team on the planet. Thanks for being respectful while doing an excellent job reporting what will undoubtedly become known as the biggest scoop in history. You've earned the title, Martin."

After joining the approaching governor and his group, David allowed the Secret Service escorts to whisk him to Air Force One in Bozeman to begin the journey back to Washington.

Major Kohler stayed behind and continued to direct her search-and-rescue mission. Martin and Kevin had been ordered to relocate as closely as they could get to Grand Teton National Park.

As they prepared to go in opposite directions, Major Kohler and Martin shook hands and acknowledged their mutual appreciation for one another. Major Kohler started to turn to walk away, then turned back, took a card from her BDU pocket, handed it to Martin, and said, "Call me."

47

The Streets of Gold Evangelical Church, Tulsa, Oklahoma
The first Sunday following the day of

THE REVEREND DOCTOR BRYAN LARSON III glanced at his watch: 2:10 a.m. The founder and senior pastor of The Streets of Gold Evangelical Church had almost finished with the most important task of his life.

Last night, Saturday evening, Dr. Larson had let himself into the church's main sanctuary, carrying the first load of what he considered to be the Lord's tools. He unlocked the door at the rear of the building and made his way up the steep stairs leading to the church attic. He cautiously moved down the narrow, dimly lit catwalk until he reached what he knew was the space above the two double doors that opened into the foyer.

Pine two-by-fours ran parallel to the catwalk. Along with connecting studs every twenty-four inches, they formed the upper support for the church's false ceiling. Reaching into his oversized canvas duffel bag, the reverend removed the first of four folding fiberglass sawhorses and positioned its feet on two of the wooden beams. He repeated this three more times, until he had a contiguous sixteen-foot sawhorse spanning the attic space across the two rear aisles.

In the center of each of the four sawhorses, he attached a remotely controlled cargo release hook. Dr. Larson had borrowed the idea from the now-ubiquitous Amazon delivery drones. In this case, the hooks used the same radio frequency and could be opened simultaneously with the remote-control device the reverend would be using later Sunday morning.

After the sawhorse mounts were in place, Dr. Larson made two trips back to his Lexus SUV, retrieving four glass apple-cider jugs. The jugs did not contain cider.

Years earlier, when he was still just Bryan Larson III, he had overheard one of his older, far-from-religious uncles—a Vietnam vet—telling his father how to make what he called "foo gas," essentially napalm.

"You make a mixture of three parts gasoline and one part diesel. Then you start stirring in crushed-up chunks of styrofoam. Plates or cups or packing material—anything made of styrofoam will work. As you stir, the gas will dissolve the styrofoam, and the mixture will start to form a gel. That's all there is to it. Pour the gel into a jar, put a firecracker on the outside, and you're ready to make some crispy critters."

Reverend Larson wouldn't need a firecracker.

He wasn't tired even though he had been working feverishly since ten o'clock. The reverend knew he was one of the chosen and this was God's work, his crowning glory on this earth. He knew what he had to do. And he knew when he was supposed to do it.

His preparations were almost complete. The reverend attached a glass jug of foo gas to the release hook on each of the sawhorses. They hung about three feet above a fiber tile on the ceiling.

Each of the jugs weighed six pounds. This was more than enough to send it crashing through the flimsy ceiling tile when it was released by the remotely controlled hook. He knew because he had tested his design numerous times in his garage using Clorox bottles filled with six pounds of water. The main thing to remember was to shield the buttons on his remote control. It would not serve the Lord if the jugs were released prematurely.

The next task was a lot easier. Dr. Larson returned to his SUV and removed another canvas duffel bag. Inside was an AR-15 equipped with an illegal bump stock and three one-hundred-round dual-drum magazines. The magazines were manufactured in what had been South Korea for use by the ROK Army. He had purchased them online from Classic Firearms at a special price of $79.99 plus state tax and shipping.

He had loaded tracers into the last twenty positions of each drum magazine; they would be the first to fire. Tracers didn't have the penetrating power of regular AR-15 ammunition, but they could still blow the heart out of a target at one hundred meters. Besides, penetrating power wasn't their primary objective. Not today.

The bump-stock-equipped AR-15 was capable of firing four hundred rounds of 5.56 mm ammo per minute. And the dual-drum magazines gave it more continuous firepower than the US Army's fully automatic M-16. To be on the safe side, he had also packed a twelve-gauge Street Sweeper shotgun and two twelve-round drums. This little goodie had cost him over fifteen hundred dollars at a gun show in Dallas.

The reverend loaded each weapon and made sure a round was in each chamber. He did click on each gun's safety. He wanted to be ready, but as with the foo gas, he didn't want an accidental discharge. That could really mess up his plans, and the Lord would not be pleased.

Finally, he hid the guns and their spare ammo inside the pulpit. He covered its rear storage space with the white cloth he used to conceal the props he sometimes used in his sermons.

As was his custom, he would be the first to arrive for Sunday service. He would make sure neither any of the choir nor one of his associate pastors came near the pulpit.

It was after three by the time Reverend Larson made it back to the parsonage. Still running on pure adrenalin, he was not the least bit tired. The reverend realized he would never be tired again.

He went to the master bedroom and took his clothes off, planning to take a shower and get dressed in his most expensive Sunday suit. He wanted to look his absolute best today.

After getting undressed, he walked over to the California king bed, where his wife of forty-nine, almost fifty years lay sleeping. Gentle snores accompanied her shallow breathing. He was careful not to wake her, she seemed so peaceful. He thought she was still beautiful even after all these years, and he realized he loved her as much as he had the day they were married.

He picked up the aluminum softball bat that was kept for protection at the head of his side of the bed.

Swinging with all his might, he brought it down on the pterion region of his wife's skull. It sounded like a cantaloupe had been dropped on a kitchen floor.

"Tell Jesus I'm coming, darling. I'll see you directly." Dr. Larson laid the bat on his bed, then went into the master bathroom and showered. He let the steaming hot water wash his wife's splattered blood from his hands and chest. Then he shampooed his hair, rinsed, and repeated. His hair was his signature. He tried not to be prideful, but he did love his coiffure.

After putting on his tighty-whities and a T-shirt, he went into the kitchen, made a half pot of coffee, and put a Pop-Tart in the toaster. He wasn't terribly hungry, but he knew he was going to need the little extra push the caffeine and sugar would give him.

Reverend Larson arrived at the sanctuary at seven thirty, well in advance of the nine-thirty early service, his largest and most inspired congregation. For the first time in years, he didn't need to review the notes for today's sermon. There weren't any notes because there wasn't going to be a sermon.

At nine fifteen, the reverend hung the Street Sweeper on a sling attached to the center of his belt. He then slipped on his long black pastor's robe and the rose-colored Easter-season stole he had received as a gift from the congregation at the consecration of The Streets of Gold Evangelical Church.

He made sure his robe didn't show a bulge from the dangling shotgun. He was confident that none of the worshipers would notice the significance of the stole's color. Nor would it matter if they did.

At promptly nine thirty, Sister Dorothea sat down at the vintage Hammond organ. She pressed a single key, producing a chime that could be heard throughout the sanctuary, signifying the beginning of the service.

As she started playing the processional music, "Lord, Here We Are Again," the choir began marching in, led by an associate pastor carrying a cross mounted on an eight-foot pole. When the procession took its place at the front of the sanctuary, the associate pastor said an opening prayer and asked the congregation to take their seats.

Pastor Larson got out of his chair and took his place behind the pulpit. "Brothers and sisters, welcome to what will be a unique worship service, one the likes of which you have never experienced. I'm going to start things off a little differently today.

I would like for the choir and our associate pastors to come down and join the congregation. If you can't find an empty pew, just stand in one of the aisles. You as well, Sister Dorothea."

At his bidding, those sharing the stage with the reverend filed forward, filling the pews and clogging the aisles.

Then the Reverend Doctor Bryan Larson began speaking: "It may have gone unnoticed by most, if not all of you, that today is the first Sunday after the first full moon, which occurred after the eruption of what is now called Mount Shoshone. You may ask, Why is that significant?

"Over two thousand years ago, our precious Lord and Savior, Jesus Christ, was crucified and buried. The third day he rose from the dead. You know that to be a fact. That is the very basis of our faith.

"What you may not know is that in 325 CE, the Council of Nicaea decreed that Jesus ascended into heaven on the first Sunday after the first full moon occurring on or after the vernal equinox. This was based on interpretations from the book of Luke when the New Testament was translated from Greek to Old English.

"In those days, the people didn't have access to iPhone calendars and had to base their records on seasons of the year and celestial observations. At any rate, this was the same divine logic that directed me to select today, the first Sunday after the first full moon after the eruption, the final sign, to do what I have to do.

"Ever since the United States destroyed the heathen North Koreans, I knew the time was coming. And I knew I had been singled out to do the Lord's bidding.

"As is written in the Gospel according to St. Matthew, 'And ye shall hear of wars and rumors of wars: see that ye be not troubled: for all these things must come to pass, but the end is not yet. For nation shall rise against nation, and kingdom against kingdom: and there shall be famines, and pestilences, and earthquakes, in divers places. All these are the beginning of sorrows.'

"The war with the DPRK was the first sign. The awakening.

"I heard the voice which made no sound.

"I have felt a spiritual presence at night, and when I was all alone.

"I knew the time was near. The eruption, the earthquakes, and the thunderous sound which kept circling the globe have announced the coming.

"The time is now!"

The congregation sat motionlessly and stared transfixed as the tenor of the reverend's voice rose to a crescendo.

"Now, fall to your knees and prepare to meet thy maker!"

Almost as one, the congregation dropped to their knees in reverent awe. As they fell in front of their pews and in the aisles, the Reverend Doctor Bryan Larson removed the cover from the remote control that he had placed inside the pulpit.

He pressed the release button.

The four cider jugs of foo gas dropped from their perch, crashed through the fiber ceiling tiles, and smashed on the hardwood floors below. The gasoline mixture fell over twenty feet, splashing all over the floor and onto the congregation kneeling in the last four pews. They paid little notice.

Dr. Larson reached behind the cloth covering the pulpit's storage space, grabbed his AR-15, and started firing at the people in the last row. The first tracer ignited the foo gas, and the screams began.

48

Washington, DC
The day following the Tulsa massacre

Hoping to enjoy a rare relaxing Sunday morning, the president and First Lady had just finished brunch in the White House family-residence dining room. David was halfway through the business section of the *Washington Post* when CNN was interrupted by a breaking news announcement.

"This just in from our affiliate station, KJRH, in Tulsa, Oklahoma, where there has been another mass shooting. Reporter Mandy Middleton is on the scene. Mandy, what can you tell us?"

"Shane, I'm at The Streets of Gold Evangelical Church on Seventy-First Street on the east side of Tulsa. As you can see, firefighters are battling a raging fire at the entrance of the church, and the streets are filled with police and emergency vehicles. Apparently, someone started shooting inside the church during today's early-morning worship service. Witnesses tell us there was a muffled explosion followed by continued fire from an automatic weapon."

"Oh my God, David, this is horrible!" Kelly gasped.

David stared transfixed at the television screen.

Mandy stepped away from a falling timber. "We just spoke with the Tulsa PD spokesperson, who confirmed numerous gunshot and burn casualties. There is no official word on the number of casualties or the status of the shooter. But based on what we are seeing, this could well be the worst massacre our country has ever seen."

"This is insane," David roared. He leaped from his chair, the *Post* dropping onto the floor, his face morphing into a mask of rage. He glanced at Kelly and reined in his emotions.

"Hold on, Shane," Mandy said, cupping her hand over her earphone. "We've learned that the police have confirmed seventy-four dead and over a hundred wounded, some critically. These counts are sure to rise after emergency personnel gain control of the fire."

David's eyes remained fixed on the TV. "Commanding officers have a maxim in the army: you are responsible for everything your people do or fail to do. I haven't been at the helm long enough to change this country's course, but I've got to start trying. It's time for one person, and that's me, to finally accept responsibility for this lunacy and put a stop to it.

"It may be political suicide, but as God is my witness, I'm going to do something besides offer thoughts and prayers. Whatever it takes to end this madness."

Kelly stood and took both of David's hands in hers. "I totally agree with you, sweetheart. It sucks that up until now, no president has given gun violence anything more than lip service. Just kicked the can down the road to the next guy. And now it's in your lap. And that means it's in our laps.

"David, something occurred to me just now, one of those blinding flashes of the obvious. Do you recall telling me that when you were at the Farm, during that last election strategy session, Milt said that it would take a constitutional convention to bring about the changes in the Centrist platform?"

David nodded slowly.

"And do you recall him saying that it would take a disaster of biblical proportions to make that convention happen? Well, Mr. President, I don't mean to sound the least bit flippant, but you've got your disaster. Two of them. Back to back.

"As much as I hate to add to the burden that you're already carrying, you've got to leverage this crisis. The intersection of these two events will be the only opportunity you will ever get of this magnitude. Use them as a force for good and create something that will move this country forward for another two hundred years."

David pulled Kelly toward him, kissed her on the forehead, then placed his hands on her shoulders. "You're right, Kelly. Thanks for legitimizing what I was thinking." He stared into Kelly's eyes. "Things are going to get messy, politically speaking, but I take comfort knowing you're in there with me. You are there with me, aren't you?" David grinned.

"Of course, I am, Mr. Grand Potentate." With a hint of a smile, Kelly fired back, "Well, at least I'm pretty sure I am."

David muted the TV. "I'm going to call my chief of staff and have him schedule a cabinet meeting for first thing in the morning. I need to give them an overview of my plan of action. And I'll have one by then. Then I'll ask the CoS to arrange a news conference for tomorrow afternoon. I want the American people to know we're not just sitting up here wringing our hands. Plus, I want to start getting the public on board while they are still as shocked and pissed off as I am.

"The Second Amendment extremists will never come around. They'll start screaming their 'you can't take my guns' battle cry even though no one has any intention of taking their sacred toys.

"I'll try to send a positive message from the Executive Office, at least to those who will listen. But first, I'm going to secure Skype with Judson Ballard, Milt Freeman, and Elton Kirby, the current Envision president. Milt knows more about constitutional law than anyone I know. And he's been waiting for this day since Sandy Hook. I'll need Judson and Envision-2100 to start pulling financial and political strings at the state level. Your thoughts?"

"You know where I stand, and I love watching you swing into action. I just hate that it had to come to this before a president had the *huevos* to stand up and do something. But I'm proud that it's you!"

"Thank you, Kelly. That's all the encouragement I need."

An hour later, David and Mia Lopez were in the White House Situation Room. Milt's and Judson's images filled the giant split screen on the wall at the head of the conference table.

"So, from a thirty-thousand-foot level, that's what I'm thinking," David said. "It took Kelly less than a millisecond to remind me that, as we discussed at the Farm, we should look for the opportunities brought about by these two catastrophes."

"You've got a sharp wife, Mr. President," Judson said. "Tell me what you need from me, and I'm on board. What say you, Milt?"

"This is a cookie, to use one of Nelson's baseball terms—a pitch that's easy to hit," Milt replied. "Now, let me qualify that. It won't be easy, by any stretch of the imagination. It will be the most onerous task anyone in your position since Franklin Roosevelt has chosen to take on. And it will most likely be a long, drawn-out dog fight. Frankly, I don't see it coming to fruition during your first term of office. But as an old buddy of mine used to say about the lottery, you can't win if you don't play."

"Well, based on what I'm considering, I might not get another term of office," David interjected. "So I'll do what I know needs to be done; to hell with the consequences!"

"That's why we hired you, Mr. President." Judson pounded his desk with his fist.

"Agreed," Milt said. "Now, as I stated at the Farm, the only way we will get our amendments enacted is through a constitutional convention. This has never been done in the history of our country.

"Under Article Five, a constitutional convention can be called when formally proposed by two-thirds of the states. That's thirty-four in case you're an Auburn grad. To date, twenty-eight states have made application for a convention under Article Five. These applications remain in effect until they are officially rescinded by an individual state. Right now, we're six states shy of getting the process started. We've got to focus on all the holdouts to make sure no one state feels neglected.

However, I suggest we concentrate on the political heavies, initially California, Oregon, Washington, Virginia, New York, and Illinois.

"There will be several parallel threads in our strategy. For example, there are no established rules for a convention. Many scholars, myself included, are worried that without some parameters, an Article Five convention could get out of control and potentially destroy the constitution that it's trying to protect. We must establish boundaries. I suggest that it be convened only to address the specific changes we have on the table.

"And we have to develop rules of order. There aren't any. Not even recommendations about who the states should send as delegates or how many. Since one of our amendments deals with term limits, we damn sure don't want them sending someone who is currently in office.

"I could and will go on and on, but suffice it to say this will be a long, arduous process. You'll kick it off with your news conference tomorrow afternoon. Then you and Mia can hit the bricks with another blitzkrieg and start whipping up support at the state level. Judson and the Envision-2100 members can start pulling corporate strings, and I'll put together a legal team to draft up a charter around what I just presented. These are all recommendations, of course. I wouldn't want to appear to be taking liberties I don't have."

"This is perfect, Milt," David said. "Precisely what I was looking for. Judson, make it happen. Mia and I will get things started on our side. I'll have the chief of staff set up on-site and virtual status meetings. Milt, I'm going to assign the attorney general to your team in an oversight role. I don't want anything coming back on any of us."

David stood up, facing the camera and everyone on the Skype call. Pointing at his friends and in the voice of an old-time tent revivalist, he said, "All right now, let's go change the world!"

Epilogue

All across the United States of America
After the event, out of crisis

THE PHYSICAL SCARS OF THE YELLOWSTONE supervolcano eruption would take years to heal, but they propelled global governments to action.

What had once been an impotent climate change conference was transformed into a multinational organization with actual monitoring and enforcement power. The planet's only hope was that it wasn't too late.

The eruption and the crisis that followed also propelled transformation in the US government. As Milt predicted, despite the herculean efforts of the president and vice president, it was three years before the requisite number of states filed their applications to convene an Article V constitutional convention.

The convention was eventually scheduled for what would be the second year of President Stakley's second term in office.

As was fitting, the convention was held in Philadelphia, Pennsylvania. President Stakley addressed the opening and closing sessions. Unlike the first and only other convention of its type, in 1787, it did not result in a new constitution. But it did produce a set of amendments to the existing time-honored and long-cherished document that mainstream Americans knew in their hearts was necessary to reunite the United States.

And so it would be: the beginning of the beginning.

Acknowledgments

I DEDICATE THIS BOOK and every good thing I have done or tried to do to my wife. She is the source of my strength and encouragement. She comforts me when I am down in the dumps and kicks me in the butt when I need to be motivated. I love you, Trisha!

And a boatload of thanks and appreciation to my lifelong friends Jim Ledford and Roy Stafford and my brother-in-law, Kenneth Spann, for their assistance and encouragement. Also, a heaping helping of gratitude to my editor, Deborah Froese, who epitomized the concept of "there's no such thing as good writing, just good rewriting."